MW00488232

COURAGE TO BE COUNTED

A CLUBMOBILE GIRLS NOVEL

BUGLE CALL BOOKS
www.buglecallbooks.com

ELERI GRACE

COURAGE TO
BE COUNTED

A CLUBMOBILE GIRLS NOVEL

Copyright© 2019 by Eleri Grace

All rights reserved.
Printed in the United States of America.

No part of this book may be used or reproduced in any manner whatsoever without written permission except in the case of brief quotations embodied in critical articles and reviews. For information, address Bugle Call Books, P.O. Box 25347, Houston, TX 77265.

This book is a work of fiction. References to real people, events, establishments, organizations, or locales are intended only to provide a sense of authenticity and are used fictitiously. All other characters, and all incidents and dialogue, are drawn from the author's imagination and are not to be construed as real.

First paperback edition published 2019

Cover designed by Rafael Andres, Cover Kitchen
Map designed by Rafael Andres, Cover Kitchen
Layout by Suz Whited

ISBN 978-0-9600445-0-4 (pbk.)

Published by Bugle Call Books
www.buglecallbooks.com

*To the spirited and courageous women who served
as Red Cross Girls during World War II*

*To Elizabeth,
who would make a perfect Red Cross Girl,*

*and Harry,
my young flyboy who provided expert aviation advice*

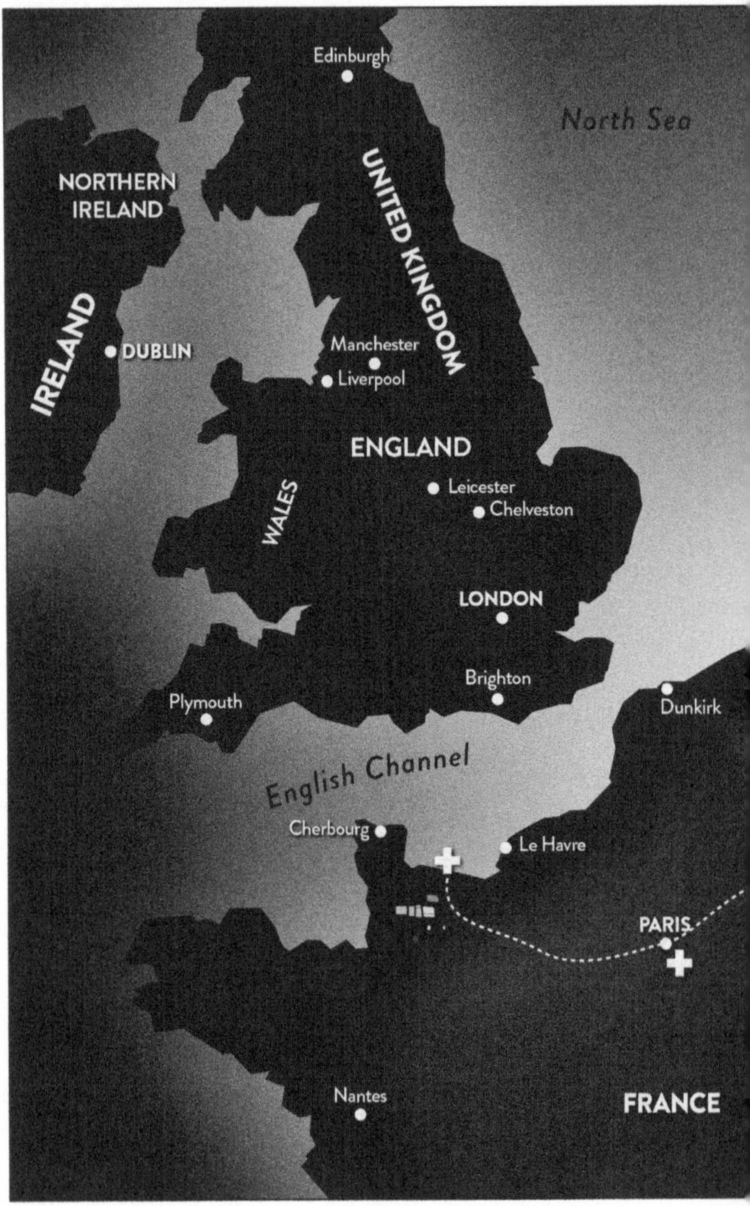

Edinburgh
North Sea
NORTHERN IRELAND
UNITED KINGDOM
IRELAND
DUBLIN
Manchester
Liverpool
ENGLAND
WALES
Leicester
Chelveston
LONDON
Brighton
Plymouth
Dunkirk
English Channel
Cherbourg
Le Havre
PARIS
Nantes
FRANCE

CHAPTER ONE

October 1942
Darr Aero-Tech Flying School, Albany, Georgia

Dressed in men's flight coveralls and boots, Vivian crouched beside her friend Zanna and squinted at the distant flight line. Still no clear path to the Stearmans and PT-19 training planes. Cadets, instructors, and ground crew workers bustled in every direction. Too many people between them and the planes. Too many people who might see they weren't men.

Vivian rocked back on her heels. She shook her head and turned to Zanna. Riotous red tendrils framed her friend's face. Vivian motioned for Zanna to push them under her leather aviator helmet.

Zanna peeled back each side of the helmet, shoved her curls beneath, and ran a finger over the edges to seal it. "You too."

Vivian crammed wayward strands securely inside her cap.

Sneaking into an Army Air Forces pilot school to fly one of the planes wasn't the best idea. Zanna had cooked up this scheme and worn Vivian down.

Today was Wednesday, not a lazy Sunday afternoon when the men had passes into town and the training planes sat idle and available for civilian pilots like Zanna. Thunderstorms were forecast for the weekend, and Zanna needed more flying hours by next Monday when she reported for the Women's Auxiliary Ferry Squadron. Enjoying a glorious fall day from the skies or indoors with her mother hovering over her packing efforts? For Vivian, an easy choice.

Her only goal for the day had been to finish packing. Vivian would spend six weeks training with the Red Cross in Washington before shipping out to an overseas posting. Even the drudgery of packing couldn't dampen her excitement. Yet, she would do almost anything to escape her mother's smothering company for a few hours. Mama was not happy to be sending both of her sons *and* her daughter off to war.

Zanna pulled Vivian to her feet. "We can't wait much longer. Besides, we look like regular cadets."

"Cadets with boobs. I'm sure that won't draw any attention at all on a base with hundreds of men." Vivian patted the edges of her helmet again.

"Just look purposeful. Hank'll walk us to the flight line. We'll get in a plane like usual and be on our way. Easy-peasy."

"Not a problem for you, Zan. They might slap your wrist for bending the rules, but the army needs you to ferry planes all over the country."

There weren't enough qualified women pilots to replace all the men enlisting in the service. But plenty of women would jump at the chance to take Vivian's place and go overseas with the Red Cross.

Zanna gestured toward the dwindling number of planes at the hardstands. "The war could end before there's a clear path. Let's go."

"Fine, fine, but hurry."

Vivian strode forward at a fast clip and kept her gaze trained on their destination, the flagpole near the flight line. "Is it my imagination or is every man looking us over?"

Zanna didn't answer.

"Zan?" A quick glance left and right confirmed Zanna was no longer beside her.

Vivian looked over her shoulder. Zanna and her shorter legs lagged behind. Vivian circled her arm to urge her friend to pick up her pace. Head still turned and continuing to walk with the same brisk stride, Vivian slammed into someone.

A stab of pain shot from her elbow to her shoulder. One of the RAF cadets. He must have come out of his barracks directly into her path.

He stumbled back from their collision and raised his hand to salute. "Sorry, sir." As his eyes met hers, his segued from deferential to dumbfounded.

"Are you—?"

Vivian tugged Zanna's wrist to urge her to keep walking and waved at the stunned cadet. Vivian hoped he wouldn't tip off anyone else. Would the American officers listen to him? Darr was one of the American flying schools designated to train the RAF pilots Britain so desperately needed.

"This is crazy. Crazy, cockeyed, cockamamie scheme." Vivian huffed out each word, renewing her brisk gait. "What if they boot me out of the Red Cross? Canned before I've even made it to Washington for training."

Zanna snorted. "For crying out loud, Viv, even if we're stopped, who would report you to the Red Cross? Can you slow down?"

Vivian slowed her stride. "Last week's paper ran that piece about me going to Washington, about the Red Cross Girls."

"You think these men read the local happenings column?"

Probably not. Still, the rigorous Red Cross screening process hadn't been a cakewalk, and Vivian had no desire to squander this opportunity. This was her best chance to help the soldiers in the combat zones without becoming a nurse or enlisting in the women's auxiliary services, where they would assign her to a typing pool. Not many women had the qualifications to secure an overseas assignment with the Red Cross. Vivian intended to put her best foot forward with her choice of wartime service and give Georgia voters another good reason to put her in office someday.

They turned in front of the hangar. Vivian spotted Zanna's younger brother waiting by the flagpole. As an instructor, he had arranged clearance for their flight with one of his buddies in the control tower, though he had concealed their gender.

"There's Hank. Should we salute when we're closer?"

Zanna laughed. "He might find that sexy from *you*."

"That's all I need." Guilt, buried for months, years, an entire childhood, squiggled in her gut. Since she moved home in June, Hank had been a constant presence. Delivering a fresh peach pie from his mother. Offering a lift downtown for Vivian's shopping. Bringing cold bottles of Coke to Daddy and her brother Danny while they repaired Danny's 1935 Buick.

The war had everyone rushing to the altar. What Hank hoped would happen in its sweet time took on a pressing urgency.

No. No whirlwind wartime courtship and wedding for her. Not to Hank or anyone else. And no staying home and missing her chance to be part of it all.

When they reached Hank, his brown eyes gave Vivian's coveralls a once-over. His head tilted to one side, and his lips tugged up at the corners.

Zanna crossed her arms over her chest and cleared her throat.

A flush crept up Hank's neck, and he motioned for them to follow him to an open-cockpit PT-19.

Vivian was glad they were taking a PT-19 today. She preferred the open cockpit with the wind in her face, especially in nice weather.

Zanna extracted a Gosport tube from the pocket of her coveralls and held out the end with the earpieces to Vivian. "You want to hear today?"

Vivian shook her head and pointed at the end with the mouthpiece. "I'll talk."

Zanna rolled her eyes and fitted the end with the earpieces over her helmet. "What if you gave up some control for a change?"

Vivian laughed. This wasn't about control; it was logical. Vivian wasn't a pilot, so Zanna shouldn't need to tell her anything during flight.

"Fine, Nervous Nellie. I'll pass the mouthpiece to you when we're strapped in," Zanna said.

Zanna and Hank conducted a preflight inspection of the plane. Then the women donned seatpack parachutes.

Hank gave his sister a stern glare. "No hot pilot stunts and shenanigans, Zan. Got it?"

Zanna stuck out her tongue at him before using the wheel as a boost to hoist herself on the wing. She hopped into the front cockpit.

Hank moved closer to Vivian. "Give you a lift?" He laced his hands together, palms up, and raised his eyebrows in question.

"I bet you don't give a boost to those RAF boys, do you?" Vivian didn't give him a chance to answer. She put one foot on the wing, hauled the other one up, and climbed into the rear cockpit.

Zanna held the mouthpiece end of the Gosport tube over her shoulder. Vivian pushed it under her thigh to grab it later.

Zanna pushed the starter button, and the engine rumbled to life. The prop's initial half-hearted spin soon churned into a frantic whirling.

Hank hopped on the left wing to talk to Zanna, presumably about the flight path. Several other planes in various state of takeoff readiness crowded the taxiways, their rumbling, roaring, racing engines vibrating in unison.

He edged over the wing to the rear cockpit. Leaning close to Vivian's ear, he said, "Strapped in tight?"

If it wasn't so loud, she could have told him. Vivian had been flying with Zanna for years and knew perfectly well how to secure the seat belt.

Zanna gestured to the left.

One of the base officers strode toward them at a fast clip, jabbing his hand first toward the control tower and then to the line of planes waiting behind them. They needed to get on their way and pronto.

Hank jumped down and moved the wheel chocks before stepping out of the way.

The control tower gave Zanna a green light, and she signaled for takeoff. The plane clattered and bumped, gathering speed down the runway. Air, hazy from the prop blast, rolled in slow waves. The plane pulled away from the ground, and Vivian's stomach flipped. Wind whipped against her face as the plane gained speed and altitude.

Farms, the river, and other landscape features she knew so well looked so different from this vantage point. Vivian had flown with Zanna countless times, but she had never lost her awe, her sheer exultation with the experience. Flying on such a gorgeous day was the perfect segue to the next chapter in her life. When would she be this carefree again?

Zanna leveled the plane and turned southeast. Vivian had been too preoccupied with avoiding trouble at the base to wonder about Zanna's flight plan. Several times before, Zanna had taken them south of Tallahassee and over the Gulf of Mexico. Once, she had gone due east to the Atlantic coast. That was before the war. With tighter wartime coastal security in place, Hank couldn't have authorized that sort of flight.

Vivian brought the Gosport tube close to her mouth. "Are we staying in Georgia?"

Zanna shook her head in exaggerated fashion.

"South toward the Gulf again?"

The back of Zanna's leather helmet bobbed.

After crossing Tallahassee but short of the Gulf, Zanna banked back to the north. By the time Zanna skirted them around Tallahassee again, Vivian judged they had been in the air over an hour. The lakes below were south of the Georgia border.

Vivian pushed the sleeves of her coveralls up. She spoke into the mouthpiece again. "So warm up here. Wish we'd worn bathing suits under these coveralls."

Zanna gave her a thumbs-up sign. She wiggled and twisted in her seat. The plane's nose dipped in response. She waved an arm, displaying the sleeve of the apple-green blouse she wore under the coveralls.

Great idea. Vivian unzipped the coveralls to her waist, eased the parachute pack strap off each shoulder, and shrugged out of the sleeves. She pulled the pack straps back up. Her red rayon blouse ruffled in the wind, cooling and soothing. So much better.

The plane took a few successive dips in altitude. Vivian's stomach dropped with each one.

"What are you doing now?" she yelled into the mouthpiece.

Zanna twirled her blouse overhead. Pink bra straps stood out vivid against her pale, freckled shoulders and the khaki of her parachute straps.

"Are you crazy?" Vivian shouted into the mouthpiece before exploding with laughter.

Zanna whooped and whirled the blouse in a spin. She wasn't buzzing airfields or buildings or people. Or doing unauthorized aerial acrobatics. But Zanna flying the plane in only a bra qualified as acting the "hot pilot" Hank had warned her against.

Vivian's helmet had slid farther and farther back on her head in the heat. Strands of hair plastered against the side of her face.

The hell with it. The disguise function was unnecessary up here. Vivian pulled off her goggles, then the helmet.

Wind whipped her hair in front of her face. She saw nothing through the thick curtain of her sandy-blond hair. Each time she swiped her hair back, it blew over her face again.

Goggles. They would hold her hair off her face. She patted around on her lap and next to her leg. Dammit, she must have dropped them.

Vivian nudged her foot against something. She bent forward as far as the lap belt permitted, stretching her hands. Her fingertips grazed the canvas material of the goggles strap. She strained farther, enough to grasp the strap between two fingers.

Straightened upright in her seat once again, Vivian felt the seat belt's pressure around her waist ease. She blew out a long breath and flattened the goggles strap across her lap.

Male voices whooped over the steady drone of the plane's engine.

Vivian gathered her swirling hair into a loose ponytail and swiveled to one side in her seat, looking for the source.

Another training plane cruised a short distance away.

Her hair swirled free from her hands to obscure her vision again. Vivian pulled the strap over her head and brought the goggles over her eyes.

She angled herself on the far right edge of her seat for a better view.

The cadet in the front cockpit punched his fist in the air and mimicked Zanna's twirling motion. The instructor in the rear cockpit saluted, grinning widely. He was dishy. Vivian could see that, even from this distance. Without a helmet, his blond hair glinted in the sunlight.

Zanna spun her blouse even higher.

The men's yells grew louder.

Vivian shouted, "No one will believe them if they say they spotted a woman in a pink bra flying a training plane."

Zanna cheered.

The men's voices seemed louder than before. The distance between their planes when she first spotted them had narrowed. Narrowed enough to cause concern. Zanna made no effort to change direction. Was she too wrapped up in egging on these fellas to pay attention?

Vivian's gut lurched, this time with nerves rather than the exuberance she had felt on takeoff. The wing tips of the planes were close, too close. Dangerously close. An RAF cadet and an American instructor from Darr had lost their lives in a training accident last month. That might have been due to weather or inexperience, but a stunt like this could also prove fatal.

Vivian's fingers tightened around the mouthpiece dangling in her right hand. She raised it to her mouth and screamed, "Zanna! We're too close!"

Zanna's green blouse rippled through another revolution.

Vivian opened her mouth to scream again, but Zanna lowered her arm and their plane banked into a sharp left turn. She craned her neck to the right, trying to see the other plane's location. Thankfully, their plane had turned in the opposite direction.

She puffed out a deep breath and swiped at sweat trickling down her face.

The instructor held up a hand in a casual wave. Despite the nonchalant gesture, he would surely chew out the cadet when they landed. The student had gotten too wrapped up in Zanna's antics to pay attention.

Zan waggled the wings of the plane in a wave at the men. Her blouse went sailing over the side before the plane smoothed out.

"Shit! Shit! Shit! I loved that blouse!" Zanna screamed.

Vivian laughed, giddy with relief. "Serves you right for grandstanding."

The other plane disappeared from sight, following what appeared to be a course back to Darr. Could they beat it? Ideally, they would land, check in with Hank, and leave the base without attracting notice.

They eased back into their coveralls when Darr came into sight.

Vivian peered over the side of her cockpit. A crowd of uniformed men had clustered near the flight line, right where they would return this plane after they landed.

Swell.

So much for an ordinary, incognito landing. The cadet and the handsome instructor must have beaten them back to Darr and wasted no time spreading the word.

Two men stood apart from the others, one of them wearing a uniform bearing the unmistakable black armband emblazoned with MP in large white letters.

Military Police.

Vivian leaned over the edge for a better look. The other man wasn't wearing an aviator helmet or a service cap. His fair hair glinted in the sunlight. The same instructor who had seen them in the air. He must be reporting them to the base police.

The flips and dips in Vivian's stomach had little to do with Zanna's descent.

CHAPTER TWO

Jack transferred the goggles dangling in his right hand to his left and shook hands with his hometown friend. Chuck's uniform sported the black armband of the Military Police Corps. "Hadn't heard you were an MP, Chuck."

"Enlisted right after Pearl. Army aptitude tests showed I'd be a good fit for police corps. Hoping I won't be here long. Want to get overseas." Chuck gestured at the milling cadets. "'Course, what you're doing here's important. That's different. Someone's gotta train these fellas to fly a plane. But MP on a home-front base feels like a second-rate assignment."

Jack shifted his weight from one foot to the other. He didn't want to be here any more than Chuck. "They don't keep the same MP here very long. Probably ship you out before long."

Chuck nodded. "Hope you're right. Heard Eddie's sweatin' it out in the jungle. Guadalcanal."

Jack winced. Marines were still fighting for every inch of that tiny island. "Pop told me Eddie joined the marines. Didn't know he was already in it."

"Rough duty over there." Chuck pressed his lips together. "Speaking of rough duty, I was sure sorry to hear about Ace."

Pressure gripped Jack's chest like he had tightened a seat belt around his heart.

He backed up a few paces and jerked his thumb over his shoulder. "Gotta go give a report to that cadet." Expelling each word took effort. He needed to summon enough air to end the conversation on a friendlier note. "Hey … uh … find me when you have time off. We'll go into town and have a beer."

"You bet, Jack. Tell your folks hello."

Jack gave Chuck a casual wave and walked toward Cadet Easton. He took successive shallow breaths, sucking in as much air as his tight lungs could hold. It did little to relieve the compressive clutch.

He stopped a few feet in front of the waiting cadet.

Easton saluted.

Jack returned the salute. He filled his lungs with more air and fixed the cadet with a withering stare.

Splashes of red flush blotched Easton's neck. He bit his lip and blurted in a rush, "Sir, I shouldn't like to use a woman as an excuse. Not even one flying in a brassiere."

Easton was nearly done with training, due to take his final sixty-hour check ride next week. He could earn his wings, a distinction still eluding more than half the RAF cadets in American training schools.

"I waited, Cadet Easton. Waited for you to recognize the danger we were in and change course. Waited nearly too long. Could have collided and killed both of us and those women."

"Yes, sir. I know, sir." His eyes were trained on a point over Jack's shoulder. Had to give him credit, Easton wasn't blinking. No half-assed excuses or pleading either. Didn't he realize what happened to cadets who washed out of pilot training in the RAF?

Dammit, Easton was too fine a flyer to face being demoted to a gunnery course. Darr also didn't need another washout. The British were already touchy about the high attrition rate under American instructors.

Jack leaned closer and injected a dash of easygoing Tennessee boy into his voice. "Today's your lucky day in more ways than one, Cadet Easton. I'm gonna cut you some slack."

"Thank you, sir." A sheen of sweat beaded on Easton's upper lip.

"You don't see half-clothed female pilots up there every day."

Jack tamped down his amusement at the memory and forced his expression to match his words of warning. "I expect to take you up for your final check ride next week. Between now and then, I don't want to hear you've put one toe out of line. Are we clear?"

"Yes, sir. Very clear, sir."

Jack waved him toward the ground school and turned toward the ready room. He would check the boards and see if he could take up another student.

"Nielsen!"

Major Harrison motioned for Jack to follow him into the headquarters building.

Harrison closed his office door and stepped behind his desk. They exchanged salutes, and Harrison motioned for Jack to sit. "At ease, Lieutenant."

Jack hadn't been carousing during his off-hours. Well, not much. He and the other instructors had played a few pranks on these RAF flyboys. Nothing serious. Nothing that should warrant Harrison's involvement.

Harrison rocked forward on the chair legs. "Why didn't you come to me first?"

Jack straightened. A tingle in his toes, a jabbing jump in his pulse, all alerts signaling the need to watch his step. "Sir?"

Harrison brandished a sheaf of papers. "Transfer to active duty? Why in hell would you want to do that? Thought this had to be a mistake. I called, and the adjutant informed me *you* filed the request."

He had. Jack had driven to Savannah on a rare day off last week to put in the request in person. He hadn't expected they would grant it. The army needed trained combat pilots, but Jack was twenty-four years old and had been in the reserve for over three years. They might think his instructor rating more valuable and prefer he continue to train younger men. His local draft board had informed him he had an indefinite deferment on the basis of essential war occupation.

Jack jiggled his knee. "I want to do my part, sir. I asked to be sent to transition school for training in the B-17."

Harrison leaned across the desk. "We need first-rate instructors. As many as possible."

Jack drew in a gulp of air, released it in a slow stream. He needed to get overseas. He couldn't be stuck here for the duration, pushing paper, trying to make boys who could barely shave into combat-ready pilots. Besides, he'd promised Ace.

"With all due respect, sir, I request my transfer to active duty be honored, effective immediately."

Harrison picked up a glass paperweight from his desk. He shifted it from one hand to the other before putting it down again. "I don't have enough instructors as it is. You know that, Nielsen. That's why Maxwell sent you here last spring. Takes too damn long to move a cadet class through the program."

"Pilots returning from combat will have the best experience to share with these green cadets." Jack traced his thumb over the embossed letters of Ace's dog tag in his pocket.

"If—and it's a big if, Lieutenant—if airmen return to stateside duty after completing their tours, they won't be here until next summer at the earliest."

"Sir, the adjutant in Savannah told me command expected to receive a transfer of several pilots who saw duty in the Pacific."

Harrison's eyes held a flicker of paternal concern, perhaps the fleetest dash of envy. After a moment's pause, he slapped the papers against his desk. "If I get a replacement for you, I'll sign this. That's the best I can offer you. Until then, consider yourself on duty, Lieutenant."

Jack stood and saluted. "Thank you, sir."

To be sure Harrison signed his transfer, Jack would drive to Savannah on Friday, see if he couldn't finagle the speedy transfer of at least one qualified flight instructor.

In the meantime, he planned to round up officers and head to the Victory Club in town tonight to celebrate his opportunity to finally fly one of the bombers. Best of all, he would stand a much better chance of working with a commercial airline after the war. Since he hadn't finished college, Jack's chances of getting one of those coveted positions were slim. A good combat record ought to substitute fine. He might not have to go back to school after all. Besides, he had promised Ace back in July he would ditch his cushy stateside job.

Ace, his best friend since they were four years old, came through Albany to see Jack on his last leave before shipping overseas. Over beers, Ace urged Jack to get in on the action. Ace had been allowed to say he was "somewhere in England" in the letter he sent in August. His first letter, his only letter, his last letter.

Jack gulped air and pressed his palm flat against his chest, as though counterpressure would relieve the crushing, constricting grip.

He blinked, looked around to see if anyone had noticed, if anyone was watching. Jack couldn't ever judge how much time passed when he experienced these episodes. He hadn't bothered to mention it to the base doctor. It would pass; it always did.

Jack intended to carry through on the deal he had struck with Ace. Ace had been right. Jack's talents were wasted here. He wanted to do his part. His part and Ace's part too.

He walked outside and shaded his eyes against the glare. A quick glance confirmed the ready room was empty. Jack shrugged and strolled across the grassy field to the flight line.

Worry about his performance and possible consequences hadn't deterred Easton from telling the story about the woman pilot flying a plane in her bra to some of his fellow cadets. The circle of men waiting near the flight line had grown during Jack's conversation with Major Harrison. The flying brassiere and her passenger must be back.

He stopped short of the crowd.

The two women had put on coveralls since he and Easton had seen them. From what he could see, the pilot was holding court. She had charm all right. Her dynamic, flirtatious manner had a magnetic effect on the men crowded around her.

Her friend, copilot, pilot-wannabe, whomever she might be, was the one who drew Jack's eye. He had spotted her caramel-colored hair flying all around her face before he noticed the pilot in the pink bra.

Hank Davenport motioned for the women to follow him. Now that Hank and the redheaded pilot stood side by side, Jack recognized the obvious family resemblance between them.

As they drew nearer, Jack overheard Davenport's frustrated admonitions. "Great way to blend in, Zan. One of the cadets claims he saw a girl pilot flying a plane in nothing but a bra. I told you no hot-pilot stunts. Isn't that the last thing I said to you?"

"That's what I was trying to do, Hank. Keep from being a 'hot pilot.'"

The other woman held a finger to her lips. When her green eyes met his, Jack nodded to her. A signal he hoped she understood—that he wouldn't make complaints.

She winked at him as she passed.

Damn, she was cute. He should ask Davenport for her name. Jack would be leaving soon, but no reason he shouldn't have a little fun before he left.

CHAPTER THREE

"When were you planning to pack all this?" Vivian's mother gestured around the room at the stacks of clothing Vivian had purchased from the Red Cross packing list. "Between the farewell lunch with your friends and the party tomorrow night, you're not likely to have a minute to spare."

"Don't worry, Mama. I'll get to it." Vivian kissed her mother's cheek as she passed. Her outfit, a green short-sleeve ribbed sweater paired with a black A-line skirt, needed something more. She opened her jewelry box and held up a necklace. "Pearls?"

"Always pearls." Mama took the necklace. "Here, I'll do it, honey."

Mama stood behind her and fastened the necklace clasp.

Vivian let her hair down. She leaned closer to the mirror to apply lipstick. Puckering her lips to check the effect, Vivian caught sight of Mama's reflection behind her own. Dark under-eye circles signaled strain and tension.

Mama chewed on her lower lip. "Vivi, sugar, are you sure? You could roll bandages or make care packages. Go work in one of the factories, even. I don't see why you feel you've got to go clear across the world to do something for the war effort."

"Children and older women can roll bandages, Mama. Like the Red Cross recruiter said," Vivian put her hands on her hips and went on in a bright falsetto tone, "I'm young and educated and ... *spirited*."

Mama's expression shifted from worried to hurt.

Vivian dropped the dramatics. "I want to do my part."

Her mother didn't understand how lucky Vivian was to have this job. The Red Cross had turned away plenty of qualified applicants. Having a college degree and being a career girl wasn't enough. The Red Cross hired women who could think on their feet, lift a fifty-pound bag of doughnut flour, and jitterbug with the fellas at an evening dance.

They also wanted women who were comfortable working with men. Vivian had spent childhood summers swimming, fishing, and riding bicycles with her brothers and their friends. To her mother's chagrin, Vivian got a newspaper route at age twelve, the only girl in town to have one. She had taught French at an exclusive boys' prep school, bypassing her male colleagues to secure promotion to director of the school after only two years. Yes, she could hold her own with men.

Vivian picked up her purse and walked out of her room to the stairs, Mama right behind her.

"What about staying closer to home? Apply to work in one of those Red Cross clubs in Atlanta?"

Vivian gave her mother a quick hug and hurried down the steps. "Don't wait up. I'm not sure how late I'll be with Zanna and Hank."

"You could marry that boy and stay right here," Mama called after her.

That was exactly what her mother hoped would happen.

Mama pushed a strand of gray-flecked honey hair back in place as she leaned over the banister. "Blanche says Hank's promised to join his father's law practice after the war. Did he tell you? Why, he'll be a real up-and-comer, Vivian."

"I'm sure there's some lucky girl, probably right here in Albany, who'll appreciate that, Mama. You can send the wedding notice to me overseas."

Daddy, seated in an armchair near the radio and listening to the war broadcasts, shot her a furtive smile.

Vivian kissed him on the cheek as she passed. "Bye, Daddy. Hank and Zanna are waiting."

She hadn't even made it to the porch swing before her mother's voice sounded through the screen door. "Ed, how many times in the last week have I asked you to fix this loose stair board? One of us is going to fall and break our neck. Didn't you see Vivian step over it? Turn off all that gloomy war news and get your toolbox, why don't you?"

Poor Daddy. Frustrated at her dwindling opportunities to control Vivian's life, Mama would probably turn up a dozen more tasks for Daddy before the evening was over.

***

The Victory Club was crowded with a mix of locals, RAF and American cadets, and the unmarried women who flocked here in hopes of snagging one of the dashing uniformed pilots.

Hank went off to get drinks. Vivian stopped at the pool tables to chat with some RAF cadets who had been to Mama and Daddy's for dinner. As she turned to scan the crowd for Hank with the promised drink, she found herself face-to-face with the handsome blond officer who had seen them in flight this afternoon. His irises were ringed with a dark blue, which made the shimmery silver at the center all the more striking.

"Hoped I'd run into you again before I leave." His voice was like a Hershey chocolate bar dunked in steaming coffee, deep and rich and soothing.

"You're … " she began, losing her chain of thought. "You're leaving? Where are you going?"

"Active duty. Just requested a transfer."

"Thought they wanted experienced instructors to stay here?" That's what Hank had said anyway.

"It's my ticket to flying for one of the airlines after the war." His eyes clouded with something like defiance. He pursed his lips. "Gotta do my part." That you-can't-help-but-smile-back-at-me expression returned. "Besides, I'm too good a pilot to sit this out."

Most flyboys had a cocksure flair, a strong strut in their step. This one had something more, something better. He exuded infectious élan, tempered with an alluring assurance and dishy good looks. Butterflies flitted in her stomach.

Vivian made a show of looking him up and down. "I'm going to guess fighter planes?"

He shook his head. "Nah, too tall to fly a fighter. Gonna go train for B-17s."

He *was* tall. Well over six feet.

"So, Lieutenant—"

"Nielsen. I'm Jack Nielsen."

"Nice to meet you, Lieutenant Nielsen."

"Jack."

"Jack," she repeated, her lips curving up. Shame she hadn't seen him around town. They could have had some fun over the summer.

He tilted his head to one side. "You might be a Carole."

Vivian laughed and shook her head.

"Rita? Or Hedy?"

He couldn't possibly be comparing her to screen stars Carole Landis, Rita Hayworth, or Hedy Lamarr. "I'm afraid it's nothing as exotic as that. I'm Vivian."

"Vivian. As in Vivien Leigh? Also known around these parts as Miss Scarlett?"

Vivian batted her eyelashes coquettishly, mimicking the famous Southern belle. "I had never made the connection until you mentioned her, but we do share the same initials. My surname is Lambert."

An RAF cadet jostled into Jack's back, nearly spilling his drink. "Sorry. So sorry, sir."

Jack waved him off.

Thanks to that cadet, Jack stood much closer now. Close enough for Vivian to inhale the fresh scent of his Burma-Shave soap.

"I'll be here in Albany until my transfer goes through. Could I take you to a movie sometime soon, Vivian?" His voice swirled her name like melting marshmallow cream.

She would leave the day after tomorrow "for the duration" as the saying went. Why complicate things with a date, with someone new that she might never see again? Jack's eyes, holding more than a hint of daring joie de vivre, probed hers. His laugh lines deepened perceptibly. Yes, he might be worth the trouble.

"I'd love to. Tomorrow afternoon?"

"Hey, Nielsen." Hank's voice sounded behind her.

Vivian started. Hank wore what might pass as a smile, but she read tension in the set of his shoulders. He gave Jack a quick once-over. Thank goodness Zanna was right behind him.

Hank handed Vivian a daiquiri. "Thought you were coming to our house tomorrow afternoon to decorate for the party?"

"Oh, Hank, it's Vivian's last free afternoon. Besides, you know darn good and well Mama and her hospital league friends did most of the decorating already." Zanna hooked an arm under Vivian's elbow and pulled her toward the back. "Come watch me throw darts with Mitt and Clyde."

Vivian allowed Zan to tow her a short distance away before hissing, "Zan, couldn't you see I was enjoying myself?"

"You don't want to let Hank give that dishy pilot the idea you're his girl, do you?"

Fair point.

Vivian stood off to the side to watch the darts games. She sipped her drink, enjoying the fresh tart flavor. Hank must have remembered to tell the bartender she liked it with extra lime juice. He was a sweetheart. He would make a good husband. For another woman.

Time and distance would solve the problem with Hank. Flight instructors were in high demand. The navy might try to poach Hank for their aviation training programs, but with his valuable instructor rating, he wouldn't be called up in the draft. He would be staying here, or at the very least, stateside.

Vivian took another drink and looked away from the dartboards. A glint of golden hair drew her roving gaze. Several cadets stepped around one of the pool tables, and Vivian found herself locking eyes with her gorgeous would-be bomber pilot.

His expression held hers fast, delving and discerning. There was that teasing half smile again.

Vivian swirled a cool, melting ice cube around in her mouth, watching him. Watching him watching her.

"Awww, goddammit!"

She whirled to face the dartboards again. Mitt Jenkins held up his hand, speared with one of the darts. Blood pooled around the edges of the dart.

Sweat beads popped on Vivian's neck, around the edge of her face.

"We ought to go to the hospital and get a doctor to pull that out," Tab, Mitt's wife, said. Her voice sounded far away.

"Nah, we don't need a damn doctor. I've pulled one out of my foot before," said another man. And before anyone could react, he pulled the dart out with a sharp tug. Blood spurted and gushed out, covering Mitt's wrist.

Blood was all Vivian could see. Dartboards, pool games, and tables of chattering people disappeared.

Coolness. No, cold.

She jerked, suddenly aware that her eyes were open.

"Viv?" She heard Zanna's voice, but it took a few seconds before her friend's face swam into view above her. Why was Zan so large, so close?

Vivian gasped and tried to move back from Zan's looming face. Her head pushed against something hard. A metal button? Vivian blinked in confusion and craned her neck to look above her head. No mistaking the bright hair, more white than golden under the overhead light. Why was she in Jack's arms? She had been watching him across the room while Zan played darts.

Darts. Mitt's hand. Blood. She fought back a surge of nausea.

"She's always had issues with blood," Zanna said. "I'll get her a glass of water now that she's rejoined us." Zanna handed a wet napkin to Jack before walking in the direction of the bar.

Jack traced the wet cloth around the edge of her face. His eyes never left hers.

Zinging flutters swept through her in response to the gentle brush of his fingertips. She shivered.

"Vivian! What happened?" Hank hurried toward her.

Jack helped her into a sitting position. Vivian grabbed his thigh for support. The room tilted before settling. She put her head toward her knees, willing the wave of dizziness to recede.

"A dart jammed into Mitt's hand. He was bleeding like a stuck pig." Zanna gave Vivian a glass of cool water.

She sipped and looked around the room. Losing time was disorienting.

Hank knelt next to her, shaking his head. "Does the Red Cross know you faint at the sight of blood?"

"I guess it's obvious why I didn't apply for nursing training."

The small circle of people around them laughed. Hank stood and offered her a hand. Once she landed on her feet, he pulled out a chair. "Rest here a bit."

"Honestly, Hank, I'm fine." She had only fainted one other time. Vivian didn't much care for the vulnerability any more than the physical sensations.

Vivian fiddled with her pearls and watched people disperse back to the dartboards and pool tables. Jack had disappeared.

Some RAF men invited Vivian and Zanna to play a game of pool. Vivian lost spectacularly since her focus was more on keeping an eye out for Jack than on her game. She waved off the offer of a rematch and left Zanna in flirtatious conversation with one of them.

Hank was at the bar with some buddies. Whether it was the fainting spell or the effects of the daiquiri, fresh air sounded good.

Once outside, Vivian paused for a moment to let her eyes adjust before taking a gravel path to the park. She took a seat on a bench under a cluster of trees.

Still no sign of Jack. It would be for the best if the date fell through. What good could come of it? They were both leaving. She would never see him again. Her employment mirrored the military enlistment: for the duration. No one could guess what that meant.

The uncertainty of it all troubled her parents. They were proud she would serve overseas, yet they worried. How long before she could come home? Would she come home? Red Cross workers stationed overseas would be given the military's substantive rank of captain on their ID cards, so that, if captured by the enemy, they would receive a higher standard of POW treatment. If the Allies lost and she was a prisoner, how long before she might be released? Truth be told, crippling anxiety had woken her more nights than not in the last month. Whatever chirpy spin she might put on for her mother's benefit, Vivian understood the risks, the danger, and the open-ended nature of her obligations.

"Penny for your thoughts?"

Vivian didn't need to turn and confirm. Hank.

"I was about to go back inside." She made to stand, but Hank forestalled the motion and sat next to her.

"Hoped I'd be able to catch you on your own. Before you leave on your big adventure." Hank rubbed the back of his neck.

"Going into a war zone wasn't how I pictured my first international trip." Vivian squelched irritation from her tone. She had been surprised by the number of people who believed she was headed off on a sightseeing jaunt. Finally having the opportunity to go overseas was exciting, but this was no lark. It would be hard work.

"They shouldn't send women into combat areas." Hank held up both hands, palms out. "I know, I know. You'll be back away from the actual fighting and all, but still, things happen. Just gettin' there's dangerous."

Vivian suppressed the doubts she had been mulling moments earlier. "I want to do my bit for America, for the Allies, same as men. I want to do something real."

"Viv, from what you've said, you're gonna be serving coffee and doughnuts to the soldiers. What's important about that?"

Her cheeks tingled with a hot rush of blood. Should Vivian not take pride that she had been chosen for an elite position? "They only interview college-educated women who've had a career. Not many women get this opportunity."

Hank raked his fingers through his reddish-brown hair, leaving it standing on end. "Vivian, I'm making a hash of this. I didn't follow you out here to debate what you're gonna be doing over there. It's … look, might as well say it. I've loved you my whole life it seems like." He turned his face toward hers. "I'm in love with you. I know you're still gonna go, but …"

He lifted his jaw, locking his eyes with hers. It was too dark to see it, but Hank carried a thin, ridged white scar along the underside of his chin where he had once hopped on his bike to chase after the school bully on Vivian's behalf, slammed his chin on a sharp edge of his bike's headlamp, and skidded over a rut in the road. Affection and warmth for Zanna's kid brother swelled inside her.

Hank edged closer, his knee pressed against hers.

He might misinterpret her nostalgia if she didn't say what needed saying. "Hank, I'm sorry." Her breath caught slightly and she exhaled, determined to push out the words that would hurt him so much. "But I don't feel the same way. And I don't think I ever will."

Longing in his eyes morphed into an unfathomable hurt. Hank kneaded his hands and stared at his feet.

She ought to have remembered. Same achy constriction around her heart, same hollow feeling in her gut. Breaking off with her college sweetheart had been simpler. Truth be told, he had probably wanted it as much as she had.

Vivian stood and laid a gentle hand on his shoulder. "You probably don't want to hear it right now, but I know there's a lucky, lucky girl out there waiting for you." She paused and squeezed his shoulder. "You've got such a big heart, Hank. I'm so sorry it wasn't meant for me."

She had walked only a few paces when Hank called out, "Wait, I'll give you a lift home."

"I'm gonna walk. You go on, Hank."

She followed the path to the river. Croaking frogs and cicadas humming in the trees replaced the faint strains of "Sleepy Lagoon" from the bar's jukebox. Their natural rhythm soothed her senses. If only nature's choir could erase Hank's hurt and her guilt. She had tried so hard not to give him the wrong message.

Vivian swept her fingers over the top of a log near the riverbank, checking for branches or knots that might snag her stockings, then sat. She stared out at the dark water. She would be in Washington in two days' time. Once she left and he took some time to let her words sink in good, he would move on. Hell, if he was like most men, Hank would cast the story as him rejecting her. He would be all right.

Footsteps crunched on the path behind her.

Vivian glanced over her shoulder. A quick flash of blond hair glinting in the moonlight confirmed what she had deduced from his strong carriage. Jack. Her heart thrummed at a fast clip. When he reached her, he motioned to the log. "May I?"

She nodded.

Jack sat next to her and stretched out his long legs. "Came out to get a little fresh air. Stifling hot in the bar." He had pushed up the sleeves of his uniform shirt, revealing lean, muscular forearms.

Vivian licked her lips. "The cool breeze blowing through the open windows and the fans weren't enough?"

Jack winked. His mouth curved up teasingly. "Okay, that was applesauce."

"I thought you dishy flyboys had all the smooth lines." Good thing darkness hid the blush heating her face. Lordy, she had told Jack straight out she found him dishy.

"Not sure that rumor's on the level."

"Probably covered in advanced training," Vivian said.

Jack laughed. "Maybe. What about you? You're gonna work for the Red Cross—something that doesn't involve blood?"

"I'll be a recreation worker. Posted overseas after I've finished training in Washington."

"And what does a recreation worker do?" Tone was everything. That same question from her mother or Hank might have put Vivian on the defense. Jack's voice held genuine curiosity and interest.

"Run entertainment clubs for the soldiers. Places where they can play a game of ping-pong, listen to music, grab a burger and a milkshake. Supposed to be a slice of America."

"Just in the big cities, like London?"

"No, everywhere soldiers are based. All those towns in England and Australia where we have air bases or naval ports will have a Red Cross presence."

Jack whistled. "That'll take a lot of workers. Are y'all volunteers?"

"Oh, no, the pay's tops. More than I made at my old job."

"One of my younger sisters is working in a factory in Nashville. Makes great money. Can the Red Cross compete with the defense plants?"

"Yes, but it's a different pool of workers. You can't interview with the Red Cross without a college degree and career experience."

"Career experience." Jack tilted his head toward her. "Any job? Or is there a professional ping-pong player requirement?"

Was he ribbing her? No, Vivian sensed Jack respected what she was about to do.

She laughed and nudged her elbow into his ribs. A sizzle zipped from her arm and landed somewhere south of her gut, catching Vivian off guard.

"What did you do before? If you weren't a professional ping-pong player." Jack shifted. His arm pressed against her shoulder. And stayed there.

Butterflies skittered against her ribcage.

"I … uh." Good grief, she hadn't been tongue-tied around a man in years. Vivian started over. "I taught French at a school in Savannah and then became the school director. A friend told me about the Red Cross positions in the spring. Once I got the job, I gave my notice to the school and moved back here to my parents."

"You're going to Washington for training, did you say?"

Vivian nodded. "My train leaves Friday morning."

"Ah." He raked one of his boots in the dirt, tracing circles with the heel. After a moment's pause, Jack looked up. "So that movie date tomorrow?"

Now that he knew she was leaving so soon, did he want to cancel? A note of hopefulness in his tone suggested the opposite.

Shame she hadn't met him earlier in the summer. It had been a long while since Vivian had a steady boyfriend. Plenty of casual dates with no hurt feelings on either side, but no one special. In normal times, Jack might have proven a good prospect. More attractive than his swoony good looks was her sense that he had smarts and spirit to match hers.

Vivian met his gaze. "I'd still love to go. Can you get away in the afternoon? My friends are hosting a farewell party for me tomorrow night."

"I'm due some time. Should take it before I leave." He took her hand and interlaced their fingers.

A warm tingle slid down her spine. She scooted closer and squeezed his hand.

"Have you thought about where Red Cross might send you?"

She shrugged. "Could be anywhere. Obvious places are England and Australia. But, my recruiter said they've got women all over the world already. North Africa, India, China. Even Iceland. Guess it would be my luck to get stationed in Iceland. Georgia girl goes to the

Arctic."

"I hear the bombers headed to England do a fueling stop in Iceland. I'll look you up."

"I hope not." She held up her free hand. "Wait, that didn't come out right. I didn't mean I wouldn't want you to look me up. But I hope we're both somewhere warmer than Iceland."

"Warmer and more exciting?"

Vivian laughed, tightening her hand in his. "I admit, Iceland wasn't at the top of my travel list."

A comfortable silence fell between them for a few moments. A whippoorwill sounded in a nearby tree.

"Are you scared at all? Not knowing where you'll be, how long you'll be there?" His questions, more than a whisper but soft and relaxed, invited confidences.

"Sometimes I lie awake at night and fret I'm making a huge mistake." She cast him a wry smile. "I'd never admit any of this to my mother. She would try to convince me to get out of it. Truth is, I've committed myself to huge unknowns. Destination unknown. Duration unknown. Dangers unknown."

"Soldiers have those same worries, trust me."

"And you? What are you worried about, Jack?" Vivian traced her thumb up and down one of his fingers.

He leaned toward her, only a slim sliver of air separating them. "Same things. Want to do my part. Same as you, right?"

Before she could answer, he pressed his lips against hers.

Vivian moved her lips against his. Warmth circled her heart, radiating and rippling and redoubling.

She moved her hands to his neck and pulled him closer. Jack tasted slightly of beer, and his lips were soft and pliant against hers.

When they broke apart, Jack leaned his forehead against hers, a puff of warm breath against her mouth. "This all right?"

In answer, Vivian scooted nearer, circled one arm around his waist and tangled the fingers of her other hand into his thick hair, bringing his lips to hers. As the kiss intensified, her pulse raced, and she reveled in the bristly scrape of his masculine stubble against her skin. Jack groaned, pulling her tightly against him and teasing her mouth open wider.

This kiss wasn't gentle or tentative. Rhett Butler telling Scarlett O'Hara she needed to be kissed often and by someone who knew how came to mind. Vivian had been kissed plenty. But she had never been kissed like this. Jack knew what he was doing all right.

Of all the luck. To meet him now, right at the edge of momentous change.

"This is the start, isn't it? The start of something," Jack whispered.

Yes, it was the start. The start, and perhaps the end.

CHAPTER FOUR

November 1942
Washington, D.C.

Jack leaned back against the train seat cushion, no longer as comfortable as it had been when he boarded hours ago in Smyrna, Tennessee. He looked at his watch.

Late. Late and cutting into his leave time. Late and keeping him from Vivian.

Next week, he moved to a new base. Vivian was shipping out any day. They had to grab this chance to see each other one last time before the war parted them for who knew how long.

The daily flow of letters between them wasn't enough. Hearing her voice, smooth and honeyed, in a weekly phone call wasn't enough. The pictures she had sent weren't enough.

He couldn't wait to touch her, kiss her, breathe in her perfume. Its light flowery scent reminded him of the white blooms in his grandmother's garden from spring into summer. Gardenias maybe.

Vivian had sent him a Redskins game program autographed by quarterback Sammy Baugh as an early Christmas gift, shipped before she knew about this leave. Jack had her gift in his kit bag. He had stopped himself from buying what he really wanted to give her.

A ring.

She would think it was too soon.

They would be separated, maybe until after the war, and Vivian would spend her time overseas surrounded by thousands of soldiers. He trusted her, but he sure as hell didn't trust them. A ring would signal her status to all those fellows. It would affirm their courtship, anchor their commitment, assure their constancy.

Jack had found the perfect ring in a shop in Nashville—an emerald-cut diamond set in a simple platinum band with engraved flowers. He returned several days in a row, and the jeweler teased him, "Son, if you're this unsure, you probably don't need to be buying a ring yet."

He hadn't bothered to explain he wasn't the one with reservations.

The train chugged into Union Station, three hours late. Jack grabbed his kit bag and made a beeline for the door. He couldn't locate Vivian anywhere. She must have gone back to her hotel. He pulled out one of her letters with the address and asked a station clerk for directions.

At her hotel, Jack hurried through the hotel lobby to the reception desk. "Excuse me, my girlfriend, Vivian Lambert, is staying here. She's with the Red Cross. Can you ring her room?"

A young woman looked up. "I'm sorry, sir, but the Red Cross personnel checked out earlier this afternoon."

Jack's pulse quickened. He raked his fingers through his hair. "Do you know where they were going?"

"No, but a few of them left notes." She opened a drawer and pulled out a small handful of envelopes. "Your name, sir?"

"Jack." A neck muscle seized, and he moved a hand to knead it. "Uh, sorry, Nielsen. Jack Nielsen."

She pulled an envelope from her stack and passed it to him.

Jack moved away from the desk and ripped it open. Not in Vivian's usual tidy handwriting, the note had been scrawled in haste.

Jack,

I can't believe what bad luck! I was waiting at Union Station when I learned we had our orders and needed to leave. Your train must be late.

No one has any idea where we're going or how we're getting there.

Honey, I'll write you at your APO once I get to my assignment. If only we could have shared a few kisses and made a plan. Must leave now.

Hugs and Kisses,
Vivian

Damn. Flushing heat crept from his chest to his neck. He loosened his tie.

She was on her way to New York or San Francisco. It was an open secret that all the troop ships left from those two ports.

Jack had never been to New York, but there would be too many hotels for him to check them all. Not to mention, she might be heading west. San Francisco was out of the question. He only had a four-day pass. Maybe someone at the Red Cross could give him more information.

He stepped back to the front desk. "Can I get directions to Red Cross headquarters?"

A clattering noise on the lobby's tile floor behind him drew Jack's notice. He turned around. A housekeeper wheeled a trolley with neat stacks of clothing. Red Cross uniforms. A slip of paper was pinned to the top garment in each stack.

"Irene, I got all these piles of clothes from that Red Cross lady. Where do you want me to leave 'em?"

"Leave that there, Sadie. I need to clear a spot after I've helped this gentleman."

The clerk's face, tilted winsomely toward him, was tinged with flush. She smoothed her hair. "Red Cross headquarters, you say?"

Jack knew that stance, that smile, that look. He also knew how to use it to his advantage. He bestowed his widest, most dazzling smile on her. "Could you write it down? Maybe find me a city map?"

While she was occupied looking for paper and a map, Jack inspected the trolley. Vivian's name wasn't on the slips of paper pinned to any of the stacks on the top rack, but one girl had written more than a mailing address: *We were told we won't be needing this type of clothing, so you can guess as well as I can what that means!*

Jack confirmed Irene was still looking for a map, turned back, and sifted through the stack. Lightweight clothing. A summer dress. Silky blouses. A lightweight seersucker Red Cross Girl uniform.

Vivian's stack was on the bottom rack. Same lightweight clothing. She wasn't headed to the Pacific if these clothes were being shipped to her parents in Georgia.

New York. Had to be.

"Irene? I don't need that map after all. Thanks anyway, doll."

***

After being bumped from the first two departing trains in favor of soldiers with orders, Jack secured a seat on an overnight train. Noisy soldiers, crowded in the compartment, kept him awake far into the night, and he disembarked into the chaos of Penn Station in a fog of disoriented exhaustion.

He pushed open the door into the bustle of New York City's unfamiliar streets. The bite of a crisp morning breeze cleared sleep from his head. Uniformed men were everywhere, some with weekend passes, some moving into a different phase of training, some preparing to ship out for overseas duty.

Colder than he had been in Washington, Jack turned up the collar on his flight jacket against the brisk wind. Looking at the surrounding skyscrapers, he figured he could search all weekend without catching sight of her. Finding the Red Cross headquarters here should be his first stop.

Jack ducked into the first coffee shop he spotted. He would buy breakfast and try to find someone who could give him directions.

The waitress poured steaming coffee into his mug. "You here all alone? Soldiers always come in large groups."

"Hoping to find my girlfriend while I've still got leave. Missed connecting with her in Washington. She's shipping out with the Red Cross. Do you know where the Red Cross building is?"

She shook her head. "Nope, sorry. I'll ask back in the kitchen for you."

Jack skimmed the menu and ordered the morning special.

Serving his order a few minutes later, the waitress said, "You're in luck. Girlfriend of one of the cooks works with the Red Cross. He says they're on West 49th Street, not too far from Times Square. You know where that is?"

"Can you draw me a map?"

She returned a few minutes later with a map drawn on the back of a ticket. "If you don't have luck there, I'd look around Broadway, Rockefeller, all the places visitors want to see. I see big groups of soldiers going to see shows and whatnot before they ship out. Women going overseas are probably no different."

Jack stopped at a USO canteen not far from the diner. After storing his bag for the day, he headed west into Times Square. Might as well look for her at tourist attractions on his way to the Red Cross headquarters. Vivian and her friends were more likely to be sightseeing than at their hotel at this time of day.

The waitress had been right. Large groups of soldiers milled around the streets near the popular venues.

He spotted a small cluster of women with insignia on their coats approaching the ticket window at a theater on Broadway. One of them opened her clutch, the same deep green leather as the one Vivian carried. Light brown curls spilled out of her woolen winter cap.

Jack pushed his way through the waiting patrons, muttering apologies.

He caught hold of her around the waist and pulled her into a tight embrace from behind.

Her startled exclamation didn't sound like Vivian.

She turned around, and in the instant her shocked brown eyes met his, Jack's heart, thudding with escalating anticipation, deflated.

"I'm sorry. You looked so much like my girlfriend from behind," Jack said, quickly releasing her.

Her coat's insignia wasn't Red Cross either. These women were with the Coast Guard reserve.

He walked another few blocks and noticed another large group of women across the street. Their heavy gray woolen coats lacked any insignia, but the identical styling sparked hope.

Without thinking, Jack stepped into the road to cross. A driver, blaring his horn, stopped short.

Jack hopped back on the sidewalk, cursing himself. He wasn't in a small town in the South. He backtracked to use the crosswalk and hurried to the other side of the street. Crowds of people jammed the sidewalk, most of them trying to gain entry to the Stage Door Canteen. He finally made his way through the crush of soldiers.

The theater's marquee advertised a show called *Oklahoma!* It was a hot ticket, judging by the number of people clustered around the ticket window. Jack scanned the clusters of patrons with mounting frustration. Where had the women in gray coats gone?

He caught the faintest whiff of familiar perfume and whipped his head around in time to see them headed toward the stairs in front of him.

"Ready, Vivi?" one of them called to a woman who lagged behind, her head turned the other direction.

She was Vivian's height. Despite the cloche pulled tight over her head, light brown tendrils grazed her shoulders.

His heart pounding, Jack stepped forward and put a hand on her elbow. "Vivian?"

She turned with a questioning look at his hand on her arm, and the thrill of excitement died in his throat.

"Sorry, my mistake," he muttered. He gave her a tight smile and a small wave.

He should continue on to the Red Cross. Parking himself in the lobby of her hotel all day might end up being a better use of his precious leave time.

Jack walked to the end of the block. When the light turned, he stepped into the crosswalk, buffeted and jostled by pedestrians pushing around him.

"Jack!"

He turned instinctively at the sound of his name, but couldn't see who was calling out. Jack was a common name.

He turned to see if he could still cross, but stopped at a louder feminine shriek of his name.

"Jack! Jack, wait!"

Jack looked back, and his heart launched skyward.

Vivian.

She was across the street, trying to extricate herself from a congested knot of people crowded at a crosswalk.

He waved to show he had seen her, that he was waiting. Jack moved closer to the edge of the sidewalk, desperate to reach her and enfold her in his arms at last.

Vivian stood on her tiptoes and waved back. She turned to a group of soldiers and gestured toward Jack and then to the crowds between her and the crosswalk. A navy sailor hooked his arm under her elbow and pulled her to the front of the waiting throng so she could be the first to cross.

The light changed, and she ran, a hand pressed against her cap to hold it steady.

Jack pulled her out of the crowd at the corner and swung her into a tight embrace. He burrowed his head against her hair, inhaling the scent of her flowery perfume.

Vivian pushed his cap up and swiped hair off his forehead. "Jack, what are you doing here? How did you know?"

"Long story. I'll tell you later."

She laughed. "I was afraid I was chasing and yelling at a total stranger."

Jack wrapped his hands around Vivian's waist, tugged her against him, and kissed her. A long, slow kiss. A kiss that sent tingles radiating out from his racing heart and enveloped him in warmth.

CHAPTER FIVE

Vivian towed Jack by the hand to one of the shop windows on Fifth Avenue. Fur coats and formal dresses filled the displays.

He pulled her close against his side and pointed to a beaded, green floor-length evening gown. "You'd be stunning in that dress."

She smiled and shook her head. "I won't have any need for such a fancy dress where I'm going."

"If you won't let me spoil you with a ritzy dress, how about that carriage ride?" Jack squinted at the nearest street sign. "The park should be only a few blocks from here."

She squeezed his hand as they strolled away from the shops.

Jack had found her. In this colossal city, congested by the crush of soldiers crowding the normal population, he had found her.

Technically, she had spotted him. But he was the one who had worked out that she was here, even though her note left him no clues. Vivian didn't realize she was bound for New York until she was told to leave her warm weather clothes behind. There hadn't been time to add a postscript to her note.

Vivian stole sideways glances at Jack. Aglow, they were here, together. He had been desperate enough to see her to come haring to New York on a long-shot hunch.

Though the trees were bare, the lakes frozen, and the playground equipment empty, Central Park exerted a magical pull. Jack hired a carriage to give them a ride. Snow fell softly and the noise and bustle of the city all but disappeared as the horses clip-clopped them into the wooded interior of the park. The afternoon took on a fairy tale quality. Vivian leaned her head against Jack's shoulder in contentment. The war seemed distant, illusory.

Jack leaned close and brushed his lips against her cheek. Shivers unrelated to the cold weather zipped from her neck to her toes.

"Earlier, I felt overwhelmed by the city, trying to think how I would find you." He circled his hand at the distant cityscape. "Now, with you by my side, I want to see it all and experience everything it has to offer."

"Let's see as much as we can." Vivian slid her hand around his waist and snuggled against him.

Jack tightened his arm around her shoulder. "Where were you going with your Red Cross friends?"

"We weren't sure. Some of us wanted to go to the museums, others wanted to shop. We thought we would see a show this evening, the Rockettes or a musical on Broadway. Oh, and the Empire State Building. The views would be incredible on such a clear day. What do you think?"

Jack's lips quirked up. "I'm game to see the museums."

"There's also ice-skating at Rockefeller Center. I've never ice-skated, have you?"

"Never had any chance to learn that in Tennessee." He winked at her. "But I'm willing to try it, if you are."

Vivian pulled her trusty Argus camera out of her bag and asked the carriage driver to take their picture together before they got out.

She pointed across the street from the park. "After we go to the museum, let's backtrack and have tea in the Plaza Hotel. Ever since I read *The Great Gatsby*, I've wanted to see it."

"Sounds swell." Jack wrapped an arm around her shoulders and pulled her close against him. Vivian's heart flipped in her chest.

They passed a couple of hours in the Museum of Modern Art. Vivian had visited the National Gallery in Washington, but Jack had never had the opportunity to visit a large art museum before. She might have stayed longer, but they agreed they should allow themselves time to see more of the city. They might only have today.

Seated later at the famous Palm Court restaurant for afternoon tea, Jack leaned across the table and took her hand. "What a relief you spotted me. I was already worried it might be hard to get any information from the Red Cross. I was prepared to be as charming as all get out, but glad I don't have to worry about that now."

Vivian laced her fingers tighter with his and squeezed. "Not sure your Southern boy charm would work as well up here."

He laughed. "Yeah, maybe not."

"Washington is still a Southern city at heart." Vivian released Jack's hand so their waitress could serve their drinks. Coffee for him and tea for her.

Jack gestured around them. "How's it compare to here? The Big Apple?"

"Hmm. Definitely very different cities." Vivian's fingers grazed against Jack's hand as they both reached for the cream pitcher. Warm tingles zipped through her.

He licked his lips and pushed the cream toward her.

Vivian tore her gaze from his and tipped the pitcher to splash cream into her steaming cup, watching as it turned the tea to a shade of pale caramel.

"Can you see yourself living somewhere like here?"

"Here?" Vivian took a sip of fragrant tea. The cream added the perfect flourish of sweetness. "I can't see these people wanting to elect a Southern belle to represent them, can you?"

One night last month, she had gone out to dinner with her suitemates Hadley, Audrey, and Maggie to celebrate completing their training. Hadley ordered them a round of French 75 cocktails, a specialty in her hometown of New Orleans. That round led to a few more. When Jack called later that night, Vivian had been tipsy enough to confide her hopes of a future in public service. "You'd be tops at that, Viv," he had said.

Jack hadn't laughed, hadn't made patronizing references to big dreams, hadn't asked how she might do that and still be a wife and mother. Heart swelling, Vivian had stretched the hallway phone cord farther to plop down on a nearby window seat. She had kicked off her heels, drew her feet underneath her, and grinned soppily at the phone even though he couldn't see her.

"Once people got to know you, they'd love you." Jack plunked another cube of sugar into his coffee. "Besides, not everyone lives smack-dab in the city."

The waitress delivered a tiered stand piled with tea sandwiches, scones, and small crocks of butter and jams.

"You don't want to live here, do you?" Vivian tilted her head.

Jack shrugged. After inspecting several of the tea sandwiches, he chose chicken salad. "Lots of the airlines are based here."

"That's the headquarters though. Surely the pilots and crews don't all live here."

"Probably not," he conceded. "But I figure a pilot spends more time at home if he lives close to the airline's hub."

Vivian could picture it, just like the ads in all the magazines: a cozy home where he would expect to find a cheerful wife and rosy-cheeked children and a hot dinner waiting for him each night. Not messy and disorganized chaos because Mom was off on the campaign trail or writing legislation.

She reached for a scone, avoiding Jack's gaze.

Mama had said it all along. Career girls couldn't expect to keep working once they had a husband and family. Mind you, that hadn't been the only thing holding Vivian back from marrying her college sweetheart, but it had loomed large in her thoughts.

Jack laid his hand over hers. "We aren't making big decisions today."

No, they weren't. They both had an important job to do before they could make any long-term plans. No point in letting something so far in the uncertain future spoil the fun they might share in the here and now.

Vivian nodded and laced her fingers with his.

Their eyes locked. She traced her thumb in circles over his palm, brushed it down the side of his index finger. His long, firm, slender finger. Her mind flooded with images of how and where he might touch and caress her with that finger. Feathery light skims and fiery hot strokes.

Rippling tingles cascaded down to her center. She gulped.

Jack's eyes were wide and bright, his cheeks tinged with flush.

The waitress held a tray of cookies aloft over the center of the table, right over where their hands were clasped.

Vivian startled as though the waitress had peered right into her bedroom-only thoughts.

They each pulled a hand back to allow her space to set the tray.

Jack cleared his throat. "Uh, have they told you what your assignment will be?"

Vivian closed her mental bedroom door. She tore her eyes away from Jack and his sensual hands to focus on the sandwiches. "Not yet. Since we're traveling from here, we know we're going to Britain or Africa. Most of us will be assigned to base clubs or Clubmobiles. Did I write you about those?"

He shook his head, and she explained, "Lots of our bases are located out away from towns, so our fellows can't get to the clubs. Someone had the idea to convert old buses into a club on wheels. A team of us will drive a Clubmobile to smaller bases each day."

The waitress reappeared and poured more coffee for Jack. He added another sugar cube and stirred.

Flush heated Vivian's neck and earlobes. She pulled some of her hair forward.

Jack's Adam's apple bobbed once in his throat. His gaze roved from her eyes to her finger twirling a strand of hair.

Butterflies skirted and darted deep in her core. Vivian knew where that look in Jack's eyes might lead. She had seen it before, with other boyfriends.

Always before, she had shut it down before things went too far. Even with Curt, her college sweetheart. Not because the desire wasn't there or out of a sense of propriety. No, she had held back before because of the inevitable expectations those men would assume. Expectations she had no intention of fulfilling. Not until now.

Jack leaned closer. "You've talked a lot about Zanna in your letters, but you haven't mentioned her brother."

"Hank?"

"Hank Davenport, Esquire, isn't it?"

Vivian smiled at him over the rim of her teacup. Jack respected her education, was proud she had the qualifications to get one of these coveted positions with the Red Cross. Even so, insecurity about her having a degree he lacked popped up now and again.

Jack had completed the two years of college required for him to get his commission with the Army Air Corps. He could always go back and finish the degree. Vivian didn't doubt his intellect. From what he had written to her about his college years, she guessed Jack had been restless and frustrated by the tediousness of the classes, not the academic rigor. Several of her former students fit that mold. Bright students who felt caged in the classroom.

"I got the feeling he was sweet on you." Jack's knee jiggled under the table.

Vivian steeped her tone with calm reassurance. "He's written a few times. I wrote back innocent pen-pal letters."

Hank's letters assumed there wasn't someone else in the picture, that he still had a shot. And why wouldn't he? He didn't know Vivian had seen Jack every available moment that last day in Georgia. He didn't know they wrote to each other every day without fail, and that strong bonds of friendship and mutual respect had sprung up alongside intense physical attraction. He didn't know that on an evening when Jack said he would try to place a call, Vivian stayed in, close to the phone, desperate not to miss a chance to hear his voice. He didn't know she wanted to talk to Jack for hours, for forever, and that she ached with an intense yearning after she hung up from these treasured calls.

She set down her teacup. "He wrote a few weeks ago to say he was coming to Washington for a visit. I called to let him know about us. I half hoped the operator would cut in and ask us to cut off our call. He didn't want to accept it."

Jack's eyes were intent on hers as he pulled her hands into his. "Accept what?"

Vivian held his gaze, squeezing his firm, smooth hand, lacing her fingers tighter with his. "That I've fallen for you. That I can't imagine there ever being anyone else for me."

***

"I know you mentioned seeing a show, but how would you like dinner and dancing? It would give us more chance to talk than if we're in a theater." Jack offered her his arm to descend the steps leading from the Plaza Hotel to the street.

"That would be fun, but my uniform isn't exactly a dinner-and-dancing dress."

"Do you have something else back at your hotel?"

"We aren't supposed to, but yes, we all hid one or two civvies. I'm not sure what I've got is up to New York standards. It's nothing like those fancy dresses we saw in the shop windows earlier."

"You'll be more beautiful than anyone in the city. Let me take you out for a nice dinner and dancing while I still can."

Jack's wide grin was irresistible.

Vivian's lips curved up in response. "All right, dancing it is."

Together, they figured out the subway route back to her hotel in Brooklyn. Women finishing their Saturday afternoon shopping, children skipping alongside or playing street games, and shopkeepers hawking the last of the day's goods assailed their ears as they exited the station. Snow had stopped falling, but the brisk quality present in the air suggested it might start again.

Vivian pointed out the imposing facade of the St. George Hotel to Jack, who whistled appreciatively at its enormous proportions.

They stepped into the lavish lobby. Vivian steered him to the left from the main entrance and waved at the seating near the elevators. *Wait here, I'll be back in a jiffy.* What she intended to say, ought to say, tried to say.

Jack would board a train tomorrow. She might be ordered to the port at any time. She didn't want to part from him until one or both of them had to leave.

The elevator clanged shut. Now she would have to wait for it to return.

Vivian traced her fingers over the smooth polished wood of a nearby chair.

Jack placed a gentle hand over hers, stopping the nervous progress of her fingers. He pulled her to a more secluded area near a window. Vivian's heart fluttered, both from his proximity and the escalating anxiety of warring impulses.

"I have a feeling I know what's on your mind," he said in a low voice. "I'm thinking about it too, believe me."

Jack swept aside stray curls escaping her hat. He traced his fingertip along her cheek. His light touch sent chill bumps goosing down her arms.

She brought her lips to his. His unshaven scruff scraped against her cheek, and she pulled him closer, kissing him harder. That hint of sunshine in his scent, the gentle pressure of Jack's lips moving against hers, the soft groan that escaped his mouth. *Oh, Lordy.*

Jack slid a hand inside her coat to circle her waist and pulled her tight against him.

She ran her fingertips over the smooth leather of his flight jacket and then threaded them into his hair.

They broke apart and cast sheepish glances at passing hotel guests.

No one paid attention. It was New York.

She swallowed and started to speak, but he put a finger over her lips and shook his head. "Sweetheart, one thing at a time. For now, go get one of your pretty dresses. After dinner … we'll see what we want to do."

Vivian pressed on her toes and kissed him again. "I'll meet you back here."

She pushed the call button and heard the *kathunk-kathunk* of the car descending. The doors clanged open, and she told the elevator conductor to take her to the tenth floor.

Jack was right. She should enjoy a fancy evening out on the town with her boyfriend. No reason to get too caught up questioning what might or might not happen between them later. They had tonight. Of course, that was the problem. They had tonight. Tonight was perhaps all they had, all they would have for an uncertain amount of time, all they might ever have.

Vivian reached her room. *Get your dress, let the evening play out naturally, stop trying to control every detail.*

She unlocked the door and stepped inside.

Her roommates Audrey and Daisy and three other women were in the middle of a card game.

"What, you already lost that drooly fella of yours?" Daisy teased.

"He's waiting downstairs. We're going dancing, so I need my nice dinner dress."

Vivian opened her trunk. She extracted her black dress that she had stashed deep in her bedroll.

She stood and held it up to her form, smoothing it out.

"Do you have heels to go with that?" Audrey asked.

She did. Vivian pulled them from a pillowcase and held them by the ankle straps. The others nodded approval at the cute patent leather heels.

Audrey contributed a pair of nice black gloves. Daisy unearthed a beautiful beaded silk wrap from her trunk.

Vivian pulled her small silk pouch out of her trunk to retrieve her pearls. They weren't supposed to bring valuables, yet Vivian had been loath to part with them. She put the necklace on and tucked it under her blouse collar.

She put her dress and heels into her musette bag. They weren't supposed to be out of uniform, and it would be her luck to run into one of their supervisors.

Taking her musette bag for the dress gave her the perfect cover to pack a few other items. She slid a fresh blouse, underwear, a nightgown, a hairbrush, and a few other toiletries into her bag.

Vivian buckled the straps on the bag and stood. "What are you gals doing tonight?"

"Not having as much fun as you! Doesn't your fella have buddies with him who could take us out to paint the town red?" Audrey pouted her lips in exaggeration.

"Don't mind her—have fun. We won't wait up." Daisy shuffled the card deck.

Vivian had already stepped into the hallway when Audrey called, "Vivian, there's a rumor tonight might be the night. Probably smart if you left a message with the desk clerk once you know where you'll be tonight. It could be a false alarm, but you never know."

"Thanks, I will."

Vivian closed the door and leaned against it. *Tonight?*

CHAPTER SIX

Jack and Vivian stepped from the subway station into the hubbub of Times Square. Traffic and crowd noise blared at them from all directions.

They stopped at the USO canteen where Jack had stored his kit bag earlier in the day. He asked the receptionist for recommendations for nearby hotels. She wrote the names so quickly Jack felt compelled to say, with a quick glance over his shoulder at where Vivian was waiting, "Nice though, right? Not a place swarming with soldiers looking for a cheap night's stay?"

Her eyes cut to Vivian. She took the paper back, crossed out the places she had written and added three more names. She noted "dancing —Terrace Room—Benny Goodman?" next to the New Yorker Hotel. That sounded good to him.

Once he had signed the hotel registry and secured a room key, Jack turned to look for Vivian.

He spotted her hanging up the phone at the concierge desk across the lobby. She gazed out the window, oblivious to his approach. She had removed her hat and smoothed her wind-tussled hair. Caramel-colored waves fell to her shoulders, a looser style than the tight curls many women favored.

Jack slid his arms around her waist and whispered in her ear, "You're so beautiful."

Her eyes clouded with some emotion Jack couldn't peg.

"Were you making a call?"

She nodded. "Audrey says there's a rumor we may be shipping out tonight. I called my hotel's desk clerk to leave a note for her that we're at the New Yorker. The concierge says they can bring me a message at the restaurant or to your room."

He kissed her forehead. "If the Red Cross is like the military, rumors are almost always just that."

"I hope you're right." Vivian grabbed his hand. "But we shouldn't waste any more of whatever time we have left."

"Good news. Benny Goodman's playing upstairs tonight. Orchestra doesn't start until eight o'clock though, so how about we go to the bar and have a drink first?"

After a second round of drinks in the lobby bar, Vivian suggested they should go change for dinner.

Jack looked at his watch. "Good idea. Orchestra starts soon."

He took her hand and walked toward the elevator. "Room's on the twenty-second floor."

The elevator conductor told them that every room higher than the fifteenth floor had blackout curtains.

"I wonder how they chose the fifteenth floor. Seems like all the lights ought to be dimmed," Vivian mused as they stepped out.

Jack read the brass direction signs on the wall in front of them and turned them to the left. "Something about disguising the skyline from the air. That's what I overheard someone say at a diner this morning."

He unlocked and held the door open, ushering her in ahead of him.

Vivian stepped inside and paused by the armoire. She pulled off her uniform jacket and hung it over a chair.

Jack unzipped his kit bag and fished around the inner pocket for his toothbrush and toothpaste. His hand closed around a small box. His Christmas gift for her. He paused, considering when would be a good moment to give it to her.

"Oh, Jack, come look. You won't believe. We can see the whole city from here."

He turned.

Vivian stood at the window, holding the blackouts open. Pops of light from lower stories of buildings broke the darkness.

Jack walked to stand behind her and peeked over her shoulder. God, this city was massive. Buildings and buildings and still more buildings. Buildings as far as the eye could see, their hulking shapes evident even in the dim-out.

"See how tiny the cars look. Headlights moving every which way. Like fireflies zipping here and there on a summer night." Vivian pointed.

Jack edged closer and looked down.

Oh shit.

Cool, moist sweat popped at his hairline and slid slickly down the sides of his face into his collar.

"That's got to be the Empire State Building, don't you think?" Vivian's voice was muffled, far away, yet she was standing right next to him.

A wave of dizziness washed over him. He simultaneously tried to step backwards and sideways. He lurched clumsily. Jack paused and planted his hand firmly on the interior wall and used his other one to cover his eyes, which he squeezed shut.

"Jack?"

He uncovered his eyes and blinked to clear his vision.

Vivian leaned against the glass, her eyebrows raised in concern.

"Don't lean … God, move away … from there," he rasped.

Every urge he had was to grab her, pull her back to safety.

No, he might push her in his panic. She might go crashing out the glass. Falling, falling, falling. He pulled his hands close to his side, determined to resist making any moves that might cause her to fall.

Jack fell to his knees, nausea rising in his throat, almost gagging him. He pressed his palm flat and hard against his pounding forehead. His heart rate escalated at odd intervals, and his breath came in shallow gasps.

Vivian knelt next to him. She wasn't leaning against the glass any longer.

Breathe. Breathe. Breathe.

Nausea ebbed away.

He ignored her whispered entreaties to tell her what was wrong, only shaking his head emphatically when she asked if she should call for a doctor.

Vivian pulled a handkerchief out of his jacket pocket and sponged the sweat from his face. She took one of his hands in hers.

He finally looked up.

Her face was chalky white, and her eyes were huge. "Jack?"

"Sorry." His voice crackled still with that odd panicked rasp. He swallowed. "Heights."

"Heights?" she repeated. "But, Jack, you're a pilot."

"Doesn't bother me in the cockpit." He pushed back on his hands. He needed water.

Vivian pushed him back down. "Stay here for a while longer. You're still white as a ghost."

"Water," he muttered.

"I'll get it. You stay put."

Ice clinked into the glass.

He kept his head down. *Don't look at the window. Don't look up. Don't look.*

Vivian knelt next to him and placed the glass into his hand.

He drained it before he tried to speak again. "Didn't think about the view bothering me. Sorry."

"You've had this happen before?"

"Not often. No tall buildings in Tennessee. I didn't think about it when they gave me this room."

"I still don't understand why flying a plane at incredible heights wouldn't affect you. That doesn't make sense."

Jack had experienced dizziness and a racing heart when he started flight training. He had managed to hold it in check long enough to get a chance to solo, and for reasons he had never understood, those symptoms disappeared on his first solo flight and never cropped up again in the air. Not when he was piloting. Some of the cadet trainees had given him cause to feel mild motion sickness, but he could take over the controls any time. He had trained at high altitudes in the B-17 with no problem.

"The elevator ride didn't bother you?"

"No. I was okay until I looked down from the window. I think I'll be all right once the curtains are closed. Supposed to be closed for black-out anyway." Jack swiped his face again with the handkerchief.

Vivian stood and pulled the curtains closed. "We're quite the pair. A pilot with a fear of heights and a Red Cross worker who faints at the sight of blood."

Jack laughed. "Hadn't thought of it like that, but you're right."

She held out a hand to pull him to his feet. He kept hold of her hand for a moment, testing his balance, and then went into the bathroom.

Jack splashed cold water on his face and neck and studied his reflection in the mirror. Not as pale as when he walked in moments ago. He should change into a fresh shirt. This one was soaked through. Jack pulled off his jacket, tie, shirt, and undershirt, and slung them over his arm. He stepped through the bathroom door, leaving it open enough for a shaft of light to filter into the now darkened room.

Vivian was sitting on the bed and looked up at once. Her eyes widened as they traveled over his bare torso, and her cheeks flushed pink.

"How are you feeling now?" She pulled her necklace from under her collar, worrying the smooth pearls through her fingers.

"Better." His eyes locked with hers. She was sitting on his bed and eyeing him like he was the cat's meow. Hell yes, he was better.

Her eyes flicked several times between his eyes and his bare torso.

Jack balled up the soaked shirts he was holding, hastily stuffed them in his laundry sack, and yanked the drawstrings closed.

As he moved to sit next to her on the bed, Vivian continued to toy with her necklace. Jack joined his hand with hers on the piece. His fingers rolled through the pearls, the smooth stones slipping in and out between his fingers.

His hand slowly strayed from the necklace and found her slender neck to be as smooth as the pearls. Jack moved a fingertip behind her ear, caressing, as his other hand cupped her face and tilted it back. Her lips parted, and the pulse in her neck quickened.

He should get dressed. He should buy her dinner, take her dancing, like they planned. Even if food was the last thing on his mind. Kissing her right now, right here, on his bed, would not get him up and back into his uniform. He exhaled, his breath a puff away from her Cupid's bow lips.

Jack slid his fingers underneath the pearls again and let his other hand drop from her face. "Are you wearing these with your dress tonight?"

Vivian scooted closer to him and rested one hand on his thigh. "I think I'd rather wear them here …without my dress."

The tempo of his heartbeat tripled. Vivian wearing nothing but her pearls? *Yes. God, yes.*

He brushed a trembling fingertip over the smattering of pale brown-sugar freckles on the tip of her nose and high along her cheekbones. "Benny Goodman?" The pitch of his voice was lower, deeper.

The hand she had rested on his thigh pressed down with greater pressure as she leaned closer. "No. This."

He didn't want her to look back and worry they had been swept up in the moment. "You don't want to go dance?" His voice was strung taut with anticipation.

She laughed, her breath warm and soft. "No, and you don't either."

Jack could bear it no longer. He pressed his lips against hers, circled his hands around her waist, and pulled her against his body.

She opened her mouth, and her tongue urged his open. Vivian ran her thumb in slow circles over one of his nipples. It wasn't the only part of him hardening.

Her fingernails skimmed his bare back. His pulse skittered. "Viv, you know I—" *He wanted to marry her, intended to marry her, would marry her.*

"Jack, I want you as badly as you want me. Maybe more." Vivian's tongue darted inside his ear, sending a shower of shivers down his spine.

Jack's hand snaked underneath her blouse. His fingers roamed restlessly over the cups of her bra, part lacy, part silky smooth, craving the ability to touch more than fabric.

God, he couldn't resist. He teased his fingers inside one of the cups and caressed the side of her breast. Her small groan emboldened him, and he cupped her breast in his hand, tracing the tip of her nipple with one finger. It stiffened at his touch.

She kissed up his neck and moved to an earlobe, sucking it lightly into her mouth. He shivered convulsively, the sensation at odds with the heat spreading through his body.

Jack shifted and guided her head toward the pillow. He unbuttoned her blouse but was caught short with the Red Cross pin fastened over the top button at her collar.

"I'll get it." She deftly removed the pin and placed it on the bedside table.

Jack undid the last button, opened her blouse, and lowered his lips to kiss the top edges of the pale pink bra cups, running his tongue over her warm skin. He pushed her open blouse up and circled his hands around her back, then moved his lips back up her chest and neck to close over her mouth again. His fingers popped the hook so her bra fell open.

Vivian slid her hands inside the waistband of his pants and cupped his ass through his undershorts. He groaned.

Eager to see one of the attributes of her figure he appreciated most, those glorious breasts he had imagined every time he pleasured himself these last few months, Jack pushed her unhooked bra up. He trailed his lips over the light dusting of freckles across her chest and the tops of her breasts. Jack lowered his mouth to one breast, flicking his tongue over her nipple, featherlight at first and then stroking the nub with rough, coarser licks with the tip of his tongue.

Rap, Rap.

Jack paused.

Vivian raised her neck and shoulders off the pillow.

"Probably the door across the hall," Jack whispered.

A louder rap sounded.

"Mr. Nielsen?"

Thank goodness he still had his pants on. Jack slid off the bed and strode to the door.

He framed himself in the partially opened door, blocking the bellboy's view.

"Sorry to disturb you, sir. I was told to deliver this. Apparently it's a matter of urgency." The young man handed an envelope to Jack and shifted his gaze discretely to a portrait hanging in the hallway.

Jack extracted some coins from his pocket and handed them over with a muttered thanks.

He shut the door with a sinking feeling.

Jack turned to find Vivian standing behind him, one hand holding her blouse closed, the other outstretched. "That must be for me."

CHAPTER SEVEN

Jack stepped behind her at the bathroom mirror. "Almost ready?"

Audrey's message urged Vivian to rush back. They were expected to be at the docks by midnight. The other women would pack her bags, but none of them could carry her gear and their own.

Vivian set her hairbrush down and met Jack's eyes in the mirror. "If we'd only had one more hour."

Jack turned her toward him and laid a finger across her lips. "We can't think about what-ifs."

"It's hard not to," Vivian whispered.

Jack shook his head. "No. I wouldn't have wanted it to be rushed and cut short, and neither would you. It's supposed to be special. It *will* be special," he emphasized. "We're gonna be fine, both of us."

Were his odds of coming through as good as hers? Jack had been flying for years. Surely his odds were better than the thousands of young men who hadn't seen the inside of a cockpit a year ago and were now headed into combat.

"Here, you don't want to forget this." Jack held out his hand. Her Red Cross pin was nestled in his palm. He slid a finger under her blouse to fasten it.

Jack picked her cap off the counter and set it on her head at a jaunty angle. "My beautiful Red Cross Girl."

Vivian averted her gaze. She picked up the hairbrush and turned to squeeze past him.

He laid a gentle hand on her shoulder. "What is it?"

Vivian didn't know how to explain the contradictory emotions swirling. She wished they'd had another hour. Another hour, another day, another week. Not only so they could have finished what they started and made love. They had been separated almost from the moment they met. She wanted more time with him, more time to laugh, to dance, to create the connections to sustain their relationship for the duration of the war.

She ran her fingers over her Red Cross pin. Training had been very specific on this point. They must conduct themselves in a manner that would reflect well on the Red Cross. Technically, she shouldn't have had drinks in the bar downstairs in her uniform, but no one paid attention to that rule.

"I hope I haven't wrong-footed myself already, that's all."

Jack frowned. "I'm not sure I know what you mean."

"Gotten myself off to a bad start. You know, with the other women, with my supervisors." Her supervisor might have asked her roommates about her whereabouts and made a notation in her file.

"When you went to your room, what did you tell them you were doing tonight?"

"I said we were going out for dinner and dancing, and that's why I needed my dinner dress."

"Why would that be a problem?"

When Vivian didn't answer, Jack cupped his fingers under her chin, tilting it up. "As far as your friends know, the bellboy handed us the note on the dance floor. You used the ladies' lounge to change into your dress, then we had a drink in the bar, went to dinner, and had a few dances before our evening was cut short. Why would anyone suspect that wasn't the case?"

The rational part of her brain knew this made perfect sense. Audrey and the others wouldn't have reason to imagine anything other than Vivian returning to their room by curfew after an evening of dinner and dancing with her fellow. She no longer needed to consider whether she might have stayed all night with Jack and how she might have explained her absence. Her supervisors would be too caught up in the flurry of getting them off to the docks to question her. By the time they were at sea, no one would remember to ask what she did tonight.

Guilt fueled a different picture. The bellboy called back to her hotel and reported he had delivered the note to Mr. Nielsen's room. Their supervisor overheard the women gossiping about this, and when she arrived, Vivian was discharged from her position, forbidden to accompany the others to the docks.

No, she was being ridiculous. Jack was right. If anyone asked, all she had to do was repeat the picture he had painted. "You're right. I guess I'm jittery now that it's time."

"You're not the only one. That's normal. Fellas shipping out feel the same." Jack's lips curved up. "They show it a little differently, but it's nerves. Heading off to war is a big, black gaping hole of uncertainty."

Her stomach flipped and fluttered. From the moment the ship set out to sea, she would cede control, and her life would be subject to untold dangers and sheer caprice. Her training had prepared her to handle the expected dangers. She knew how to use her gas mask and how to react to the screech of an air-raid siren. Unpredictable risks presented more of a challenge. She would need to call on her instincts and resourcefulness when confronted with unexpected perils and vagaries.

"I'll be fine."

"That's more like it." A fierce note of pride in his voice vied with adoration shining in his eyes.

Vivian stroked the side of his face. "We better go."

"One last thing to add." Jack pulled out a small box from his coat pocket and handed it to her.

Vivian's heart rate jumped. He knew she wasn't ready for an engagement, didn't he?

"Go on, have a look."

Her fingers trembled as she opened it. A filigreed heart-shaped silver locket nestled against the box's red velvet interior.

Vivian exhaled. Her racing pulse slowed.

She traced her index finger over the raised pattern. "Oh, Jack, it's lovely. When did you get this?"

His answering smile had a boyish, almost shy quality. "Got it in little shop in Nashville last month. It's for Christmas. And ... for us."

Vivian opened the heart. Jack had put a picture of himself in his dress uniform on one side, but had left the right side empty.

"I'll leave it to you to add one. One of the ones we had taken together today. Or one of you, that'd be nice too. Whatever you like."

Vivian's vision blurred.

Jack snapped the locket closed. "No tears splashing on my picture," he said, kissing her forehead. "Can I put it on you?"

She nodded, shivering at the light touch of his fingers on her neck as he fastened it.

"Looks pretty."

Vivian smiled at her reflection and at him. "Remind me to tuck it inside my blouse, out of sight, when we get to my hotel, all right? We're not supposed to have jewelry, and I don't want Miss Terrill to make me mail it home." She had already removed her pearls, put them in a silk pouch, and buried it deep in her musette bag.

They hurried through the front lobby doors a few minutes later. Jack put his crush cap on his golden hair and signaled for the doorman to hail them a cab.

Neither of them said much as the cab sped them through the darkened city streets and over the Brooklyn Bridge. They sat close together, knees touching, hands clasped tightly, Jack's arm slung over her shoulder to hug her against his side. She nestled her head on his shoulder, breathing in his scent, wanting to ingrain its sunshine freshness in her memory.

It didn't take long to reach the St. George Hotel. Its large facade, a source of wonder earlier, now loomed dark and cold against the skyline. It would be here where the next chapter of their story began, where she would be forced to part from Jack, where she would bid him good-bye.

She stepped from the cab. The cold wind whipped her hair. Vivian grabbed her cap to prevent it from blowing away.

Once inside, Jack pulled her by the hand to a small alcove near the elevators.

A growing cold pit formed in Vivian's stomach. Her heart might cleave in two, and it wasn't doing any good to remind herself of the thousands, if not millions, of other couples facing the exact same separation.

Jack pulled her into a tight embrace, then lifted her face to look into his eyes.

"Vivian," he whispered close to her mouth. "Viv, I love you. I know how you feel about wartime brides, so I won't make that mistake." He laughed softly, his lips almost brushing hers. "But I love you, and we'll figure it out together when this war's over."

"I love you too. I love you so much." She took a deep steadying breath and tightened her arms around his neck. "Oh God, Jack, I didn't realize how hard this would be."

Jack leaned his forehead against hers. "I know." He leaned in to kiss her for a lingering moment.

This was it. She might well stand here and prolong their good-byes all night, but Jack was trying to be strong. Strong enough to be the one to break apart, the one to pull back and wave, the one to say the final good-bye.

"Keep yourself safe for me." Jack slid the heart locket inside her blouse and tucked the chain underneath the edges of her collar.

"You too."

His silvery blue eyes stayed intent on hers as she backed toward the elevator.

She pushed the button to call the elevator without looking away from Jack. When the doors opened, Vivian stepped backwards into the car, put her fingers to her lips, and blew him a kiss. "I love you."

"I love you too," she heard him say as the doors clanged shut.

She told the elevator conductor her floor number in a voice strangled with emotion.

Vivian closed her eyes, wanting to imprint in her mind that last image of Jack, standing tall in his formal dress Air Corps uniform, love for her shining in his expression.

CHAPTER EIGHT

December 1942
USAAF Station 105, Chelveston, England

Vivian leaned toward the rain-spattered windshield, anxious for a first look at the base it had taken her three weeks to reach. Three weeks since she left New York. Three weeks since she had seen Jack.

Mist and fog, swirling and receding, revealed an immense base stretching for miles in every direction.

Their driver rolled down the window. The MP stepped out of the guard station, pulled his poncho hood over his head against the rain, and peered inside the car.

"Captain Fred Clarkson with the American Red Cross. Delivering these ladies to establish a recreation club on base." Clarkson took laminated ID cards from Vivian and Mabs and passed them out the window.

The guard returned their cards. He directed them toward a low concrete building a short distance from the gate.

Inside the headquarters building, they were introduced to successively higher-ranking personnel before shaking hands with the group commanding officer, Lieutenant Colonel Curtis LeMay.

"Miss Vivian Lambert of Albany, Georgia, and Miss Mabel Kirk of Kenosha, Wisconsin," Clarkson said.

LeMay didn't smile. He gave off a taciturn manner. His piercing olive-green eyes traveled from their caps to their pumps. A similar appraisal by another man might have put Vivian on her guard, but she sensed LeMay wasn't judging their appearance so much as taking their measure, sizing up their character, fortitude, and commitment.

"You'll find Miss Lambert and Miss Kirk are well up to the task of organizing recreational opportunities for your soldiers. Not been in the field long, but they've got a strong training record and are enthusiastic about the Red Cross mission. Exemplary character and hard workers. If one of your men can give me a lift to Wellingborough, I'll catch a train to London from there," Captain Clarkson said.

LeMay's heavy eyebrows crinkled together. "You're not staying? Red Cross promised we would have a club by the end of the week. Without on-base diversions, my men will be climbing the walls."

"That's still the plan. It won't be a problem, will it, ladies?"

Vivian infused her voice with a smidge of Southern charm and a shot of self-assurance. "Don't worry. We'll have entertainment in place for the men by the end of the week."

LeMay shot her an I'll-hold-you-to-it look. "You might be in the right place, Captain Lambert. Our group's motto is 'Can Do.'"

He offered no pleasantries to wind up the meeting. LeMay was all business. He stood, opened his office door, and called his executive officer, who led them out.

"We've got a car for you, sir," the executive officer said. He waved his hand at a tall, gangly redhead who was barely past enlistment age. "Lieutenant Thompson here will take these ladies and their trunks to their quarters."

Clarkson tugged on his gloves. "Very good, thank you."

He turned to look at Vivian and Mabs. "Any questions before I leave?"

Vivian and Mabs exchanged a nervous glance, shook their heads, and wished him a safe trip back to London.

"Er, if you'll follow me, I'll give you a lift to your quarters. I already loaded your trunks." Thompson opened the door.

The truck roared over bumpy, mucky trails. Cold, damp air seeped inside. They passed clustered rows of oddly shaped buildings, half cylinders of corrugated steel arching over a long flat space. Large numbers of bicycles rested against the outside of each building.

"Nissen huts," Thompson said. "Army can put those up quick and cheap, so you'll see 'em on all the bases over here. Cold and drafty sons of ... er ... they're none too warm. No insulation at all in between two layers of corrugated steel."

Airmen in leather flying jackets outside the huts waved as the truck rumbled past.

"Those were for the enlisted fellows. These ahead are for officers. They're settling in. Got here today," Thompson explained.

Officer huts had bricked entrances, the only visible difference from the others.

"Everything's sure spread out." The base was larger than Vivian's initial impression.

"Supposed to make it harder for Germans to damage too much if they bomb us."

Vivian's heart jittered in her chest. Of course, the airfields would be a prime target.

Thompson drove farther past the officer quarters and swung the truck in front of an isolated group of two smaller Nissen huts. "Home sweet home."

Vivian stepped out of the truck. Chill, wet wind spattered her face. Her heels sank into mud. Soggy, slimy, squishy mud.

Mabs grimaced as she too picked her way through the thick muck to the door, which Thompson held open for them.

A shaft of dim afternoon light illuminated three cots on each side and a small narrow coal stove in the center.

The door swung shut and cast the hut into darkness.

Thompson opened the door again and looked up. "Ah, right, there you are." He pointed to the three light bulbs suspended from the ceiling. "Give one of those a pull, get you some light in here."

Mabs pulled the cord on the bulb closest to her. Nothing.

Vivian walked a few paces and tried another one. Nothing.

"Hmmm," Thompson muttered. "I'll go check the other hut."

The interior plunged into total darkness again. "Typical. He might have propped the door open." Mabs's exasperated voice sounded from somewhere behind her.

"Probably didn't even cross his mind." Vivian walked toward where the light had disappeared. She patted around on the front wall and located a rough canvas material covering one of the windows. She held it up so the fading light filtered in through the small four-paned window.

Thompson pulled the door open, bent to prop it open with two bricks, and came inside.

Mabs raised her eyebrows, and Vivian suppressed a grin.

"Nothing doing. Must not have connected the electricity for these huts yet," Thompson said. "We transferred from another base. Guess the outfit stationed here before didn't use these."

"Well, they're wired." Vivian gestured at the hanging bulbs. "Shouldn't be too hard to fix."

"'Fraid nothing here is easy," Thompson said. "Brits provide the electricity, see, so I bet they'll have to send someone out. And today's Saturday."

"We'll bunk somewhere else until this is fixed." Mabs slung her musette bag back on her shoulder.

"Uh, I dunno about that." Thompson looked at the useless bulbs. A hint of peach fuzz on the underside of his jaw. He was too young to be here. Too young and inexperienced to improvise a solution.

"We can camp on the floor of one of the admin buildings, can't we? Make a pallet with this bedding?" Vivian pointed at the neat stacks of sheets and blankets on each cot.

Thompson scuffed his toe on the concrete floor. "I'll report the electricity and ask about where you should sleep when I get back to headquarters."

Vivian picked up two stacks of bedding. "We'll bring these and come with you."

"It's almost chow time, and the mess isn't far. Probably ought to eat first."

"How about a flashlight?" Vivian asked.

"Lemme check the truck. Think I've got one I can give you."

Thompson reappeared a few minutes later, clicking a flashlight on and off again.

"Works." He passed it to Vivian and brought their trunks in, setting each one at the end of a cot. "Come on outside, and I'll show you how to get to the mess hall."

They followed him, and he pointed to a large building across a field. "Reckon you gals are supposed to eat with the officers. That's the officers' mess. You can't see it through the fog, but about a half mile that way" —he pointed southeast—"is the enlisted men's mess."

Thompson hopped in the truck and started the engine. He leaned out the open window. "I'll report the electricity problem."

"Hang on." Vivian stepped around to the driver's side. "Where are the latrines?"

"They're back that direction." He jerked his thumb. "But hell, you can't use those."

"You aren't suggesting we hold it, are you?" Mabs said.

"Shit," he muttered.

"That too," Vivian said.

He flushed red but laughed. "Hop in. I'll give you a lift and stand guard. Have to report *that* issue too."

The men Thompson rousted out of the latrines whistled at the sight of women on base.

"Nature calls for us too." Vivian strode into the cleared building.

"Where's the Lysol when you need it?" Mabs held her nose.

Mud caked the floor. Four toilets, spaced less than a foot apart, faced the wall of urinals.

"Did your Red Cross interview cover this?" Vivian claimed one of the end ones.

"I suspect this is only the beginning of things our training didn't cover."

One grubby bar of soap. A trickle of ice-cold water from the taps. No towels. They wiped their hands on their skirts.

No mirror either.

"Is my hair standing out about four feet from my head?" Mabs patted the back of her head and frowned at the obvious volume. Her mass of dark red curls was several inches bushier than when they left London.

Vivian giggled. "A headscarf might help. At least you've got curls." She ran her fingers through her limp hair.

They exited the latrines. Thompson pointed to a low building about a quarter mile from where they stood. "Truck'll get stuck if I drive you across the field. That's the mess hall."

"We're going to need boots." Mabs yanked her heel out of another mud bog.

"And bikes." Vivian pointed to the groups of men biking from the direction of their quarters.

Even before they entered the mess, they were something of a sensation. A ridiculously large number of men waited to escort them in. Jostling each other to get closer, they all vied for attention. Questions came at them fast and furious from every direction.

"All right, fellas, let 'em have some space," a strong voice ringing with authority cut through the chatter. "These women are with the Red Cross, and they'll be stationed here to open a club for all you louts. You'll have plenty of opportunity to talk with them."

The press of men dispersed, granting them breathing room again.

Though he was taller than most men in the room, his height bore no relation to the command he yielded. His boyish, rounded face and dusting of freckles notwithstanding, Vivian guessed he was about her age.

"Captain Archie MacLeod," he said.

"I'm Vivian Lambert, and this is Mabs Kirk. How does everyone already know we're here?"

"Word spreads fast. Especially concerning members of the fairer sex." MacLeod held the door open for them.

Vivian and Mabs followed him to the serving line.

MacLeod seated them in the center of one of the long tables and took a spot for himself across from them.

Chipped beef, lumpy mashed potatoes, limp green beans, and sliced peaches. Canned peaches in syrup. Sacrilege. Peaches should be fresh. What she wouldn't give for a slice of Mama's peach pie. Warm peach filling in Mama's perfect flaky crust. Vivian's mouth watered. Mess hall dining would be an adjustment.

The men were in high spirits, acting like they hadn't seen a woman in years. Banter, mild innuendo, and a barrage of questions punctuated the meal.

Vivian would have to be adept at letting these men know about

Jack without giving offense. She ran her fingers over the filigreed pattern on her locket. He had given it to her only three weeks ago. Vivian's heart contracted with the sting of homesickness.

Not so much missing home or the familiarity of America. Missing Jack.

She would locate the base's mail facilities tomorrow. Jack had probably mailed many letters. She had written to him during the long two weeks zigzagging across the Atlantic's rough winter swells and posted the letters when they docked in Liverpool. During her week of training in London, Vivian shipped him a package with a few tourist gifts and copies of the photographs of the two of them in New York and some of her and her new friends sightseeing in London.

The dining hall radio crackled with a sudden burst of static in place of the music program.

"Germany calling, Germany calling," a nasal voice intoned.

Many of the men waved their hands at the radio set, muttering curses about the traitor Lord Haw-Haw and his propaganda broadcasts. Vivian had heard one of his programs back home. Naturally the Germans would also transmit them to Britain and aim them at both military personnel and civilians.

"Bastard turncoat … sorry, ladies," said Lieutenant Mel Simmons, a navigator seated next to Mabs.

"Hey, Pinkerton, turn it off, will ya?"

The captain rocked back on his chair legs and stretched his arm toward the knob on the radio. He froze as the nasal voice said, "Greetings and welcome to the officers of the 305th Bomb Group, who moved from Grafton Underwood to Chelveston today."

Static crackled.

Every man in the room exchanged sideways glances with the others.

Vivian's pulse jumped, accelerated.

"Officers of the 305th, look at the clock on the west wall of your dining hall. You will see it is ten minutes slow."

The watch on the wrist of the officer seated next to Vivian showed six twenty; the long hand of the wall clock pointed squarely at the numeral two.

Ten minutes slow.

"You will fly a mission tomorrow, men of the 305th. The Luftwaffe will have a special welcome waiting—"

Click.

Commander LeMay turned from the radio and faced the silent room. "Jerry and his lapdogs want you to think they've infiltrated us, that there's a spy in our midst. That you can't trust each other. That's bullshit, and I won't stand for it. Nothing's more critical than teamwork and trust in our ships. I'll focus on base security. You focus on your mission and your crewmates. Hit the target and work with your crew to get back home. That's all."

A chill coursed through Vivian's core. Was there a spy in their midst?

CHAPTER NINE

December 20, 1942
Dyersburg Army Base, Halls, Tennessee

Jack led the officers of his crew to the hardstand. His enlisted crewmen, some of them smoking a last cigarette before takeoff, clustered around their assigned B-17 bomber, their ship. Enlisted fellows often joked they must have been drunk and mistakenly signed on for the navy rather than the USAAF. Airmen had simply shortened airship to ship.

The new waist gunner stepped out from the group, snapped to attention, and saluted. Like the rest of the enlisted guys, he was young.

Jack returned the salute. "We can dispense with the saluting, all right? We're a crew, and we're all in this together. I'm not too bothered about rank, and none of these other fellows are either. We're all matchsticks in a box."

Jack was commander, but each of his men played an important role. Each individual contributed to the success or failure of the team. No place on the crew for rivalries, petty disputes, disrespect, or slacking off. The bonds they forged now were critical to their survival.

"We're a team. Gotta look out for one another up there." Jack emphasized the word *team*. "Now, what's your name, sergeant?"

"Louis Olin Becker, sir."

"Drop the sir business too. All right, what name do you go by? Louis? Louie?"

"Lou. Lou would be good, sir. Sorry—"

"Jack. You can call me Jack. I'll also answer to Nielsen."

"Or Chief." Bowie pulled his cap off and ran a hand over his short cropped brown hair.

"Or Chief," Jack agreed. "Some of our crew have taken to calling me Chief when we're in flight. Understand I'm not encouraging this, but I'll answer to that too. Lou, this is Bowie Coates, our copilot. He's from Texas, and he'll tell jokes in a constant stream over our intercom until I tell him to shut the hell up."

Jack motioned to the lean redhead who stood nearly as tall as Jack. "This here is Chaz. He's our navigator."

"And then we've got our bombardier, Gibson Turrell." Jack clapped a hand on the shoulder of the fourth officer. "Don't make the mistake of challenging Gib to drinking games."

Jack circled his hand at the cluster of remaining men. "Did you get introduced to all these fellas?"

Lou nodded.

"Good. You'll know us all a lot better after today's mission. Today, let's all use our real names on the intercom so Lou can learn who's who. Come closer, and I'll brief you on what we're doing. We've got sandbag bombs so Gib can use his bombsight. Which you need to go get now," Jack reminded Gib.

The top-secret bombsight was locked away after each use and could only be carried to the ship by the bombardier, escorted with an armed guard. Gib had taken an oath to destroy it if the plane was in danger of landing in enemy territory.

Gib headed to the storage facility.

Jack continued with summation of their day's mission. "Chaz will use dead reckoning to navigate us to the target and back. I'll turn the controls to Bowie once we've completed our bomb run. Everyone else will man their station and try to simulate actions you would take in a combat scenario. Then, we're gonna swing out over the Gulf to some barrier islands so you can use your guns. I'll tell you when. Any questions?"

"Weather briefing?" Chaz prompted.

"Go ahead, navigator."

"The weather is expected to present no issues for the duration of our flight, men." Chaz snapped his notebook closed.

"Good. And here's Sergeant Mack with our chutes." A trailer pulled beside them.

"If it doesn't work, you can bring it back and get another," Sergeant Mack joked. He handed a parachute to each of them.

"You deliver a replacement if this one don't work on the way down?" Bowie asked.

"Don't hold your breath," Sergeant Mack said.

"That's not what I'll be trying to hold if this little cord don't work when I need it." Bowie tucked the chute under his arm.

Jack toyed with the cords holding the parachute pack closed. His throat went dry. He lurched, courtesy of a free-fall sensation his brain ordered up, then scuffed the toe of his boot as though a rock was to blame for his misstep.

"Chief? Okay to board?"

"Yeah, yeah. Let's get moving."

Gib arrived back with the bombsight and collected his parachute.

Jack swung up through the forward hatch after Bowie. He ducked into the cramped cockpit, stowed his flight bag, and maneuvered his long legs into the seat. The dry sensation in his throat disappeared.

He patted his pant pocket and ran his thumb over the embossed lettering of Ace's dog tag. What he wouldn't give to tell Ace about each of his men. Ace had been a navigator for his crew. It had been clear from his last letter that Ace thought his pilots were tops. Yet something had gone badly wrong for Ace's crew. No survivors.

Jack inhaled and yawned wide, trying to pull more air past the weights sitting at the bottom of his lungs.

Bowie's flight bag nudged Jack's knee as Bowie crammed it under his seat.

Bowie took the right seat and looked left at Jack. "Ready?"

Jack leaned out the window. "Clear number three."

"Number three clear," the ground crew sergeant said.

Jack started number three's engine. Its propellers jerked a few times before they fired and caught. He twisted around in his seat to look at Ira, their flight engineer. Ira cocked his head, listening intently to the engine, and nodded at Jack, who started the remaining engines. The ship vibrated powerfully and roared to life.

Bowie took intercom check-ins to confirm each crew member was at his designated spot, ready for takeoff.

After he heard Stan's check-in from the tail, Jack set the flaps and slats to taxi the ship. It bounced and rattled around the taxiway.

Poised at the edge of the runway, Jack set the parking brake and reversed each engine. She was eager for takeoff, taut tension against the power of the brake holding her back. Jack called the tower to request clearance for takeoff, then pushed the four throttle handles forward to maximum power and released the brake.

She gathered speed, smoothing out before lifting into the air in a powerful arc.

Jack told Gib and Chaz to move into the nose section.

"Pilot to crew: Put on your oxygen masks. I'll be taking us to our cruising altitude of fifteen thousand feet. Confirm one at a time when you're at your station with oxygen working." Jack fitted his mask.

One by one they confirmed, and Bowie ticked them off on a log.

"Chaz, give me the course to target at regular intervals."

"Will do, Chief."

Bowie took advantage of the lull to tell a joke poking fun at the navy.

Before the laughter died down, Bowie spoke into the intercom again. "Did y'all hear the one about the soldier whose fiancée wrote him to break off the engagement and asked him to return her picture?"

"What'd he do?" Tink asked.

"He went to his buddies and collected a whole stack of pictures of women the fellows didn't want and sent 'em to her with a note that said, 'Sorry I can't remember which one you are. Please keep your picture and return the rest.'"

The jokes and stories continued until Chaz reported they were five minutes from their target.

"I see the range ahead," Jack reported. "Gib, I've turned the controls of the ship to you for the bomb run."

"I have the controls, Chief."

"Bomb bay doors open," said Gib moments later.

A minute or two ticked by. A biting gale-force wind whipped into the plane and seeped into the flight deck.

"Bombs away," Gib called.

Jack took control again and executed the turn to take them away from the target. The bomb bay doors closed.

Chaz gave the coordinates for the next stop on their flight plan, the uninhabited barrier islands outside Mobile Bay where the army had placed targets for in-air gunnery practice. Bowie and the others continued to tell jokes and share stories.

Jack ought to enforce radio silence as he would under combat conditions, but this was a monotonous stretch. Besides, Lou could learn more about them all if he let it slide.

Some time later, Jack lined up his approach to the targets and called into the intercom, "Gunners, prepare to shoot."

The cockpit rattled from a series of concussive blasts from Ira's top turret guns, positioned two feet above them.

Jack turned flying duties over to Bowie. He cautiously navigated the narrow catwalk through the bomb bay, leery the doors might open again if he put too much weight on them, until he reached the entrance to the waist belly of the ship.

Stooping and stepping through to the waist section, he exhaled in relief. Jack stopped to watch Ford swivel his guns and take aim from the cramped confines of the ball turret. Lowered below the bottom of the plane in flight, the ball turret was more exposed and vulnerable than where Gib and Chaz sat in the nose.

It looked like his waist gunners Lou and Walt knew what they were doing. He looked in on Stan perched on a stool in the tight confines of the tail section before making his way to Tink's radio room.

"Say, Chief?"

"Yeah?" Jack peered around Tink's compartment, crammed from one end to the other with communications equipment.

"Hey, what you said earlier about us being a team? I know they'll have a nice Christmas dinner in the mess, but it'd be swell to have a crew celebration too."

Jack had put in for a two-day pass to go see his family in Jackson.

"Sure thing, Tink. We ought to do that soon. Hoping I'll get leave to visit my folks on Christmas."

Jack edged across the treacherous catwalk in the bomb bay and reentered the flight deck.

Technically they should head back to base. But they were ahead of schedule, and Jack had a short detour in mind. He squeezed back into his seat and resumed flying duties.

He asked Chaz for a heading to the beach areas near Panama City, glanced sideways at Bowie, and winked.

Bowie raised his eyebrows.

Folks would be on the beach on this warm December day in coastal Florida. They might enjoy seeing a powerful B-17 bomber up close and personal.

They descended to a lower altitude over Panama City, and Jack banked due southwest, toward the sandy beaches. "I think we ought to inspect these beaches, be sure we don't see German U-boats lurking nearby. What do y'all think?"

"I think Chief oughta bring us a little closer. I see some gorgeous dolls on the beach, and I'd love a better look," Gib said.

Resounding whoops from the rest of the crew sounded on the intercom as Jack swooped the bomber lower, about two hundred feet above the water. Beachgoers shaded their eyes and waved at them.

"I reckon we need to inspect this beach again. Those nice folks of Panama City can hand us a few cold beers," Jack said. "After all, we're ensuring their safety from Nazi saboteurs."

"Hell, yeah," Bowie yelled.

"Whoo-hoo!" Jack buzzed fast and low over the beach again.

The crew cheered as Jack continued to make low passes over north Florida seashore beaches before turning north and following Chaz's directions to get them back on their scheduled flight path.

He shouldn't have indulged that whim. Still, not a bad idea for his fellas to see Jack wasn't all business, that he enjoyed a good time. The stunt had been harmless enough.

Jack checked his watch. Only a few minutes off the radial. They could make up time, especially with a tail wind. No one would be any the wiser that Lieutenant Nielsen had bent the rules.

This was one of their longest training missions yet, and even Bowie fell quiet as the bomber droned on into their final hour of flight time.

A short while later, Bowie informed the crew they could disconnect from oxygen. They would be under ten thousand feet for the remainder of the flight.

They removed their masks, and Bowie stretched his arms to the ceiling. "I'm gonna go be sure no one's asleep at the wheel back there."

He could have used the intercom, but Jack wasn't fussed if Bowie wanted an excuse to stretch his legs.

Jack glanced at the altitude and speed gauges. Everything was on track.

The fellas were going out to a bar tonight. He might stay on base instead and write a letter to Vivian. He wrote her every day, but lately his letters were dashed off in between training assignments and meals.

Her letter from yesterday relayed she had been assigned to a bomber base "somewhere in England." He was relieved she was out of London. From what he had heard, the Luftwaffe wasn't regularly targeting the Allied airfields. She should be safe enough there.

Safe enough from enemy action, that is. Her letter had also been filled with references to men she had met on base.

It's what she had been sent overseas to do. He knew that. She couldn't establish a recreational club for the soldiers without interacting with the soldiers. But for crying out loud, did she have to mention so many of them by name?

She hasn't been there three weeks yet. She can't have forgotten you already.

Besides, she had closed her letter with reassurance: "I tell all the fellas here I'm taken, that my boyfriend is the best pilot in the USAAF."

That was some comfort, but no denying she was daily in the company of thousands of young men. How did the army make sure she and Mabs were protected? He trusted Vivian. It was those men, many of them on the make, that worried him. He ought to ask her more about that in his letter tonight. What would stop some guy from forcing his way into their quarters?

A flash out the left window jolted Jack out of his head. Was it lightning?

Jack blinked and looked left and right. Bowie's seat was still empty.

The altitude gauge was lower than when he had last checked. Dammit, he should have monitored those gauges. He needed to adjust.

A flash to the left again. What was that? He looked out his left window.

Ice cubes tumbled into his gut. All the air left his lungs.

Another B-17. Another B-17 flying in a straight path directly toward them.

Climb, climb, climb. Come on.

Jack gritted his teeth, pulled up on the yoke, and pushed hard on the throttles for more thrust.

He looked down, waiting, praying. Had he climbed fast enough, high enough, far enough?

Jack stretched in his seat, craning his neck to check out Bowie's window.

Cruising below, at a lower altitude, the bomber had descended, perhaps in response to his climbing maneuver.

Jack took shallow breaths in short succession, pressed one palm flat against his chest. He needed air. Sweat ran in rivulets off his forehead into his eyes. Why hadn't the other pilot seen him? A new pilot perhaps. Or one as distracted as Jack had been. Chaz and Gib flew in the nose. Why hadn't either of them sounded the alert? Or Ira, the flight engineer? They too ought to have been paying better attention.

Yet, he was hardly in a position to berate his men on this point.

It didn't matter whether it was his impulsive diversion to joyride over the beaches or being distracted by worries about Vivian. Either way, he bore the responsibility and needed to be sure he didn't make those mistakes again. They were all damn lucky to be alive. How easily they might have become another statistic, another ten men added to the tally of thousands losing their lives in training accidents.

Jack was the commander, the leader, and these fellows depended on him. The crew was a team for purposes of achieving their missions. But he alone was charged with the overall safety of the plane and its crew. His decisions could mean life or death for them all.

"What did I miss? Anything exciting?" Bowie squeezed back into the copilot seat. "Did you forget about the altitude gauge? You were climbing fast just now. I nearly slipped on that catwalk in the damn bomb bay."

CHAPTER TEN

December 1942
USAAF Station 105, Chelveston, England

"A Christmas party? Here?" Vivian frowned at the dark, gloomy space.

"We've got four days to get this place shipshape," Mabs said.

"It would be easier to transform this musty hut into a funeral parlor." Vivian tugged a cord on one of the pendant lights hanging from exposed beams.

Brainstorming produced a list that prioritized things they needed to host a Christmas party over improvements that could wait.

"I'm not clear on what the army provides versus what we're supposed to obtain from Red Cross or find ourselves," Mabs said.

"I say we requisition whatever they'll give us here. What did you find out about our electricity?"

After dinner they had discovered they had no supplies to use the coal stove in their quarters. It had been a cold night. Cold and short. Thunderous roars of B-17 bomber engines starting the day's mission woke them before dawn.

"They'll bring us our coal ration, matches, and fire-starter supplies. They're *aware* of our lack of electricity and will put in a request with the Ministry of Something Something tomorrow." Mabs rolled her eyes.

Vivian held up their list. "Let's start with the quartermaster."

Without the vastness of the base and the unavoidable muck they had to traverse, they still would have made slow progress. Every soldier who caught sight of them wanted to stop and chat. Who were they, what would they be doing, how long would they be staying, where were they from?

The base had no signs, and the roads were nothing more than circuitous muddy footpaths. Bicycle tracks meandered every direction through the grass and mud.

They located the quartermaster's depot but had missed him. One of his subordinates kept up a running conversation for half an hour before admitting he didn't have the authority to release anything to them.

Vivian shoved the notepad back into her coat pocket. "Oh, for God's sake, half the morning's gone, and we've got nothing to show for it."

They trudged back outside into the drizzle.

"Let's go to the mess and talk to the cook about food supplies."

At the mess hall, they got their first lesson in the bureaucracy they would need to master to do their job.

"Army provides food for the *men*," Sergeant Dupre emphasized. "Hell, not sure whether I'm supposed to keep feeding you gals meals, let alone cater this party you're planning. And even the army's gotta go through the limeys and provide ration cards for everyone who's eatin' on base."

"We have ration cards. We will have, once Red Cross sends them," Vivian assured him.

"Want to eat? Need a ration card." He turned back to chopping onions.

"It's Sergeant Dupre, right?"

"Yep." *Chop, chop, chop.*

"Okay. Want to be sure I use the right name when I explain to Commander LeMay why we'll need someone to take us into the village so we can *eat*."

They had reached the door before he called, "All right, all right. We'll feed you meals, Lady Captains, but I need your ration cards soon, else I'm cuttin' into supplies already allocated for the men."

They stood outside the mess hall, trying to decide where they should go next. "There's British staff somewhere on base, right?" Mabs pulled the flaps on her winter hat lower over her ears.

"Should be," Vivian said. "I can't remember what his title might be. As if all the American military jargon isn't enough to master."

Each man they stopped to ask for directions had endless questions. Did they know who won the Army-Navy game this year? What was playing in the movie theaters back home? Could they serve hamburgers and milkshakes in the Aero Club? When would it open?

"Never, if we can't get the supplies," Mabs said under her breath, while Vivian waved off yet another cluster of men shouting questions.

They located the correct building and asked the clerk if they might visit with the British liaison for the base.

"You'll be wanting Sergeant Jimmy James, Clerk of Works. Have a seat please, and I'll inquire if he can see you."

"Claarrck of Works," Vivian whispered, and Mabs shook with silent laughter next to her.

The derivative Jimmy didn't suit the dapper British soldier in the least. Uptight appearance and clipped accent aside, the man impressed her as a fellow who made things happen. Sergeant James invited them to follow him into his office.

Vivian and Mabs took seats in chairs in front of his desk, and Vivian pulled out the notepad with their lists. "What we need, sir, is an understanding of who we should speak to about supplies we've spent the morning identifying. The building is dark and gloomy, and we want to whitewash the walls. Who can get us paint?" She looked up, her pen poised to record his response.

"Paint is an improvement to the building, which will revert to His Majesty's Royal Air Force at the end of the war."

"Which ministry do we need to see about a few buckets of paint?"

"I can get you the paint."

"And brushes, buckets, supplies to put it on the wall?"

He arched one thin eyebrow. "Will the two of you be painting the walls yourselves?"

Mabs scooted her chair closer. "We could. But—"

"Or," Vivian cut in, "we can get on with all the other work to hold a holiday party by week's end if you send us a small crew of men to do the labor."

"Two men already assured me they would do the work once we have the paint." Mabs turned to Vivian. "When you went to headquarters to ask about ladies' latrines, I found them whitewashing another building. They said they could start this afternoon."

Mabs's voice held a strong current of assertiveness. Zanna had employed a similar cue to signal Vivian to tone down her instinctive bossiness. The Red Cross had hired overachieving, intelligent women with strong, confident personalities. If Vivian wanted a good working relationship and friendship with these women, she couldn't afford to alienate them.

"That's swell, Mabs. That'll save us all some time."

Food would have to be acquired through the local market, with ration cards and other approvals to come from the Ministry of Food. Furniture and equipment could be sought through the Ministries of Works and Supply. If they wanted to hire cooks and other staff for the club, they needed to speak with the Ministry of Labour.

"Most local women have compulsory war service occupations, so your safest bet is to try and find elderly women or young teenage girls. Be careful. There are fines for making a bad hire," Sergeant James said. He pushed his chair back.

"Oh, wait, we've got a personal list too," Mabs said.

"Pray, go on."

"Boots." Vivian pulled off one of her shoes and held it up so he could see the partially dried mud caked in a thick layer all around the clunky square heel. "Preferably the ones lined in fur we've seen some of the men wearing."

"Crew members have priority for the fur-lined boots. It's minus fifty degrees for much of their mission time."

Vivian gulped. She had no idea the crews operated in subzero temperatures. "Regular combat boots will suit us fine."

"Bicycles? We've noticed most of the men have them."

"The men bought them in the villages."

A clerk poked his head inside the door. "Almost time, Sergeant."

"Right, thank you. Ladies, the bombers are due back. If you care to walk with me, I'm going to the control tower to watch the mission return." He pulled on a wool overcoat.

Vivian and Mabs put on their coats and scarves and followed him out.

Men on bicycles converged on the control tower from all directions.

The control tower, a square concrete block building with glass windows all around, had a railed balcony at the second-floor level and around the flat roof. A number of men in leather flight jackets lined the balcony and roof railings, some using binoculars to scan the sky.

"The roof is the best view of the formation coming in," Sergeant James said.

They scrambled up the steps after him.

"Y'all gonna help us sweat out the mission?" Lieutenant Sellers said.

"Kind of cold for sweating." Mabs tightened the head scarf knot under her chin.

The men laughed.

"It's what we call it when we're gathered here to wait for our ships—the bombers—to come back in," Sellers explained. "Anyone who didn't fly the mission, ground crews, engineers, mess hall staff."

And medical personnel. He made no mention of the ambulances parked outside the runways, but they were there. Waiting.

Sweat beads pooled improbably at her hairline. Vivian swiped the sweat with a gloved fingertip and looked away from the ambulances.

Vivian noted the comradeship among the men gathered in the light misting rain. A steady flow of wisecracks masked the undercurrent of tension. Rank didn't have a place on this roof. Everyone on base was united in the collective wish for the safe return of all the crews.

"Here they come," called one of the men with binoculars.

Mere specks from this distance, especially with the cloud cover. The specks grew larger. They might have been a flock of birds.

Some of the men counted out loud.

"No point counting yet. Some of 'em may be continuing on to another base."

"Twelve."

"Eleven, twelve ... thirteen ..."

Vivian didn't want to ask how many planes had gone out. Tension etched in every face told her there were still planes unspotted.

A low droning sound grew louder with each passing minute, like the buzz of a single bee gradually transforming into the cacophonous thrum of a hive. One plane moved into a landing pattern. It came in with a smooth landing, gradually slowing its speed before coming to a final stop.

Vivian hadn't seen a B-17, the famous Flying Fortress, up close before. Jack was now behind the controls of one of these enormous, powerful machines. Vivian's stomach twisted.

Devil's Playmate, the name painted on the nose, was visible from a distance. The men had already explained that most crews named their plane. The nose of the plane carried its name and artwork, often a scantily clad or suggestively posed woman. This one featured a woman in red bra, panties and high heels, holding aloft a red cape that ended in flames.

It had sent up a flare as it approached for landing.

"Why did it send out a flare?" Vivian asked Sellers.

He pointed to the ambulance that had roared down the perimeter track and parked beside *Devil's Playmate*. Two medics climbed aboard through the front hatch. "Means they've got someone on board who's been hurt or ..."

Or killed.

Waves of dizziness buzzed across Vivian's forehead.

Medics carried the first man off the plane to a gurney and began treatment.

Captain MacLeod trained his binoculars on the wounded man. "Frostbite."

Nine other crew members came out of the hatch and gathered near the medics. One knelt beside the wounded fellow and offered him something Vivian couldn't see.

"Lettin' him have a smoke." MacLeod chuckled. "Must not be too bad off."

The man hauled out of the next bomber, *Long Tall Sally*, wasn't so lucky.

"They're givin' him plasma," Sellers said. "Must've got hit, lost some blood."

Vivian turned away and inhaled deep breaths of the cool misty air.

Now six planes had landed, and one man called, "I got seventeen."

No one whooped or cheered, but the palpable drop in tension signaled the group hadn't lost any bombers. Crews piled into jeeps to ride to the interrogation room.

"We should go see if we can help serve food to the crews," Vivian said. "At least find out what the fellas would like to have when they're back."

"Scotch. Ciggies. More scotch. Then coffee," Captain MacLeod said to much laughter and general agreement.

Vivian spotted the tall Clerk of Works headed toward the stairs. "Sergeant James?"

He stopped and waited. "Well, what did you make of the sight of the returning bombers? Quite something, isn't it? Nice that it was a good day."

At least four cases of frostbite, the one guy getting plasma and who knows what, and a dozen or more battered and shot-up planes. A good day.

Vivian quashed her incredulity. "Erm, yes. Could we serve food and drinks to the men in the briefing room? When the Red Cross gets a doughnut machine to us, we'll meet the returning crews with coffee and doughnuts. In the meanwhile, if we can help, we'd like to."

He nodded. "I expect the mess cooks have sent coffee. I can escort you."

Vivian followed Sergeant James and Mabs inside the large Nissen hut that served as the base debriefing room. A pungent blend of cigarette smoke, sweat, leather, and alcohol permeated the room.

At each of the eight tables, an intelligence officer sat with a crew for debriefing. Other crews stood around the perimeter against the walls, waiting their turn. Many of the waiting men had glasses of Scotch. A trolley near the windows held several open bottles of Scotch and glasses.

Vivian spotted two large coffee urns next to a stack of cups and saucers across the room. She pointed them out to Mabs. "Let's move those near the entrance. We can offer the fellas a cup of coffee before they leave."

They each grabbed a side handle on one of the coffee urns and lifted it.

"Aw, hey now, dolls, let me move it for you. Where do you want it?" A slight young man hurried toward them.

Vivian suppressed a smirk. She might be bigger than him. Their eager helper looked too young to have a newspaper route, let alone bomb Nazi Germany.

She gestured to a small empty table near the door. "We want to move the coffee service, so the men can have a cup of coffee after debriefing."

"Oh, right." He motioned to one of his crewmates. "Give me a hand, eh, George?"

Vivian and Mabs loaded cups and saucers on trays, which the men also insisted on carrying for them.

Once everything was in place near the door, Vivian turned to the younger one. "Thank you. Sorry, I didn't catch your name."

"Johnnie Huntley. I'm the ball turret gunner on *The Lone Ranger*."

"Oh, the one that lost some of the tail section, right?"

"Our tail gunner had a narrow escape. Gave him my shot of Scotch."

"We'll serve food next time," Vivian said. "You're bound to be starving. Coffee's not good on an empty stomach. Or mixed with Scotch."

***

December 24, 1942

Village children bundled in heavy coats stepped through the door of the Aero Club, holding fast to the hands of mothers or grandparents.

The Aero Club was serviceably ready for the party. Four weeks of hard labor compressed into four days.

Christmas decorations added a festive touch, but the permanent artistic contributions were even better. The USAAF had hired Bruce

Bairnsfather, a famous British artist, to decorate the facilities at American air bases. Men loved the pinup girls he painted on barrack walls and the noses of bombers.

Bairnsfather, conveniently living on this base, had painted his well-known WWI "Old Bill" character standing alongside a bomb illustrated above the Aero Club's fireplace. He had also painted a large model Luftwaffe plane supplied by one of the soldiers that hung suspended from the rafters in a death spiral. Vivian suspected the men appreciated that dangling Focke-Wulf 190 more than the holiday decorations.

The children's eyes locked on the Christmas tree near the stage. Vivian and Mabs had decorated it with a few strands of "fairy lights" donated by a shopkeeper, strings of popcorn, gingerbread men fashioned out of cardboard, paper chains made from old newspapers painted red and green, and tinsel in the form of strips of tinfoil called chaff that the men dropped from the bombers to jam the German radar defenses.

Packages spilled out from under the tree, wrapped in old newspaper or parcel paper painted with white paint and tied with colored yarn. Vivian and Mabs had wrapped candy bars, cigarette packs, gum, comic books, combs, and razors as token gifts for the men. Red Cross provided toys, books, candy bars, and special treats for the children.

To their amazement, a village family had donated a piano to the Aero Club. A local farmer had transported it to them in his horse-drawn hay wagon. Lieutenant Coble played Christmas carols.

Vivian and Mabs paired each arriving child with a soldier. When they ran out of children, they told the remaining eager men to join in already-formed groups.

Commander LeMay came to the party. With his barrel chest and florid face, he would be perfect for the role of Father Christmas, if only she or Mabs were brave enough to ask him.

They settled on Doc Burke, the base doctor, as a more approachable substitute.

"Doctor Burke, may I see you a moment?" Vivian beckoned him to follow her off to the side.

"This is wonderful," he said. "You've done good, fast work. Look at how much fun these kiddos are having. The men too." The children, most of whom had been shy and reticent at first, were laughing and playing with the airmen.

"Thank you, Captain. Listen, we need some special help to round out the party tonight." Vivian pulled a red felt jacket and cap with cuffs of white snowy material and a fake snowy white beard from a box, keeping them folded out of view. She lowered her voice. "We need someone to play Father Christmas when it's time to give out the gifts for the children. Would you do the honors?"

Captain Burke guffawed. Vivian smiled and put a finger to her lips. "Shhh, it's meant to be a surprise."

"I'll be happy to do it, but where on earth did you find this costume?"

"The village school teacher in Yelden offered it."

Vivian waited until everyone was served and eating and then prompted Captain Burke to step outside to transform into Father Christmas.

"The gifts in the white sack are for girls, the ones in the canvas bag are for boys. All the children receive one of the small red sacks. Those are treats from the Red Cross."

Vivian held the door open for him, and he made a big show of his entrance. "Ho, Ho, Ho! Merry Christmas!" he called in a booming voice. He made his way through the center of the Aero Club to the Christmas tree, and some of the men called, "Hey, look, kids, it's Santa Claus!"

"Father Christmas, boys, Father Christmas." Smart of him to remember the British children didn't know the American name of Santa Claus.

Mabs stood on a chair and motioned for quiet. "All right, listen up, men! You can bring the child or children you're hosting tonight to see Father Christmas. He has presents for everyone, no need to rush. A few at a time."

The table of men closest to the tree stood.

One of them hoisted to his shoulders a small boy who was staring at Father Christmas with trepidation. The airman approached the tree. "This is Niles, Father Christmas. Niles loves airplanes and wants to be a pilot when he's bigger."

Vivian dug around in the bag to be sure the boy would get one of the model planes and handed it discreetly to Doc Burke.

Laughing and joking with the children and each other, the men helped them open the gifts. Delighted boys engaged in a mock battle with their new model airplanes, with the grinning men calling out tips.

After all the presents had been handed out, Lieutenant Coble called some men he had persuaded to sing carols with him. They sang the ones that would be most familiar to British children first, including "Good King Wenceslas." Burly Lieutenant O'Neill surprised them all with his clear tenor solo of "The First Noel."

Vivian and Mabs turned off most of the electric lights and passed around lit tapers to each table. Lieutenant Coble played the opening chords of "Silent Night." The men stood, some of them holding the candles aloft, others holding sleepy children, and they all began to sing.

Vivian shivered and blinked back an unexpected rush of hot tears, swallowed hard against the lump in her throat. The evergreen scent of the tree and the familiar carol should have reminded her of family, home, Georgia. But it was Jack's face she saw in her mind's eye, Jack she wanted with a fierce longing. He seemed a world away. Vivian's heart beat faster. Her fingers fiddled with the locket hinge.

Everyone blew out their tapers. Vivian and Mabs matched coats with their owners and settled their guests into the army trucks waiting to deliver them back to the villages.

They came back into the club to find many men still milling around. How should they communicate the party was over and the club wouldn't open for real for another week? They stacked plates and glasses on a trolley so they clanged and clanked and clattered. They reached around the chattering and oblivious men to pick up dishes, glassware, and discarded wrappings.

Someone had spilled milk. Vivian turned to get a mop and nearly slammed into a man who had approached behind her.

"What a lovely party. Thank you for hosting it," said the smiling English pastor. No wait, they weren't called pastors here.

"Joe Chapman, Vicar of St. Mary's Church in Yelden." He clasped her hand warmly in both of his.

"I'm pleased to meet you, Vicar Chapman."

He patted her hand and released it. "Joe, my dear. You may call me Joe. Your lads have taken to calling me 'Chappie,' whether because of my surname or because I seem to be falling in as an unofficial chaplain for them, I'm not sure."

"We're glad you came to the party, Joe. I'm Vivian Lambert." She waved her hand toward Mabs, maneuvering around another group of men with an armload of discarded wrapping paper. "That's Mabel Kirk, known as Mabs."

Mabs piled the paper on a table. They would smooth it out to be reused. Joe reached out to shake her hand. "It's lovely to meet you both. I hope to see you at midnight mass tonight."

Vivian looked around the club. Crumbs and wrapping paper covered the floor. Dirty dishes, cups, and utensils still littered many of the tables.

Joe followed her gaze, then called in the clear tone of a man accustomed to making himself heard. "Gentlemen, these lovely ladies who organized and hosted tonight's festive party can now use a hand in cleaning up. I'm sure you fine chaps will be happy to assist them, am I right?"

Throngs of men answered his summons. Before long, the club was spotless again. Several men pushed a cart laden with dirty dishes to the door and told her and Mabs they would see that they were delivered to the mess hall.

Joe clapped his hands together and smiled at them. "I'll see you both a bit later. You should have no trouble finding suitable escorts to see you safely to the church. Oh," he leaned conspiratorially close to them and whispered, "and I've been told they will deal me into a poker game after services. Officers' Club if you care to join us."

CHAPTER ELEVEN

December 24, 1942
Jackson, Tennessee

Jack slung his kit bag over his shoulder and stepped off the bus. He paused to pull on his shearling-lined gloves.

War hadn't changed the Christmas decorations on Main Street. Garland wrapped the overhead electrical wires and wreaths hung on lampposts.

He made a quick stop in Cox's Drugstore to buy a gift for Pop before heading up Cumberland toward home.

He had planned to bypass 261 Elm Street. Too many memories. Too much chance he would see Ace's family before he was ready. Yet, his feet had led him here all the same.

No Christmas wreath on the door. No Christmas lights on the roofline. No Christmas tree in the front window.

What was clearly visible was the service banner for Ace and his twin brothers, Stu and Rob. Edged with a broad red border, the center white rectangle displayed the stars representing each son's military service in a vertical line. Two blue stars on bottom. A gold one at the top.

The tire swing on the front oak tree moved in a gust of wind. Jack's lungs compressed to the size of Ace's gold star.

He should stop in, pay his respects to the Pattersons. He hadn't attended Ace's memorial service in September. Told his parents he couldn't get leave. Truth was, he hadn't asked.

The dog tag had arrived a week later, enclosed with a handwritten note from Ace's mom. *I kept one, and I'm sure Ace would want you to have the other.*

Jack slid his hand in his pocket and rubbed the dog tag between his thumb and forefinger. He would see Ace's family tomorrow.

"Francie isn't doing too well. I expect your mom has told you?"

Jack turned around. Ellen Norton, the Pattersons' across-the-street neighbor, had come out to pick up her evening newspaper.

He stepped closer to her. "Mama says she takes them a casserole every week. Drives Francie to church Sunday mornings."

"Ralph wasn't ever much of a churchgoer. Now, well, he won't hear of it. Folks said he didn't want to go for the services for Ace. Believe it was your pop who persuaded him he had to do that much, for Francie's sake." Ellen turned her gaze to the gold star in the window.

Yes, that was something Pop would do.

Jack's eyes wandered to the end of the block, to the neighborhood baseball field.

"Why can't you hit the curveballs, son?" his father once said. "Ace can hit 'em every time."

Jack had squared his shoulders and raised his bat, ready for the next pitch.

Another curveball. Another strike. Another disappointment.

He had glared at Pop, cast his bat aside, and stomped off.

Ace had stuck around. He could always anticipate Pop's pitches.

Jack had good reflexes, better than Ace. But he could never read his father, on or off the baseball field.

Jack turned his gaze back to Ellen Norton. "I ought to head on. Mama'll be anxious to see me."

"Will you look in on Ralph and Francie? While you're here?"

Jack nodded. He should see them. Ace's folks were family.

Ellen smiled and patted his arm. "They'll like the chance to see you."

Jack waved to her and set out again. Rounding the corner, he spotted his youngest sister, Rosie. She was leaning into a car parked on the street, passionately kissing some young man.

"Is this any way to welcome home your big brother?"

Rosie leaped back from the car. Her blond hair was shorter than when he had last seen her.

"Jack!" She ran forward and hugged him. "Pop would have come to get you."

"A walk sounded good, Rosie-Posie. Besides, he needs his gas ration. Now, introduce me to your fella here. Leastways, he better be your fella, based on what I saw."

Jack hid a smile as the young man scrambled out of the car and saluted. "Private Jimmy Morris, sir."

The kid's garrison cap was askew, probably from smooching Rosie.

Jack returned the salute. "Where's your home base, Private Morris?"

"Tyndall Field, Florida, sir."

"Tyndall. Gunnery?"

"Yes, sir." The young man's eyes flicked to Jack's wings. Had he washed out of pilot training?

"My crew has some of the best gunners in the service. One of them, fellow by the name of Stan Markham, trained at Tyndall. He's our best shot, our tail gunner. How much longer before you finish?"

"First of January, sir."

"Jack, can't you all drop the 'sirs' business?" Rose interjected.

Ignoring her, he asked, "Home for the holidays on a pass, Private?"

"Yes, sir. Arrived sixteen hundred hours, sir."

"And what are your intentions with my sister?"

"Jack! Stop it." Rose punched his arm.

He laughed. "All right, all right, Rosie-Posie. I'll lay off."

Jack cast a you-better-not-do-what-I-know-you're-thinking-about glare at Private Morris over her shoulder. "Are the others inside?"

"Mama and Phoebe are. Phoebe's friend dropped her off about an hour ago. Pop's still at the plant."

"All right. I'll go in so you can carry on with your good-bye." He cleared his throat and added, "Within reason, Private."

Jack climbed the steps to the front porch. Its wide planks had hosted numerous games of marbles with neighborhood buddies. Ace, of course. But also Chuck, Eddie, Dave, Roy, Fred. All in the service now.

Christmas tree lights flicked on. Mama or Phoebe must have plugged them in and failed to notice him standing here. He threw one last look at Rosie and her boyfriend. They held hands, clearly waiting on him to disappear from view before resuming anything more.

He pushed the door open to find Phoebe straightening up from beside the tree. Her mouth curved into a smile. "Jack's here, Mama," she called.

Jack pulled her into a hug. She stood on tiptoe to kiss his cheek.

"You look nice, Feebs. Are you meeting a boyfriend tonight too?" Jack leaned sideways to look through the front window. Rosie and Private Morris were locked in a clinch.

Phoebe laughed. "I see you met Rose's Jimmy on your way in. Nope, no local fellas for me."

"No one *local*, huh? And plural? Got more than one on the line, do you?"

She rolled her eyes. "What about you, Mr. Big Time Operator? I'm sure this flyboy getup isn't hurting your dating life." Phoebe ran her fingers over the eagle on his crush cap.

"No more BTO for me." Vivian's face swam into view. What he wouldn't give to have her here by his side this holiday, introducing her to his sisters, his parents.

"No time for dating? You?" Phoebe tilted her head, her lips tugging up on one side. "No, that's not it, is it?"

"Nope."

"Who is she?"

"Her name's Vivian. Met her in Georgia." Jack unbuttoned his left breast pocket and pulled out one of Vivian's pictures from when she was in D.C. He passed it to Phoebe.

"You have her picture in your pocket? You must be completely gone. What's this uniform she's wearing? And isn't that the Lincoln Memorial behind her?"

"Yeah, she trained in Washington with the Red Cross. Shipped out overseas earlier this month. She's in England now."

Phoebe looked up from the photo and grinned. "Aw, Jack, you're in love, aren't you?"

Mama came in from the kitchen, wiping her hands on her apron. Her eyes widened. "Jack! Oh my goodness."

"I told you he was here. Didn't you hear me?" Phoebe said.

Mama hurried forward to pull him into a tight hug. She stepped back but held fast to his arms. "It's been too long since you came home, Jack."

Mama wasn't going to be excited about his immediate plans. His folks had assumed he moved from Albany to Smyrna and then to Dyersburg as an instructor. Jack hadn't wanted to correct that misimpression with a letter or a phone call. Now that he was here, it dawned on him Christmas Eve dinner was hardly the time either. Before he left. Long as he told them before he left.

"Why didn't you come find me in the kitchen?" Mama swiped nonexistent lint from his uniform coat.

"He was too busy showing off this picture of his dreamy new girlfriend," Phoebe teased, holding the photograph out to Mama. "Our Jack's in love."

Mama took the picture from Phoebe. "Oh, why, she's lovely, Jack. You should have brought her with you. I suppose she's with her family for Christmas though, isn't she? When can we meet her? What's her name?"

Jack could all but see visions of wedding dresses and cradles dancing in his mother's eyes.

"Her name's Vivian, and she's with the Red Cross, overseas in England now. We …" Jack stopped. He had been about to say he and Vivian hoped they would end up in the same theater of operations so they might take leave time together.

Mama passed the photo back to him. She didn't seem to have noticed his pause. "Overseas? Oh dear. I know some of the girls have joined the WACs and whatnot. Call me old-fashioned, but I don't think young women have any business going off into a war zone. It's bad enough they're doing so much work in the factories here." Mama frowned at Phoebe. "I still think it would be much nicer, honey, if you would enroll yourself back in college and do something else for the war effort. Besides, it's more likely you would meet a nice young man if you were back in college instead of working with a bunch of women in that factory. Don't you agree, Jack?"

"I love my job, Mother," Phoebe said.

The front door opened. From the sounds of the conversation floating in with them, Pop had caught Rose and her fella in a clinch. "On a public sidewalk isn't seemly, Rose Louise, that's all I'm saying."

Rose followed Pop in the door, rolling her eyes. She stood on tiptoes to kiss Jack's cheek. "I'm glad you're home for Christmas, Jack."

She headed to the staircase.

"Dinner's almost ready, Rose," Mama called.

Mama turned to Pop. "What was all that about?"

"Drove up to find her and that Morris kid smooching right on the sidewalk outside the house," Pop said.

His consternation with Rose dissipated as he clapped Jack on the shoulder. "No problem getting a pass? Figured they would want instructors to stick around and carry on with training."

A squiggle of guilt twisted Jack's stomach. No, he shouldn't fess up now, not with Mama putting dinner on the table.

They sat for dinner some half hour later. Pop reached back to tune in the radio, but Mama waved her hand. "Not tonight, John. It's Christmas Eve. Let's enjoy our family together again without the war news."

"Might be the last time it's just the five of us." Phoebe winked at Jack.

He fought the urge to kick her under the table.

"Oh, that's right. Did you show your father the picture? Jack has a sweetheart, and it sounds serious." Mama passed Rose a platter of sliced ham.

"You and Phoebe inferred serious," Jack muttered.

"Aren't you going to show Pop her picture?" Phoebe passed him the rolls.

"Pop doesn't want to fuss over a photo," Jack said.

"I'd like to see the picture," Rose said.

Phoebe mouthed the words "Jack's in love" to Rose.

Jack and his father exchanged a familiar look of commiseration as Jack pulled the photo out and handed it across the table to Rose.

"Tell Pop and Rose about her," Phoebe said.

"Butter's not scarce yet?" Jack pulled the full crock toward him.

"What's her name, Jack? She's a doll, even in uniform," Rose said.

"Uniform?" Pop reached his hand out for the photo.

Jack repeated the details he had given the others earlier. "And we saw each other in New York before she shipped out a few weeks ago. She's working on a bomber base in England now."

"You're right," Rose said.

Jack looked up. "What?"

"Phoebe's right. Jack's in lurrrvve." Rose rolled and stretched the word into multiple syllables.

"How do you get one of those Red Cross jobs overseas?" Phoebe asked.

"You are *not* going overseas," Mama said. "Bad enough you've cut your education short and taken work in a factory."

Before Phoebe could argue, Jack said, "You have to be at least twenty-five, Feebs, and you'd need that college degree too."

Phoebe glared at him as Mama started in again about her going back to school. He winked at Phoebe's scowl and picked up the snowman salt shaker to add salt to his potatoes.

"What was Vivian doing before she signed on with the Red Cross? Did you say her family's in Georgia?" Mama passed him the creamed corn.

"She was a French teacher for a few years, then she got promoted to be director of a fancy boys' school in Savannah. She's sharp. Wants to go back and get a graduate degree after the war's over."

Mama waved a hand. "She won't need another degree, not if the two of you are going to get married and start a family."

No point denying Mama's assumption about imminent wedding bells. As far as he was concerned, they would be getting married. "She wants to continue with her career. Might go into politics."

"Oh, she'll change her mind once the first baby comes along, I imagine," Mama said. "Besides, you're the one who needs to go back to school. Finish what you started."

Jack fell silent and speared another bite of baked ham. Truth was, of the pair of them, Vivian was the one better suited to pursue more education. All he wanted to do was fly. He had only gone to college because the Army Air Corps required at least two years. Jack had done exactly that and no more. Before the war, his chances of flying outside the military without a degree were low. The war might change all that.

"How much time do you both have away?" Pop looked from Jack to Phoebe.

"I'll need to catch a bus back the day after tomorrow," Jack said.

"I've got the early morning shift, so I have to leave tomorrow night. My friend Doris drove us. She'll be by to get me late afternoon," Phoebe said.

"Is the Vultee factory still hiring?" Rose asked.

Phoebe shrugged. "I expect so. They're running round the clock. Do you know someone?"

"Well, I was thinking I might—"

"You'll do no such thing, Rose. You've got another term yet of high school," Mama interrupted.

"Besides, you'll be closer to that fella of yours if you stay right here. He's been in gunnery training, right? I imagine he might end up in Dyersburg with Jack before too long. Don't you think, son?" Pop said.

He wouldn't be in Dyersburg much longer. He should tell them.

"The army isn't always logical about where it sends men." That much was true.

Rose spooned more green beans on her plate. "You said that gunner on your crew trained where Jimmy's been in Florida, so that makes it more likely."

The ritual sounds of their meal—the scrape of utensils against china, chewing, swallowing—magnified like a drumroll in the slim pause that followed Rose's observation.

Shit.

Jack waited, his glass of water raised halfway to his mouth, his pulse accelerating like B-17 engines lumbering to life in full-throated whining fury.

"Crew? What crew? Are you training crews now?" Pop's

eyebrows drew together. His mouth tightened.

Jack put down his glass and jiggled his knee under the table. "I'm not instructing pilots or crews, Pop. I put in for a transfer to active duty a few months ago. I'm lead pilot for a bomber crew, shipping out in a few months."

Mama's fork clattered to the table.

"You had a deferment based on being a flying instructor." Pop slammed his glass on the table so hard the dishes rattled. "A deferment … Goddammit, Jack, what were you thinking?"

"After what happened to Ace," Mama whispered, tears welling in her eyes. "Oh, Jack, how could you?"

Jack drew in a deep breath. Like trying to breathe through a straw when his chest was this tight. "Don't you see? That's exactly why I have to do my bit."

"There's patriotism and then there's stupidity." Pop's voice rose and his tone moved straight through aggravated to antagonistic. "You were already doing your part, dammit. Why in the hell would you want to throw yourself into the line of fire when you were already performing an essential task? You weren't playing it safe in some goddam desk job. You were doing something the army needs, something not just anyone can do."

"Plenty of fellas can step into that cushy instructor job and be glad to do it." Jack pressed three fingers against his pounding head.

The derision in Jack's tone was lost on Pop.

"Then they've got a hell of a lot more sense than you do." Pop balled up his napkin and threw it on the table. "Going overseas won't bring Ace back."

"No, it won't. But if we win the war, he won't have died for nothing." Jack struggled to pull enough air into his lungs.

Pop snorted. "You think you can win the war singlehanded, do you? You'll get yourself and others killed if you go into combat cocksure and spoiling for revenge."

"Jeez, Pop, where was all this common sense when you enlisted and left Mama to have me all on her own, huh? You didn't lay eyes on me until I was over a year old. Least I'm not leaving Vivian knocked up and coping with an infant."

"As far as you know," Pop retorted.

"John!" Mama said, waving her hand at Phoebe and Rosie, who had abandoned any pretense of continuing to eat.

Jack had half-risen from his seat without realizing it. "Sit down, Jack," Mama said. "Your father didn't know I was pregnant when he enlisted."

"He knew you could have been."

"Enough." Mama stood. "It's Christmas Eve. It's a time for peace, a time for family. No more war talk tonight. Phoebe, come help me slice fruitcake for dessert. Rose, please bring the dishes back to the kitchen."

"I'll help you, Rosie." Jack had no desire to be left sitting alone with Pop.

He pushed open the pocket door that closed the kitchen off from the dining room. He leaned against it so Rose could pass through and glanced back at his father.

Pop was slumped back against his chair, hand over his eyes, eyeglasses held loosely in one trembling hand.

CHAPTER TWELVE

January 27, 1943
USAAF Station 105, Chelveston, England

"Raise by a dollar." Vivian tossed her coins in the kitty, eliciting groans from Bill and Tad, both ground crew chiefs, and Mel, a navigator too laid up with a sinus infection to fly today's mission but not too ill to play a few rounds of poker.

"Hell, Georgia, you must like your hand," said Steve, an aerial engineer.

"Fold. Again, dammit." Bill tossed in his cards and rubbed Pep's neck. Pep, a sheepdog adopted by *Bomb Boogie*'s crew, stuck close to Bill when his crew flew a mission.

One by one, the others folded.

"What about you, Chappie? Still in?" Mel looked at his watch again. He twisted around, eyes squinted at the overcast afternoon sky visible through the window.

Vicar Joe drummed his fingers on the table and looked back and forth between his hand and Vivian.

"Might be gettin' a little rich for ya, Chappie?" Tad lit another cigarette.

"Call." Joe extracted an American bill from his pocket.

"Ooooh, whoo-boy, Chappie must have a good hand if he's parting company with that much money," Bill said. "You may lose for once, Georgia."

Vivian had a full house. Joe had only discarded one card. He might have four of a kind. A straight flush? She had observed that he pulled out of the games when betting got too high stakes for his pay grade. If he called her, he must be confident. Moreover, he could use the money more. If she raised once again to increase the value of the pot, he might fold.

"Ready to show?"

Mel whistled when she laid her cards out, but whooped when Joe showed a royal flush.

Vivian hid a smile. She snapped her fingers in mock disappointment. "Even the best have to lose now and again."

"Peaches here doesn't lose too often. Nice show, Chappie," Bill said.

"We got time for another round?" Tad asked.

"Mel's been antsy for the last half hour," Eddie said. "Don't know why you'd expect them back already. Today was no milk run to France."

"Last mission I flew to France was no fucking milk run, lemme tell you," Mel said. "Germans are pretty intent on protecting those U-boat pens."

U-boat pens, the fellas had explained, were facilities at French ports that the German Navy used to repair and re-equip their U-boats. The Eighth Air Force had been targeting them mercilessly for months.

"Still, point is, they weren't goin' to France today, so we shouldn't expect 'em back yet." Bill looked out the window.

Today marked the first mission to Germany for the American bombers. Tension hung heavy as a blackout curtain. Given how much flak and fighter resistance the Germans put up at France's U-boat pens, no one expected their defense of the Fatherland to be anything less than intense.

Joe was a frequent guest at the base, a steady presence on mission days. He arrived in the predawn hours to meet with crews after they left the briefing room, before they piled into the jeeps to go to the flight line. Joe had taken a special interest in the men at Chelveston and yet hadn't usurped the official base chaplain, Father McClarahan.

Always before, Joe walked back to St. Mary's Church to attend to other matters after the ships took off. Today, he had stayed.

Vivian stood. "I should help Mabs take the doughnuts and coffee to the interrogation room."

She found Mabs and their British staff in the small Aero Club snack bar kitchen. The temperamental doughnut machine was running smoothly for once, churning out hundreds of sinkers to offer to the hungry crews. Jittery pre-mission stomachs caused many men to skip breakfast.

The fellas claimed they weren't hungry at the post-mission debriefing, but they were ravenous. Once they tasted the first hot doughnut, their stomachs sent a quick SOS to their brains. At that point, Vivian and Mabs couldn't keep them coming fast enough. Today they also had sandwiches.

The British women urged Vivian and Mabs to go join the gathering crowd at the control tower. "Go watch the lads coming in," Mrs. Tillman said.

At the base of the tower, Vivian looked up and shaded her eyes. Dark specks interspersed with the white clouds. Droning engines grew louder.

The first ship in the landing pattern sent out a flare. *Grin and Bare It* whizzed past. The crash truck and two ambulances drove parallel to the runway and met the ship at the end of the runway.

Vivian couldn't see anything, but a man with binoculars called out, "Two wounded on board. Loading them both into the ambulance. Others are coming out the hatch okay."

Tall Temptress also sent out a red flare before landing. Three wounded men came off the ship, two of them treated outside the bomber.

Vivian made her way to Mel. "Any missing?"

He shook his head. "The ones that are down look pretty beat up, but they all made it back. There's Bill and his gang heading over to meet *Bomb Boogie*." Mel pointed to a jeep waiting by the runway. It rumbled to life and roared across the field. Pep sat with his paws on the open passenger window, anxious to see his crew again.

Vivian exhaled. Some of the wounded men might not survive, but they now had a chance. A chance far too many men lost on every mission.

"Good. Gotta go serve the crews now."

"Hey, you and Mabs coming tonight?" Mel asked.

There wasn't a dance tonight. Not here. Not at the nearby bases. Not even one at a British base. A rare night when they weren't expected to socialize with officers. Vivian planned to get as warm as possible in her bed and catch up on correspondence. She wrote to Jack almost every day, but she owed letters to her parents, her brothers, and Zanna.

"What's tonight?"

"We're going pub crawling. Bring your bikes. Meet at the back gate, near the path to Yelden. Twenty hundred."

Vivian waved but didn't commit. She had her heart set on a simple no-fuss evening. Besides, she would have to close the club since Mabs took the opening shift today.

"Be sure Mabs knows, all right?" Mel called.

She waved, laughing. They never stopped trying, but the men now understood she was taken. Mabs was a different matter. They besieged her every day with everything from flirtation to outright marriage proposals.

Vivian jogged a short distance to catch up with Mabs.

She couldn't resist adding a razzing note to her tone. "Mel wanted me to tell you *specially* that a group of officers are going pub crawling tonight. He said to bring your bike and meet at the Yelden gate at twenty hundred."

No flirtatious response. No goading her about joining the fun. Shining streaky paths stood out among the freckles on Mabs's cheeks.

Vivian pulled on Mabs's elbow. "What's up?"

"We need to go help them serve," Mabs said, her voice closed off.

"That first crew hasn't even loaded up yet."

"No, I expect they haven't. They'll need to." Her voice broke, and she gulped. "They'll need to have another bombardier take their bombsight off the ship for them."

"I couldn't see. Was their bombardier one of the ones they loaded into an ambulance?"

Mabs swiped at tears. "Chuck Langston."

"Chuck ... the Green Bay fan? Dark hair, kind of looks like Glenn Ford?"

Mabs nodded, her brown eyes round and glistening. "MacLeod was in the control tower. He said ... said their pilot told control tower that one of their gunners had been holding Chuck's head up for three hours, trying to keep him from bleeding to death."

The interrogation building, the fields, and the runways behind them blurred. Bile rose acrid in Vivian's throat. She wanted a gulp of fresh, rain-drenched air, but inhaling filled her nostrils with the pungent smell of sticky mud. She grabbed Mabs's elbow to keep herself upright.

Mabs must have interpreted this as Vivian offering support. "I'll be all right. Just hit me hard." She ran a fingertip under each eye and wiped her tears on her skirt. She looked over her shoulder. "First jeep is loaded and heading this way. Let's go in."

Vivian linked her arm through Mabs's elbow in both a show of empathy and a means of keeping herself moving.

Before the sweaty, grimy crews arrived with lit cigarettes, Vivian inhaled, filling her senses with the familiar aroma of coffee and sugary doughnuts. She tried to push aside the searing image Mabs had painted of a crew in distress, wounded men thousands of feet in the air with no trained medical help on board. Was it wrong of her to hope the army would change its mind and demand Jack stay stateside as an instructor?

The first crews stamped in. Vivian focused on the task at hand, offering a cup of steaming hot coffee to each of the cold airmen.

"Aw, hot joe. Boy does that smell good," the first one said.

"We still get the Scotch, right?" another one said, his eyes scanning the room.

"Yes, yes, you can have the booze too," Vivian assured them. "But start with this coffee and a doughnut."

Some of their hands shook too much to hold the cup steady for her to pour coffee. In those cases, Vivian discretely took the cup, set it on the table, and poured a half cup so the man wouldn't slosh it on his hands when he picked it up again.

Vivian recognized some of the men from *Grin and Bare It*'s crew when they came through the line. Their pilot's hand was steady when she poured his coffee, but he didn't smile, joke, or flirt.

Their navigator waved off the coffee and food. "Can't hold it," he said in a cracked voice.

Navigators flew in the nose of the plane with the bombardier. Vivian tried to slam her mind shut against the unbidden image of what the navigator would have seen, heard, and smelled while working in proximity to a gravely injured man.

"Whoa, sweetheart. I don't need the whole pot," said Sergeant Corcoran. His mug was filled to the rim. One more pour and she would have doused his hand in hot coffee.

"I'm so sorry. Here, put that one down, and we'll start over."

"'S all right, doll. I'll sip a little off the top so it's not so full." He drank a few sips, smiled, and moved on.

The room was soon noisy: ongoing interrogations at eight separate tables, arriving crews joshing with one another and with Vivian and Mabs, and debriefed men imbibing liberal shots of Scotch. Some of the crews were directed back to the hardstands for group photographs to mark the momentous occasion of the first daylight raids on Nazi Germany.

Vivian and Mrs. Sanders, another of their British staff, rounded up a few men to help them transport the dirty dishes and coffee urns to the mess hall kitchen. In the hour since the first Fortress landed, the men had consumed fifteen gallons of coffee, a thousand doughnuts, and four hundred sandwiches. They had piled a dozen empty bottles of Scotch on the trolleys.

Mabs and Mrs. Tillman hurried to open the Aero Club. It would be swarming with men within minutes.

***

Vivian closed the ledger book just before midnight and locked the club's door.

Her eyes were slow to adjust to the darkness.

Normally the route between the club and her quarters teemed with men, but the base was quiet tonight. Many of the men had received a pass after today's mission and were likely whooping it up in London.

Her quarters were situated some distance from the men's accommodations and within shouting distance of a guard post. Vivian usually appreciated the security of that separation and didn't mind the walk. Tonight, the cool mist and odd silence on base created an eerie atmosphere.

She shivered, tightened her scarf, and picked up her pace.

The shortcut across a field was tempting, but it would be muddy and difficult to navigate, not to mention deserted. Vivian continued on the main perimeter road.

A pair of flickering lights in the darkness caught her eye. Cigarettes. By the fuel stores? No man on base would smoke so close to the fuel tanks. Maybe a man had snuck his girl on base and, in the throes of a tryst, forgot how close he was to the combustible aviation fuel. Or it could be village children, enjoying an illicit smoke. Children snuck under the base fences all the time. It would be the sort of dare local boys might think was a lark.

Vivian turned and walked toward the glowing circles.

Wharrrrr ... WHAAAARRRR ... Wharrrrr.

The distinctive rising and falling wail of the air-raid siren blared from every direction.

Vivian stopped. Heart pounding, she looked wildly around. Shelter. She needed to get to a shelter. The closest one was near the club. She turned to backtrack, then hesitated.

If those were village kids, they would be scared and unsure where to go for shelter. Worse still, if the Germans dropped a bomb anywhere near those fuel tanks, they would have no chance.

Vivian whirled around and stepped off the perimeter road. She trained her eyes on the red circles and ran flat-out, her breath visible in the misty air before her face.

Her toe stubbed against some unseen obstacle in her path. Before she could react, Vivian pitched forward and landed hard on her right knee.

Searing pain pulsated from the impact. She pried her palms out of the muck and stood, wincing with pain.

The incessant blaring of the siren reverberated in her ears and set her teeth on edge.

Vivian hobbled forward tentatively, then, once she was confident the knee wouldn't give way, with greater urgency.

An airman with a local lover would have already run straight into her path. It must be children. They might try to run for home. Trouble was, they were a good distance in any direction from the fences separating the base from neighboring villages.

The pinpricks of light faded and vanished.

The immediate area was pitch-black. She hadn't needed a light to follow the perimeter road from the club to her quarters.

Luftwaffe be damned, she needed her flashlight to locate these kids. Vivian pushed her hand first into one coat pocket and then the other. Oh, hell, the mission left late today. She wouldn't have needed a flashlight to serve the pre-mission doughnut run and must have left it behind.

Shouting was pointless. They wouldn't hear her voice over the siren.

Vivian stood stock-still and focused on the area where the red dots had faded, assessing her location. A dark building outline to the left. That was headquarters. The lights had come from the above-ground fuel stores situated near the closest hardstands, to the northeast of headquarters.

Vivian cut a diagonal course from headquarters, the heat-laced pain radiating from her knee dictating a slower pace.

The breeze shifted, and she caught a faint whiff of cigarette smoke. How far away could one smell smoke?

The siren shut off. The last thrumming chorus of wails rang in her ears for a few moments.

Vivian cupped her hand over her mouth and shouted, "Hello, Hello?" No response.

She plowed ahead and continued to call out. Perhaps they had run too far away to hear her.

Fuel drums loomed in her path.

Jack, who closed every letter with pleas to keep herself safe, wouldn't like this one bit. Vivian could pay a steep price if the Germans unloaded bombs in this vicinity.

Bzzzzzzzttttt. A humming, droning, thrumming sounded from somewhere above. Vivian's heart pounded. Airmen would know at once if a plane was friendly or hostile, but she couldn't tell the difference.

Vivian forced herself to run again. If she didn't find them near the drums, she would head to shelter, put distance between herself and the combustible fuel. The strange humming sound grew louder, and Vivian looked up at the pitch-black sky. Pointless. No crisscrossing searchlight beams here.

She slammed into something solid. Someone solid. "Ooof."

Vivian flung her hand forward and closed her fingers around a wool coat sleeve for support.

Two boys, perhaps twelve or thirteen years old.

Her breath came in gasps, and her voice came out louder than she intended. "I'll take you to a shelter. Come with me! Do you have a flashlight?"

"A what?"

They didn't call it a flashlight. What was the British word? Vivian mimed. "A light ... you know, a ... a torch? That's what you call it, right?"

"Oh, a torch, yes'm." The taller boy pulled one out of his coat pocket and passed it to her.

Vivian clicked it on and motioned for the boys to follow. Their shoes crunched on the frost-coated grass, their panicked breathing the only other sound. The droning noise faded away.

She nearly missed the entrance to the shelter. It was camouflaged, hard to spot even in daylight.

They stumbled down the steps, with the bricked walls on either side pressing close.

The concrete door looked heavy and shut tight. No telling if anyone had sought shelter at this one tonight. But when Vivian tugged, it opened, the bottom scraping against the brick.

Light flickered from inside and someone called, "Come on in."

Vivian shone the light on the concrete steps leading farther into the shelter and motioned for the boys to go first.

She pulled the door closed and followed the boys. Her knee objected violently to yet another set of steps, and her heart thudded in her chest, a reaction to the shrill heart-stopping siren and the pace she had set to get them far from the fuel storage.

A few candles had been lit, illuminating the faces of the men sitting on the duckboard seating that lined each side of the long cylindrical shelter.

"Well, well, who do we have here?" Captain MacLeod trained his flashlight on the boys and Vivian in turn.

Vivian laid a hand on the shoulder of each boy. "I had closed the club and was headed to my quarters when the siren sounded. I found these young fellows on my way."

Captain MacLeod cocked an eyebrow, his lips twitched up for a slim moment before settling into a more neutral expression. His eyes locked with Vivian's, and she gave him a brief nod. She would tell him later how she had happened on two village children in the pitch-black of this labyrinthine base.

"Come on over here, lads." Sergeant James, the Clerk of Works, patted the seat to his right.

"You'll be Jed Smithson's boy, will you?" he asked the taller boy.

"Yes sir," the boy mumbled.

"Go on, introduce yourselves properly. Let's have your names. We shall all be good friends in here before the night's out." Sergeant James winked at Vivian.

"Peter. I'm Peter Smithson," the taller boy said, his eyes trained on his shoes.

He nudged the other boy with his elbow, who whispered, "Uh, my name's Ron. Ron Allred."

"We won't worry what you were doing on this base so late at night, lads. I expect your families are worried, so we'll deliver you home straight away once the all-clear sounds. For now, settle in and make yourselves comfortable," Sergeant James said.

Captain MacLeod extracted two candy bars from his coat pocket, which he passed to the boys. They mumbled their thanks but sat quietly, apparently too contrite to even unwrap the candy.

MacLeod gestured to the seat beside him. "No need to stand, Captain Lambert. Where's your partner in crime?"

Mabs. In the flurry of trying to locate the wayward children, Vivian had forgotten her friend. On a pub crawl, they would have a pint at one village's pub and then set out on their bicycles to the next village to make the rounds. They might have been between villages when the sirens went off.

"She went out to the pubs with Lieutenant Simmons and some of the others. They were going to Yelden first." The words tumbled out faster than normal.

"They'll find shelter." MacLeod's firm assurance didn't allay her growing anxiety.

"But they were doing a pub crawl tonight." Vivian couldn't force her mind away from the picture of Mabs and the group of airmen on bikes on a country road between Yelden and one of the other area villages. Exposed, vulnerable.

Her hands trembled. She shoved them deep into her pockets.

"They'll be all right. Probably a false alarm," said Captain Talbot.

The Red Cross in London had trained them in air raid procedures and how to use their gas masks. The training had seemed relevant for London or one of the big industrial cities. Vivian didn't know why it hadn't occurred to her before now. American air bases, clustered tightly together here in East Anglia, presented a dense and appealing target for the Luftwaffe.

Vivian looked at MacLeod. "Does Yelden have an actual shelter? Or only Andersons that the villagers might have?" Back garden Anderson shelters could only hold a few people and were often mucky with accumulated rain water.

"Andersons. We're the target, not these little villages," MacLeod said.

Except those little villages and farmhouses abutted right against the boundaries of the base on all sides. On takeoff, the Forts barely skimmed over the tops of thatched roofs of farmhouses. If the base was the target, those village homes were in the crosshairs.

One of the men had brought a dog to the shelter. He lifted his head, pawed at Vivian's ankle, and whined.

A series of low rolling thuds. *Boom. Boom. Boom.*

It might have been a thunderstorm rumbling off in the distance. Tremors reverberating through the ground above suggested otherwise.

"Well, shit." Captain Talbot looked up at the roof of the shelter.

Another succession of thuds and crackle of explosions.

Vivian's heart raced.

This was no newsreel in the cinema back home. This was real. This was war with all its dangers.

"How far away?" One of the men leaned over to rub another dog's ears.

"It's not the base," MacLeod said. "We would hear and feel more impact."

"No, it's not here," Sergeant James agreed.

"Not yet. Could be any minute." Captain Talbot stared upward and wiped his sleeve across his forehead.

"We'd hear the whine of the bombs coming down if they were closer. We're feeling more than hearing," said MacLeod. "Must be a few miles at least."

Vivian wiped a few flecks of concrete off the dog's shiny black coat.

The thuds and explosions ceased after what might have been hours but was more likely minutes.

All was silent.

Waiting seemed an eternity, but long before the all-clear siren sounded, Vivian knew the Germans had gone. Both dogs had settled.

Once they exited the shelter, Sergeant James motioned for the boys to come with him. "I'll make sure these lads make it home."

He clapped a hand on Ron's shoulder. "Don't you boys have anything to say to Captain Lambert?"

After they each thanked her, they followed the tall Clerk of Works toward headquarters. Their woebegone expressions suggested spending the night in the cold, dark shelter was preferable to facing their families.

Captain MacLeod smiled at the boys' retreating backs and cut his eyes to Vivian. "How about I walk you back to your quarters, and you can tell me how you came to find those boys?"

* * *

When they reached her hut, Captain MacLeod offered to come in and start the coal stove. "I can wait with you until Mabs returns."

He wasn't worried about her safety. The manned guard station was less than a hundred yards away. Yet, Vivian didn't question his motives or worry that he might make a move on her. Archie was devoted to his girlfriend, Sara, a field director with the Red Cross's

London headquarters.

"You don't happen to have anything to drink in here, do you?" He fed kindling into the stove.

Vivian stood and crossed to the shelves over one of the bunks. "As a matter of fact, we do."

She found a bottle of bourbon and a set of touristy glassware she had bought in London to send as a gift back home. Mabs hadn't touched a bottle of Coke from earlier, so Vivian grabbed it to use as a mixer. The room temperature had kept both beverages cold.

MacLeod frowned as she walked toward the center of the room with the drinks and glasses. "Thought you were limping earlier."

"I fell while I searched for those boys. I'll take an aspirin and be fine by tomorrow." Vivian poured a measure of bourbon in each glass and topped it off with Coke.

"I can bring a jeep to take you to sick quarters. Let Doc have a look."

"That's not necessary. I'll be fine." Vivian handed him a drink and moved to the small table near the coal stove. "I'll drop in on Doc tomorrow if it's not better in the morning."

MacLeod pulled out a chair for her. "You might've run for the shelter and told one of us what you'd seen, that you thought it might be kids who had snuck in."

Vivian picked up the deck of cards on the table and shuffled them, raising an eyebrow. When he nodded, she began to deal. "Honestly, it didn't occur to me. Once I decided it might be children, I had to search them out. I hope Sergeant James will impress on them not to sneak a smoke close to combustible matter."

"I suspect once their parents are done with them, they won't be sneaking cigarettes for a long while." MacLeod laughed.

They played at least three hands of gin rummy before they heard the sound of approaching voices outside. Vivian stood and hurried through the door, colliding with Mabs, Mel, and two other officers, Norm Jackson and Ab Hart.

"Am I glad to see you." Vivian gave Mabs a quick hug and stepped out of the way so they could enter.

"Now *that* sure looks like a good way to celebrate living through a Luftwaffe bombing raid," said Norm, eyeing the glasses of bourbon and Coke.

"And how," agreed Ab.

"Plenty of bourbon, but we'd need more Coke," said MacLeod.

"To hell with Coke. I'll take a straight shot of that." Mel pulled off his overcoat and hung it over a chair.

Mabs laughed as she untied the scarf around her hair and took off her coat. "Sounds good to me too."

"Where were you? Do you know what they hit?" MacLeod poured four more glasses and handed them around.

"We started out at the Chequers and had a pint. Then we biked to the Swan, you know, in Newton Bromswold? We took that little footpath that runs alongside the river. We got there all right. Had settled in with a new drink when the village siren sounded."

"The pub's proprietor herded us all out, and we went to an underground shelter," said Norm.

"I don't think Yelden has one. Lucky we'd moved," said Mabs.

"And lucky you weren't out on your bikes on that footpath," Vivian said.

"Well, odds weren't high the Krauts would drop bombs randomly in the countryside at no target at all. Turns out, that may be what happened." Mel took a sip of his drink.

"What?" MacLeod said sharply.

"Didn't sound close enough that they hit here, but we figured fellas at the main gate might know something. The MP told us those bombs dropped at Wellingborough. They're not sure about damage or people hurt," said Norm.

"Wellingborough? Nothing there, is there? Nothing they'd be targeting, I mean." Vivian looked around at the others.

"Nah, nothing military. I bet they were aiming for us and missed," said Mel.

Vivian shivered and downed the last of her drink. Mel was right. They were the most likely target for miles.

CHAPTER THIRTEEN

May 2, 1943
USAAF Station 105, Chelveston, England

Three tiny pairs of legs dangling out of the underside hatch caught her eye.

Vivian braked and slid off her bike. She stared at *What's Cooking Doc*, parked in a nearby hardstand.

The ship's ground crew chief, Sergeant Tad Winters, came around from the front of the nose and waved at Vivian. "Hey, Red Cross."

She set the kickstand. "I thought I saw——"

Now she was closer she heard the unmistakable sound of childish giggles. Tad grinned and pointed up. "Wanna come up and join our young friends? They're enjoying a cold bottle of Coke and a look inside."

Vivian clambered up, grateful she was wearing the drab gray battle fatigue uniform the Red Cross supplied a few months ago. Skirts were impractical for Red Cross work, though headquarters hadn't realized this until women in the field lodged complaints.

Three children from Chelveston were in the cockpit. The two boys jockeyed for position in the left pilot seat, while the little girl hovered at the side.

Tad rapped the boys on the shoulder. "Hey now, no shoving. You don't want to go breaking those Coke bottles, or we've got a big mess to clean up."

The boys stopped the overt jostling, though the older one continued to nudge his thigh subtly against the other one.

"Another visitor today?" Duck Howard, one of Tad's ground crew, squeezed in behind them, clutching three Hershey's chocolate bars. "Sorry, doll, I didn't know to get one for you."

"That's all right. I just came up for a quick hello."

Duck handed candy bars to the boys. "Hang on to those until after you're out of the cockpit, all right?"

"Kiddos, we're about to run an engine check. You can see what it feels like when this ship is running if you don't think the noise will be too loud," Tad said.

The boys exchanged excited looks.

Duck knelt at the little girl's level and handed her a chocolate bar. "What do you say, Ivy?"

She still looked uncertain, and Duck said, "How about if I sit in the copilot seat, and you can sit in my lap?"

Once Duck and Ivy were settled, Tad said, "Keith, Alan, you'll need to let me sit in the pilot seat long enough to start the engines. Then you can come back."

The boys, carefully carrying their Coke bottles with both hands, crowded next to Vivian in the cramped space behind the pilot seats.

Tad leaned out the window and signaled to one of the crew below to clear the first engine. He pushed the start button, and the propeller whirred, the engine roared, and the cockpit vibrated. Noise and reverberation crescendoed with the addition of each of the engines.

Tad moved the throttles. He raised his voice and explained what he was doing, what the various gauges in the intimidating instrument panel showed, and what functions they served.

In his letters, Jack referred to the bombers he flew with feminine pronouns. So did the men here. Both the flight crews and the ground crews who maintained the ships with painstaking care. There was something of a lover's relationship between the ship and the men who flew or looked after her.

"I need to try to catch Mr. Parrish at the bakery," Vivian yelled over the roar as the final engine added its voice to the choir.

Tad waved to show he had heard.

Vivian climbed out the hatch and retrieved her bike. She had made it to the main road leading to Yelden when she heard someone calling her name. She braked and turned.

"I came from the club. Mrs. Tillman said you were in Yelden." Johnnie strode to where she had stopped.

"I'm going now, got stopped with something else." Vivian surreptitiously glanced at her watch. Village shopkeepers in England didn't always adhere to an exact schedule.

"Oh, right." Johnnie scuffed the toe of his boot in a semicircle, eyes on the ground.

Vivian climbed off the bike seat and set the kickstand. "Did you need me for something, Johnnie?"

"Er ... well, I ... er ... I wondered if you could ... Well, I didn't know who to talk to exactly. My squadron commander, well, I don't think he'll be too helpful. Thought about talking to Doc Burke."

Did he want to discuss whether he had picked up some disease on his last leave?

"Johnnie, Doc is who you should seek out, if you've ... er ... not been feeling well."

"No, no. It's not me. I don't know if you've met her. She's come to a few of the dances. Her name's Elsie. She's one of the Land Army girls, works on the Tillman farm."

Elsie. Dark hair, elfin features, large eyes. A certain sweetness. Memorable in that she didn't have the brash manner or the worldliness of the other Land Army Girls, most of whom were from London or large industrial cities.

"Oh, yes, I know who you mean." Vivian waited for him to go on, and when he didn't, she prompted, "Elsie is the one who has a problem?"

"Well, not exactly a problem. Wait, yes. Yes, a problem. A ..."

The moment he turned his flushed, tormented face to look at her, she understood. Yet another thing that wasn't covered in her Red Cross training.

"Elsie's pregnant," Vivian said.

"Yeah. And Colonel Tedders, I know what he's gonna say. He's told the other fellas who landed in the same fix they should pay for the girl to go see someone in London. He advanced them money and put 'em on a tight leash around base. It's not me I'm worried about. Elsie wants to keep the baby."

"And what do you want, Johnnie?" She doubted he had seen his nineteenth birthday.

"I want her to have the baby. I want to marry her. She's willing to go back home with me to Springfield. I've got seven missions left."

Seven missions. Seven dangerous missions. Seven more missions than any crew at this base had yet survived.

No one knew yet what would happen with a crew that did finish those missions. With the heavy losses the bomber crews were sustaining, the men had reason to doubt they would be allowed to go back to the States after finishing one combat tour. They had too much valuable training and experience, and there weren't enough replacements coming in.

Vivian ran her fingers through her hair. "How ... er ... does Elsie know how many months gone she is?"

"About three, she figures. She can still do something. But, we don't want to do that. I ... well, do you think they'd let me marry her?"

"I'm not sure, Johnnie. I'll ask around, all right?"

"That would be swell, Vivian. We know I might have to do all my missions first, but we'd like to get married quick as possible. Maybe fudge the dates a little, you know?"

So innocent. A Yank airman marrying a British girl who has a baby six months later, and no one would suspect anything?

"Let me see what I can learn, and I'll find you when I have more information." Vivian patted his shoulder and smiled. "Where is Elsie's family?"

"She hasn't got any to speak of. Her parents are both dead, died when she was a teenager. She lived for a time with an aunt in Manchester. After the war broke out, she signed on with the Land Army. Her older brother was killed in the Blitz."

"Oh, I'm sorry to hear." So Elsie didn't have ties, probably liked the idea of starting over in America.

"Johnnie, don't rush into a marriage, okay? You haven't known one another too long and—"

"No, I know what you might be thinking. Elsie isn't trying to trap me. We love each other. Please. If something happens to me, I want someone to know about Elsie, about the baby. I'd want my family to help her and be part of my kid's life," Johnnie said.

Perhaps he still saw uncertainty in Vivian's expression, for he plunged on.

"I know every time I go up, my odds of coming back safe are lower and lower. All of us know. I'll feel better knowing I told someone what I wanted."

Vivian couldn't argue with this. Every mission now had losses. Entire ships went down, sometimes with all or some of the crew parachuting to be taken prisoner, sometimes not. Ships returned, but with gravely injured or dead men aboard.

"Should I write it up? I didn't do a will or anything earlier, seeing as how I didn't own anything."

"That's a great idea. Bring it to the club. Mabs and I can both act as witness," Vivian said, relieved she wouldn't be left trying to communicate Johnnie's verbal wishes.

***

Vivian stopped her bicycle at the base of the grassy mound the locals said was the site of a former castle. The limestone bell tower and spire of St. Mary's Church looked picturesque against the uncharacteristically blue sky. Surrounding fields were thick with a flowering yellow plant the English farmers called rapeseed. Some of the men said it reminded them of the wild mustard that grew this same time of year back home on the West Coast.

Joe probably knew how an American soldier could be married over here. He was more likely in his study in the vicarage at this time of day, but Vivian went to the church first.

Since first coming here on Christmas Eve, Vivian had loved this old Norman church. She attended Sunday morning services with Mabs and groups of men from the base, but she most enjoyed the peace and solace she found on her own time.

Vivian paused to read some names and dates on crumbling tombstones in the churchyard and leaned her bicycle against the outside wall when she reached the portico entrance. She scuffed her boots at the bricked entrance before pushing on the heavy wooden door. She breathed in the undefinable smell of age and walked up the center aisle of brick and stone pavers. Dark timber roof beams and pew benches contrasted with light limestone walls and arches. Someone had come in and drawn the blackout curtains back. Natural light filtering in through the stained-glass windows on this sunny day added to the serenity.

Vivian took a seat in one of the front pews and closed her eyes, enveloped in peaceful solitude. She came to St. Mary's in hopes of finding answers that would help Johnnie marry Elsie. But another aspect of her conversation with Johnnie propelled her in the church doors rather than cycling on to the vicarage where she would be more apt to find Joe.

Johnnie was right to recognize his statistical odds of survival. They had lost so many men in the few months since she and Mabs arrived. Chuck Langston wouldn't see his beloved Green Bay Packers play another game. Chris Coble wouldn't play the piano for them at their next party. The entire crew of *El Lobo*, at least four presumed dead. The entire crew of *Boomerang* were POWs. *Devil's Playmate* ditched in the North Sea in February, with no survivors. T*he Hun Hunter. Chuck Wagon. Available Jones.* No survivors, no survivors, no survivors.

And her Jack was coming into this god-awful mess. She had a letter from him yesterday that said so. He hadn't written the word Britain. The censor wouldn't let that pass. But he wrote that they had their orders, were packing, and he would see her soon. He had signed the letter "Jack Sprat." Vivian had no doubt he was coming to England, to the Eighth Air Force. A jolt of frustration-fueled panic pierced, encircled, gripped her heart. She squeezed the locket Jack had given her between her fingers. If only her heart was as invulnerable as the one patterned on her locket.

He wouldn't appreciate the odds stacked against him until he experienced it firsthand. Missions fraught with danger from the moment ships started down the runway. Hastily constructed runways weren't as long as would be ideal for heavy, fully-loaded bombers. Once airborne, catastrophic possibilities multiplied: bumping or crashing into another Allied plane in the tight formations inside heavy clouds that hung over England so much of the time, enemy fire from Luftwaffe fighters, flak from the anti-aircraft batteries defending the targets, mechanical failures, bailing out behind enemy lines, or ditching in the frigid North Sea.

How did these men muster the courage to board their ships for a mission with the casualties mounting all around them? She and Mabs now served doughnuts to the crews before each mission. The Charge of Quarters woke them at three o'clock before he made his rounds to the men's barracks to wake the crews.

Yesterday morning, she had watched from the briefing room doorway. Watched the men, shrouded in the dawn's cool misty fog, as they collected their parachute packs and Mae West life vests. Watched the silhouetted figures, tall and proud, gather around their ship to hear their pilot's pre-mission pep talk. Watched those courageous men follow their pilots into a ship that might serve as coffin rather than shelter.

"May I join you?"

Vivian looked into Joe's kind face. His eyebrows creased, and his welcoming smile flagged.

Her chin trembled, her throat tightened, and a hot rush of unexpected tears fogged her vision. She brushed impatiently at them and waved at the seat beside her.

How could she cry when the British had sacrificed so much more and for so much longer? Were these tears for those men, little more than boys, she had known and loved such a short time, or were they for herself and for Jack?

"You know, the war is closer here. It's natural you should feel it more keenly," he said, breaking the silence.

"I'm not worried for myself," Vivian managed to choke out.

"No, no, my dear, you misunderstand what I meant. Yes, in the main, we're all of us in more danger due to our proximity to the battles, to the reach of the Luftwaffe. What I meant was you can see the realities of war here in a way that wouldn't be possible back home. You become friendly with men who may be here one day and gone the next. You may play a few hands of poker with a man who doesn't return from his mission the next day. You may dance with an officer one evening, only to learn the next day his ship is missing. You may serve doughnuts to a man one morning and find out his plane ditched into the sea hours later. Your work over here adds an immediacy to your wounds."

Vivian swiped at more tears.

"I should imagine you are wondering how can God allow so many fine young men to be slaughtered in the prime of their life? How can God not see the justness of our cause against fascism and tyranny and evil? How can God not spare more of our young men who are on the right side?"

Vivian knitted her trembling hands together in her lap. "Something like that, I suppose."

"I wonder if it might help to think about how many of the enemy soldiers are simply doing what their leaders tell them must be done. They too are young men who have little or no say in what they are commanded to do in the name of their country."

She turned to look at him. "So God will stand by? Let mankind do its worst until we're all wiped off the face of the earth?"

Joe sighed. "Since Cain first raised his hand against Abel, God has wept at our capacity to choose the path of violence and death over life and love. I should not think that God likes war and bloodshed. I imagine He weeps at what His children have done to one another, what they will continue to do for the foreseeable future. God, I believe, knows that when confronted with evil of this magnitude, His children will use their God-given power to rise up against the despots and protect the innocent."

Vivian pulled her clasped hands against her stomach. "And in the meantime, thousands of young men will lay down their lives against evil."

"It's natural we wish for divine intervention. But God didn't start the war, man did. And man must end it. I know this isn't what you want to hear. I wish I could give you better answers." Joe extracted a handkerchief from his pocket and passed it to her.

Vivian wiped her face.

No, it wasn't what she wanted to hear. Joe was right. What she wanted to hear was that there was some easy way to stop all death and destruction. Some way to assure Jack's safety. Some way to assure her brothers would make it home safe and sound. Bob's latest letter confirmed he was "somewhere in Britain," and based on several lines of Dylan Thomas's poetry he quoted, Vivian suspected he must be in Wales. Danny expected to be assigned to a naval squadron on one of the aircraft carriers any day now. Given the infrequency of his correspondence, he might already be at sea.

They sat in silence for a bit.

Joe rose, using the back of the pew in front of them as leverage.

"Oh, Joe, I came here to ask you a question. How would an American soldier go about getting married over here?"

"I thought your young man was still in America?" Joe raised his eyebrows.

Vivian smiled. "He is. Well, in truth, his last letter says he was shipping out, and I think he's coming here. But, it's not me we're talking about. One of the men on base has, well, has need to get married as soon as possible."

"Ah, I see. Well, tell him he'll need to secure a marriage license from the town hall. If he's planning to marry her in a church, this church for example, the banns must be read out for three Sundays prior to the wedding. If waiting more than three weeks presents a problem, he can buy a special license from the town hall. That expense at least shouldn't be a problem for your Yank soldiers." Joe winked.

"Right." Vivian stood and stuffed the handkerchief in her pocket. "I'll pass that information on to him."

"Good. Tell him to come see me straight away if he wants the banns read this coming Sunday. I'll come round the base tonight for poker with the boys if he wants to find me. Are you playing tonight?"

"Thanks, Joe. I'm not sure about poker. I'm closing the club, and some of the fellas are leaning on me to come to Chequer's tonight for a pint."

"Some of those boys are all too happy to keep you away from their poker games," Joe said.

Vivian waved and walked back up the aisle. She pushed open the church door and stepped into the afternoon sunshine.

She parked her bike against the side of the Aero Club and headed toward the entrance. Vivian wouldn't have been surprised to find Johnnie waiting outside the door, anxious to hear what she might have learned since she had left him scarcely an hour ago. The men relied on her ingenuity. Whatever she didn't know off the top of her head, well, they were sure she could find the answer within minutes, hours at most.

What she hadn't expected was Mabs to be waiting to hand over a telegram from Red Cross Headquarters in London.

Vivian tore it open and scanned the message.

```
VIVIAN ELAINE LAMBERT
USAAF STATION 105,
CHELVESTON, ENGLAND

YOU ARE HEREBY DIRECTED TO REPORT TO RED
CROSS   HEADQUARTERS,   GROSVENOR   SQUARE,
LONDON,  BY  AFTERNOON  OF  4TH  MAY  1943
REGARDING PENDING IMMEDIATE REASSIGNMENT
TO CLUBMOBILE UNIT 337, LEICESTER.
```

"Well?"

"I'm being reassigned to one of the Clubmobiles."

CHAPTER FOURTEEN

July 1943
Leicester, England

"Vivian? Come away, love. You're the early bird today."

Louise Hadaway, proprietress of the boarding house, stood framed in the doorway in the slim shaft of light from the hall. "I can send you off with a cuppa if you like."

Neither Dottie nor Jean stirred when Vivian returned from the frigid hall bathroom. She had spot-cleaned her battle fatigues last night, yet they still reeked of doughnut grease. Only way to get rid of that stench was to dunk the fatigues in aviation fuel at a bomber base and hang them out to dry.

She padded into the kitchen, carrying her combat boots so she wouldn't disturb the others. Besides the room she shared with fellow Clubmobile girls, Dottie and Jean, Mr. Jones, a retired music teacher, and Misses Claudia and Gloria Snell, elderly sisters, had rooms here.

Vivian stepped into her boots and laced them. She pulled out a chair and sat.

"Remind me again why you're doing the early shift for the third morning in a row." Louise pushed a bowl of oatmeal and a steaming hot mug of tea across the table to Vivian.

"My friend Mabs wants me to come to Chelveston tonight for a dance. She's sending a couple of officers to pick me up around six. I'll stay overnight with her on base, and someone will bring me back tomorrow evening. I'll have all of tomorrow off."

"Well now, that sounds lovely and worth losing sleep," Louise said.

Vivian took a sip of the aromatic tea. Perhaps. She was utterly exhausted, and only the promise of catching up with Mabs prompted her to accept the invitation. That and an entire day off.

A stack of letters tucked between a vase of flowers and the salt and pepper shakers on the table reminded her. "No letters for me yesterday?"

"Sorry, not anything yet, duck. Took time before the army got Dottie and Jean's mail sorted. Why doesn't the Red Cross handle your mail itself?"

"I'm not sure." All she cared about was that Jack was somewhere in Britain by now, but until she received another letter from him, she didn't have any chance of discovering where he had been posted.

Vivian stood and pulled on her field jacket, which now sported insignia patches from the army ordnance units based near here in addition to all the 305th bomber group's squadron patches. "Thanks for the breakfast, Louise. I'll see you tonight before I leave."

"Be careful, dear. I do wish they'd send a man to see you girls safely over there in the mornings."

"I'll be fine. I know the route well now," Vivian assured her. Besides, the dark was already giving way to the first bloom of dawn on the horizon. Vivian enjoyed the solitude of her walk through the empty streets of Leicester to the 820th engineer battalion's base on her early shift mornings. It was the only peace she would know all day.

She exchanged morning greetings with the MP at the guard station and walked through the quiet base. No loud whine of the generator as she approached the mess hall where their Clubmobile, the *South Dakota*, was parked. Damn.

Rather than walk around to the entrance, Vivian pushed against the back door of the mess. Locked. She pounded on it. Waited. Nothing but clanging metal pans and various voices of the staff making breakfast for the hundreds of hungry men based here. She pounded longer and louder. She finally heard approaching footsteps.

"Who the fuck would make all this racket at this hour?" The door pushed open with such force that if she hadn't taken an anticipatory step backward, it would have knocked her flat.

"Aw, shit," the mess worker said. Turning toward the kitchen, he called, "Which one of you lazy fucks was supposed to turn on the generator for Red Cross?"

A skinny private clad in a stained white undershirt and fatigue pants hurried past her and his still-swearing supervisor.

He returned a few minutes later, apologizing again.

Vivian smiled and thanked him. Loud chugging from the generator meant the *South Dakota* had power.

She flipped the heat switch on the doughnut machine. If she was lucky, it would put out some warmth into this freezing bus. She wrapped her scarf tighter, reluctantly stashed her mittens in her fatigue pockets, and rolled up her sleeves.

A radio and early morning music programming, that's what she needed. She could put a record on the Victrola, but she couldn't change out the records once she started mixing dough. Their English driver, Charlie, also hadn't yet figured out how they might play the Victrola without the music blaring through the outside speakers mounted on the *South Dakota*. The last thing Vivian needed was for a load of soldiers to show up at the Clubmobile while she was cooking doughnuts. They would offer to help, and it would be a disaster. Work space was cramped, and extra people underfoot always resulted in spilled ingredients, mess, and more work.

Vivian dragged one of the hundred-pound bags of doughnut mix, slit it open, and measured out the fifteen pounds she needed for the first batch of dough into a pail. She ran water into a large pitcher in the sink, sifted the flour into the metal dough container, and poured in the water.

Now came the hard part. Her poor, red, chapped hands were happy with the overnight respite. Vivian gritted her teeth and plunged her hands into the cold dough, kneading it until thoroughly mixed. She stuck her gooey hands under the taps, wincing at the even colder water temperature.

She pressed the metal disc on top of the dough mix inside the canister. It would force the dough through to the cutter and into the hot fat. She clamped the top on and hoisted the heavy canister on the machine.

Vivian set out as many wire trays as would fit on the counters and located the tongs. She lugged a large metal pail to the side and measured out another fifteen pounds of the flour mix and refilled the water pitcher.

Now that the next batch was prepped, she turned to the machine. Hot doughnuts slid down the chute. Vivian transferred them to wire trays.

And so it went. Mixing dough, filling trays, preparing the coffee urns.

"Good thing I have a college degree for this job," Vivian muttered, circling and shrugging her aching shoulders.

The Red Cross only wanted college-educated career girls, but the actual work hadn't correlated too closely with the exacting qualifications.

Dottie had groused a few nights ago that any bimbo with a pretty smile and the ability to mix flour and water could do the job. Vivian and Jean hadn't contradicted her.

Granted, starting and running an Aero Club required some business know-how. Keeping account ledgers, deciding where to cut expenses, hiring and firing workers, and procuring supplies wasn't easy. Each Clubmobile crew also had to keep detailed records—the expenses of the raw materials used, how many men they served, how many doughnuts, gallons of coffee, packs of gum, and cigarettes they gave out.

The job was more exciting and more of a career boost than if she had taken a defense plant job back home. But it became harder with each passing day to ignore the nagging worry that her brain was less useful than her hands and her pretty face.

Perhaps she was simply worn down by the brutality of war. All those months of watching too many bomber boys get killed or maimed had taken a toll. She ought to take leave, more than the overnight stay she was taking tonight. Yet, now that Jack was in England, Vivian was more determined than ever to hoard her accumulated leave time.

She grabbed the tongs. Doughnuts piled up. Worrying about Jack wouldn't get the job done or improve her mood.

By the time Dottie and Jean arrived at ten o'clock, Vivian had a good start on the food and coffee they would need for the day's route.

"Ah, the aroma of fresh, hot doughnuts," Dottie said. "It's the first thing I'll do back home—seek out a doughnut shop."

"Won't we all," Jean said.

"The boys love 'em." Vivian wiped perspiration from her brow with her forearm. Her hands were matted with gooey dough.

Now that the others were here and the base was wide awake, they could have music. Jean turned on a record. Before long, clusters of GIs stuck their heads inside the Clubmobile to chat or beg for a doughnut. Several lounged on the benches in the back near the Victrola and changed the records.

Charlie arrived by noon. Bangs and vibrations reverberated through the Clubmobile as he fueled it and switched off the generator power.

Dottie shooed the last of the GIs out the door, while Vivian and Jean secured the trays of doughnuts and coffee urns.

"'Lo, ladies." Charlie opened the driver's door and slid in. He consulted the schedule taped to the dashboard. "Army depots at Gaddesby and Ashby Folville today."

Vivian took the seat next to Charlie, the perk of doing the early-bird shift. Dottie and Jean were left with the benches in the back. As the *South Dakota* lurched down bumpy, rutted roads to today's destinations, they would be buffeted from side to side into one another.

It took an hour to drive the fifteen miles to Gaddesby. Narrow country roads weren't easy to traverse, and Charlie couldn't drive very fast in the awkward, loaded-up *South Dakota*.

Before they chugged through the gates, Charlie stopped. Dottie and Jean moved to the front, so they too could lean out the windows and call greetings to the excited soldiers who waved and ran beside the Clubmobile.

"You betcha! We'll save a few, don't worry," Vivian called in response to the guard soldiers' pleas for them to bring doughnuts on their way out.

Clubmobile work meant longer days and fewer breaks, but the men they served were infantry soldiers who weren't yet jaded by the losses endured by the airmen. They were training hard and they missed America, but they weren't bloodied and beaten down like the bomber crews and fighter pilots.

Charlie pulled up to the base mess hall and hopped out to connect the *South Dakota* to the mess's electricity so they could play the Victrola through the PA system.

Vivian and Dottie opened the windows to create the serving counter and joked with the large cluster of men who had surged to the front of the Clubmobile.

"Where are the sinkers?"

"Have you got any recent newspapers?"

"Heard there's a new record by Dinah Shore—do you have it?"

Vivian moved a wire tray of doughnuts to the counter but swatted at the hands of the first men in the line. "Hold your horses. Coffee isn't set up yet."

"C'mon, Georgia, just one?"

"You want coffee to dunk it in, don't 'cha?" Dottie said.

Charlie signaled they had electricity, so Jean started the music. Men cheered when the PA system crackled and the opening strains of "A String of Pearls" sounded. Jean fiddled with the PA knobs, cranking the volume.

"You gonna dance with me today, Seattle?" A man demonstrated his dance moves with an imaginary partner to the amusement of his buddies.

"After we get everyone squared away with doughnuts and coffee, I'll come out and dance," Dottie promised.

"All right, fellas, we're ready now." Vivian handed a cup of coffee to the first guy in the line and held up her finger to indicate he could take a single doughnut. He grabbed two and smirked at her.

"You want any sweetener with it?" Vivian poured coffee for the next in line.

"Stick your finger in it, and that'll do," he said.

She grinned and laughed as though she had never heard the overused joke.

COURAGE TO BE COUNTED

The line to the Clubmobile snaked out for what seemed like a mile.

Jean pulled out a tray of doughnuts. "I'm gonna take these to the back of the line. That way if some of these fellas only want a doughnut, they don't have to stand in this line."

"Looks to me like this base is big enough now they oughta get their own club." Dottie pulled more coffee cups from the cabinets and set them next to Vivian.

"They're movin' most of us outta here soon, I hear," one of the men who had overheard her remark said. "Somewhere nearer the coast. Can I have a pack of gum while I'm here?"

Vivian pulled a pack out of her pocket, transferred it into his hand, and hoped the men nearest wouldn't also clamor for gum, candy, and cigarettes. They offered those items after the main service of doughnuts and coffee.

Jean was back in short order, swinging an empty wire tray. "Boy, are they hungry."

Vivian passed another loaded tray out the door to her and slid the empty one into one of the racks.

Dottie changed the record again and leaned out the door to call to the cluster of men who had already finished their coffee and doughnuts. "Any of you fellas wanna come in and change the records for us?"

Vivian smiled but barred the door with her arm after seven or eight GIs clomped inside. "Maximum occupancy is ten." Clods of dirt from their boots caked *South Dakota's* central aisle. Vivian kicked one out of her way.

After they finished the doughnut and coffee service, the women stepped out of the Clubmobile. True to her word, Dottie danced with some of the men.

Vivian circulated with a tray filled with free goodies. British soldiers, already resentful of the higher pay earned by their American counterparts, were charged for food and amenities in their base clubs. To curtail some of their ally's resentment, the army dictated the Red Cross must charge money for everything offered in its on-base Aero Clubs. The average American soldier didn't understand the underlying political justifications, and the Red Cross's reputation suffered unfair accusations of greed. Clubmobile service, on the other hand, could offer everything for free because the British weren't running a similar mobile service. Vivian handed out large amounts of gum, cigarettes, candy bars, razors, and comic books.

"Next stop should be a little quicker. Smaller outfit there." Charlie started the engine to head out.

"Don't forget to stop at the guard station," Jean said.

Charlie laughed. "I don't think they'd let us through if we didn't stop."

They got out and handed around doughnuts, gum, and candy. Jean poured coffee into their canteen kit mugs. They didn't like to shortchange the guards out of a little conversation to go with the food and coffee.

Charlie beeped the horn, leaned out the window, and called, "They're expecting us at Ashby Folville, ladies."

Late afternoon sun peeked behind the clouds when Charlie maneuvered the *South Dakota* back to its parking spot near the 820th's mess hall in Leicester.

Vivian opened cabinet doors and set dirty cups and saucers on the counter to be washed.

"I was going to clean the urns first." Dottie shifted the stacks of saucers to one side.

"It's so much more efficient to put the clean cups and saucers away first. Besides, I've already got them stacked and ready to be dunked in the soapy water." Vivian unlatched the next cabinet and pulled out another stack of dirty cups.

Jean cleared her throat. "*Besides*, you don't need to be back here doing anything. *Besides*, you're supposed to be off-duty. *Besides*, your ride to Chelveston will be arriving soon."

Vivian set the cups in her hands back into the cabinet and straightened.

Dottie raised her perfectly groomed eyebrows. Jean had a hand on her hip, a mixture of exasperation and laughter evident in her expression.

Vivian exhaled and smiled. "I'm sorry. I'm doing it again, aren't I?" She had reached an understanding with Jean and Dottie shortly after her arrival that they shouldn't mince words if she was attempting to take over.

Dottie waved a hand at her. "Don't worry, Vivian. But please go on and have fun. We'll deal with all this just fine."

"See you tomorrow night," Vivian called as she climbed out.

A few minutes later, Vivian pushed open the door to their boarding house. She paused in the front entryway to remove her muddy boots before moving into the kitchen.

"Well, hello, dear. How was your day?"

"Good, but smelly, muddy, and tiring. Like usual." Vivian leaned over the pot to see what Louise was making for dinner. "Umm, bean soup. That smells delicious. I'm sorry to miss it."

"Shouldn't you be changing your clothes?"

"Yes, I thought I'd check with you ..." Vivian trailed off without finishing. The answer was written in Louise's expression.

"Sorry, dear. I know you're anxious. It also took time before Jean got her mail."

A month without mail was torture. She had continued to write to Jack, assuring him she was fine but wouldn't receive his letters until her mail sorted itself out.

Louise nodded at the combat boots Vivian was carrying. "You won't need those while you're gone, will you?"

Vivian shook her head, and Louise reached out to take them. "I'll clean them and leave them to dry outside in the garden tomorrow."

"Oh, that would be swell, Louise. Thanks."

"Don't mention it. Now off with you. Go make yourself smart for those Yank airmen." Louise shooed her out of the kitchen.

Did she have time to run a bath? It would be only a few inches of tepid water, but a big improvement over her toiletry for the last several days.

Jean had left a small stack of new American magazines on her bedside table. Vivian picked one up and flipped through it. How tempting to stay here. Have a leisurely bath, wrap up in warm clothing, crawl in bed, and read these magazines. She never had a moment to sit in peace. Not once in six months had she taken an entire evening to herself.

Her bath didn't take long. No point lingering in four inches of cool water. She had put on her underthings, powdered her face, and brushed out her hair when Louise knocked on the door to offer her hot curling tongs. Vivian thanked her and rushed to the mirror. Her hair, stubbornly resistant to taking and holding curl, looked only passably better when she gave up.

She had pulled on her uniform skirt and blouse when Louise knocked on the door again. 'Two nice looking young men from Chelveston are downstairs waiting to collect you."

"Thanks, I'll be right there." Vivian pulled on her uniform jacket and picked up her cap and musette bag.

Her mood perked up when she entered the sitting room. Stephen Sellers and Mabs's boyfriend, Mel Simmons, chatted with Louise and the Misses Snell.

Stephen and Mel asked a lot of questions about her Clubmobile work on the drive to Chelveston. Which units they served, what morale was like in the various army units, were those men as much fun as the fellas at Station 105, was it more work to drive around?

Vivian was grateful the men were keeping the conversation light and cheerful. She would learn soon enough which men had been killed or gone missing since she left Chelveston. But she would rather attend the dance in a more festive frame of mind.

Several familiar faces stood out in the groups of men they passed on the drive into the base. Many of them waved and called greetings. Stephen parked a short distance from the Officers' Club.

"If Mabs wasn't busy closing the Aero Club, she'd be outside waiting. She can't wait to see you again," Mel said.

"Changed much in the weeks you've been gone?" Stephen asked as they stepped through the door of the Officers' Club.

There was an immediate crush of men. "Hey look, Georgia's back again."

A glint of golden hair shimmered under one of the pendant lamps.

Vivian's eyes focused on the one face that stood out among the sea of familiar faces crowded around the bar.

Jack.

CHAPTER FIFTEEN

"Jack!"

Jack turned, and his heart swelled in his chest.

Vivian stood framed in the Officer Club entry. She hurled herself through the airmen crowding the path between them.

Jack hurried forward and enfolded her in his arms. He buried his face in her hair and inhaled the fresh scent of her shampoo.

"You're here. Oh my God, you're here." Her hands locked around his neck as though she would never let him go.

"Thought I might have to call every base in the country to find you," he murmured in her ear.

Jack dipped his head and closed his lips over hers. Her fingers threaded into his hair, and her lips moved hungrily against his. His breath quickened, and he tugged her closer. If Vivian was bothered by the wolf whistles and teasing remarks of the men surrounding them, she gave no indication.

Damn but it felt exactly right. Even in this crowded room reeking of smoke, sweat, and beer, Vivian flooded his senses.

At last, he pulled back and kissed her forehead. His heart thumped hard in his chest. She was here. Here and in his arms.

In the weeks he had been in Ireland awaiting assignment, Jack had realized the daunting challenge of finding Vivian, armed only with the knowledge that she was "somewhere in England." The USAAF had at least a hundred bases, and the Red Cross maintained hundreds more off-base clubs. Holding his girl securely, Jack silently thanked God, Lady Luck, or whomever had a hand in their unexpected good fortune.

He stole another kiss and whispered, "Can't believe it."

"Now, now, would the Red Cross approve of canoodling on the dance floor?" Resonant baritone notwithstanding, the man's voice held a teasing note.

A tall boyish-faced captain stood behind Vivian. He winked at Jack.

Vivian turned her head and burst out laughing. "Archie!"

"Hiya, kid." He nodded at Jack. "This fella your pilot?"

Vivian squeezed Jack's hands. "Jack, this is my friend Archie."

MacLeod shook Jack's offered hand. "Captain Archie MacLeod. Haven't been here long?"

"No," Jack said. "Got here yesterday."

"Figured. I would have known you from Vivian's pictures if I'd seen you around. Which squadron?"

"Three sixty-xix. Haven't met too many people outside of my barracks."

"I'm three sixty-five. See you around in the officers' mess."

Moving toward the bar, MacLeod patted Vivian's shoulder. "Good to see you around here again."

Jack's heart settled somewhere near his ribs. "Wait, I thought this was your base."

"It was until last month. I got transferred to a Clubmobile operating out of Leicester. Mabs invited me to come back tonight for a visit. Have you not been getting my letters?"

"Not since I left the States. They said mail will catch up to me here."

Vivian nodded. "My mail hasn't started forwarding yet either. It's been making me crazy. Your last letter said you had orders, and then I didn't hear anything else. At least we know where to find each other."

Small comfort. Jack wanted nothing more than to never let her out of his sight again. "How far away is … where'd you say you are now?"

"Leicester. It's about an hour from here."

Not ideal, but at least they were no longer separated by the Atlantic Ocean.

"Hey, Red Cross! How ya doin'?" A short, pudgy lieutenant with a thick northern accent barreled toward them. Still more men trailed behind him.

Jack took her hand. She smiled and locked her fingers with his.

Dammit, he should have spirited her away from the crowds. Now they would be stuck here being polite for God knew how long. All Jack wanted was to make up for lost time.

It took half an hour for all the men to ask Vivian about her new assignment, exchange a few jokes, shake Jack's hand, and proclaim him a lucky guy.

No wonder her letters had been filled with the names of so many men. Every man on base seemed to know her. Jack had believed her when she wrote that the men respected her and understood she had a boyfriend. It wasn't that he didn't trust her. But he figured at least some of the fellas were on the make, no matter what they told Vivian.

Jack watched closely, but saw no evidence of that tonight. This notion that a woman could be a buddy was new to him. It seemed the war was changing everything.

When the last fella had finally wandered off to the bar, Vivian squeezed his hand. "I thought you left the States at the end of April. Did they delay you?"

Jack shook his head. "Been waiting in Ireland for six weeks. Fellas on my crew used the time to sample every ale and lager the local pubs had on tap."

"They'll find plenty of that around here too. Pub crawls are fun, especially ..." Vivian's eyebrows knit together.

"Especially?" Jack prompted.

"Especially between missions." She averted her eyes and tightened her hold on his hand.

"Expect that's a good way to spend evenings in these little villages. No movie theater, no bowling alley, no skating rink."

Vivian didn't answer. Had she had a bad experience in one of the pubs? A fella got too rowdy or pushed her boundaries? A flush heated

Jack's neck.

He paused long enough to infuse a note of nonchalance into his tone. "You don't like the pubs?"

"The pubs are good fun. It's only ..." Vivian took a deep breath. "It's only that, well, you're here now. You'll be flying missions. Combat missions."

Right. The US Army Air Forces didn't bring him to England for dances and pub crawls. They brought him here to take the war to the Luftwaffe, to the Nazi war factories, and if need be, to the German people.

Jack pressed his lips together. He had picked up on despair in her letters. Based on context around the places the censor had snipped from her letters, he guessed the Eighth Air Force had sustained large losses.

"Hey, I'm the best pilot in the US Army Air Forces, remember? Isn't that what you bragged to all these fellas?"

It was the wrong tack to take. Red blotches popped on Vivian's neck, and a sheen of unshed tears clouded her eyes. She brought a hand in front of her lips. "Jack, no. You don't understand. It's got nothing to do with your skill."

Jack pulled her into his arms. Her heart hammered wildly against his chest. "I shouldn't have said that. I know, Viv. Didn't mean to be flippant."

She would have known many men who had been killed. Men like Ace. Jack gulped air.

It wouldn't serve any purpose for him to make the assurances on the tip of his tongue. His skill would play a big part in how he and his men fared in battle. Years of flying experience won him the left seat and command of his ship. Jack took pride, and yes, dammit, a certain measure of confidence, that his experience would stand him in good stead when it counted.

He tilted her face up and stroked her hair away from her forehead. "Let's enjoy this fine band that's about to start. Let tomorrow take care of itself."

Vivian swallowed and nodded, her eyes locked with his.

She pulled him closer. Jack nuzzled her neck.

Was it possible for them to disappear from this dance?

He had heard outlandish tales of men taking lovers into parked bombers at the flight line. No, he had no intention of making love to Vivian for the first time in the waist belly of a Fortress. Or a haystack in the surrounding fields. Or in the Nissen hut he shared with seven other men. Vivian deserved romancing with privacy, candlelight, and flowers.

Whatever options the base might offer lovers, it couldn't measure up to the standards he had in his head. For now, he would dance with her and show her a good time.

"Want me to get you something to drink before the band starts playing? Another beer?" Her friends had supplied them both with a beer earlier.

"Thanks, honey, but not now." Vivian kissed his cheek and stepped out of his arms. "I need to make a trip to the bathroom."

Jack looked around. He had seen men coming and going from one small bathroom near the back. "Is there one for women in here?"

"No. There's one at headquarters. I'll be back in a jiffy, don't worry." Vivian had taken only a few steps when a woman in a Red Cross uniform hurried forward, called her name, and enveloped Vivian in a fierce hug.

She pulled back from their embrace but grabbed Vivian's hands. "Oh, Viv, I've missed you so much, you have no idea. It's not the same around here without you."

"I've missed you something awful. Jean and Dottie are tops, but it's not the same." Vivian nodded her head toward Jack. "This fella look familiar?"

The woman glanced up at him and clapped a hand flat against her chest. "Uff da!"

Vivian laughed. "We've surprised her if she's lapsed into Wisconsin-speak. Jack, this is my friend Mabs. Mabs, Jack."

Mabs's brown eyes met his. Her friendly smile told him he had passed muster.

He grinned back at her. "Vivian mentioned you in her letters. Good to meet you."

She turned to Vivian. "Golly, Viv, I'm sorry. I would have called you if I had seen your fella around base. It's been crazy around here since you left, but I can't believe I missed him."

Jack held up a hand. "Oh, no, I got here yesterday. Barely unpacked."

Mabs swiped dark red curls off her face and dabbed away beads of perspiration at her temples. "I have been working long hours, but, whew, glad to know I wasn't that distracted."

"Why the long hours? You look wrung out, honey."

"Everything got loused up at headquarters. Big surprise." Mabs rolled her eyes. "Your replacement has only been here two days. She's swell, don't get me wrong, but it's been hard to do it all alone."

Vivian frowned. "You've been on your own for more than a month?"

"I'm exhausted. We're so glad you're here and can help us out tonight. Not much of a night off for you, but you know how it is."

"I came prepared, wore my dancing shoes." Vivian held out a foot to display a scuffed, low-heeled black pump.

Jack couldn't wait for the excuse to hold her close on the dance floor and twirl her around with the faster swing tunes.

"The band will start any minute," Mabs said, her eyes traveling over to the stage where the musicians tuned their instruments in a cacophony of discordant noise.

"Mabs and I booked the Sky Liner band months ago. You're in for a treat tonight," Vivian told him.

The musicians all wore USAAF uniforms. "Haven't heard of them before. They're all in the service?"

"Yep," Mabs said. "Some of the soldier bands are better than others. These fellas are tops. They're booked all the time."

A slender freckled officer, approaching Mabs from behind, put a finger to his lips. He circled his hands around Mabs's waist to pull her against him and kissed the back of her neck.

"Ooh!" Mabs startled.

"Band's about to start, sweetheart. I get first dance, right?"

"First and last." She turned in his arms and smiled up at him.

He tilted his head toward her. "Just the two?"

Mabs swatted at him. "You know the rules."

"Rules are meant to be broken."

"Mel, stop it already. Introduce yourself to Vivian's fella or haven't you noticed him?"

"Vivian's boyfriend is here?" He straightened, let go of Mabs, and held out a hand. "Melvin Simmons."

Jack shook his hand. "Jack Nielsen."

"You're part of the group that arrived yesterday?"

"Squadron 366," Jack said.

The microphone crackled, and the band leader introduced the musicians.

"Better get your dance in, buddy." Mel grabbed Mabs's hand and towed her toward the dance floor.

Fast-paced "Hep-Hep! The Jumpin' Jive" wouldn't have been Jack's first choice. He was relieved when the band played "Manhattan Serenade" next. Now he could pull her close.

"Only one more, Jack," she murmured.

One more dance? They had all night.

Dancing close, holding tight to her hand, was heaven. He tilted his head toward her and leaned in to steal a quick kiss.

"Thought smooching was off-limits, Georgia," said a man dancing with one of the local girls.

"He's my boyfriend. He's allowed as many kisses as he wants."

"Lucky fella. Don't let her near your poker games, buddy. She's got a corner on all the luck."

"You play poker?"

"Yeah. Daddy taught me and my brothers one summer. Mama wasn't keen on my doing it, but I'm sure glad I know how. It's a good way to pass time, especially when it's too wet and miserable to go out to the pubs. I do have uncommonly good luck. Joe says the fellas are trying to hide their games from me." Vivian laughed.

"Joe?"

"Joe Chapman, the vicar at Yelden. I might have referred to him as Chappie in my letters. That's what all the fellas here call him. We've become good friends."

"So all the guys here *and* Joe, huh?"

"Joe, the *vicar.*" Vivian playfully shoved her hand against his chest and grinned at him.

"Is he a married vicar?" Jack widened his eyes mockingly and tilted his head.

Vivian pursed her lips to hide her smile. "Widowed. Older. No reason for you to be jealous."

His stomach clenched. Even if the vicar wasn't a problem, Jack was still unnerved by the easy familiarity and banter between Vivian and all these men. Apart from the Red Cross Girls, there were perhaps twenty local girls. The men crowded around the dance floor far outnumbered the women.

The song ended, and Vivian gave Jack a swift kiss on the cheek. "Listen, I have to dance with the others now. I'll save the last dance for you."

Jack's jaw tightened. Mabs had told Mel he would have her first and last dances, but that shouldn't apply to Vivian. This wasn't her assigned base.

"But I'm your fella, don't I get dibs?" His voice oozed charm with whipped cream and a cherry on top.

"Sorry, honey. It's my job to be sure all the soldiers have a good time at these dances." She squeezed his hand.

"This isn't your base anymore. So it's not your job, is it?"

"I'm in uniform."

He leaned in close. "I can take care of getting you out of uniform," he whispered against her neck and discretely nipped her earlobe.

She inhaled deeply. "Don't torture us both."

Some scrawny dogface lieutenant tapped her shoulder and asked if he could have the next dance.

Jack's jaw pulsed with aching tension, but Vivian shot him a look that communicated he should back off with good grace. Dammit.

"I'll find you when the band takes their break," she called as the man swung her away.

Jack stood off to one side, scowling. Watched her dance one dance after another. Sometimes the final notes of a song had barely faded away before the next fella was beside her to claim his turn.

"I find it helps if I poke fun at the fellas she's dancing with." Mel held out a bottle of beer. "Maybe one of them's losing his hair already. Another one might as well have two left feet. Having a few drinks usually makes my commentary even more entertaining—or brutal, depending on your perspective."

Jack's lips twitched. He took the beer and clinked it against Mel's bottle.

"Take this fella here." Mel pointed at an awkward, gangly young man dancing with Mabs. "Doubt he's shaving yet, and I happen to know he snores louder than a flight line of bombers revving up for a mission."

Jack laughed.

Mel was right. Good-naturedly abusing her dancing partners was better than getting all in a lather and stewing with jealousy. Vivian waved and smiled at him as she twirled by, unaware that he had just pronounced her partner a drip.

Bowie, Chaz, and Gib joined them. Bowie, ever the wisecracker, was happy to mercilessly skewer the hapless men who danced with Vivian and Mabs.

"Hey, we'll each go dance with her, Chief. Three less dance partners for you to worry about," Chaz offered.

Jack nodded his agreement.

Chaz ground out his cigarette and cut through the dancers to reach her.

He watched as Chaz introduced himself and smiled when they waved at him.

At last, the band leader announced an intermission. Jack snagged a glass of water from the bartender. Vivian would be thirsty after all that dancing.

She waved off several men trying to engage her in conversation and squeezed through the crowds to Jack. Her face shone with perspiration, and she beamed when he handed her the water. "Thanks, honey. That's exactly what I need, and then I need to make that trip to the loo I missed earlier."

Vivian drained the glass and set it down.

At last, the perfect cover to get her alone.

"How about I escort you?" Jack winked at her.

Vivian smiled, took his hand, and steered them through the crowds.

Twilight hovered, though the full black of nightfall's inky cloak edged closer.

"Do you keep a flashlight with you if you're out after dark?" Jack steered her around a large rut in the road.

"Yes, but you're not supposed to use it more than you have to. You'll get used to doing without it."

The hubbub of conversation and laughter from the club faded. The crackle of their footsteps on the gravel path magnified in the stillness.

When they reached the low concrete headquarters building, Jack stopped. He cupped her face in his hands and whispered, "You're even more beautiful than I remembered."

She raised up on her toes and brought her lips to his. Jack's hands encircled her waist, tugging her against his body. Her mouth opened under his, and her cool, slim fingers twined in his hair. Jack's pulse roared in his ears like a chorus of bomber engines poised to take flight.

He eased his fingers inside the waistband of her skirt and under her blouse to caress the smooth skin of her back. He trailed kisses down her neck. Her breath came faster, tinged with a frantic edge. Hair on the back of his neck zinged to attention at her touch.

"So about your uniform?" Jack whispered against her neck.

Vivian's shoulders shook, and her light, feathery giggle sounded in his ear.

"Is there some place on base we could go? Other than those hay stacks on the other side of the fences?"

"The Aero Club has a sofa," she said.

Jack raised his eyebrows. Tonight's dance was in the Officers' Club, but the Aero Club must be open for the enlisted men. "Is it closed tonight?"

"No. The British staff will close it for Mabs, since she and Nancy are busy with the dance over here. I could get the key from them or Mabs."

He pressed his forehead to hers. "I'd rather take you to a nice hotel in London. Something more along the lines of the New Yorker."

"Being together is more important than the where." Vivian's eyes locked with his. Ardor and determination warred with anguish in her expression. She didn't trust the odds for his survival, not enough to leave it to chance. Capricious and uncertain, time in the furor of war was a risky wager.

"But Jack?"

"Hmmm?"

"I really have to go to the bathroom."

He laughed and released her. "I'll wait here."

Vivian opened the headquarters door and disappeared inside. He heard her greeting someone before the door closed.

Jack leaned against a wall. A sofa in a Nissen hut wasn't nearly good enough for her. It was better than a damp haystack or the rough wood and dank heat inside a parked bomber, but that wasn't saying much.

He would make it up to her on his first leave. Shouldn't be hard to get recommendations for the swankiest hotels and nicest restaurants in London. Vivian would have the candlelight and romance she deserved.

Vivian stepped out the door again.

Jack moved toward her. He wrapped his arms tightly around her waist from behind, snuggling her back against his chest and burrowing his face into her sweet-smelling hair. "How soon does that club close?"

"Not soon enough," she murmured. She turned in his embrace, and her lips found his.

Jack crushed his mouth against hers, thrilling at her soft, whispery gasp, at her fingers clenching harder in his hair, at the taste of her, a hint of hops mixed with spearmint gum. He pulled her more firmly against his body and backed them up against the wall of the headquarters building.

She must feel how hard he was. The way she pushed back against him? Oh yeah, she felt him all right.

Vivian groaned, locked her arms securely around him, and deepened her kisses.

Oh, God. He might have to reconsider the haystack options if they kept this up.

Boots scuffed against pebbles on the path. Rowdy laughter sounded at the tail end of a ribald joke.

Jack glanced over his shoulder. Red pinpricks of lit cigarettes moved in their direction.

"Maybe they'll pass by," Vivian whispered.

They would move on all right, but probably not before trying to get any eyeful of Jack and Vivian and ribbing them. Jack took a step back from their clinch, grabbed Vivian's hand, and towed her toward the path.

The men called greetings the moment they saw Vivian. Of course they knew her. Ground crews, ordnance men, medics, so many of the base's workers had been here since the beginning and would remain until the war ended.

While Vivian chatted with those fellas, several people drifted in and out of the Officers' Club in search of fresh air or a break from the noise. The clamor of tuning instruments wafted outdoors each time the door opened, signaling the band would soon start its next set.

After waving to the ordnance boys, Vivian looked up at Jack. "Sounds like the band is about to start playing again."

He blew out a breath and nodded. They had waited this long. Besides, he wouldn't want to risk them being seen. Waiting for the Aero Club to empty and close was the best option, even if every second out of her arms was torture. "Hate turning you over to dance with all the others."

"I know, but it's only for a short while. A couple more hours, and the rest of the night is ours." She lifted her chin, smiled, and stroked the side of his face. Her light, feathery caress sent shivers spiraling down his arms.

Jack held the door open for her. He followed her and moved to her side, intending to reclaim her hand. Might as well continue to signal her relationship status to these fellas, even if he did have to endure watching her dance with them for the rest of the night.

An older woman and a man wearing Red Cross uniforms stood a few paces from the door. Vivian towed him toward them. "Captain Sutherland, Captain Clarkson, what brings you here from London?"

The woman turned and smiled. "Oh, Vivian, hello. Fred and I are touring all our clubs in the area."

"Aren't you with one of our Clubmobile units now?" The man removed his glasses and cleaned the lenses with his handkerchief.

Vivian nodded. "I'm based in Leicester. Mabs invited me to come back for the dance tonight."

Fred put his glasses back on. "You ladies did an outstanding job with the club here. It's one of the best we've seen. If you're staying overnight, you should join us for breakfast tomorrow morning."

"I won't go back to Leicester until tomorrow afternoon."

"They've got me bunking with you gals tonight," the woman said. "I'll look for you later. You can escort me back to the women's quarters while Mabs and Nancy shut this down."

Jack's heart dropped into his stomach. He didn't need the quick anguished glance Vivian threw his way to know their plans had just been upended.

CHAPTER SIXTEEN

October 14, 1943, 8:15 a.m.
USAAF Station 105, Chelveston, England

The group intelligence officer unveiled the map displaying today's target. A line of yarn ran from their base at Chelveston to a spot deep inside Germany. Jack groaned and cursed with the hundred other men crammed into the briefing hut.

Schweinfurt.

Their last deadly mission to Schweinfurt in August, fresh in everyone's mind, had ended in devastating losses.

Jack's ship had been out of commission, and they had also missed the more disastrous run to Stuttgart three days later. The bomber stream went over the Stuttgart target three times. Three times through the barrage of lethal flak, using three times more fuel than usual. Scores of their bombers had been forced to land in France or ditch in the Channel because they had run down to nothing. Desperate crews broke radio silence with a babble of Mayday calls to give their coordinates so the British land sea rescue teams might find them.

Today the Eighth would take another shot at finishing the job in Schweinfurt.

It would be the biggest challenge Jack and his crew had yet faced. Missing both Schweinfurt and Stuttgart struck many in their group as too charmed by half. Despite today's dangers, Jack would be glad to vanquish any lingering suspicions about his crew. Or him.

"Sure you don't want one of these today, Chief?" Gib held out a pack of cigarettes.

Jack shook his head and swung into the back of the army truck behind the others. The truck belched to life and spewed foul exhaust into the damp air. They bumped through a field toward the perimeter road.

Gib lit a cigarette and held out his match for Chaz, who lit his smoke. Gib tossed the match and ground it under his boot. Bowie groused that Gib hadn't passed it to him.

"No three on a match," Gib said gruffly.

Bowie rolled his eyes but fished his matchbox out of his pocket. Bowie had little patience with flyer superstitions. Soldiers in the Great War learned the hard way that Germans would spot a match light across the trenches, zero in on the second light, and fire on the third light off the same match. Lore had expanded such that death might strike any of the three men who lit up on the same match.

First stop was *Lucky Strike*. Her officers hopped out of the truck. No calls of good luck or other farewells from the other men. Conversation was minimal on mission mornings. The truck rumbled on.

Their hardstand was the next stop. They received their ship after they arrived in June. His guys ribbed him, but no one argued when Jack announced he would name her *Vivian's Victory*. He let the others have a say in the artwork painted on the nose, with a few caveats. With Vivian's name on the plane, he hadn't wanted the woman to be half-naked like so many of them. Curvy and suggestive was fine, but nothing lewd.

Gunners were already in the ship installing their guns, except for Ira, who was deep in conversation with Tad and Duck.

"Chaz, before you settle in, tell Walt and Lou to come down. I want them to go rustle up extra ammunition for us," Jack said.

"One step ahead of you, Chief," Duck said. "When we heard it was Schweinfurt again, Tad figured you'd want extra on board. We sent our guys to ordnance with a truck." He pointed at four large wooden crates.

"Good thinking, thanks. I'll buy you a round of drinks when we're back. Chaz, tell the gunners to come load these, would you? Be sure they know to distribute the weight evenly." An extra thousand pounds, but worth it if they needed it.

"They brought around an extra fuel tank for all the ships. It's in the bomb bay," Tad said.

The gunners set about lugging the heavy crates of ammunition up through the rear hatch, while Jack and Bowie did the walk-around with their ground crew. Tad said he didn't like the sound of the ailerons but hadn't been able to find anything wrong.

Jack looked at Ira. His butt was on the line too.

"Tad and his guys have checked it out. I can't think of anything else to check," Ira said.

Jack pursed his lips. Another idle day wouldn't help his men get mission credits. Not to mention the mess hall chatter that would follow them if the *Vivian's Victory* fellas missed another big one.

He ran his hand through his hair. "Monitor it, and let me know if you change your opinion," Jack said to Ira.

Bowie told the others to come down for their pre-mission talk.

Once they stood circled around him, Jack looked steadily at each of his men in turn. "We all know this won't be a milk run. It'll be a tough one. But look here, a lot went wrong with that last Schweinfurt mission that won't repeat today. We stay focused. We go by the book. We stick together, get the job done, and head home. Nothing more to it. Matchsticks in a box, fellas." Jack's shorthand for reminding his crew that none of them were more important than the others, that each had a potential for sparking and each might step in and take over for one that failed to light or burnt out. "All right, let's go up."

Jack slid his hand inside the lining of his jacket pocket and closed his fingers around the edge of Vivian's picture, then patted the outline of the dog tag buried deep in the bottom of his pants pocket. Once he put his gloves on, he wouldn't be able to check.

Before he took his seat, he covered his parachute pack with an extra flak suit apron. If he needed to bail out, he didn't want to find the chute had been shredded by a shell. He pushed it under his seat and checked twice to be certain the flak apron was in place as protective cover.

"You not using that extra apron on your lap, protect your goods?" Bowie said, raising an eyebrow.

Jack laughed. "I've got one for that too." He pulled it out of his bag and placed it over his lap.

He and Bowie ran through the preflight checks and started the engines one by one.

Jack twisted around to look at Ira in the jump seat behind Bowie.

After listening for a few moments, Ira said, "Sounds okay to me right now, Chief."

Jack looked at Bowie. "You hear anything off?"

"No. What did Tad think he heard?"

"Described it as a high-pitched grinding. Might have been the ailerons, but they checked out. Whatever it was, it's gone," Ira said.

Jack leaned out the cockpit window and gestured to Tad. He mimed the question over the roar of the engines. Tad gave a thumbs-up sign.

"Tad doesn't hear anything. What's the worst case fallout?" Jack asked Ira.

"Sounds like abort to me," said Gib through the intercom.

Jack had forgotten the rest of the crew could hear the cockpit discussion on the intercom.

"All in favor of aborting this mission to Schwein-fucking-furt and its fucking flak field?" said Gib.

"This is not a democracy, Turrell. If Chief says we go, we go." Bowie rolled his eyes.

Jack had taken three aspirin at breakfast, for all the good that had done. He kneaded his throbbing temples.

He could abort. Pilots had a certain amount of latitude, and his crew chief had handed him a decent reason to abort. It would pass the smell test, if only barely. Still, an abort wouldn't give them mission credit.

Jack didn't want the shirker label. Missing the third tough mission in succession wouldn't do him or his men any favors around the base. As pilot, he would bear the brunt of the snide remarks and sideways looks.

Yet, could he risk the lives of his nine friends for the sake of his pride?

Jack peered out the rain-spattered window. Tad and Duck stood waiting for his signal to remove the wheel chocks. Was he a fool if he didn't take the out Tad had offered up?

"We go."

***

Leicester, England, 10:45 a.m.

"What are we supposed to do with all these doughnuts?" Vivian waved her hand at the fully laden trays stacked in the racks on the Clubmobile.

The Clubmobile's engine hadn't turned over this morning. Sputtering noises, followed by curses and clanging for half an hour. Charlie poked his head in the door, grimy with grease and sweat, to inform them the *South Dakota* would need to spend a few days in the repair shop.

"We" —Jean pointed at herself and Dottie— "will distribute the doughnuts here with these nice engineers. They'll be happy to have them. Since we'll be out of commission through the weekend, why don't you go pack a bag and catch a train? Go see that swoony pilot of yours."

"Jean's right. You should go have fun," Dottie said.

Jack had said he would be eligible for leave very soon, whenever he completed his next mission. This could be their lucky day.

Dottie shooed her hand at Vivian. "If you hurry, you can make the late morning train."

***

Somewhere over southeastern England, 12:00 p.m.

Jack looked sideways at Bowie. They should join the formation in the high squadron, but in all the confusion caused by the dense cloud cover, the 381st bomb group had beaten them to it. Jack followed Dave's *Leading Lady* and moved into a low position in their segment of the bomber formation.

Hundreds of droning bombers moved toward the English coastline, painting white contrails across the clear blue sky. Sunlight beamed on the white-capped waves of the sparkling blue channel.

A few miles over the water, Jack ordered the gunners to test their guns. "Don't do more than test. Conserve the ammo for when we need it."

"Navigator to crew: We will reach the Belgian coast in fifteen minutes."

"Pilot to navigator."

"Go ahead."

"Inform me when we're five minutes out."

At the Belgian coast, German fighters would rise up to meet them. If they needed to abort for mechanical issues, they must do it soon. Breaking away as a straggler in sight of the Luftwaffe invited disaster.

"Pilot to flight engineer: Status report on the health of the ship?"

Ira's voice crackled over the intercom. "All systems A-OK, Chief."

As long as his ship was sound, Jack could handle whatever Schweinfurt threw at them.

Ralph Patterson came over the other day, son. Said they'd had a letter from one of the officers with Ace's group. Ace's crew chief claimed he had warned the pilots about something that wasn't up to par, said he told them they shouldn't go up until was fixed. Ralph says Ace never had anything but praise for his pilots and the men he served with. But his folks are heartsick to think his death could have been avoided. I know you realize it—the lives of your men aren't yours to squander.

"Pilot to crew: Prepare for action."

***

USAAF Station 105, Chelveston, England, 1:00 p.m.

"Is this young woman trying to sneak on base?"

Vivian turned at the sound of the familiar voice. "Joe! I've missed you." She hugged him and bestowed a fond kiss on his cheek.

Vicar Joe looked startled, but pleased, by her unexpected show of affection.

"I'll vouch for Captain Lambert," he said to the bemused guard.

Once the guard was convinced neither of them was a German spy and were familiar figures on the base, he let them pass.

"What brings you here?" Joe's eyes traveled to her bag. "Is this a planned leave trip?"

"No, my Clubmobile died this morning. The other girls convinced me I should come here and visit Mabs."

Chappie laughed. "Mabs and a certain pilot too, I imagine."

She laughed. "Perhaps."

They walked the footpath from the Yelden side entrance, and Vivian looked toward the runways. Only a few bombers in the hardstands.

"They must be flying a mission today." She looked up at the thick cloud cover. There must be good visibility over France or Germany.

"Yes, they are. Maximum effort."

Vivian's mouth went dry. Maximum effort meant they were striking deep into Nazi Germany against a heavily defended target. A dangerous mission.

That must be why Joe was here.

"Do you know when they're expected back?"

"I came for briefing and takeoff. They left around ten, a late start for such a big mission."

"They won't be back until much later this afternoon?"

"I shouldn't think so. I came to find a poker game. Interested?"

Poker would provide a welcome distraction. "Of course. I'll find Mabs first and leave my bag with her."

***

Somewhere over Belgium, 1:15 p.m.

"Shit! A dozen, at least," came Lou's voice.

"Bandits, six o'clock high," Stan called.

"Damn that was close!" Walt's normally level voice was several octaves higher than usual.

"Got one! I got one! Didja see that, Lou? It's the one blazing straight down your side. You see it? Got him dead-on. Chaz, you copy me?" Ford yelled into the intercom.

"Copy. Recording it in the logbook," said Chaz.

Allied fighter escorts came to the end of their fuel range and turned back for England. German fighters swarmed the bombers moments later. That was normal. The number of fighters careening through the bomber stream wasn't usual.

Waves of yellow-noses, the dreaded Focke-Wulf 190s. Swarms of Messerschmidtt 109s, launching rockets that exploded in the air all around the bombers. Dive-bombing Stukas joined the fray, pelting into their midst like a hawk swooping down on hapless prey.

Jack gripped the yoke, his jaw clenched tight, fighting his instinct to take evasive action. It had never been harder to hold steady course and keep his ship tucked snug into the formation.

"Chief! Oh, fuck, she's coming straight toward us! Move, move, move! Fuck, move!" Ira screamed.

Frost on the windshield affected Jack's visibility, and they didn't have much maneuvering leeway. But, he managed to jink them out of the path of a falling bomber.

"Holy fuck, that was close! Might've been inches from our wing. Christ!" Gib yelled.

Jack's heart pounded in his ears. He gulped air into his tight lungs. Sweat streamed from under his flak helmet and seeped under his goggles. Dammit. With his heavy gloves on, he couldn't swipe underneath the goggles. Unchecked, that moisture would freeze and obscure his vision. He yanked off his goggles, mopped his hand around his face and the goggle lenses, and snapped the goggles back in place.

"No chutes out of her," Ford reported from the ball turret.

Bowie pointed up, miming his question. Could they move into the spot vacated by the one that nearly hit them? It was in the high squadron they were supposed to be in. Despite the fatal hit that poor ship had suffered, they would be much, much safer there.

Jack pulled back on the yoke and pushed up on the throttles, accelerating and climbing rapidly.

He leveled off and pulled into one of the 381st's elements. *Miss B. Haven* had been trying to maneuver to this spot and was forced to fall back. Bowie's quick eye had given them an edge.

Jack raised a hand in greeting to the copilot in the adjacent bomber.

"Nice move, Chief," Chaz said.

Jack kept his focus on the instrument panel. They ought to keep intercom chatter to a minimum. He would give Bowie his due later.

"Navigator to whoever wants to know: We're approaching Aachen. We're expected to encounter some flak as we pass over."

"Well, that's swell. Just swell. Last hour of fighter action hasn't been exciting enough," Bowie said.

***

USAAF Station 105, Chelveston, England, 2:30 p.m.

Vivian patted the snoozing sheepdog. *Bomb Boogie* and its crew were lost in the August mission to Schweinfurt, and the crew's dog Pep had attached himself to Bill, their crew chief.

Bill now served *Lucky Strike*, but Pep seemed disinclined to give his heart to Bill's new crew. Even the animals had adopted emotional detachment defenses.

Mabs stood, stretching. "I better call it quits and go check whether the food's ready."

"Remember they started out late today. You can't be expecting them back yet," said Tom, one of the ordnance crew.

"No, I know. Mel already told me their ETA, but the club opens in an hour."

Mel had elected to stay on as operations staff after completing his combat tour last month.

"You need help?" Vivian asked.

Their fellow poker players insisted Mabs must need Vivian's help and what a shame Vivian would have to leave them to more games.

Mabs laughed. "Nancy and I've got it under control. You stay and have fun."

***

Near Schweinfurt, Germany, 2:45 p.m.

"Bandits peeling off," Stan said.

It was obvious already why the German fighters were abandoning the bomber stream they had harassed incessantly for two hours.

Puffs of black smoke, soft and wispy like black cotton balls, filled the air from exploding flak shells. Deadly, no matter how deceptively harmless they appeared.

The ship jerked violently against the upheaval in the air from the flak explosions.

"Hold on tight, gentlemen. Schweinfurt's putting up a show for us," Bowie said.

"Copilot to radio operator: Release the first bundle of chaff. Repeat, release the first bundle of chaff."

Tink responded moments later. "Radio operator to copilot: First bundle of chaff released."

Moving closer to the IP, the point where they would form up for the bomb run, the flak increased significantly, rattling and pinging against the ship. Smoky bursts from exploding shells created a carpet of black cotton candy.

"Another one going down at nine o'clock. I count four chutes," said Lou.

"It's from our group," said Stan.

"Anyone know how many total from our group? Chaz?" Ira asked.

"Too many. Too fucking many," said Chaz.

They all fell silent. Jack's gut twisted. Thank God he had moved up while they had the chance.

"Navigator to crew: Approach to target."

"Bombardier to crew: Bomb bay doors open."

A blast of flak shook the bomber, her nose dipped sharply in response.

Rattles and pings. Buffeted by the flak bursts, *Vivian's Victory* dipped and swooped unpredictably. Jack and Bowie fought hard to keep her steady. Gib would use the toggle switch to release the bombs after the lead ship initiated its bomb drop, but a stable platform helped them all.

"Bombs away! Let's get the hell out of here!" Gib's voice reverberated on the intercom.

Jack banked sharply starboard.

Shit. German fighters returned in force, refueled and desperate to avenge the destruction the Allied bombers had unleashed on the Schweinfurt ball-bearings factories.

"I saw goddamn night fighters! They're putting everything they've got against us!" Tink called.

Blackness crushed from both sides. Jack blinked. No. He couldn't afford tunnel vision, not now. He turned his head in each direction, blinking hard. He focused on Bowie for a few seconds. *Breathe, breathe, breathe.* He toggled his oxygen regulator to pure.

His crew called out tail numbers or squadron positions of so many burning, spinning, damaged bombers that Jack wasn't surprised when Chaz cut in, "One at a time. I can't get all this with you all talking at once and going so fast."

Onward they swept due south, before turning west-northwest. Their formation was no longer tight and protective. Too many holes, too many stragglers, too many vulnerabilities.

"Navigator to crew: We'll reach Metz in three minutes."

Metz should be the last place they would encounter heavy flak. American Thunderbolts or British Spitfires would be waiting to escort them home not far outside Metz.

Crack!

Flames shot in front of the windshield and his crew mates screamed curses into the intercom.

Vivian's Victory plunged into a steep dive.

CHAPTER SEVENTEEN

October 14, 1943, 3:45 p.m.
USAAF Station 105, Chelveston, England

Vivian called good-byes to Joe and the other men from the afternoon's poker games. Working would distract her from scanning the sky for the return of the bombers, focus her mind on something other than worry about Jack, and relieve her restless fidgeting.

She set out on the familiar route, now worn into a serviceable path rather than the mucky bog she and Mabs had been forced to traverse when the 305th first moved to this base. It wound past headquarters before ending at the Aero Club. She could pop in and say hello to the headquarters staff.

A jeep approached from behind. Vivian moved off to one side to let it pass.

"Heard a rumor you were here," Captain MacLeod called out. "Give you a lift?"

"I'm headed to headquarters. Figured I'd see you there." Vivian hoisted herself into the passenger seat.

He shifted gears, and the jeep rumbled forward. "Not for much longer. LeMay's moving me to Suffolk with him."

LeMay had been promoted to Brigadier General and awarded command of the entire Third Bombardment Division, which oversaw operations for fourteen bomb groups from Elveden Hall, an estate near Cambridge.

"Good for you." Jack should talk to MacLeod about doing something along those lines when he completed his tour.

MacLeod laughed. "I dunno know yet if it's good or not. Doubt Iron-Ass will be any easier to work for in Suffolk than he was here."

"But he respects you enough to offer you the position, and it's a promotion."

MacLeod made a noncommittal noise. He pulled to a stop in front of the headquarters building. "Well, here we are. I've got to make a run out to the bomb dump. I'll see you at chow tonight."

Vivian hopped out and waved.

She pushed open the door and stepped inside. The executive officer usually seated near the entrance wasn't there.

The door behind his desk was ajar.

Vivian moved behind the desk toward the door, intending to peek in and wave hello.

"Ours are in the high squadrons. If it's the lower ones getting hit hard, we may be all right." The group operations officer paced behind his desk.

"They're under radio silence. Where are these reports from?" LeMay's normally brusque voice held a note of unease.

"Reports from two separate bombers that aborted and are already back. Jerry fighters shredded our forces today, well before they reached the target."

Vivian's hand clutched at the doorjamb, her heart pounding. They had been on rough missions before, this group. Jack was spare in the details he recounted, but Vivian could fill in the blanks.

Her heart thumped in her tight chest.

***

October 14, 1943, 4:15 p.m.
Near Metz, France

Jack pushed the throttles forward to increase power. Still flames and smoke.

Bowie turned the internal fire extinguisher knob on the fire control panel to the right outboard, but it had no effect.

Jack nosed her down more sharply still.

Garbled, crackling shrieks and disjointed curses from the crew blasted through the intercom.

"Hold tight. Do not bail out, and that's an order!" Jack commanded.

A raging roar of blood coursed under his temples and across his forehead.

"Air-speed 210," Bowie reported. "Ten thousand feet … Nine thousand feet … Eighty-five hundred feet …"

The cockpit shuddered, vibrating and rattling, a whining crescendo of engine noise as she dove fast.

One shot. That's all he had. Neither the engine's internal fire extinguisher nor Jack's quick action to shut off the gas and booster pump for that engine had worked. All they had left was a dive that might kill the fire with rapid cooling air drafts. She wouldn't have enough power to climb back high enough to try the dive maneuver again.

Jack's stomach dove right along with his ship.

"Air speed 250. Six thousand feet and dropping," Bowie said.

The intercom sputtered and someone said, "Bail out! Bail out now, or we lose our chance!"

Who the fuck was that? Gib?

Jack's muscles, straining from his exertion at the controls, jittered and spasmed.

"Pilot to crew: Do. Not. Bail. Out. Repeat, do not bail!"

He gestured for Bowie to make an assessment. Bowie shook his head in a way that indicated he couldn't tell whether the fire was out.

"Cockpit to crew: Can anyone see if the fire's out?"

"Ball to cockpit: Smoke's so thick, it's hard to say. I don't see any flames."

"Three thousand feet," Bowie said.

"Pilot to ball: Come out of the ball turret. Waist gunners, assist Ford into the ship. Copy me?"

"Yes, Chief. Coming up." Ford's voice was thin, shaky. Must be terrifying to watch the ground rushing up from his vantage point.

"Waist to pilot: Ball turret retracted. Ford in the ship," Walt reported.

Jack leveled her out shy of a thousand feet. Clusters of farmhouses and grazing livestock were visible.

Air drafts from that steep dive did their job. The engine was shot, but the fire was out, unable to spread or cause other issues.

Bowie closed the throttle to the damaged right outboard and cut its mixture control, then pushed the button to feather its prop. Jack turned off its magneto switch and trimmed to adjust for the lost engine.

"Copilot: Check out the crew." Jack's throat had gone completely dry, his voice was raspy and raw. He swiped at sweat trickling from his flak helmet.

The flak blast had likely done more than set one of their engines ablaze. But checking out the crew took priority before they assessed the mechanical functions.

Gib responded to Bowie's check. Jack pursed his lips and narrowed his eyes. Yes, he was damn near certain that had been Gib trying to incite a bailout.

"Stan? Copilot to tail gunner: Respond please," Bowie called.

Silence.

"Walt, go check on Stan and report back," Jack said.

He and Bowie examined the instrument panel while they waited.

"Waist to cockpit: Tail's all shot up, Chief. Big holes blasted through here. Must have severed Stan's oxygen line. I hooked him up to a walk-around oxygen, and he's coming around."

"Stay with him. Check him over in case he's been hit and it's not obvious." Jack inhaled and flipped his oxygen switch from pure back to normal.

What else was wrong? If the tail was as bad off as Walt said … yes, the vertical stabilizer was out. No functionality in the rudder.

Was it that flak burst? Or was whatever worried Tad and Ira earlier this morning lurking, possibly exacerbating the damage from the flak? If the ship lost much more functionality, he should give a bailout order. Imprisoned was better than dead.

"Pilot to radio: Don't send our coordinates. We don't want

unwelcome guests joining us." They were still outside the range of Allied fighters, and Germans might intercept their call for assistance and send fighters to finish them off.

"Walt here, Stan was hit. Piece of shrapnel's stuck in his lower leg. Don't think I ought to try and pull it out. I gave him the morphine shot from his kit, bandaged him best I know how. Lou's gonna help me move him into the waist."

Stan might not be able to bail out. The fellas wouldn't leave him, none of them would.

"Pilot to waist: Keep an eye on Stan and report back if anything changes. Is the tail gun functioning, do you know?"

"Lou tested it out. It's working. Pretty exposed, not sure how stable it is."

"Pilot to engineer: Check out the tail. If it's stable enough and you can get oxygen, I want you to man the gun back there. I'd rather have a man there than at the top turret."

"Will do, Chief," said Ira.

"Tink, be prepared to man the top turret gunner position if Ira is gonna be in the tail."

"Copy," said Tink.

"Pilot to navigator: Confirm our position."

He and Bowie took her up in slow intervals, not wanting to tax her too much on three engines. They couldn't locate the formation. It was long gone. They would have to limp home at whatever pace and altitude *Vivian's Victory* could manage. With any luck, a Spitfire or two might have hung back at the coast to watch for stragglers.

With one engine out, they were also burning fuel at a faster rate.

Wait, they had an extra fuel tank in the bomb bay.

"Pilot to bombardier: There's an extra fuel tank in the bomb bay. Get us set up with that."

"Bombardier to pilot: Copy."

The intercom crackled a few minutes later. "Bombardier to pilot: That tank got knocked around in here. Must've broken open when it got slammed against the hatch. Fuel leaked out everywhere. Hope nothing catches fire near here."

"No extra fuel left?"

"Correct, none left."

Fuck. Fuck, fuck, fuck.

"Pilot to navigator: Give me two headings. One to home. One to Switzerland."

***

October 14, 1943, 5:45 p.m.
USAAF Station 105, Chelveston, England

Vivian wound her scarf tighter against the brisk autumn breeze. Everyone was gathered around the control tower as usual. Vivian stationed herself nearest the path to the interrogation hut. She would surprise Jack on his way in.

She picked up snatches of conversations from those closer to the control tower.

"Should have known. Fucking Schweinfurt again."

"Never been this late."

Vivian twisted the end of her scarf, rolling and grinding the fabric between her thumb and index finger.

"There they are," someone called.

Most of the small black dots continued on. No, not most of them. All but two.

These two must have gotten attached to another group. The others would arrive any minute now.

Monkey's Uncle and *Hip-De-Ditty* taxied down the runways. Not *Vivian's Victory*. She would be with the main force.

Ground crews, the other men, everyone continued to scan the skies for the rest of their bombers and crews. No one paid much attention yet to the two crews who had come out of their ships. Vivian's heart skittered when she looked their way. Something about the set of their shoulders, the way they walked toward the interrogation hut. Post-mission letdown or something more?

She stole into the interrogation hut behind them.

Mabs turned to her when the last of the twenty men had moved on with coffee and doughnuts. "You want to help serve? I figured you would wait outside for Jack."

"These crews came in ahead of the others. I ..." She didn't know what made her come inside, other than watching the empty sky made her more anxious.

Mabs frowned and started around the serving table toward Vivian. She collided with Mel, who hurried out of the interrogation room, his jaw tight, his freckles popping in stark relief against his pale face. He gripped Mabs by the shoulders, saying wordlessly what Vivian's instincts had been telling her from the moment those two bombers detached themselves from the others.

They were the only two bombers that would return.

***

October 14, 1943, 6:30 p.m.
Somewhere over the English Channel

"Come on, sweetheart, you can do it. You can make it," Jack whispered. His taut arm muscles quivered from sustained exertion at the controls.

Not here. Not over the water. Not when they were so close.

Chaz said they were fifteen minutes out from a RAF base near the coast. They could land there if they reached it before they ran out of fuel. They had been taxing her fortitude and her fuel supply for more than two hours. It would be dark soon. Ditching into the frigid waters of the Channel in the dark through a thick cloud cover did not sound like a promising survival plan.

They could have gone for Switzerland. Realizing his overwhelming desire to get back to Vivian might be clouding his judgment, Jack had asked the crew to vote whether to divert to Switzerland or take the risk and try to make it home to England. "Know she's in a bad way. If we try for home, we might have to bail out over France, ditch in the Channel, or crash land once we're over England," Jack had warned.

They had all voted to continue on. No one wanted to be interned, even in neutral Switzerland.

The left outboard engine sputtered. Smoke furled out of it. It pulled almost no power.

The tight band that had wound around his chest for the last few hours constricted another notch.

"Damn lucky it's the other outboard," Bowie said. Failure of either inboard would destabilize the ship and send them hurtling down into the water in a hurry.

The crew had already tossed out all remaining ammunition. They had to lighten her load again and quick.

"Pilot to crew: Everything out! Throw out the ball turret. Rip out the gun mounts and anything else you can. Flak suits go! Get it all out. Tink, send out our call sign and position to British Coastal Command, in case we have to ditch in a hurry. Then establish contact with that RAF field."

Jack pushed the two inboard engine throttles to emergency power and said a quick prayer they could withstand the additional strain.

Tink sent out their coordinates three times in succession, then sought contact with the nearest RAF field. "Hello, Lumba, Hello, Lumba, this is Grubby L. Lumba Traffic, Grubby L inbound to land. Again, Grubby L inbound to land. Emergency on board. Expected landing time eighteen hundred forty-six."

"Pilot to waist gunners: Can Stan walk?"

The intercom crackled. "Chief, this is Lou. Negative."

That would complicate ditching, especially if they lost whatever daylight was left. Not much time after impact before the ship filled with water. Everyone had procedures to follow. Someone would need to do Stan's jobs and two or more of them would have to assist him out to one of the dinghies.

"Lou, you and Walt move Stan to the radio control room. Everyone else, keep tossing shit. I'll give you an intercom warning and sound the ditching bell signal if you need to assemble in the radio room to brace for imminent ditching. Get Stan in place now, in case."

"Chief, this is Walt. We copy, and we're moving Stan."

"Radio to pilot: I established contact with Lumba. We have permission to land."

"Pilot to radio: Pass any instructions to me once Chaz has navigated us in closer."

Vivian's Victory shuddered and jerked up in response to whatever the crew tossed out. Bowie flicked the fuel gauge knob between both remaining inboards. They both continued to drop precipitously.

Dammit.

"*Everything*! Everything out! Everything but us and Tink's radio goes! *Now!*" Jack bellowed into the intercom.

Blood thundered in his ears. Black squares, like horse blinders, pressed closer on each side of his face.

Jack purposefully tore his eyes from the gauges and swiveled in his seat. He couldn't afford to lose his peripheral vision now.

Bowie tossed his and Jack's flight bags and flak suits to Gib to throw out.

Fuel levels dropped another notch. The left outboard engine sputtered and faltered again. Bowie cut the fuel supply to the engine and feathered its prop. No point feeding it any more of their dwindling fuel.

Rolling waves of vibration rocked the ship from nose to tail, building and intensifying. Near impossible to read the instrument panel. Jack and Bowie both braced and strained to maneuver the controls.

"Navigator to pilot: We've got land underneath our wings again. Hold course for five minutes and begin the descent."

"Just a little longer, darling, come on," Jack urged, his hand clutching the yoke in a death grip.

They wouldn't have to ditch in the Channel. But, they might yet need to land in a meadow of grazing cattle if she couldn't stay aloft long enough to see them safely to the emergency landing strip at RAF Hawkinge.

"Pilot to tail: Getting dark. Keep a sharp eye out while you've got visibility. Copy?" German night fighters sometimes flew silent and menacing behind straggling bombers after nightfall, shooting them down as they approached their bases.

"Tail to pilot: Copy."

Tink passed on the landing instructions from the control tower. "They're reporting dense cloud cover down to three hundred feet but trying to get the FIDO going."

FIDO or fog dispersal involved pumping petrol into pipelines situated on either side of a runway and then out through burner jets at intervals, creating walls of flame on either side of the runway. They hadn't given RAF Hawkinge much time to act.

Jack glanced at the altimeter. Fifteen hundred feet. Even without fire markers, he spotted it through a swirling mist. A single runway. That was all they needed. Fuel was perilously low, but they were over land and approaching a cleared landing strip. Jack's tight muscles relaxed perceptibly. He inhaled, slowly exhaled. They could make it. They would make it.

Swirling clouds pillowed across the entire windshield. A low-hanging cloudbank, as the control tower had warned Tink.

Jack's eyes flicked between the altitude indicator and air speed gauge. He continued to descend, relying on his instruments rather than sight.

"Can't go around again." Bowie pointed at the fuel gauge, with the arrow sitting at two gallons.

No, they had no reserve fuel for circling around for another go at the landing. They must nail it.

Bowie toggled the fuel boost pump switches for both inboards.

Jack held the control column with one hand. His right hand pushed the throttles to both the inboards forward. Bowie deployed the landing gear.

"Eight hundred feet," Bowie intoned.

Nothing but swirling clouds, dense and smothering.

"Five hundred feet."

Jack's heart lodged in his throat, pulsating and pounding. He tightened his hold on the yoke.

Through the whirling moisture, he caught a flash of light. Jack strained to look out the small window on the side of the windshield. There it was again.

"Three hundred fifty feet."

They broke through the clouds right at three hundred feet.

The runway, illuminated with flames on either side, was directly below. Too directly below. Dammit, they could not overshoot the runway. Jack pushed forward on the yoke and pulled back on the throttles.

The wheels touched down in an inexplicably soft landing, but Jack pumped the brakes to keep the ship headed straight down the middle. He didn't want to get her too close to the flaming petrol on either side.

Bowie sent out a red flare for Stan.

"Hail, holy Queen, Mother of mercy, our life, our sweetness, and our hope," Ford's voice crackled on the intercom.

A chorus of "Amens" sounded in his headset.

Jack set the parking brake and cut the mixture while Bowie feathered the props on the remaining engines. Too close for comfort. Way too damn close. Jack pressed his forehead against the yoke, gulping deep lungfuls of air.

Bowie squeezed out of the seat and stood. He paused, then clapped a hand on Jack's shoulder and squeezed.

He lifted his head from the yoke and glanced up at Bowie.

Bowie saluted. "Damn fine flying, Chief. Mighty fine flying."

Jack exhaled and raised his hand to return the salute. "Couldn't have done it without you. And the others."

Dusk had deepened to full nightfall by the time Jack and Bowie swung out of the hatch.

Covered in grease and grime, faces pale and reeking of sweat, his men stood huddled, waiting on him and Bowie.

"Stan?" Jack asked.

"Medics have taken him. They'll take us to the hospital to check on him after we get chow. His lower left leg was pretty mangled. I don't think he'll lose it, but I'm no doctor," Walt said.

Jack glanced at the tail section of *Vivian's Victory*. The tail had suffered extensive damage, visible even in the dark misty fog enveloping them. Hard to read her serial number.

Several RAF officers assured them they could get food in the mess hall. "Right this way. We'll get you fed and set up in bunks for the night."

"Can I radio or telephone our base to let them know we landed?" Tink asked.

"You're based at Chelveston, you say? We'll radio them you have arrived, though a bit southeast of where you hoped to be tonight," said one of the officers.

The men laughed.

"Our man can come take the tail number off your plane. You go eat and get some sleep. No inspecting damage until morning anyway," the officer said.

Jack fell into step beside Chaz and pulled on his sleeve to signal for him to hang back. When the others were a few paces ahead, Jack said in a low voice, "Was that Gib who shouted for a bailout?"

Chaz hesitated.

Jack stopped, grabbed hold of Chaz's upper arm, and looked directly in his eyes. "Was it?"

Chaz pressed his lips together and bobbed his chin.

He shouldn't air their dirty laundry in front of the RAF men. This could wait.

No. No, it couldn't.

Jack shouldered his way into the throng of his men.

Tension he had held in check for the last hours unleashed itself as cold fury. Grabbing roughly at Gib's uniform jacket sleeve, Jack slammed him back against the side of the mess hall building.

"Hey, what the—?" Gib began.

"If you *ever* countermand one of my orders, whether we're on a mission or otherwise, you're off my crew. You've spent your one chance, and you'll get no others. Do you understand me?" Jack's voice was controlled and clear but laced with combustible violence.

"I was—"

"Save it. I don't want to hear it. No excuses. No one else panicked. No one else doubted me. No one else tried to subvert my authority. If you no longer have confidence in my ability to command our ship, you can find another crew. If you're gonna stick with us and fly under me, you'll obey my orders without question." He gave Gib's shoulders a firm shake. "Are we clear?"

"Yes, sir."

Jack released his hold on Gib. His heart thudded in his chest.

He signaled for his men to go in the mess hall. The fellas averted their eyes and moved cautiously around him and through the door. Gib shrugged away from Chaz, who had clapped him on the back.

Jack paced past the door to the mess, finally lashing out and kicking a nearby post.

"You should go on in and eat with them. You've asserted your authority, and now they need to see you don't bear your crew member any personal ill-will," said an older RAF officer, career military perhaps.

Jack stopped pacing in circles. "I'm not hungry."

"Probably not. It was a rough mission, or you and your men wouldn't be here. But it's important for you to make a pretense of it, break bread with them again. Otherwise, you risk this becoming an insurmountable wedge in your crew. I suspect you know already you can't have that and expect to survive."

Jack raked a hand through his hair, then nodded curtly at the RAF officer. "Yeah, I'll go join them. Thanks."

He paused at the door, his hand on the knob. Goddammit all to hell, he shouldn't have let loose on Gib. He should have used it as the basis for a morale-boosting talk with his fellas. He should have waited until his head was clear, when he was less strung out and tense. Now he had to figure out how to put things right. Not just with Gib. Earning back the respect he had squandered wouldn't come easy.

He would start by giving Bowie credit for the move higher earlier. He would repeat his favorite metaphor for the crew, they were all matchsticks in a box, none more important or as integral to success as any other. Ten little matchsticks lined up in a box.

CHAPTER EIGHTEEN

October 15, 1943
USAAF Station 105, Chelveston, England

"Did you sleep at all?"

Vivian looked up. She hadn't expected Mabs to find her so early. The base was eerily quiet. No mission going out today. Most of the ground crews no longer had a ship to maintain, so there weren't even normal sounds of maintenance work, done at night and in the open.

"Yes, a little." She might have dozed sitting out here near the runways.

"Scootch over."

Vivian shifted down the small wooden bench. Mabs sat, hooked her arm through Vivian's, and ran her fingers across the sleeve of the thick woolen overcoat swamping Vivian. "Jack's?"

"Mel brought me all his things." He told her she should keep whatever she wanted before they shipped his trunk home to his parents. Vivian couldn't bear to look through the trunk yet, but she had pulled out the overcoat, more to be enveloped in his scent than because she needed warmth.

Mabs interlaced her fingers through Vivian's and squeezed. She rested her head against Vivian's shoulder. "Your bed didn't look slept in. Have you been out here this whole time?"

"I thought I'd feel it, feel him, one way or another, out here by the runways. But, I don't. I don't have any sense."

Jack could vanish from the face of the earth in an instant. She had thought she would intuit his fate, but only emptiness, a vast and desolate emptiness, stretched out in her mind. They might never know what happened to him.

Bitter anger coursed through her, a consuming rage. At the Germans. At all the forces conspiring to put so many people in peril. At a God who turned a blind eye.

"Honey, it can take months before they report his status."

"He's not a prisoner."

"We won't know until there's been enough time."

"No, I know he's not. I heard the reports." The officers didn't expect many of their missing men were prisoners. From what other groups and their two surviving crews reported, most of the 305th's losses were sudden, violent, and explosive. No time for a bailout. Especially not for the pilots, who stuck with their ships long enough to give everyone else a shot at getting away. Maybe he hadn't had time to be afraid or feel pain.

"Viv, there were parachutes—"

"I don't want to prolong it. There's no point. Not when the odds are so low." Vivian stood. She had spent her time communing with the universe. No reason to stretch that out any longer either. "My Clubmobile is bound to be repaired by now. I'll take the afternoon train back to Leicester." That was a lie. Her Clubmobile wouldn't be repaired yet, but Mabs was sure to let the point pass.

"You need to give yourself time—"

"No, I don't need to wallow. What good will that do? I need to … Well, I need to not be here. That much I know. Could you … ." Vivian's throat constricted. She tried again. "Could you go through his trunk? Keep whatever you think I might want later, and let Mel ship the rest."

"Of course. But—"

"I'm gonna take a walk. Can you find one of the men to give me a lift to the station?"

Without waiting for Mabs's response, Vivian wrapped Jack's coat more securely around her and walked toward the perimeter road.

***

Vivian was relieved to find the church empty. Joe tried to speak with her yesterday at the base. Someone found him when they realized *Vivian's Victory* was missing. No, not missing. Gone. She couldn't allow herself to think missing.

Joe offered words of comfort and solace, but Vivian hadn't wanted to hear them. She wanted to hear them even less today.

She checked her watch. No, not late enough yet. She couldn't endure the sympathy, the platitudes, the commiseration of her friends, Jack's friends.

Vivian shouldn't have been here. If the *South Dakota* hadn't quit working yesterday morning, she would have been hard at work in Leicester, unaware of Jack's fate. Her thumb traced the filigree pattern of her locket.

There would be a memorial service later, if someone confirmed his plane exploded or crashed with no parachutes. If that wasn't confirmed, they would wait until it was clear he hadn't made it to a POW camp or escaped back to England. By then, he would be long forgotten. His bunk stripped, his possessions removed, his space on base made ready for the next eager young airman who would replace him. It would be as though he never existed, never lived, never loved.

Her heart constricted. Vivian had known it would come to this. She should have prepared herself better. Jack told her the moment they met back home, he was going into combat. She hadn't appreciated what that meant for the bomber crews. If she was being fair to herself, she couldn't berate herself or regret falling in love with him initially. She had been as blind and naive as any other home-front soldiers' sweetheart. They had no idea what their men faced.

Once he arrived here, it was a different story. She had known he had a one in four chance of surviving his tour. At best. She had *known*. She had seen so many men not return from their missions, knew of so many funerals and memorial services. And yet she had still harbored that small spark of hope that he would beat the odds. She had let herself picture him still standing at the end of it all, picture the two of them riding off into the sunset. Stupid, stupid, stupid.

Vivian was surprised to find herself consumed not with weeping or the numb coldness that had cloaked her heart since the previous evening, but anger. She wanted to curse, scream, throw something. And why was she here? Here of all places. In a church, a place of worship for a God who allowed this senseless slaughter to continue.

Tires crunched on the gravel outside.

The church door creaked open. Vivian refused to turn and look to see who had come to attempt to offer her comfort.

Footsteps clumped down the center aisle to where she sat in a front pew.

Muddy sheepskin-lined flier's boots.

Those could belong to almost anyone on base.

It must be her imagination. A slight whiff of intangible freshness cut through the distinctive aroma of mud, grease, gasoline, leather, and wool most fliers carried with them. It couldn't be.

Gentle, firm fingers slid under her chin and tilted her face up.

And there he was.

Jack.

Unbelievably, solidly in front of her.

She clapped her hand to her mouth, her eyes blinded by the tears she had been unable to shed until now.

Jack's eyes, a sheen of moisture clouding their pale blue cast, locked with hers. Unspoken words passed between them. Experiencing life without him, however mistaken and brief, underscored life's fragility, upended Vivian's thinking, unsettled her resolve.

He sat and wrapped her in his arms. She buried her face into the soft leather of his bomber jacket. He stroked her hair and kissed the top of her head as she clung to him.

She raised her face, and he leaned his forehead against hers, using one thumb to wipe away the tears from her cheeks.

"How? Where were you?" she asked, her voice choked with tears.

"We got shot up pretty bad. Two of our engines died. Barely made it across the Channel. Landed at an RAF field on the coast. The Brits radioed base we'd landed, but they gave out the wrong tail number.

No one here realized we were okay, or they would have told you. Our fellas expected to find Dave Gray and his crew when they came to get us this morning."

Dave. Vivian's heart constricted. How self-centered she had been. She had given no thought to the others from their group who hadn't made it back. One hundred and fifty of their men to be exact.

"And the others? Do you know what happened?"

His expression hardened. "We were supposed to be in the high squadron, but the soup was so thick yesterday that by the time we got to the assembly point, the 381st had taken our spot. We had to slide in lower. You know, in Purple Heart corner." He rubbed his eyes. "When we got over the coast, it started getting hot, Luftwaffe all over us. A bomber from 381st flying above us got a direct hit, nearly clipped us. I moved up fast and took its spot."

Jack paused, then said bluntly, "Bowie's quick thinking saved our lives. The other two ships, the ones that came back yesterday? They also got lucky breaks and moved to safer spots in the formation. Everyone down low was shredded."

Biting her lip, Vivian interlocked her fingers with his, still unable to believe he was there. "Did you—?"

"Did we see? Yeah, yeah we did." He turned anguished eyes to hers. "I'm glad my guys were spared. But, God Vivian, hardly anyone else ..." His voice cracked, and he stared at their clasped hands.

If only they could escape this madness. Jack would never desert, and she would never propose it. She wished a thousand times over, not for the first time, that he was safe at home doing his bit as a flight instructor. If he survived his tour, she would persuade him to go home or shift into a training job here. No. Even better, working with the division headquarters, where he would absolutely positively not fly any more missions. She should be sure Jack spent some time with Archie MacLeod.

Jack's free hand rubbed restlessly over the dog tag he kept in his pocket at all times. His friend Ace's tag. Jack spoke of Ace often, but always in the context of stories from his childhood. He cut off questions about Ace's death or how it had affected him.

Jack heaved a deep sigh and looked up again. "If you hadn't been here, I could have said we had a rough one and left it at that."

If she hadn't been here, hadn't experienced the blinding panic, searing terror, and heartbreak of imagining him dead, she might not understand what was now crystal clear. They had to seize every moment, live each day to its fullest.

Vivian ran a fingertip along the dark blond stubble on his cheek. "You look done in. Did they feed you? Were you able to rest?" He hadn't bothered to change his clothes before setting out to find her.

"Yeah, they were fantastic, the RAF 'chaps,' as they say."

"Did you fly back?"

"Nah, your namesake is still at the RAF base, and I'm sorry to say she's pretty beat up. We're gonna send Tad and Duck to get her in shape to fly, then Bowie or I will bring her back."

"They won't send you out again any time soon, will they? In another plane?"

He shook his head. "They'll have to wait for a new influx of planes. And crews." He stood and pulled her to her feet. "They've given us a three-day pass to London."

"My Clubmobile's out of commission—that's why I was here. It won't be fixed for a few more days. I'll be able to take good care of you." She rubbed a smudge of grease off his chin.

He pulled her close, and Vivian breathed fully for the first time in hours. His lips pressed against hers, softness yielding to a gentle pressure before giving way to promise.

CHAPTER NINETEEN

October 15, 1943
London, England

Jack tossed a few bills on the table. "No flying tomorrow, men. Live it up."

"Recognizing your need to be appraised of all situations involving the men under your command, we'll stop by your room later. Let you know we made it back." Bowie put his hands behind his head, leaned back in his chair, and winked.

"Blackout's pretty hazardous," Chaz observed.

"You'll rest better knowing we're all accounted for." Gib lit another cigarette and signaled for the barman.

"Anyone who shows up at my door tonight will do a week's work with our ground crew," Jack said. In response to their jeers, he added, "I outrank every one of you."

"Ooh, he's pulling rank," said Gib.

Just good-natured ribbing, though the fellas clearly assumed she and Jack would share his room tonight. A flush crept up Vivian's neck, and she busied herself with retrieving her purse.

When they reached the hotel, Vivian waited on a chaise in the lobby while Jack obtained his room key.

Jack returned a few minutes later and slung his kit bag and her musette bag over his shoulder. He took her hand and led her toward the staircase. "I signed the registry as 'Mr. and Mrs.' just in case," he said in a low voice.

Mr. and Mrs. Jack Nielsen. Would that ever come to pass? Were they tempting fate with the pretense? Jack had wanted to marry her almost from the moment they met. The Red Cross wouldn't stand in the way of a wedding. If something happened to him, wouldn't she regret they hadn't seized the chance? She knew the answer, for it had been one of the many regrets running through her head this time last night.

She loved him. Vivian was more certain than ever before. Believing she had lost him had shaken her into confronting her emotions. Perhaps her fear, her escalating panic about his survival odds, was keeping her from making the commitment she knew he wanted. She couldn't banish her terror, but she resolved it wouldn't keep her from loving him fully and freely.

Jack unlocked the door and motioned her inside.

She strode forward to pull the lamp cord while the hallway light still illuminated the room.

Jack closed the door and set his bag on the luggage rack, placed hers on a chair. He removed his cap, set it on the bedside table, and gestured to the china carafe on the table. "You want me to fill it with water?"

"Not unless you want some," Vivian said.

He shook his head. "No, but I'm gonna use the loo."

The door clicked closed behind him.

Vivian removed her jacket and hung it in the armoire. She stepped out of her pumps and used her toes to slide them under the luggage rack.

She opened her musette bag and rummaged through her clothing. Her lacy pink nightgown was back home in Georgia. These days she slept in a warm flannel nightgown, topped with her jacket or overcoat, and paired with at least two pair of socks in her cold billet. Hardly a sexy look for tonight. Her dressing gown wasn't apt to inspire ardor either, but it wasn't a schoolmarm flannel number. She left it on top of the bag.

Vivian crossed the room and pulled on the sash to raise the window. A trace of musty odor hung about the stuffy room. A waft of cool, damp air left a light mist on her face. She closed her eyes in contentment.

She should move back and let the blackout drapes fall closed, but the delicate spray of mizzle continued to beckon, refreshing and relaxing.

"How's the view?" Jack whispered against her neck. Her heart raced. Vivian hadn't heard him return to the room. His hands circled her waist and pulled her against him.

"Dark. Nothing to indicate we're in London, apart from the fog," Vivian murmured.

His lips brushed against her neck, sending shivers spilling down her spine.

"We might be anywhere," Jack whispered in her ear, his lips sucking and tugging on her earlobe. "Where do you wish we were? If there was no war?"

"Anywhere as long as we're together." Vivian let the faint scent of his soap and the wool of his uniform coat tantalize her senses. She ran her thumb over his hands, still interlocked tightly around her waist. "You?"

"Hmm, same. Anywhere's fine if we're together. Together and alone." His voice, close to her ear, was imbued with an uncharacteristically husky timbre. Her heart thudded against her chest, and her stomach clenched in anticipatory pleasure.

Alone. She would no longer have to content herself with imagining how they might finish what they started in New York. So many nights had passed since they parted. Restless nights where her imagination conjured a cascading torrent of physical and emotional sensations. Nights where she brought herself over the edge and smothered the noise into her pillow, hoping her roommates were sound asleep.

That longing hadn't dissipated.

Jack moved his lips to her hair. "Viv, nothing's changed for me since New York. I haven't stopped loving you all this time." He paused. "But I want you to be sure. I don't want you to be worried about the Red Cross, or anything else."

With Jack's tongue making delightful swirls in her ear, it was hard to be too worried about her employer's guidelines for her personal life. She might not be ready to marry him yet, but she would become his lover tonight. She understood what he was up against. This time last night she grieved his loss. He was here now, and they weren't guaranteed more than this moment.

"I'm not worried about that now." Vivian turned in his embrace and kissed him.

His soft lips moved against hers, gently at first, then with more pressure, more urgency.

Vivian wrapped her arms around his neck, drew him closer, and tangled her fingers into his hair. She pressed her body against his, heard his breath quicken, felt his growing arousal.

Sharp, successive blasts sounded through the open window, and Vivian startled, bumping her nose against his.

"Only a car horn," he whispered against her mouth.

God, please no air-raid sirens tonight.

Jack untucked her blouse from her skirt and unbuttoned it from the bottom. He fumbled a bit with the Red Cross pin, then set it on the table next to the carafe before lowering his mouth to her throat. He trailed his tongue over her clavicle and across the tops of her breasts.

She moaned, and Jack looked up from her chest, his eyes intent on hers. "You're sure?"

"I've imagined this moment a hundred different ways since we left off in New York, how it would be between us when we found each other again." Vivian traced a fingertip around the edge of his face.

Jack's lips twitched up on one side. He straightened and slid a few fingers under her chin, tilting it up. He leaned close, sucked on her lower lip, and whispered, "Tell me how. Tell me how you imagined it. Tell me the best way you imagined it, Vivi." The sultry tone, the look in his eyes, his full lips, moist and enticing, sent ripples of shivers slinking across Vivian's shoulders.

He slipped one of his fingers inside her bra cup, circling and tracing patterns over her sensitive breast and moved to her hard nipple. "Do I undress you first? Or do you remove my jacket, my shirt, and my pants? What comes first?"

She might be inexperienced, but Vivian couldn't mistake her body's reactions to his seductive questioning. "You might ease my blouse off my shoulders next," she whispered.

His fingers brushed her shoulders, guiding her blouse down her arms. Her blouse fell to the floor, and Jack pulled her against him. His hands roamed her back, and his lips skimmed across her shoulders, her neck, her chest.

"I might do this next," he murmured and used a featherlight fingertip to trace the ribbon stripes on one of her bra cups, "if that feels nice."

Vivian exhaled audibly.

"Does it? Feel good?"

His hand cupped her breast, and his thumb traced circles with increasing pleasurable pressure. His lips moved lower on her chest to her cleavage. One of his hands strayed to her back. His slender fingers deftly lifted each of the three hooks in turn. He slid his hands underneath the loosened cups, stroking the underside of each breast, and she whimpered.

"Now what do I do?" he whispered.

"You might …" Her voice squeaked, and she started over. "You might take off my bra next."

He slid one bra strap down her arm slowly, then the other, finally pulling each strap over her hands at once, letting the bra join her blouse on the floor. Goose bumps crept up both arms and across her neck.

Jack turned to her breasts. They were full and firm, her nipples erect under the attention of his tongue and fingers. He smothered her with kisses from her breasts to her neck and whispered in her ear, "What would you like me to do next?"

She moaned.

"Tell me what you imagined might happen next, Vivi," he urged. His lips quirked up on one side, and his eyes, brighter than usual, roved her face.

A growing ache between her legs told her what she wanted next. The ache would grow more intense, compelling her to satisfy it with fierce pressure, with her hand, her fingers.

"Do you think you might like it if I did this?"

Jack lowered himself to his knees, and his long fingers skimmed her thighs under her skirt. A surge of lubrication dampened her panties. The sight of him, still fully clothed in his uniform, on his knees before her, undressing her, sent her heart racing.

He fumbled with the garter fasteners. She closed a hand over his. "Careful, Jack. Those stockings are the only pair I've got left."

His shoulders shook, and he looked at her, his lips pursed together in a transparent attempt to fight back laughter.

"Don't you dare laugh, Jack." Giggles burst out before she could suppress them. How were they supposed to carry on, if she was laughing fit to die and he had joined in?

Grinning broadly, he took her right hand and guided it to her garters. "You unhook them. That way you can't blame me."

She unfastened each hook, and he whispered, "I'll take it from here. And I'll be very careful, very slow." True to his word, he took his sweet time easing each stocking casing down her leg, over her ankle, and off her foot. "See? No snags." Jack placed them next to her pin on the table.

His fingers played over the tops of her thighs under her skirt, teasing, tantalizing. Their laughter from moments ago hadn't ruined the mood after all. She moaned at the feathery caresses under her girdle skirt, his fingers skimming her inner thighs, frustratingly stopping short of where she most wanted his touch. Her muscles quivered with tension and need.

"What happens now, love?" He rocked back on his heels and smiled. His hands caressed underneath her skirt, the velvety strokes of his fingers giving way to a pleasantly firm massaging motion.

When she didn't answer, he said, "I think your skirt could come off."

She swallowed, unsure she could speak.

He unbuttoned the waistband and slid the zipper. She had lost weight over here; they all had. Her skirt didn't need any tugs to slide to the ground. She stepped out of it, and her slip followed in short order.

His scruff scraped against her soft skin as he nuzzled his lips over the tops of her thighs. He didn't wait for further instruction before he unzipped her girdle. It also didn't need much tugging to slide down her legs.

Jack pressed his hand against the thin nylon crotch of her panties. She groaned and rubbed herself against it. This was unbearable, and at the same time, she wanted the feeling to never end. An ache spread from her core to her privates, building inexorably, intensifying with his every touch.

"Your turn, Jack." Vivian kneaded her fingers through his hair.

"Not yet," he murmured. He pushed his fingers inside the elastic band on her panties and slid them off, nudging her ankles to prompt her to step out of them.

Her imagination hadn't conjured this. That she would stand nude before him, unabashed and soaking in the adoration and lust mixed in equal measure in his expression. That he would, at this point in the proceedings, still be clothed and in his uniform to boot. That him kneeling in uniform before her, ready to meet all her needs, would stir such intense physical cravings. That her lust would be so demanding, so consuming. She wanted his hand to press hard between her legs again, but better yet, she wanted him inside her. To be filled, to be linked as one.

Jack had other ideas. He used the flat of his hand to urge her legs open wider, and her inner thighs trembled. He kissed the creases of her legs, moved over the sensitive skin above where her pubic hair began. His hands roamed her bottom, and his tongue urged her to adjust her stance again, teasing against the soft folds of her labia.

Vivian's breath came in short tortured gasps.

"Come closer," he murmured. His hands urged her forward so her vagina was over his mouth.

Her imagination hadn't taken her this far either. Vivian wasn't completely innocent, but she hadn't considered he might use his mouth there, that he would excite her so thoroughly with his lips and tongue alone. She could feel how wet she was, and heat flared in her face. He wouldn't want to taste it, swallow it.

Oh, but he did. His tongue moved deeper inside her. Vivian's fingers dug into his hair. Her vaginal walls pulsed and throbbed with mounting energy. The sensation wasn't unfamiliar, though she had never brought herself to this level of intensity. For one thing, she hadn't used her fingers much, relying instead on friction and pressure to yield the waves of pleasure she craved.

He cupped her buttocks with his hands and pulled her deeper into his mouth.

"Oh, Jack." His tongue had found her nub. She had no name for it, but release followed when she applied tight pressure or friction against this sensitive part. She inhaled sharply. His tongue thrusted rhythmically against it, and Vivian simultaneously wanted to press hard against him, against something, and to relax into it, allowing the coming waves of pleasure to run their course.

Lordy. His fingers pressed against her butt, and the urge to rock her parts against the tip of his tongue grew stronger. She was almost there, right on the edge. This would be far, far better than anything she had ever done on her own. Vivian panted, huffing out her breath and whimpering, threading her fingers into his hair.

So close. She leaned her head back and closed her eyes. Her certainty she could focus her path as she did when she gave herself pleasure, focus she had suspected held her in check, was pitted against the momentum of her instinct to relax into what was building with steady intensity through her core.

Her nub spasmed against his tongue, and intense, exhilarating waves overtook her.

When she was again capable of coherent thoughts, Vivian realized Jack was still between her legs.

Heady exhilaration mixed with vulnerability, and she staggered back a few steps. She gulped in successive breaths. Nothing in her experience had prepared her for this swirl of physical sensations or the resulting emotional turmoil. What had transpired between them was much more intimate than anything her imagination might have concocted at its most feverish. Vivian had gleaned enough to know women experienced sexual pleasure, that sex wasn't just a duty she would perform for her husband. Still, women didn't discuss it among themselves. She hadn't had any idea what it all meant.

Jack stood, and one of his hands gripped around her upper arm. "Sorry, nearly lost my balance," he whispered. He had been on his knees for some time.

She tasted herself on him as Jack kissed her, enfolding her into his arms. "Did that live up to what you imagined?"

Vivian let out a shaky giggle against his mouth. "I ... Jack, I didn't realize."

"Plenty of time for us to become experts." Jack's eyes were fixed on hers, and he grinned crookedly.

"How about the feature film?" Jack's hands roved across her back, and his lips moved back to her neck, her jawline, and covered her mouth again. His kisses escalated from reverent gentleness to greater urgency and need.

Vivian thought she was spent, that her pleasure was sated. She was caught off guard by the returning urge to take Jack inside her, to sheath the length of him within her protective space. His penis pressed hard against her navel through his trousers. Her breath quickened.

Her fingers strayed to his trim waist and slid his coat belt through the loops and out of the metal frame. The metal coat buttons proved easy to manipulate. She unknotted his tie while he shrugged out of his coat.

Jack moved to encircle her back in his arms, but Vivian pushed him playfully. "You've still got too much clothing on." She unbuttoned his shirt and tugged the tails out of his trousers. She eased it off his shoulders, and it fell to the floor.

Vivian moved toward him. His arms wrapped around her waist, pulling her tight against him, and he lowered his mouth to hers again. She disengaged from his demanding kisses and, laughing, moved her lips over one of his hard nipples, while titillating the other one with her fingers.

His hands moved to cup her butt, lifting her off the floor. Heat surged through her core.

She moved her kisses to his jaw, running her tongue over the scruffy growth. Her fingers fumbled with his belt buckle, the button, and zipper to his trousers.

Jack groaned and backed them, step by step, toward the bed.

When his legs bumped against the mattress frame, Vivian pushed against his stomach. "I want to finish undressing you, Jack."

The corners of his mouth tugged into a smile. "You're the one in command in here," he said, sitting and scooting back, stretching his long, lanky legs out.

Vivian eased off his pants and tossed them over the top of the chair by the window.

She slipped her fingers inside the leg of his undershorts and ran the flat of her fingertips along the length of his stiff cock. Feathery light caresses. Shifting to light pressure with the pads of her fingers, she lengthened her strokes.

He twisted, moaning. "Feels so good. God, Vivian." His voice was much lower, rougher than normal.

Vivian moved her fingers to the waistband of his shorts, and he lifted his hips so she could slide them off.

She stretched out on top of him, lowering her lips to his. She moved herself against his erect penis. Her heartbeat *ka-thumped* in her chest.

His kisses became harder, fueled with a mounting energy.

"Mmmm," he murmured, rolling them so he was on top. His lips followed a fast trail from her neck to between her legs once again. Then he disappeared.

Vivian opened her eyes. "Jack?"

He rummaged in his kit bag and returned to the bed, opening a small tin with one hand.

Oh. Thank God he had remembered.

Fascinated, Vivian watched him roll the rubber over his penis.

He moved on his hands and knees until positioned over her once again. His eyes locked in on hers. He leaned close, the whisper of his breath featherlight against her mouth. "Yes?"

She pulled his head closer. "I love you."

Jack kissed her. "I love you too. I'll try not to hurt you, honey."

He nudged her thighs open wider and placed the flat of his hand against her vagina. She moaned with pleasure, pushing herself against his hand, aching with need. He slid a finger, then two fingers inside her again, then slid them out.

Slick with desperate desire, Vivian whimpered.

He pushed himself inside her. Vivian clenched her fingers around the sheets. No matter how welcome, no matter how wet she was, the sensation of his penis in her body wasn't painless. Her vagina both stretched and clenched at once.

Jack's voice was a gruff whisper near her ear. "Try to relax."

He raised up on his hands and made one stabbing push to go

farther within her. Vivian gasped at the sharp jolt of pain and clutched harder at the knots of sheets in her fists.

Jack tightened his arms around her and moved inside her, cautious strokes up and down. Searing pain melted away; clenching discomfort subsided into a strangely pleasurable ache. She exhaled, releasing tension with the breath. Jack pushed in deeper, and Vivian dug her fingernails into his back, wrapped her legs around his.

"Is this okay?" His tone was infused with warmth and concern.

"Yes. Much better. It's good." She moved her hips, trying to match the sync of his rhythmic movements in and out.

Her hunger to have him filling and stretching her, ever deeper, increased. Frustrated each time he pulled back or slid out, Vivian pulled against his buttocks, trying to communicate she wanted the feel of him ensconced deep within her. His thrusting motions were faster, his back slick with sweat. Intensity built through her core, and instinct took over. She moved with him.

"Oh, God. Oh, God, Vivian." Jack moved faster and faster, until he let out a long, shuddering groan.

He breathed heavily, the fine hair on the back of his neck damp from his exertions.

She clamped her legs around him. Vivian wanted him to stay buried deep within her. He was safe from danger there. She moved underneath him, trying to protectively draw him in deeper.

Vivian wasn't as sated as she might be. It was there, just out of reach. When they had been moving together frantically, she had tried to find it, to feel those clenching spasms of pleasure once again. Could he keep going? Could he continue to move like that, now his need was met?

He must have sensed what she wanted. Jack began to push within her again, and his finger strayed to her bud. He teased with the tip of his fingers at first, then shifted to using the pressure of his thumb pad. Circling, toying, stimulating. He moved his fingers up a smidge, and Vivian surged all at once, gasping and crying out. Fierce spasms rocked her, and she had no idea what she screamed.

Vivian lost all sense of how long she clutched him tight, wanting to keep him buried within her.

If only she could keep him there until this madness ended.

Later, snuggled against him, his cool even breath against her ear, it dawned on her. The war didn't have to end. Jack would be safe once he finished his tour. He could transfer into an operations role, something like MacLeod's position with division headquarters. Better still, he could agree to return to his role in flight instruction in exchange for rotation stateside.

"Jack?" she whispered.

He made an indistinct noise.

Men could finish in eight or nine months. But, weather could keep the Eighth grounded for days at a time, especially in the winter.

"Jack?" she repeated. "How many mission credits do you have?"

"Mmmph ... Twelve."

Twelve. Almost halfway. Thirteen more missions. It wasn't nothing. Vivian understood the dangers and statistical odds. But it gleamed ahead all the same, that moment when Jack's safety would be assured, and she could relax again.

CHAPTER TWENTY

February 25, 1944, 3:30 a.m.
USAAF Station 105, Chelveston, England

For the first time in months, Jack wasn't awake to hear the jeep pull up outside their hut or the banging knock on the door. Insomnia plagued him, even when the weather was so foul everyone knew none of them would fly.

Last night, he relented and took two of Gib's sleeping pills. Most of the men took them and used Benzedrine "wakey-wakey" pills to get going when rousted out of bed before dawn. Jack hated the idea of needing drugs to get the rest he needed.

The weather had been decent for the first time since December, and operations had made full use of it this week. Jack and his crew had been over Germany four days in succession.

"Another nice day over the continent, and you're all on the rosters," the Charge of Quarters yelled. He gave each of them a rough shake and pulled the light bulb chains. Curses and groans issued from every corner.

Jack sat on the edge of his cot and looked at the exhausted men around him. How the fuck were they supposed to stay alive in active combat with no sleep?

But, like the others, Jack crawled out of bed and dressed. He cast one last longing look at the framed photo of Vivian on his bedside table. As always, he couldn't stop the worries, tumbling over each other in his head like bombs cascading down to a target far below. What if that was his last look at her beautiful, smiling face? Would he hold her close again? What if the mission left him alive but severely disabled? Would she still want him? What would become of their plans, of his plans?

Bowie opened the door, and Jack followed him out into the night. A crisp bite of wind stung his chapped face and whooshed through his heavy clothing, chilling him deep in his bones. Darkness, dense and inky, enveloped them like a shroud. Occasional pinpricks of light marked a hut door opening and closing. They stumbled across the mucky footpaths by instinct, the huff of their breaths and the crunch of their boots on the frost-coated ground the only sounds.

No one talked. Not on their way to the mess. Not in the chow line. Not even as they ate powdered eggs and fried Spam washed down with black coffee. Apparently, they had been up too many times this week to merit the fresh eggs and bacon that would normally be served on the morning of a maximum effort mission.

Jack didn't eat much. The gloppy eggs were tasteless, and he hated Spam. The texture, the saltiness, the frequency it appeared in all forms on the menu—he hated everything about it. Bowie chopped his into small chunks and mixed it in with the eggs. Jack's stomach churned, and he averted his eyes. He dug around in his pocket for the pill, the Benzedrine that was supposed to clear his head. He popped it in his mouth and chased it with coffee.

Several men stood, and before long, everyone had taken the cue.

Another silent trek in the bitterly cold predawn, this time down a gravel path leading from the mess hall to the briefing hut.

Jack filed in with the others and sat on the wooden bench between Chaz and Gib. Sweat popped at his hairline and trickled down the back of his neck. More men packed into the stuffy, smoky confines. Jack unzipped his jacket, unbuttoned the top buttons of his uniform, and shifted uncomfortably.

Gib lighting a cigarette right next to him did nothing to improve his mood.

"Why you gotta light up now, with all of us packed in here like sardines?"

"My smoke is just one of many, Chief. You gonna persuade all these fellas to hold off?" Gib took a deep drag on his cigarette and blew out a lazy smoke ring. It hung in the air, swirling, its stale smell permeating every direction. Jack's stomach roiled again, and he pressed his lips together.

The door at the back of the hut slammed close. Nervous trilling chatter around the hut abruptly ceased. Jack looked over his shoulder. Commander Mustoe strode down the center aisle. Every pair of boots in the room stomped to attention with a resounding boom. Dead silence as Commander Mustoe made his way to the front of the room, the men of the 305th standing at attention on all sides.

Commander Mustoe faced them in silence. His rigid stance diverted the men's obsessive focus from the drape-covered map behind him. He held them at attention for seconds, weeks. Gib tipped ashes from his burning cigarette to the ground. Chaz's fingers clenched and unclenched around the edge of his notebook.

"At ease, gentlemen."

The executive officer made no move to pull back the drape covering the map, which would reveal the target for today's mission.

Mustoe cleared his throat. "We've been pushing you fellas hard this week. You're probably thinking you deserve a day off, even some leave. You're exhausted and probably more than a little resentful at what we've asked you to do so far, what we'll ask of you today."

His voice rung out, booming, through the unusually silent room. "But you can't think about any of that. Not right now. You must think only of today. Don't think about leave. Don't think about the girls waiting in London. And sure as hell don't think about your wife, your sweetheart back home, your kids, your mother, or anyone else. You got it? You must only think about today and your mission. Nothing else."

Jack's heart constricted. No, they weren't supposed to think about wives, sweethearts, or lovers, all right. They were supposed to consider themselves walking dead men. They were supposed to recognize it, cope with it, accept it. They were dead or as good as dead. Statistically speaking, none of them should expect to survive their combat tour. Some men had and would, but statistics said none of them could count on it.

"You may be wondering why we're going up for the fourth day in a row. Weather's kept us grounded for most of the winter so far, and this week has been our first clear shot over the continent. But, it's more than good weather, and I reckon you should know as much as I can tell you."

Jack leaned forward.

"Shouldn't come as any surprise, gentlemen, that the ground pounders are eventually gonna have to cross that channel you fly over every mission and fight their way through to Berlin. They need us to be in control of the skies above them. And they need it sooner, not later."

Jack's arm muscles tightened, and he filled the suddenly expansive space in his chest with air. On leave in London over Christmas, Jack and Vivian had noticed the sharp increase in US Army troops. Vivian said a large contingent of paratroopers were now based in Leicester. Many joked that England might soon collapse under the weight of American military forces.

Yes, there would be a ground invasion, no doubt about that. And it was up to the Allied air forces to give those doughboys a fighting chance.

***

At the hardstand, with his pulse racing and his body reacting two steps behind what his overactive mind asked, Jack motioned for his men to huddle near the left wing. He pressed his shaking hands tight against his legs.

"On the plus side, we should be back on track to finish our tour by May," Bowie said.

"One full year in the ETO in June," said Ira.

"We *would have been* back on track if bastards hadn't increased the mission count on us." Gib tossed his cigarette to the ground and extinguished it with the toe of his boot.

They were now required to complete thirty missions rather than twenty-five. Jack wouldn't have given all the money in the world to have been the brass tasked with informing the crews of this policy change. Shouted profanities and catcalls rang out until the unfortunate officer bellowed that he would court-martial the next man who opened his mouth. Public protests ended, but the bitter undercurrent of mutiny lived on.

Anger at the increase in required missions was compounded by the fact that no one had made headway into their tour, no matter what the total was. October's Schweinfurt debacle bled into months of unceasingly rotten weather, even by British standards. Runways turned into sheets of ice, and record snowfall and bitter winds penned the bored and restless men inside for weeks at a stretch. They had added a whopping two missions to their count in December and January.

"We're only focused on today, guys," Jack said. "Quit thinking about which number this is or what happens when we're done. Long as everyone does his job and helps everyone else like we've been doing, we'll come back all right. I've got faith in y'all. Teamwork, like usual. Now, listen up, Chaz'll tell us where we can expect hot action, and then everyone move into the ship so we can get going."

Jack kneaded his temples while half listening to Chaz's briefing notes. Yeah, yeah, yeah. Fighters heavy. Above-average flak. What else was new? His head throbbed, but he probably shouldn't pop an aspirin since he had taken a second Benzedrine thirty minutes ago. Moments later, he changed his mind. He dug around in his pocket, pulled out the pill, and swallowed it dry.

He told the men to board and triple-check everything. "We're all running low on sleep. Be sure you got your chute, flak suit, helmet, all of it."

Jack, Bowie, and Ira followed Tad around the ship for the preflight inspection.

They stopped near the right wing. Tad pointed to several patches they had fashioned out of spare metal, warning them about … about

… the right inboard engine. Wait, what had Tad said?

Sweat popped at Jack's hairline. He gritted his teeth, willing the rising bile to subside.

"Hey, don't rip that wing off, Chief."

What? Oh. He had grabbed the edge of the wing.

Jack could no longer pass off the acrid taste filling his mouth as inhalation of surrounding exhaust fumes. Heaving violently, he spattered vomit on the ground. He backed up and swiped sweat from the sides of his face. Tad passed him a canteen of water.

"Thanks," he muttered, twisting the lid off with a shaking hand. He took several tentative sips. There went the aspirin and the Benzedrine too, no doubt.

"Why don't we radio for a replacement pilot, Jack? You can't fly like this," Bowie said.

Jack shook his head. "I'll be all right. Got it out."

He wiped around the edge of the canteen mouth with his sleeve, closed it, and handed it back to Tad. "What did you say about the inboard?"

Bowie and Ira exchanged a glance.

"Look, I took an aspirin a few minutes ago on top of one of those wake-up pills Gib gave me." No need to tell them he had taken two Benzedrines. "Should've eaten more breakfast. I'm fine. Let's get on with this."

At a nod from Bowie, Tad carried on with their inspection.

Ira swung up through the hatch a few minutes later, and Bowie turned to face Jack. "Jack, you better be damn sure you're all right. You don't look good at all."

"None of us look good. You looked in a mirror lately?" Jack made to push past him, but Bowie put up an arm to bar his access to the hatch.

"For once, I'm being serious. You gotta be firing on all cylinders up there."

"Really? I had no idea. Drop it, Bowie. Let's go."

"Never doubted you before, Jack, but I think we oughta get another pilot. Gib's always said he can copilot, but we all know he's all hat and no cattle. Frankly, I don't want to test that theory at twenty-five thousand feet with fighters on our ass."

"I'm fine, but you're fixing to not fucking be fine if you don't move out of the way, Coates. Let's go." Jack pulled roughly at Bowie's elbow.

Bowie stood his ground and used his other hand to grab the collar of Jack's jacket. "All our lives are on the line. Is it worth you being one mission short of the rest of us? For fuck's sake, go see Doc and go back to bed. You're not the only capable pilot on this base."

"This isn't about mission count. It's about all of us sticking together. You start getting replacements on a crew, all of a sudden they're putting our fellas out as replacements and before long, they've split us all up. We're a team, and we're gonna stay that way."

If he didn't fly, their magic might break. They had made it so far, with only Stan suffering injuries back in October. And he had been back in action in time for their next mission. They were one of the few intact original crews left. Most crews had a handful of men who got wounded or a few who had been sent to a flak house for a rest period, which sometimes turned into a permanent removal from flying duties. Those who remained got split up and weren't part of a regular crew anymore.

No, them all being together, that was important, critical.

His fellas needed him at the helm.

Jack pointed toward the open hatch. "We gotta test out these engines. You gonna swing up, or do I need to issue an order, Lieutenant Coates?"

Bowie gave him a long, appraising look before nodding curtly. "After you, *sir*." Bowie withdrew his arm and waved his hand to indicate Jack should go first.

Before stepping into the cockpit, Jack pushed his fingers into the inside lining of his jacket pocket to confirm Vivian's picture was there. He stashed his chute, wrapped in the second flak vest, under his seat. The men all had their rituals, their lucky talismans secreted on their person like Jack had Vivian's photo. And Ace's dog tag. He rubbed his thumb over the well-worn embossed lettering.

"Hey, Chief, come see what we chalked today," Lou called.

Jack paused at the door into the bomb bay, managed to laugh at the messages his guys had scrawled in chalk on the bombs. "Best Wishes, Adolph, Courtesy of the Can-Do Crew," "To Hitler, Love from the Mighty Eighth," and "Run Jerry Run."

Half an hour later, the plane, with its airframe rattling, chugged around the perimeter to the runways. Jack spoke into the intercom: "Pilot to crew: Matchsticks in a box, men."

Though covered in the thick sheepskin-lined gloves, Jack's hand visibly shook when he pulled up on the throttle to start them down the runway. Feeling Bowie's eyes on his every move, he tried sending a direct message from his brain to his body to stop giving off signals of anything less than full control. No dice, but it didn't matter. They were committed to takeoff.

***

Vivian's stomach remained taut until *Vivian's Victory* came to a stop with no emergency flares. Jack's crew members piled out of the hatches one by one. They moved slowly in their heavy flight gear, stiff from the cold and the close quarters, weary from whatever challenges they had faced in today's mission.

Normally the men looked sexy in their leather flight jackets. Leather helmets, white neck scarves and crush caps added to their dashing appearance. Today, they looked far more like tired boys than the glamorous aviators the American media portrayed in glossy magazine spreads back home.

The bomber didn't look noticeably beat-up. Yet, Tad and Duck were there the moment Jack's tall, lanky frame descended the hatch. Bowie followed him, and the four men fell into conversation. They circled the ship, with all of them gesturing at various areas that would need attention before she could fly again. Duck made notes on a clipboard, holding his poncho open over the clipboard to shield it from the pelting rain.

Jack and his crew headed toward interrogation.

Vivian knotted her head scarf under her chin and stepped out into the path.

"Well, well, Chief, your day sure got a lot better," said Ford.

"I thought you promised to bring friends with you next time, doll," said Lou.

"Who says I didn't?" Vivian said.

She had brought Jean and Dottie, though it was their idea more than hers. After that mission last fall when she had feared Jack was lost, her Clubmobile friends made excuses to accompany her to Chelveston. They would go on to London once Jack returned.

"Go check out the Red Cross Girls inside. You'll see new faces." Vivian laughed as Walt, Lou, and Ford made a show of picking up their pace.

"Hey now, officers ahead of enlisted guys if there's new gals inside," said Gib.

Bowie didn't join in the joking. He looked exhausted and uncharacteristically peeved. He waved to her but didn't say anything.

She tried to embrace Jack, but he took a backward step. "I'm sweaty and dirty, honey."

Vivian was so grateful to see him she wouldn't have cared if he had dipped in slimy mud before he climbed out of his plane.

Before he could stop her, Vivian stood on tiptoe to plant a quick kiss on his cheek.

"C'mon, Viv, I said to hold off until I've cleaned up."

It was on the tip of her tongue to say, "Don't be such an ass," but Jack held up a conciliatory hand. "I'm beat, Viv. Let me go on in with the fellas so we can debrief. I'll feel better after I've gotten some food in my stomach. And a shower," he said pointedly, the barest ghost of a smile flickering across his face before disappearing again.

"Fine." She followed him inside.

He fell into step in the line for coffee and sandwiches behind Chaz and Bowie.

Jack's coffee cup clattered in the saucer. With the experience born of serving many men with post-mission nerves, Nancy took it from him, set it on the table, and poured him a half cup.

Vivian frowned. Mabs had told her before that Jack was unfazed in the interrogation hut.

His physical rebuffs could be him being uncomfortable with his sweaty and dirty appearance. But he hadn't seemed happy to see her. He hadn't even *said* he was glad to see her. For that matter, he hadn't so much as asked why she was here or how long she could stay.

***

February 25, 1944, 9:00 p.m.
Rainbow Corner, American Red Cross Club
London, England

Bowie watched Jack head to the bathroom after dinner and moved closer to Vivian. "He's not great. Don't know if you've noticed since you don't see him every day, but he's feeling it."

Vivian's stomach dropped like a dollop of doughnut dough in the fryer. It wasn't just her. Bowie had noticed it too. "His hands shake. He's jumpy and irritable, hard to please."

"Yeah, all of that and more. Look, he wouldn't like me telling you this, but Gib's been giving some of the guys sleeping pills and wake-up pills. I sleep like a log, but Jack caved this week. Got real sick this morning before takeoff but wouldn't hear of me radioing in for a replacement pilot."

She glanced around to be sure Jack was nowhere in sight. "Are you saying he shouldn't have been flying? It seemed like you were ticked off at him."

"Jack's a good pilot. A real good pilot. But I don't like what those pills did to his reflexes today. Rough up there. I reckon if you could persuade him to see Doc about taking a break …" He broke off.

Jack strode toward them.

"Right-o, I'll tell her," Bowie said to Vivian. He stood and gave Jack a casual smile. "Vivian's been giving me tips to pass on to my cousin. She's trying to get on as a Red Cross Girl."

"Oh, good," Jack said. He turned toward the games room.

Vivian followed his gaze. There seemed to be some disturbance underway in the crowded hallway.

"That sound like Tink?" Bowie cocked his head.

Jack's eyes narrowed. He strode toward the hallway.

Vivian hurried behind him. Raised voices grew louder. "Jack, wait. You shouldn't get involved in a fight." She jogged forward and put a hand on his elbow, but he shrugged her off and lengthened his stride so that he outpaced Bowie.

Jack shoved through the circle of onlookers.

"You heard me," said Tink. "Fuck off and leave us alone. We're not bothering anyone."

"Fucking kike is," someone said.

Vivian peered through the gaps between soldiers who pressed closer to the altercation. One soldier had Ira penned against the wall. Another grappled with Tink. He had lost his glasses in the struggle, and his face was purple.

Jack wrenched the man off Ira and slammed him hard against the opposite wall. The soldier struggled. Jack gripped the man's upper arms and slammed his head against the bricked surface.

"Jack, no!"

He gave no sign that he had heard her.

Gib and Chaz rushed into the fray. They each grabbed one arm of the man who was restraining Tink and shoved him into a circle of his buddies.

Jack drew back his arm to slug Ira's tormentor.

Vivian gritted her teeth and winced.

Bowie grabbed Jack's arm. "Leave it, buddy. Not worth getting tossed out of here."

"Damn straight. Kike oughta be," the soldier said. Apparently, the jarring slam against the brick wall Jack inflicted had done nothing to check the man's hostility.

Jack shook off Bowie's restraint, circled his hands around the soldier's throat, and slammed his head against the wall again. "Can't shut your yap."

"Jack, stop it!" Vivian tried to duck under the arms of onlookers, but several men closed in to block her path.

Gib and Chaz each pried Jack's fingers from around the soldier's throat.

Bowie planted the flat of his hand on Jack's chest and shoved, sending Jack stumbling back a few paces. "Cool it."

The soldier, pale and gasping, rubbed his throat. He mouthed wordlessly and glared at Jack.

Sweat trickled down Jack's temples. Tight cords stood out in his neck.

"All Americans in uniform are entitled to be here." Breathing heavily, Jack jabbed his index finger toward the man's leering face.

"Keep it up with the insults, I'll report you. Shove out. Go on." Incendiary rage simmered under the surface in his tight voice.

The soldier and his buddy groused but walked away. Spectators dispersed.

Vivian made her way to Jack and the others.

"What the hell was that all about?" Bowie asked Tink.

"We were playing pinball. Red Cross gives you the tokens free of charge to play." Tink nodded at Vivian. "They started making snide remarks about Jews and money. We were trying to ignore 'em. No money involved, so I don't know why they got all riled up."

"Bragging rights?" Gib picked Tink's glasses up from the floor and handed them to him.

"Maybe." Tink shrugged. He wiped the lenses on his shirt sleeve and put his glasses on. "Ira wasn't bragging. Decided we'd try to find you guys or get a drink. They followed us out here, and that's when you showed up."

"What's a kike?" Bowie asked.

Before Ira could speak, Chaz said, "It's a slur against Jewish people. Like when you Southerners call Negroes—"

"All right, we get the point," Jack interrupted. "Y'all come on with us. We'll get a drink, make Gib happy."

The blotchy flush had faded from Jack's neck and face. Tension had receded from his voice.

"I should go back to the hotel," Ira said.

Gib reached over and pulled Ira's cap straight. "No fucking way. I'm buying the first round."

"You don't want to miss out on history. Gib buying? That's a first," Chaz said.

"Don't worry about those bastards. They're jealous of our flyboy glamour." Bowie clapped an arm around Ira's shoulders.

Jack averted his eyes from Vivian's, but grabbed her hand, holding it fast in his.

What was happening to him? Was it the pills Bowie mentioned? Jack hadn't yet succumbed to the fatalistic mindset many airmen adopted after a few missions. Or she hadn't thought so. Even after Schweinfurt, Jack had continued to exude a steady confidence that bolstered his men. His frayed edges manifested in fits and spurts. His usual breezy joking manner might replace tense irritability in the space of hours.

Yet Bowie believed Jack needed a break. How many missions did they have left? Jack had said they flew four this week. Vivian tried to count in her head. Problem was, she didn't often know. Missions were scrubbed because of weather or aborted for mechanical failure all the time.

She had resolved in October to keep a close count, and once again she didn't have a solid number.

Tomorrow, she would think how to broach the topic of flak houses without mentioning Bowie. Jack would resent they had discussed him and that his copilot thought he needed help. He wouldn't much like it coming from her either.

Did he have enough in him to last this out? Enough for him? Enough for her? Enough for them?

CHAPTER TWENTY-ONE

May 15, 1944
Edinburgh, Scotland

Jack pushed open the door to their hotel room. The small bedside lamp cast a cozy glow, a contrast with the bite of brisk air lingering from the open window. He ought to feed a few shillings into the gas meter and try to warm the room before Vivian returned from her bath. Spring in Scotland was cooler than East Anglia.

He set the vase on the desktop and filled it halfway with water from the blue-and-white china carafe on the bedside table. After discarding the newspaper wrapped around the stems, Jack inserted the bouquet of flowers into the vase. He stood back and surveyed the result. It looked all right to him, but Vivian would fiddle with it later. Assuming she didn't throw it at him when he told her what he had done.

He had planned to tell her earlier. Vivian had been so relaxed and carefree during their week here that he couldn't bring himself to do it. He should have. She would be all the angrier that he had let her believe anything other than the truth about his immediate plans.

Jack turned at the sound of the door creaking open. Vivian

stepped in. Damp tendrils escaped where she had pinned her hair up in a loose topknot.

"Daffodils! And are those primroses?"

Jack had no idea. He had picked up the bouquet at a stall on Prince's Street, a short walk from their hotel. All he knew was they were pretty spring flowers.

She bent her face to smell the blooms. "Mmm, they smell beautiful. Thanks, honey."

Vivian crossed to him, slid her arms around his neck, and kissed him. Her soft lips moved against his. Jack inhaled her fresh clean scent. She must have taken one of her special bars of soap from home to the bath.

Jack wanted nothing more than to deepen the kiss, unknot the sash of her dressing gown, and pull her with him into bed. Judging from the fervor of her kiss, she envisioned a similar interlude before they went out for dinner on their final night of leave.

He shouldn't put this off any longer. Bad enough as it was. Jack broke the kiss.

"We can linger here for a bit before dinner, don't you think?" Vivian's upturned green eyes were soft, relaxed. Her lips parted, and she ran her index finger behind his earlobe, stroking. He shivered at her touch.

No. He couldn't make love to her and then give her this news.

Jack pulled her hand from his neck, intertwined his fingers with hers, and tried to plaster a reassuring smile on his face.

"Viv, there's something I should have told you already. I ... well, here, let's sit." He gestured to chintz armchairs near the window, but Vivian shook her head.

"What's this all about, Jack?" The ardor in her eyes cooled, and her expression turned wary.

Jack walked to the window and reached under the blackout shade to close the sash. "Sorry, meant to close this and get a fire going in here for you."

Vivian waved a hand at him. "I'm not cold, Jack. Just tell me what's going on."

"All right. Look, you've asked what I might be assigned to do, now that my tour's finished. I know I've been hedging. It's—"

"What?"

"I'll be staying in Chelveston. We'll still be able to see each other, like we've been doing." Jack rubbed the back of his neck.

"Chelveston? That's fine, Jack. What's all the fuss? I'd rather see you go back home, but that's good news. You had said they might shift you to London, and I would worry about you being there all the time."

"Mmm." Jack cleared his throat.

"Why on earth were you worried about telling me this?" Vivian opened the armoire and pulled out her pink suit. She laid it out on the bed and moved toward her musette bag. Rummaging inside, she pulled out her nylons, a slip, girdle, and bra. Vivian sat on the bed, facing away from him to pull her nylons on. She grabbed her girdle, stood to pull it up, and bent to fasten her nylons to the garters.

He ought to look away. The slow tease of her dressing ritual was distracting him from what he had to say.

She grabbed her slip. "Did you still want to go to that swanky restaurant near the Balmoral?"

"Uh, sure, that'll be fine." Jack picked up the bedside clock, turned it over, and set it down.

He had to tell her the rest.

"What will they have you doing? Ground duty with the operations staff or training exercises for the new fellows?"

"I … uh … I'll be doing what I've been doing." He swiped at sweat beading at his temples. Shouldn't have closed the window.

Vivian stepped into her slip. She pulled it to her waist and straightened. Still facing away, she asked, "What do you mean, what you've been doing? You've been flying combat missions, and you won't be doing that anymore."

When he didn't answer, Vivian turned to face him. Her lips were pursed, eyes bright and alert. "Jack? You won't be flying the missions anymore, will you?"

He nodded and cracked his knuckles. The clicks magnified in the tense silence.

"So, like Mel, right? You'll be flying a few missions as part of your duties on ops staff?"

"No. I didn't join the ops staff," Jack said.

Her eyebrows knit together, and two small lines creased her forehead. She stared at him for what seemed an eternity, then shook her head from side to side. "Please tell me you're not trying to say you've signed on for another tour."

Jack gave a short cursory nod. "We signed last week. That's why we got the full week leave."

"We?"

"My guys. We signed as a crew."

Vivian's eyes widened. "All of them? They all agreed to this, this madness? Most men can't wait to finish. I saw them come out of the plane after a final mission and kiss the ground."

Jack had known a few of his guys might want to stay on and keep going up. They groused along with everyone else, but Gib and Tink liked the flying duty pay rate. And Bowie, well Bowie wanted to fly. He had assumed Chaz and his gunners would take their points and rotate stateside.

He had joined in their raucous party at a pub in Yelden the night after their final mission. When he announced his plans over breakfast the next morning, Jack told them he would be happy to have any of them on his next crew. They caught up to him within the hour, and Bowie told him they had talked it over and there would be no need for a new crew.

"They said we're a team, and we gotta stick together," Jack said.

"And what about us? What about our team, Jack? Did it not cross your mind to discuss this with me?" Vivian took a step back toward the wall. Her face was pale, despite the flush creeping up her neck.

He bit his lip. "My decision to make."

"I haven't forgotten the Schweinfurt mission. It's all I've thought of since. You being safe. Done and safely back home." Her voice wobbled on the last word.

"It's less dangerous now, sweetheart. We've got the Mustangs with us all the way over and back—"

"Less dangerous? Less dangerous is still dangerous, Jack. Your odds of dying are not at zero." Vivian's voice rose. Her hand shook as she swiped at a strand of hair that had fallen loose into her eyes.

"No one's odds of dying are at zero," Jack scoffed. "Your odds aren't at zero, but I'm not trying to get you to go home. Doesn't mean

I'm not worried about you. I reckon you'd resent me trying to dictate what you should do."

"You resent me worrying, is that it?" Her voice grew louder with every word. Anyone in the surrounding rooms could sure hear everything Vivian said.

"Viv." He moved toward her. "Viv, honey, look, I had to do this."

"Had to? No! You did not *have to* at all, Jack. You were done. You beat the odds and now … now you've gone and made them worse." Her voice, the volume still rising with every word, was thick with suppressed sobs. She took a step toward him and jabbed a finger in his direction. "You have to undo this, that's all. You go tell Commander Mustoe you made a mistake. You finished what they sent you to do. They can't make you do a second tour. You must have enough points to go home."

Jack closed his eyes for a moment and inhaled deeply. He looked into her green eyes, pooling with unshed tears. "Honey, I've signed. I'm committed."

"No. No, Jack, no. No, do you hear me? You can't do this to me, to us."

"I have to." Jack's right hand pressed against Ace's dog tag in his pocket.

"You keep saying that. What does that mean? You've done your part. You're done, Jack. Done, done, done. You have to go home. Promise me you'll go home. Tell them whatever you have to," Vivian pleaded. Tears streamed down her face, and her hands balled into fists at her side.

Throbbing pain built across his forehead.

Jack raked his fingers through his hair and shook his head. "No. I can't promise that, honey. Gotta do my part still."

"How could they let you sign on again? You've been in bad shape for months."

"Viv, don't start on all that again. I told you, I'm fine. All the fellows have the shakes now and then." Jack strode to the window and pulled it open again. He kneaded his forehead before turning back around to face her.

Vivian swiped at tears and moved closer. "No, that's the answer. Go to Doc and tell him you made a huge mistake. Tell him how it's been. He'll send you to one of those flak houses."

"You want me sent away to a goddamn flak house? Do you have any idea what that would do to my chances of flying for the airlines after the war? That would go on my record, Vivian!" Pain roared through his ears, and he had to blink to clear his vision. A flak house? How could she think he would ever agree to that? She had brought it up once before, back in February when they were so exhausted. He thought the intensity of his reaction had shut that line of thought down for good.

"You'd be alive, and that's the most important thing."

Jack blinked to focus on her. "No! What's most important is doing my duty and keeping a good, clean record."

"Duty? You've done your duty. You can still serve, Jack, but it doesn't have to be in combat. Go to one of the rest facilities and come back into ground duty." Vivian reached out to take one of his hands, but Jack stepped backward, shaking his head.

"Don't you understand? I have to fly. The war's far from won, Viv, and I gotta do what I can. Have to be sure it wasn't all for nothing."

Vivian's brows crinkled together, her eyes narrowed. "Be sure what wasn't all for nothing?"

"All the guys who didn't make it. All those fellows back in October. All the ones since." Jack took a deep breath, his jaw clenched tight. "Ace." He extracted the dog tag from his pocket and passed it to her.

Vivian rubbed her index finger over the worn embossing. Her posture shifted, the tension in the set of her shoulders released by a small measure.

Perhaps she was thinking of all the men she had known who had lost their lives. She had confessed that she preferred her Clubmobile work because her relationships with the soldiers they served were casual and fleeting by nature. Vivian had never been good at keeping an emotional distance from the fellas she served at Chelveston's Aero Club. Jack suspected the Red Cross had a deliberate strategy of rotating its personnel for that reason, that they wanted to minimize both the personal attachments and the deflated morale that came with staying with one position too long.

Her brothers were surely also in her thoughts. Bob's letters now reported he was in "south England." He would cross the Channel with his unit in due time, any day now if the rumors were true. Meanwhile, her youngest brother Danny had at last put out to sea, working as an aviation machinist aboard one of the aircraft carriers in the Pacific.

Vivian's eyes were moist when she looked at him. "You never said his real name was Franklin."

Jack let out a smothered chuckle. "He hated it. Franklin after his grandfather and Ralph after his dad. I don't know who started calling him Ace, but I never knew him as anything else."

"I wish I could have known him. Ace is a big part of the man you are." Vivian took his hand and put the dog tag into his palm, closed his fingers around it.

He wrapped his arms around her and drew her close. "I know this isn't what you want, honey. But it'll all be fine, I promise," he whispered into her hair. "I won't let you down."

He had let Ace down, but Jack could redouble his service and recommit to his duty. And he would make damn sure he kept his promises to Vivian.

CHAPTER TWENTY-TWO

June 30, 1944
USAAF Station 105, Chelveston, England

There shouldn't be any reason to stop at Chelveston on her way to London. Mabs had been assigned to a Clubmobile operating out of Southhampton months ago. Even Nancy, whom Vivian hadn't known well, had been reassigned. The new girls running the Aero Club were probably fresh from the States.

Jack definitely shouldn't still be here.

Vivian rolled her neck side to side to release tension. She empathized with Jack's grief and appreciated his desire to bolster Ace's sacrifice. But what about her? His close brush with death in October had shaken her to her core. Why was her peace of mind less valuable than his sense of duty and sacrifice?

Besides, no matter what he said in Edinburgh and how she responded in the moment, Vivian still didn't believe Jack ought to be flying without a break. How had his superiors agreed? How could they not see how bad off he was?

Vivian had investigated Jack's claim that a trip to the flak house would stain his record. He wasn't completely correct. His time at a rest facility would be noted in his military record. However, no one outside the military had authorization to see the details in his file. He would be able to apply for a job with an airline without showing anything more than an honorable discharge.

Jack brushed off this new information. Word of mouth from other pilots would get around. The limited number of pilots who would secure post-war positions with the airlines guaranteed the airlines would hear damaging information about the candidates.

He also refused to concede his mental state put him in more danger. "We've all got the shakes." All the men suffered from some combination of insomnia and night terrors. They were all edgy and irritable.

After she walked through the guard station, Vivian shaded her eyes against the glaring sun and looked off toward the runways. Yes, they must be on a mission. Only a handful of Forts parked at the hardstands. Her hammering heart expanded until it seemed to fill her entire chest, exposed and vulnerable. *Let him be on his way back, safe and well. Let him be safe. Let him come back alive.*

Vivian fended off the shouted questions from several throngs of men she passed. She had mastered the knack of exuding friendliness while staying on task.

Headquarters, infused with the distinctively male aroma of cigarette smoke and sweat common to most military buildings, was quiet today. The man thumbing through a newspaper at the front desk wasn't the executive officer.

"Joe?"

Joe lowered the paper, his eyes twinkling. "EO stepped out to see the quartermaster, so I said I would sit here until he returns. What brings you here?"

"I'm reporting to London later today."

Joe pulled out a pocket watch. "They're not due back for a couple of hours yet."

Vivian's gut twisted with anxiety. She had hoped their arrival was more imminent. The anticipation would be torture.

The executive officer bustled back in, and Joe stood, folding the paper. He stepped around the desk. "Let's talk a walk to your Aero Club, shall we? They've got a ping-pong table now. Do you play?"

She only half listened to Joe's story about some of the village children as they walked to the Aero Club. *Please let him be safe.*

The club door was locked. Vivian should have remembered it wouldn't be open yet.

Joe gestured to a bench outside the club. "We can sit here and enjoy the sunshine unless you might like to try to find the new girls?"

Vivian took a seat. No, she didn't want to make small talk with the new women or, worse, be drawn into the endless well of questions they would have for a more experienced Red Cross Girl. She only wanted to see Jack and assure herself he was safe. She kneaded her forehead.

"You're worried about him?" At Vivian's bob of acknowledgment, Joe asked, "More than usual?"

"When I know he's up, it's harder. I hate the waiting."

Joe nodded. "Yes, it must be easier to put it out of your mind and carry on with what you need to do when you're not here."

Not entirely. Her anxiety levels had been steadily escalating, even before Bowie expressed his concerns. The odds, stacked against him, against them, from the beginning, mocked her at every turn. She swiped at tears seeping out and looked away.

"He should be finished soon, shouldn't he?"

All her anger, resentment, and anxiety bubbled to the surface. "No." She choked back a sob. "He finished two months ago, but he signed on for another tour."

"Well now, I'm sure you should rather see him heading home or taking a ground duty. Yet, he must believe he can still contribute—"

"He shouldn't have been allowed. He's ... he's in awful shape." She couldn't stop the tears. She hoped none of the fellows wandered over to see if the club was open yet. A crying Red Cross Girl was no good.

Joe patted her hand and passed her a handkerchief. "Tell me."

So she did. She poured out all her fears, everything she had observed about his worsening state, what Bowie had said months ago. "He must be hiding it. Why haven't Doc or his squadron leader realized?"

"I'm here on base often. My guess is most of men are experiencing some degree of—"

"I know, I know. That's what Jack says."

Joe cleared his throat. "What I was going to say was I've observed many men are experiencing battle stress, but it might not be amiss if you spoke to Doctor Burke. Perhaps he can assure you Jack was evaluated properly and is fit to fly. On the other hand, he might be grateful to know he should look at Jack again."

Vivian toyed with the handkerchief knotted in her hand. "Jack would hate that." He would more than hate it. He would view it as base betrayal.

Joe slapped his hands on his thighs and stood. "You might keep it in mind. Perhaps not now. There might come a time when it seems the best thing to do. I believe a poker game's going on in Hangar D. Perhaps a diversion while you wait?"

"No. Thanks, Joe. I think I'll take a walk."

Her summons to London today was sure to involve a transfer to one of the Clubmobiles going across the Channel in a few weeks. She spoke fluent French and passable German. She was certain to be among the first crews sent to France. She hated the idea of being separated again from Jack, of not having close access to his base. Yet how could she refuse? She had come overseas to help the soldiers. Important work would remain here in Britain, but across the Channel lay new challenges, change, opportunity, and yes, excitement.

This might well be one of her last visits to Chelveston. Most women didn't have this opportunity. If something happened to Jack and his crew, would she always wish she had spoken up? It wouldn't hurt to have a quick word with Doc. Joe was right. He would probably assure her he had taken Jack's mental state into account.

A jeep roared past, and Vivian waved at two local boys from Chelveston riding in the rear seats. Men would let the children ride around with them all day long when the kids weren't in school. They would also send them each back home with a gallon of ice cream. If a plane went up for a check ride, mess workers placed canisters full of ice cream ingredients in the waist and bomb bay sections. After being flown around at altitude, the canisters were full of frozen ice cream when the plane landed.

"Hiya, Red Cross. What brings you here?" Tad, Jack's ground crew chief, pulled alongside her.

"On my way to London. Thought I'd make a short detour first."

"They're up today. Due back in about an hour," Tad said.

"Yeah, I heard," Vivian said.

"Give you a lift somewhere on base?"

Vivian swung up next to him in the jeep. "Can you drop me off at the hospital? I've had a sore throat for a few days. Think I'll see Doc while I wait."

Tad would have far more daily interaction with Jack than she did. "Tad, how does Jack seem?"

Tad cut his eyes to her face, then looked back at the road. "He's wound up a little tight these days."

"Do you think that's a problem?"

"He's touchy. Fixates on stuff that wouldn't have bothered him a year ago." Tad shrugged. "His men follow him up, and I reckon that's the best evidence he's still an effective commander."

Was that enough? She thanked Tad for the ride and hopped out.

Vivian pushed open the door to the hospital and greeted the clerk on duty. A few minutes later, Doc poked his head around the corner and motioned for her to follow him.

"Sore throat, eh? Here, have a seat, and I'll have a look." He pointed to one of the beds in the open ward.

"Is there somewhere more private?"

Doc led her to a small examining room. He closed the door and waited until she had taken a seat. "When was your last cycle?"

"Oh! No. No, no, no. It's not … no, I'm not pregnant, Hugh." Vivian almost laughed, but her relief each month must mean she worried more about the reliability of the condoms than she might admit to Jack.

"If it's not that, what can I help you with?"

"I … well, I wanted to ask about Jack. He signed on for another tour, but he's not, not well."

"Jack. Lieutenant Nielsen in the 366th?"

"Yes." She couldn't account for her sudden reticence. Doc seemed to be waiting for more. "I don't mean he's sick right this moment. I mean he's not well overall. Combat fatigue, isn't that what you call it?"

Doc nodded. "Yes, that's the right term. I had a conversation with his superiors about Nielsen and his crew before they cut the new orders."

"And?"

"He's not worse off than most of the other men on this base. He's still social with his crew. He's not isolated himself. More to the point, his crew still look up to him, still signed on to keep flying with him. It said more to us than whether his hands shake a little over his morning coffee cup."

"It's not just the shakes, Doc. He's not eating well. I'm sure you've noticed he's lost weight. He's irritable. Jack's not a joker like Bowie, but he's funny in his way. Now, he might explode over something inconsequential with no warning."

Doc frowned. "Look, Vivian, the truth is I could put three-quarters of our men on fatigue leave based on that behavior. And I can't do that. You know I can't."

"He's drinking more too."

Doc raised his eyebrows. "And the pills? I know lots of the men use them, but I've tried to control it."

Jack had stopped taking them. He wouldn't risk having a drug issue noted in his file. Of course, that meant the effects of insomnia made it more likely he would fly off the handle over anything at all.

"He's not using the pills."

"All right, that's good. Vivian, these are all things our fliers experience from time to time. We'll keep a close eye on him, all right?"

"It's getting much worse. Surely that counts for something. He can't sleep. He …" Vivian paused.

Doc guessed what had tripped her up. "He's lost interest in sex?"

Vivian nodded.

"Is it lack of interest?"

A flush crept up her neck. "Sometimes. Other times, it's, well, you know."

"Sexual dysfunction is another common reaction to the stress of combat duty. I wouldn't worry about that either. He'll be back to normal once he's out of all this," Doc said.

"If he gets out of all this."

Doc sighed. "Look, Vivian, I understand why you'd be interested in getting him pulled off duty. It's natural for you—"

"It's not only Jack I'm worried about. If he's not functioning, his crew and his plane are at risk," Vivian said, her voice rising.

This wasn't her being selfish or meddlesome. There had been that time in February when they had flown all those back-to-back missions, Big Week they now called it. Bowie had been certain Jack's refusal to stand down had put them at risk. It had to put more of a burden on Bowie to be doing his job and watching out for Jack too.

Doc studied the eye chart on the wall. He returned his gaze to Vivian and said, "The crew is itself an entity. You've observed that?" She nodded, and he continued, "The crew's also a bit like a house of cards. Removing one piece can cause the whole thing to fall apart."

"His crew would be safer with a lead pilot who's less strung out."

"It's a delicate balance. Hard to know whether his crewmates would see it that way. And it's a sure bet Jack would not."

No, he wouldn't. He would be furious if he knew about this conversation. He teased her about her bossy and controlling ways, but he wouldn't find this the least bit amusing.

Doc stood. "Tell you what, I'll see if we can't get him a week at a flak house."

Vivian wanted to protest he needed much more than a week but left it at a simple thank you. Better not to press for too much.

She walked out of the hospital and turned to the perimeter road that would take her to the control tower.

She had walked a few hundred yards when Mel pulled beside her. "Hey, where you headed next?"

"Control tower if it's close to time."

"Hop in."

"Have you had leave to see Mabs lately?" Vivian asked.

"We were in London for three days last week. I know Mabs wants to tell you herself, but hell, since you're sitting here, I've gotta tell you."

Vivian laughed at his excitement, suspected what he was about to say.

"We're gonna get married! She said yes! I'm the luckiest fella ever."

"Aww, Mel, what wonderful news. I'm so happy for you both."

Vivian leaned over to kiss his cheek.

"Act surprised when she tells you, okay?" he pleaded. "She'd kill me if she knew I told you first."

Vivian laughed. "She would, but don't worry, I'm a good actress. When's the big day?"

"October. We'll both be due for a furlough. She wants you to be her maid of honor, so keep some leave time open."

October. She doubted she would be able to get leave to return to England so soon. Not if she went to the continent. She couldn't tell Mel. She couldn't even tell Jack. She would be able to write him from "somewhere in France" once she was there, but there would be no emotional farewell scene. With any luck, Jack would be in a much better state of mind by the time he received her letter.

***

July 5, 1944
Leicester, England

Someone rapped on the door.

"Vivian, there's a man here to see you. He said he'd wait outside," said Miss Snell.

"Thanks," Vivian called. One of the engineers must have come to say good-bye.

Vivian clomped down the stairs and opened the front door.

She should have hurried more with changing out of her fatigues and boots to clean up for dinner. A familiar tall, lanky flyboy lounged against the pillar, gazing off into the street.

Had he somehow found out she would ship out within days? That must be it. He had come to say good-bye, knowing they would be separated from now until the war was over.

"Jack! What on earth are you doing here?"

Jack turned around, and ice-cold water cascaded through her insides. This was no romantic gesture, no lover's farewell. He was rigid with anger. She had never seen his eyes so cold and distant.

"What's wrong, honey?" She closed the door behind her and stepped toward him. Perhaps something had happened to one of his crewmates. She stepped closer and stretched out a trembling hand to him.

"Don't pretend like you don't know," he said in a voice she had never heard him use. He took a step backward out of reach.

"Jack, I don't know what you think's happened—" she began, trying to ignore what her clenching gut signaled.

"Don't you? Did you talk to Doc, to Mustoe? Persuade them I should be pulled away from my crew? Did you?"

"I spoke to Doc about giving you a break. I didn't suggest they replace you. I wanted you to have a rest, that's all."

"We talked about this. Dammit, Vivian, we talked about this several times, and I thought I made it clear to you. I don't need time at a fucking flak house. And I don't give a damn what you think you found out about how it gets put into the records. I need a clean record. I don't want any questions. Why the hell would you do this?"

"You need a break. You can't see it, but everyone around you can. I mentioned to Doc—"

"Tell me what you told them," he said in that cold, flat voice.

"There's no 'them,' Vivian repeated. "I talked to Doc. I'm worried about you. I told him what he could see for himself. The shakes, mood swings, no appetite, can't sleep, drinking more. He must have decided I was right, that you needed a break. Is that what's happened? Are they—"

"You only told them what they already knew? You're sure?" Jack's wintry eyes locked in on hers, and another chill shot through her core.

"Yes. Doc said he'd talk to your superiors, and if—"

"Why does Doc know about our sex life if you only told them things they could see for themselves?"

"He ... he guessed. I didn't come out and say it. Doc asked if there were issues, and—" Vivian hedged.

"And so you decided to share personal details about our sex life?" His voice rose.

"Jack, Doc says it's a common reaction to combat stress. He says you'll be fine again when you're not under so much stress."

"Well, I'm glad to hear it. You won't ever know, because I'm done. We're over," he said, his volume increasing with every word.

The bottom fell out of her stomach. Her insides turned to ice. "Jack, for God's sake, that's a complete overreaction. You can't mean that."

He shook his head and turned away.

"Honey, look, I know you don't think you need to step back and rest, but you'll see. It'll all look different after some time out of all this." Vivian moved forward and placed a placating hand on his shoulder.

Jack pushed her hand away. "You always think you know best, don't you? Saint Vivian, solving all the world's problems. Well, you got this one all wrong. I asked you over and over to let it go. I told you I was fine, but you couldn't leave it alone, could you? Always trying to fix everything."

"You expected me to ignore what I see? How would I have felt if you were killed, and I had never said a word to anyone? This isn't just about you."

"The point is I didn't ask for your help. I told you to stay out of it. You shouldn't have butted in." His lashing words reverberated around the small stoop.

"Butted in? I *butted in* because I love you. I want you to be safe, and you're not in good shape right now. You're so stubborn you can't admit you're not in control, that's your problem. Obviously, Doc and your superiors agreed with me."

"Or they wanted to get you off their backs by doing what you demanded."

She bristled, and her voice rose to match his. "You can't see what the rest of us can. Bowie's mentioned it. You're not in good shape, Jack. And that's not safe for you *or* your crew. You'll see. Your crew'll be much better off when you come back rested and ready to get back into it again."

Jack's face was stark white, leeched of all color. His voice was cool. "My crew? My crew went out without me today." He paused, his eyes held hers. "They ditched in the Channel."

And with that, he turned and strode away, disappearing out of sight.

CHAPTER TWENTY-THREE

July 27, 1944
Walhampton House, Lymington, Hampshire, England

Jack peeked into the breakfast dining room. Empty and quiet. Perfect. No airmen to engage him in conversation. No staff to press him for updates on his mental state. Best of all, no Red Cross Girls to urge him to join the other men for horseback riding, picnics, canoe races, baseball games, or whatever activities were on tap for today.

He pulled out one of the ornate dining chairs. The scrape of its heavy legs on the parquet floor broke the silence of the empty room. He sat and put the napkin on his lap.

Someone had already pulled the heavy draperies open and lifted the blackout shades. Soft pink rays of dawn bloomed across the table.

Jack looked up, marveling once again at the decorative plaster ceiling medallions and trim. Damn, this house was something else. It could comfortably accommodate fifty men without doing more than doubling them up in rooms. It boasted a music room, library, conservatory, games room with billiard tables, a ballroom, and a formal dining room for evening meals that could seat all the airmen at once. Hard to believe one family could need all that.

Maybe his crewmates had been sent to another flak house. Ditching and getting fished out of the Channel by the British sea rescue team surely entitled them to a stay at one of these homes. They deserved the rest, same as him. More importantly, it would prevent his crew being split up. Split up from him, that is. If they flew enough missions without him, they might get assigned another pilot.

What if they were happier with a new pilot? Jack hadn't had a chance to see them before he came here. Shortly after Mel assured him that all his men had been safely rescued, Jack had been shuttled into one of the base jeeps to come here. He hoped the fellas would forgive him. He had let them down when they needed him most.

Mrs. Corbett slid open one of the oak paneled doors separating the breakfast room from the kitchen and peeked in. "Good morning. I thought I heard someone. You'll take coffee, I believe?"

Jack nodded. Within a day after he arrived, the British staff knew his preferences and met his every need.

She bustled in, poured his coffee from a floral china coffeepot, and set it on a trivet. She lifted a matching sugar bowl and creamer from the carved sideboard and placed them in front of him. "I know you take it black, but here's a little cream and sugar if you decide you want it."

"Thanks. I've been in the habit of drinking it black because our mess hall doesn't usually have sugar. Maybe I'll try it the old way."

She patted his shoulder. "You do that, lad. Might as well treat yourself to every fancy. I'll be back with your breakfast in a few minutes." She slid the pocket door closed.

Jack tipped some rich cream into his coffee. He added two sugar cubes and stirred.

Cream and sugar wasn't easy to obtain. The army or the Red Cross must be paying a pretty penny to supplement the rations for these flak houses. Rest homes—that's what they were. He couldn't decide which term carried less stigma.

The paneled door swung open. Mrs. Corbett came in bearing a tray of dishes. She placed an individual wire toast rack with four slices of toast and small crocks of butter and jam next to the coffeepot. His plate contained two slices of rashers, two sausages, tomato slices and a large portion of baked beans. Last, she set a decorative egg cup at the left front of his plate. That single poached egg was the weekly ration for the British people, yet Jack had seen a henhouse near the stables on one of his walks around the grounds. Eggs might be one of the few foodstuffs the army didn't need to supplement in these country manor homes.

"Thanks."

"Connie, Marilyn, and Susie are in the kitchen. I told them none of the men are seated yet." She poured more coffee. "I suggested they might like to step out in the garden and pick some flowers for the table arrangements. That should keep them occupied long enough for you to enjoy your breakfast, but you might not want to linger." She winked at him and set the coffeepot down.

He grinned. "I appreciate the tip. Thanks."

Bless her. He had a running standoff with the Red Cross Girls. Each morning, a different one would try to draw him into conversation and book him into planned activities. Why couldn't they see he was getting exactly what he wanted from his stay here? He hadn't wanted to come, but now that he was here, he might as well do what he damn well pleased.

The food was delicious, a far cut above mess hall chow. He would have enjoyed savoring it, but escaping the breakfast room without attention took priority.

Jack pushed his chair back and stood. He leaned out the door, decided the coast was clear, and strode through the center hallway to the nearest door leading outside.

Peace and solitude weren't easy to come by in a house bursting at the seams with American airmen. Soon after his arrival, Jack settled on canoeing the property's lake at first light as a means of removing himself from the bustle of activity.

Jack walked around the side of the house and gazed up at the ivy-covered red brick manor house. With its dormer windows, curved bays, and decorative chimneys, it might as well have been a castle.

He skirted around the edge of the manicured gardens to the path that led to the lake. To his relief, the Red Cross Girls were nowhere in sight.

After he located a rod and reel in the small boathouse, Jack sorted through a tackle box of fancy lures. Creating elaborate lures —

probably another Red Cross Girl activity to occupy men on rainy days.

Jack stepped out to the landing for better light to attach the lure. The lake, fringed with tall evergreens and deciduous trees, was still and peaceful. Only a few ducks swimming near the edge. He cast his line.

He took a seat on the wooden planks flanking the boat slip and leaned against a stone pillar. He would take a few minutes to sit and enjoy the sunrise before launching one of the canoes.

Nothing about this view marked it as the English countryside. Not unless he turned his head to look across the estate grounds to the imposing rear face of Walhampton House. He might be in Tennessee or Georgia or any number of other places. It might be Lake Williams, south of town back home, where Jack and Ace had passed many a summer morning. Or the much larger Lake Graham some twenty miles from Jackson. Pop or Ace's dad would drive them over there. They would fish until midmorning when someone noted the fish were no longer biting. He and Ace would jump in the lake for a quick swim before they all piled back into the truck and drove back to town.

"Any nibbles yet?" said a female voice.

Jack turned. His eyes traveled from the young woman's sensible pumps to the Red Cross pin on her blouse lapel to her reddish-brown pin curl hairdo. Marilyn. One of the four Red Cross Girls. "Nope."

Marilyn tilted her head and smiled. "Recast your rod?"

Did she not realize fishing required quiet? That conversation would scare off the fish?

"I'm gonna take a canoe, get farther out into the lake." Jack leaned forward to reel his line in.

"Can I join you for a moment? I won't hold you up for long."

Jack resented the intrusion into the early morning quiet, but he had been curt and abrasive with the Red Cross Girls since he arrived. It wasn't their fault that their uniforms, their smiles, and their charm-on-legs routine cut him to the quick.

Jack blew out a breath, nodded, and settled back against the column.

She stepped out of her shoes and eased down to a seated position. "I come out here every morning too."

His eyebrows scrunched together. He hadn't seen her or anyone else.

"I kept my distance. Knew you wanted quiet. Don't worry, I won't tell the others where you've been hiding."

"Appreciate that." Jack shifted his grip on the rod.

Marilyn leaned back against a stone pillar. "This is my favorite spot on the grounds. It's got kind of a timeless quality."

He nodded. "Looks a lot like a lake back home. Swam there every weekend in the summer."

"It's a shame this water's too chilly for swimming. Too cold for this Alabama girl anyway."

"Felt pretty good to me," Jack said.

Marilyn raised her eyebrows. "You have swimming trunks?"

His lips curved up. "Nope."

Her cheeks flushed pink, but she laughed. "I'll keep that in mind when I'm walking the trails around here."

Across the lake, a tree branch swayed, bowed, and released with the ascent of a hawk. Wings outstretched in an impressive span, its hoarse screech resonated over the placid lake.

"She has such power and freedom. I wish I could soar up and away from all our troubles," Marilyn said. "Is flying like that for you?"

Jack tracked the progress of the majestic hawk silhouetted against a skyscape streaked with pinks and oranges. "There's nothing like it. It's all I ever wanted to do."

"Same for my brother Mark. Once he had the flying bug, that was it." She craned her neck for a last glimpse of the hawk before it disappeared from view. "Said nothing beat that feeling of being on top of the world and riding the clouds."

"He's a pilot?"

Marilyn picked up a pebble and rolled it between her thumb and index finger. "Was. I like to think that's what he's doing now. Flying to his heart's content."

Jack's heart clenched. Was that a flare of life from a long-dormant empathy muscle? The pervasive emotional toll of the Eighth's staggering losses exacted too high a price for most airmen. Social connections shrank to the smallest unit possible, the crew.

"I'm sorry." He bit back questions. No telling how raw her grief might be.

She bobbed her head. "Thanks. It's been a long time. And yet not." She bit her lip. "That probably doesn't make sense."

Oh, but it did. Ace might have died yesterday or a lifetime ago.

Jack focused his gaze on the mallard ducks swimming in a straight line a few yards away. Water rippled out behind them. "Lost my best friend. Really early-on. Some days seems like it just happened."

"I'm sorry about your friend, Jack." She paused. "I think the loss of someone we loved may always feel close."

"Especially if you feel guilty."

Shit. Why had he said that? That came out of nowhere. Or maybe not. Gnawing agony always bubbled under the surface.

Jack cut his eyes to Marilyn.

"Your buddy, he was a childhood friend?"

Maybe she hadn't heard his blurted admission. Or maybe she realized he hadn't meant to voice it. He exhaled and nodded. "Yeah. Our houses backed up to each other. Spent our whole childhood in and out of each other's homes. Ace. His name was Ace, and he was my best friend, long as I can remember."

Jack told her how Ace's favorite food was Mama's icebox lemon pie, how the two of them got in so much trouble for mimicking dangerous animal noises outside Phoebe and Rose's bedroom window late at night, how Ace ate too much cotton candy at the state fair and threw up all over his first girlfriend on the Ferris wheel. He pulled Ace's dog tag from his pocket and passed it to her.

She rubbed her index finger over the embossed letters and handed it back to him. "Sounds like you and Ace shared so much. Did he like flying too?"

"He wasn't a pilot. Washed out." Jack's lungs tautened tighter than his fishing line. "I should have helped him."

"Helped him with pilot training?"

He nodded, tried to force more air into his constricted lungs. "I was a flight instructor. Knew he was gonna wash out. I could have taken him up myself, made sure he could pass."

"He was at your base?"

"No." He paused. "Close enough. Could have gotten him up on the weekends."

"He gave you the brush-off?" Marilyn tilted her head, her forehead puckered in a frown.

"I never offered." Jack pressed his fist against his pulsing temple. "It was the only thing I'd ever done that he couldn't do better, smarter, faster."

"Did he ask you for help?" Her soft Southern cadence robbed the question of any note of judgment.

"He wouldn't have asked." Ace had never needed Jack's help before. He would have been too proud. Jack was the one who should have stepped up and offered.

"Hmmm." Marilyn picked up another pebble, examined it, and added it to others collected in her palm. "He was an airman, since he started with the air forces?"

Jack nodded. "They sent him to navigator training after he washed out. He was real sharp with math and science."

"Not everyone is good with figures. Maybe navigation suited him best," she said.

"But the pilot ..." Jack swallowed. "Pilot makes the biggest decisions, has the most control over the fate of his men." If Ace had been the pilot instead of the navigator, the outcome might have been different.

She rolled the pebbles around her palm. "So the pilot is the most important member of the crew?"

Jack's stomach contracted into a tight ball. "No. Not at all. That's not what I tell my men. Every member of the crew has an important job to do. We're a team up there."

"Then Ace was filling his team role, which was also important. Right?"

It was a team. Every crew was a team. Jack needed all nine of his men on their team. Without Chaz, they wouldn't make it far. He calculated and radioed adjustments to course to the cockpit for the duration of their flight. Every man had a crucial role in the overall success of the mission and the safety of their ship.

"Yeah." He hitched a deep breath.

Marilyn tossed a pebble into the lake. It plinked, concentric circles radiating out from the drop point. "You can't ask Ace, so you won't ever know for sure. But, maybe deep down, he didn't actually want to be a pilot. That could be why he never asked you for help. He might have realized that he would be happier and more useful as a navigator."

Jack had never considered it from that angle. He couldn't recall Ace ever expressing any desire to be a pilot. Sure, some small part of Ace might have wanted to best Jack at one more skill. But perhaps he had decided that navigating made better use of his strengths. Ace might have declined an offer of help.

"Were you a …" Jack struggled to find the word. "A talk doctor?"

Marilyn laughed. "Oh, golly no. I was a music teacher in Mobile. We Red Cross Girls, well, we do our best to fill whatever need you fellas have."

"I know. My girlfriend is over here with the Red Cross. Works on a Clubmobile crew out of Leicester." He couldn't bring himself to say ex-girlfriend, even though he forced her into that slot.

"I put in for Clubmobiles," Marilyn said. "I'm more optimistic about a transfer now that we're sending so many experienced Clubmobilers to France."

France. Jack's heart flipped over itself in his chest. He hadn't considered they would send women to the continent until the troops moved into Germany. "They've already got Red Cross Girls in France?"

She nodded. "First ten crews went over two weeks ago."

Two weeks? He had broken off with her over three weeks ago, been here nearly that long. Was Vivian in Normandy, closer than ever to the menace of enemy action? Jack's pulse jerked and adrenaline hurtled through his body like someone had pushed a fuel boost button on his heart.

"How would I find out if she's one of the ones over there? Would your headquarters in London tell you?"

Marilyn smiled. "She would probably note 'somewhere in France' on her letters to you."

"I haven't heard from her."

She waved her hand. "Oh, the army doesn't try very hard to get your mail to you here. There's probably a stack of letters waiting for you at your base."

"No. There won't be. Not from her." Jack massaged his aching, clenched jaw and exhaled through his nose. "You see, we had a big argument before I got here. Only reason I'm here is because she pushed the flight surgeon at my base to pull me off flying duty. I thought I didn't need to come. Thought this was only for the loonies, the fellas who'd gone round the twist."

"Ah, that explains …"

"My surliness with all the Red Cross Girls, yeah. I owe you all an apology." Jack's fingers clenched tighter around his rod.

She laid a gentle hand on his arm. "None of us are looking for an apology."

"It was your uniforms. Reminded me of Vivian, and I was still sore at her."

"You're not mad anymore?"

Jack rolled his shoulders to release tension. "Complicated. Short answer's no. She was right about me needing this break. Right about it not going on my record."

Marilyn cocked her head. "But you still don't like that she talked to your flight surgeon?"

"First time my crew went out with another pilot in the left seat, they had to ditch in the Channel." Jack's stomach clenched, and he kneaded his fist into his forehead. Coming down fast and out of control, bracing for the impact, knowing you had only moments to get ten precious lives extricated from the close interior confines of the plane. Seconds to hope and pray the rubber dinghies would detach and inflate.

Marilyn twisted her hands in her lap, her eyes downcast.

Jack realized what she must have inferred. "They made it out okay. Got picked up by one of the British sea rescue crews."

"Thank goodness," she whispered.

"If I'd been flying …" He picked up a pebble and skimmed it across the still surface of the lake.

"Your crew might not have needed to ditch?" Her eyebrows lifted.

The alternative haunted him more than anything else. What if they had faced a ditching with him at the helm, and he had choked and failed to follow every procedure to a tee? What if he had lost one or more of his men, his brothers in arms, because of his stubborn insistence that he was fine?

"Yeah. Or …" Jack's voice dropped to a whisper. "Or I might have turned a bad situation into a tragedy. Vivian was right. I didn't have any business flying then. But, it felt like a judgment. Like she thought I was flawed. Unfixable."

Marilyn was silent for a few beats, rolling pebbles around in her palm. "You've been blaming yourself for Ace not becoming a pilot, and yet … Maybe he didn't want to be one. Maybe he would have chosen to be a navigator. Maybe you've been too hard on yourself."

He nodded.

"Same with Vivian. She might have only wanted you to have a break." She paused. "Jack, most of the men who come here go back to active duty. The ones who are in truly bad shape don't get sent here. They go to a hospital or back home."

Jack bobbed his head. He had blamed his ego for contributing to Ace's death. Marilyn had a point. Perhaps his ego was also preventing him from accepting the spirit of Vivian's actions.

He inhaled a deep breath and released it in a steady stream. He looked up and met Marilyn's eyes. "Can you help me place a call to Leicester?"

CHAPTER TWENTY-FOUR

July 28, 1944, 1:00 p.m.
Somewhere south of Saint-Lô, Normandy, France

"Which way should we turn?" Vivian, wedged against the Clubmobile's passenger door, glanced to her left at the map spread on Ruby's lap. Narrow crossroads, each choice barely wide enough for their Clubmobile, confronted them.

Janie shifted in the driver's seat and swiped damp strands of dishwater-blond hair off her forehead. With the vehicle idling, not even a puff of breeze cooled the front cab, which was crowded with one more passenger than it was intended to seat.

Ruby leaned toward the map and pushed her chestnut-brown curls out of her eyes. She jabbed her index finger at their starting point at Trévières and traced through the turns they had made over the last hour. "We crossed the river right about here." She indicated a point south of Saint-Lô. "This map doesn't show new bridges, but I think it was here."

GIs had directed them across a newly constructed bridge over the Vire River about fifteen minutes ago.

Vivian pointed to a notation on the map. "This cross probably represents a church, and we saw one to the north after we crossed the river."

"Right or left, ladies?" Janie's thigh quivered to keep the heavy clutch engaged.

Vivian met Ruby's eyes. Either this map didn't depict their current location or they were lost.

They were supposed to serve the 103rd Combat Engineers Battalion near Saint Romphaire. From their instructions, they gleaned that these fellas were situated pretty far forward, closer to the front lines than Vivian's crew had gone in the weeks since they arrived in France. Engineers were often close to the hot action. Turning the wrong direction could prove deadly. The front curved and dipped and shifted, sometimes within minutes.

"Do either of you recall how hard it is to engage this heavy clutch?" All Clubmobilers bound for the continent had done a weeklong driving course in London, but Janie had proved most adept at driving over France's bomb-damaged roads.

Vivian said "left" at the same moment that Ruby said "right." They burst out laughing.

"I guess I'm the tiebreaker." Janie pointed left. "Into the hedgerows?" She waved her hand to the right. "Or into the hedgerows?"

The road in both directions was effectively a channel cutting through steep earth banks over four feet high, topped with towering hedgerows looming overhead. Hedgerows that might well mask landmines or German snipers. A shiver slid across Vivian's shoulders.

"We should turn back. I think we must have made a wrong turn." Ruby gave voice to the instinct churning in Vivian's gut.

"Turning back has its own problems." Janie drummed her fingers on the steering wheel.

Yes, it did. Mine clearing sweeps only guaranteed the roads, not the shoulders. This particular juncture also wouldn't accommodate turning around, even if they dared to try. If they were going back, they would have to reverse for some distance.

Vivian raked her fingers through the hair plastered against the sides of her face. "I say let's keep going and hope we hit another landmark that will help us decipher our whereabouts on this map."

Ruby nodded.

"Okay, a right turn is easier so we'll go right." Janie disengaged the clutch and pressed the accelerator. The *Yellowstone* lurched forward with a sharp jerk and died.

"Dammit," Janie muttered. She pushed the ignition button and moved the gear shift into first gear, with her left foot compressing the clutch.

The chugging sound from the *Yellowstone*'s engine jarred in the unsettling silence.

Was the silence an unexpected slice of peaceful countryside or a warning? No thuds and booms of artillery in the distance, no roar of tanks outfitted with bulldozer attachments clearing the hedgerows, no shouts and good-natured jibes of American GIs at work.

Janie eased them into a tight righthand turn, taking care to keep in the center of the road. Branches from trees and shrubs scraped both sides of the *Yellowstone* as they traversed the narrow passage.

Vivian peered into the thick bramble pressing close on either side, watching for any hint of movement.

Ten nerve-wracking minutes later, a break in the hedgerows loomed ahead. Good. They could assess their location from landmarks visible in the open space.

The shape of a vehicle came into view. Was it moving? Vivian's heart thudded in her chest.

"Can you tell if it's ours?" Janie slowed their speed.

Ruby scooted to the edge of the seat, wincing as her knee bumped against the gear shift, and shaded her hand over her eyes. "I think that's our white star on the back."

Vivian squinted. A white cross with a black center marked German vehicles. "Sure it's a star and not a cross?"

"Stop or keep going?" Janie asked.

"It's a star." Ruby's voice rang with certitude.

Vivian nodded at Janie. "They should be able to tell us whether we're on the right path to Saint Romphaire."

Janie changed gears and proceeded forward.

Vivian spotted the yellow tarp draped over the hood of the truck and unclenched her fingers one by one. American ground forces used yellow tarps as a signal to USAAF planes, so they wouldn't mistakenly bomb or strafe their own troops.

Ruby nudged her leg against Vivian's. "Why don't you lean out the window and wave to them, so they'll know we're friendly?"

Vivian removed her cap, shook out her hair, rolled her eyes at the other two, and leaned out the window. "Hey, fellas, want some doughnuts?"

Two of the men looked around. They set aside long-handled tools and jogged to meet them.

One of them clapped his hand around the edge of the open driver's side window. Laugh line crinkles radiated from the corners of his brown eyes. "Where are you headed, ladies?"

Ruby pointed to the map. "Saint Romphaire. There's an outfit of engineers based there."

The second man leaned over his buddy's shoulder. With his wavy dark hair, dimples and strong chin, he might be movie idol Gregory Peck's younger brother. "You found 'em."

"You're engineers?" Vivian scooted forward and peered at the men still working ahead. They moved long-handled tools with a large disc at the bottom over the ground.

"Yes, ma'am." Gregory Peck's look-alike winked.

Mr. Laugh Lines leaned in through the window. "You ladies realize you're ahead of the front line?"

Vivian's pulse jumped. "What?"

Laugh Lines jerked his thumb toward his fellow engineers. "We're the advance detail. Mine clearing."

So that's what the long-handled tools were. Metal detectors.

"You're too far south. That road about a half mile ahead is the D99." He reached in and jabbed his finger at a spot several miles south of Saint Romphaire.

"So what do we do?" Janie asked.

Movie Star pursed his lips. "Gotta get you turned around for starters. That means gotta take your truck into the hedges."

Mines Cleared to the Hedges signs had previously only kept them from hiking off the road for a pee break.

Laugh Lines opened the driver's door. "You gals better get out and go back up this road a piece. You got helmets?"

Their helmets were clustered on the floorboard near Vivian's feet.

She held one up.

"Get 'em on and move out of range."

A landmine explosion could rip the Clubmobile in half and kill them all.

Shards of ice stabbed through Vivian's ribs. She slammed her helmet on her head and scrambled out the driver's side door after Janie and Ruby.

"Hurry on up the road. When you're far enough away, we'll turn it around and drive it to you."

Without discussing it, the women broke into a jog. Hedgerows intertwined into an arch above them when they at last, panting, stopped and turned to watch.

Vivian held her breath as Laugh Lines pulled the *Yellowstone* far up over the side of the road, nudged the earthen embankment with the front bumper and reversed, repeating the process several times before straightening out.

Movie Star hopped into the front cab. Vivian exhaled as the *Yellowstone* chugged down the center of the road toward them.

When it reached them, Mr. Laugh Lines, his freckles not yet faded with age, leaned out the window. "I'm Ned, by the way." He gestured to his handsome friend. "And this is Jesse."

They introduced themselves and thanked the men.

Janie pointed to the road leading back into those threatening hedgerows. "How far before we're behind the lines? We didn't see any troops after we crossed the river."

"Hop in. We'll get you behind the lines," Ned said.

Jesse got out of the front cab. "If you gals have sinkers in the back, I volunteer to ride there."

Ruby winked at Vivian and followed Janie and Jesse up the steps into the rear of the Clubmobile.

Vivian climbed into the cab on the passenger side. "Thanks for helping us out."

Ned depressed the clutch and shifted into second gear. "Couldn't let you ladies take a risk. Besides, your friend looked like she'd had enough driving."

"I think you fellas telling us we were over the line threw her for a loop."

Ned cut his eyes to Vivian and grinned. "*You* don't look scared. Fact, I'd say you might be a little pleased."

He wasn't far off the mark. In the moment, she had been admittedly unnerved, mostly by fear of being picked off by German snipers or watching their Clubmobile explode. But no denying she thrilled with pride at their intrepid spirit. The Red Cross wouldn't approve, but the tale would impress their GI buddies.

Ned drove faster than Janie, and they were soon fully amidst those steep hedgerows. He was from Memphis, and a sharp pang of heartache flared as he reminisced about his Tennessee home. Even bone-numbing exhaustion from the pace and physical exertion of her work in the field couldn't always stave off the pain, the smothering waves of loss and remorse. Vivian clenched her jaw. No thinking about Jack or his crew. Not now.

Ned turned north at the crossroads juncture. They had lumbered forward no more than a mile when he abruptly braked. He leaned out the window and craned his neck to look overhead.

A buzzing hum in the sky grew louder and louder.

Vivian still couldn't judge friend from foe, but Ned shut off the engine. "Out!"

She slid across the seat and jumped out the driver's side after him. Ned banged on the side of the Clubmobile and shouted, "Get down in there!"

Vivian crouched on her knees at the front wheel, flattened herself, and slithered forward under the cab to wedge herself between the front tires. Ned squashed next to her, his breath against her neck.

Only ambulances could bear the red cross insignia marking them as non-combatants. From the air, the Clubmobile would have every appearance of a military vehicle. Coarse netting with moss green strips draped over the top served as camouflage when the *Yellowstone* was parked in the shade of an apple orchard, but would do nothing to help them now.

Whirring engines sounded closer and closer, lower and lower. Sharp staccato blasts of machine gun fire peppered every direction, sending showers of rocks pelting and pinging against the truck's hardy body. Vivian drew her knees close to her chest, curling herself as small as possible. Ned flung an arm over her.

Machine gun strafing fire was only the warm-up. Engines roared closer again, squealing in a crescendoing fury. A whining whistle hurtled toward them, louder and louder and louder until its shrill fury overpowered all Vivian's senses.

Pressed flat against ground roiling with waves of concussive explosions, Vivian's heart beat a throbbing tattoo in her chest. Smoke and cordite mixed with the dust filling her nostrils.

Plane engines whooshed and roared not far above.

Please let them be Allied fighter planes, fired up and hell-bent on bringing down the attacking Luftwaffe.

Another explosion, not machine gun fire or bombs. Something larger. A resounding boom shook the ground, and an acrid burning smell filled the air.

Vivian opened her eyes. Clouds of dust or smoke billowed in every direction. She coughed and squeezed her eyes shut again.

Was the Clubmobile on fire? Pungent fumes of burning metal, oil, and fuel swelled around them.

"Not us," Ned's hoarse voice choked near her ear.

The attack probably only lasted minutes, but it seemed far longer to Vivian, facedown in the dust under the *Yellowstone*, tucked into a ball.

"Stay here." Ned scooted side to side on his belly and backed himself out from under the truck.

Moments later, he tugged on her boot. "Can you get yourself out from under there?"

Remembering what Ned had done, Vivian used her stomach muscles to wiggle her body backwards bit by bit.

Ned pulled her to her feet. "You're all right?"

She nodded. Racing pulse aside, she was unharmed.

Dust clogged her nostrils. Her throat was dry and raw. She swiped around her face and wiped her grimy hands down her dirty pants legs. "Are they gone?"

Ned tapped her shoulder and pointed to their left.

Vivian blinked and clapped a hand to her mouth. Flames shot from a smoldering Luftwaffe plane in a field a few hundred feet in the distance. Smoke swirled over the menacing black swastika painted on its tail section. She shuddered.

Ned rapped his hand against the rear door of the Clubmobile. "Everyone all right in there? Come out and see what our Mustangs brought down."

The door creaked open. Jesse stepped down, turned, and offered a hand to Ruby. Janie, disheveled and improbably covered from head to toe in doughnut flour, ignored his proffered hand and hopped down, scowling.

"What happened to you?" Vivian gestured at Janie's flour-coated fatigues.

Ruby giggled. "Jesse put a sack of doughnut flour on top of her for protection. The bag, uh, must have had a hole in it."

Two P-51 Mustangs circled the field over the blazing Stuka dive-bomber.

"Confirming their kill." Ned waved at them.

Jesse pumped clasped hands overhead and whooped.

The pilots dipped their wings before flying away.

***

July 28, 1944, 7:00 p.m.
Commune of Agneaux, Normandy, France

"We missed chow, and we have to set up our own tent?" Vivian pushed her boot against the musty canvas storage bag.

Their base camp had moved farther south from Trévières in their absence. Fortunately, they passed a convoy from the 109th who alerted them to the new location.

Janie plopped on the ground. "I'm too pooped to put it up. I vote we spread our bedrolls out here for tonight. It'll be cooler."

"We'll also be closer to the foxholes, and given how our day's gone, that's probably not a bad thing." Ruby pulled a small ball of red yarn from her musette bag. She held it up. "Here, kitty, kitty."

Ike, a gray tabby, slouched lazily from a nearby copse of beech trees. His sister, dubbed Sinker in honor of the resemblance her tawny coat bore to doughnuts, came tearing from the apple orchard. She grabbed the yarn from Ruby, curled her front paws protectively around it, and glared insolently at Ike.

Ike crouched forward a few paces and batted his paw toward the ball. Sinker hissed in warning.

Vivian rubbed behind Ike's ears. He initially startled and then relaxed and purred. "You should have been faster, buddy."

GIs had found the kittens in a crumbling barn two weeks ago. The men were moving farther up the line, and Ruby adopted them on behalf of Clubmobile Group F. "Mark my words, they'll be good mousers, and we'll all be grateful to have them."

She had been right. The cats had more than earned their keep during the two nights the women billeted in an abandoned farmhouse.

Vivian spread her bedroll on the ground. "You think one of the bivouac messes would give us canned K-rations? Even those sound good. We've had a hard day."

"A hard day?" Charlotte, one of the *Kit Carson* crew, came out of a tent, holding her palms out. "We dug the new ladies' latrine. Without any GI help either, mind you. I've got the blisters to prove it."

Her crewmates Nancy and Betty followed and sat between Ruby and Janie.

"Sounds like you were doing something wrong, if you couldn't attract any GI help. They usually fall all over themselves trying to help us." Janie winked at Charlotte.

Ruby tossed a jar of Pond's Cold Cream to Charlotte. "Give your skin that 'glow of beauty,'" she said, quoting the ad copy. She had just completed putting her hair up in pin curls and smearing the cream over her face.

Nancy laughed and reached for the jar. "I'll take some. My mom's monthly care package hasn't caught up to me here."

"Mine either. I asked for a new bra, more tooth powder, popcorn, and olives. Oh, how I miss olives." Vivian's mouth watered.

"We've got popcorn if someone can locate a pan," Betty said.

Janie jumped up. "I know where a good popping pan is. I'll meet you in our Clubmobile, and we can pop it there."

Betty stood. "I'll get it and be right there."

Joyce stuck her head out of a tent. "Oh, are we having a gabfest? Did I hear someone's hungry? I've got a tin of Saltine crackers and a jar of peanut butter."

"Ooh, please. I'm famished." Vivian leaned back against a tree trunk and stretched her legs out over her bedroll.

Joyce's crewmate Lillian came out of their tent carrying a bottle in each hand. "The boys in the 109th liberated a few bottles of Sauternes and gave us these after they helped us dig our foxholes."

"We hope you all appreciate those foxholes. That's how we spent our afternoon, and here's hoping we don't spend our night there too." Francine, the third member of Joyce's crew, held her canteen cup up in toast.

Vivian clinked her cup against Ruby's. "Here's to a quiet night."

Joyce sat on the edge of Vivian's bedroll and set out the crackers, peanut butter, and a few apples they had picked from the orchard.

Vivian grabbed an apple and pulled out her pocketknife. She set slices in her mess kit lid. After spreading peanut butter on the Saltines and creating stacks, she passed some to Ruby.

"Ummm, this tastes like home, doesn't it?" Ruby bit into a cracker.

Janie and Betty returned with a pan of popcorn. They set it in the middle of their circle, and Vivian leaned forward to grab a handful.

"Too bad we can't stay in the château." Joyce poured more wine into her cup.

Their new base camp was situated near the grounds of a bombed medieval château. The young noblewoman who had lived in the château throughout the war was no older than any of them. She too had served with the Red Cross, working as an ambulance driver before France surrendered.

"She hid members of the Resistance and our own downed airmen in the tunnels underneath the château. Can you imagine? They were hiding right under the nose of the Nazi soldiers who lived in the château until last week." Charlotte took a sip of wine.

Vivian leaned forward to take another handful of popcorn. "I assume those airmen living in the tunnels have returned to England?" One Clubmobile crew had met two liberated downed airmen whom they had known at a bomber base in England. Vivian kept her eyes open, hoping to find any of the 305th's men who might have survived in hiding.

"I'd imagine so, but you can ask her yourself tomorrow. We're all going to the château for lunch." Lillian rolled another curl around her fingers and pinned it.

Francine peeled an apple with her pocketknife. "The boys say there's all sorts of German loot around the château. Lugers, daggers, flags, uniforms, who knows what all."

"We're all going?" Janie scooped a dab of cold cream from the Pond's jar.

Betty nodded. "No serving tomorrow. Not off-base anyway. What was so hard about the *Yellowstone*'s day today anyway?"

Janie and Ruby each nodded at Vivian in a you-tell-them way.

"Well, it doesn't compare to digging latrines and foxholes, but we went beyond the front lines. And then the *Yellowstone* was strafed and bombed. Can I have more wine?" Vivian held out her cup to Nancy, who had paused in mid-pour at Vivian's words, her eyes wide.

A loud babble broke out at once. "Why hadn't you told us?"

Janie laughed. "All of you kept insisting your day was worse."

"Start at the beginning." Nancy passed the bottle to Vivian.

She had reached the point where she and Ned crawled under the Clubmobile when a group of GIs called from the orchard. "Can we join you? We've got libations to share."

Most of the women were in the bobby pins and cold cream stage of the evening, with Joyce, Lillian, and Nancy already in pajamas.

Charlotte looked around. When no objected, she beckoned to the men. "All right, but you boys better not be pulling our leg. You better have legit booty."

They did.

Corks popped from "liberated" bottles of champagne. Ike and Sinker jumped and fled into the trees.

The practiced ease with which two of those boys opened the bottles was a reflection of how much looted alcohol the American military forces had imbibed in the seven weeks since the D-Day landings. These GIs, young and likely hailing from rural America, probably hadn't seen a bottle of champagne before setting foot in France.

Vivian gulped her last swig of wine and held her cup out.

One of them pulled a deck of cards from his pocket, but Betty held up a hand. "Hang on, boys. These ladies"—she pointed to Vivian, Ruby, and Janie in turn—"had some excitement on their serving run today, and we were right in the middle of hearing all about it when you turned up."

Vivian summarized the start of their story for the men and resumed where she left off. "So, then, after the Mustangs left, Ned and—"

"Swoony Jesse," the other women chanted in unison at Ruby, who grinned and dramatically mimed swooning.

"Ned and Swoony Jesse," Vivian emphasized, "walked out to the field to investigate the wreckage. They didn't find any sign of the pilot."

"What unit was this? Engineers did you say?" One of the men ran his thumb around the neck of a champagne bottle, his eyebrows creased in a frown.

Janie held her cup out. "The 103rd, based near Saint Romphaire."

The GI opened his mouth, but one of his buddies elbowed him in the ribs and shook his head.

"What?" Something stirred low in Vivian's gut.

"Who's in for some poker?" One of the GIs held up cards.

"Hold on." Janie held up a hand. "What are you not saying?"

"We made a delivery to Saint Rhompaire late this afternoon. Two engineers from that outfit were killed by snipers." He shuffled the deck, and the crackle and sizz of the cards echoed in the silence.

Ned and Jesse had left the group to help guide the *Yellowstone* safely behind the lines. It must have been two of the men who continued with mine clearing. Shivers zinged across Vivian's shoulders. Those snipers might have been lurking in the dense hedgerows while she, Janie, and Ruby drove that same road.

One of the others raked the toe of his boot through the grass. "Krauts got 'em while they were trying to reconnect with their group."

Stabs of wintry chill knifed through Vivian's core. "When?"

"Must have been about four o'clock. Trying to clear us to the D99."

They had let Ned and Jesse out around three o'clock. Jesse had said it would take them an hour to get back to the D99 juncture on foot.

Ruby's tin cup clattered against a rock. She stood, shook off Janie's hand, and strode toward one of the tents.

Vivian swallowed, staring at the bubbly remnants of champagne from Ruby's spilled cup seeping into the dirt.

"Might not have been Ned and Jesse." Janie's eyes were wide, her voice barely over a whisper. "It could have been two others who had worked separately from the main group."

Vivian tried not to signal skepticism through her expression or stance. "Could have been." She tightened her shaking fingers around the handle of her cup.

Her mind flashed rapid-fire through faces of men struck down in their prime by war's capricious hand, men who had never returned from missions, men who died in senseless takeoff or landing accidents, men who died in their ship after being wounded in battle. She squeezed her eyes shut and added Ned's friendly freckled face and Jesse's ruggedly dishy face to her mental catalogue. Janie might choose to believe German sniper bullets felled random men rather than their saviors, but Vivian's aching gut wouldn't be fooled.

She had seen too much already.

A still man, shrouded in a white sheet, carried out of a ship on a stretcher, his crewmates sinking to their knees beside him, faces buried in their hands. Shouts for Father McClarahan to come administer last rites via the control tower radio. Chappie, ashen-faced, emerging from the control tower and beckoning Vivian and Mabs to follow him to the debriefing room, saving them the horror of watching a bomber landing with a decapitated copilot still strapped into the righthand seat.

Vivian had been able to control her exposure to war's toll in England. She could avoid sweating out the missions altogether or cut her time at the tower short. Their Clubmobiles followed the troops too closely here. They had no way to avoid the sights, sounds, and smells of a very personal war.

That must be why the Red Cross chose women with strength in spades to deploy on the continent. They would need to call on every measure of resilience in their reserves to do their job over here.

"I'll go check on Ruby." Vivian placed a hand on Janie's shoulder, both as comfort and to assist herself to standing.

She couldn't remember which of the tents Ruby had entered. Parting the canvas flap on the third one, she spotted Ruby's shadowed form, lying on her side on someone's cot, her knees curled up against her chest.

Vivian threaded the strap through a loop to hold the flap open and stepped inside. Vivian knelt on the ground next to the cot and gently repinned some of Ruby's pin curls that had fallen loose. Her fingertips grazed the wetness on her friend's cheeks. "Oh, honey," she whispered.

Ruby choked back a sob, and her shoulders shook.

Would the cot support both their weight? Vivian slid gingerly behind Ruby, threw an arm over her, and inhaled the distinctive fresh scent of Pond's Cold Cream lingering at her temples.

Holding her friend, Vivian watched the light streaming through the open tent flap fold from one soft hue of twilight into another, until at last she spotted stars twinkling in the darkened sky. In war, everything could change in a sliver of a moment, a single breath, the briefest pause of inattention.

They had started a poker game outside after all. Their voices, the comforting, deeper voices of the GIs interwoven with the light, effervescent voices of her fellow Clubmobilers, drifted in. That was the way of things in war. It did no good to dwell on losses or what-ifs.

"I don't think I can do this." Ruby's voice, pitched lower and softer than normal, held notes of grief and despair.

Vivian didn't answer right away. She found Ruby's hand and laced her fingers tightly with hers. "This'll change us, harden us even, if we let it. Or, we can try to hang on to a glimmer of humanity within ourselves, for them, if not for us. Make no mistake, we'll go back different, just like the fellas. We're all in it together here. And that's something no one can take away from us."

CHAPTER TWENTY-FIVE

July 30, 1944
USAAF Station 105, Chelveston, England

"You been up with them yet?" Jack gestured to Bowie's crew, clustered at a table to the left of the bar.

Bowie now had command of a ship he had christened *Texas Two-Step*. Jack would miss flying with his friend, but didn't begrudge him the long overdue promotion.

If only Bowie's replacement wasn't Hank Davenport, Jack would have been even happier. What were the odds Hank Davenport, of all people, would be assigned to take the right seat in Jack's ship? Jack had been surprised to see him at all. Davenport struck him as someone happy to keep a safe stateside job. Still, he was here and doing a good job. Jack had no complaints about his piloting skills, at least in terms of the check-rides they had taken yesterday. Their first combat mission would be the real test.

Bowie nodded. "They're good men. Two missions down."

"Were you part of—"

"No." Bowie cut in. The army had suppressed full reports, but the decision to employ the 8th Air Force's heavies to bomb German lines as tactical support had disastrous results for the American infantry troops arrayed some thousand meters behind the marked target. Heavy bombers had never been able to bomb with any precision.

"Good." Jack took a swig and grimaced. Beer should be cold.

"Speaking of France, Simmons says his girl Mabs is over there already. She couldn't tell him anything before she left, but he's had a few letters. Vivian said anything about going over?"

Jack's heart contracted. Marilyn had helped him call Vivian's boarding house in Leicester. Her crewmates were out working, but an older woman had taken the call. She said Vivian had written to Dottie and Jean from "somewhere in France." He hung up without leaving a message.

Despite Marilyn's predictions, there had been no letter from Vivian waiting here. She had written her friends, but not him.

"Nope. Hasn't said anything about it." Jack cut his eyes away from Bowie.

"If I were you, I'd tell her to stay put. Army's probably doing its best to keep them out of harm's way, but an active combat zone isn't safe for anyone, especially women. Simmons says the gals are sleeping rough out in the fields, just like the men."

Jack made a noncommittal noise in his throat. Normally, he would have nudged Bowie in the ribs and joked about the folly of trying to tell Vivian what to do or not do. Instead, he finished the last swig of his beer and stretched unnecessarily. "Think I'm gonna head back, get some shut-eye."

Bowie put a hand on Jack's shoulder. "Hang on a sec, all right? Been meaning to talk to you about something else."

Jack eased back to the barstool.

"The fellas say you've got the idea things might have gone a different way after the Leipzig mission if you'd been piloting that day." Bowie drummed his fingers on the bar.

Jack shrugged. "You oughta know how it works. Got your own command now."

"I'd do everything in my power to bring my guys back home safely. But look here, Jack, there's a difference between the stuff you can control and the shit you can't do anything about. You know that."

"Tucker's a good pilot. I'm sure he did his best, but—"

"But nothing. He's a damn good pilot. Brought that plane down in the drink like he'd done it a hundred times before. Might have been landing it on a long concrete runway with fantastic conditions for all we felt," Bowie said.

"I'm glad to hear it went all right, as far as ditching goes," Jack said.

"As far as ditching goes," Bowie repeated, frowning. "You're thinking we wouldn't have needed to ditch at all if you'd been behind the controls?"

Jack shoved his doubts about his mental state to the side.

"Look here, we weren't in our ship that day. We took up one of those generic ships without a name. Wasn't Tad and Duck's work. You gettin' what I'm saying?"

Jack's men had said how happy they were to have *Vivian's Victory* back, how glad they were it hadn't been her sinking to the depths of the English Channel, how much safer they felt with her. He, too, was glad his ship was still in service, even if her name cut him to the quick.

"Jack." Bowie waited until Jack met his eyes. "Left fuel tank had a slow leak that got missed by that other ground crew. When the right one got hit by flak off one of those coastal batteries, we were out of luck. You being at the controls wouldn't have made any difference. Result would have been the same. Wasn't Tucker's doing. Or mine."

"Never said it was your fault." It had never crossed Jack's mind that Bowie was to blame.

"Not Tucker's fault either. He couldn't have done anything else. And neither could you, if you'd been in the left seat that day." Bowie stood and clapped Jack on the back. "Gonna go harass my crew and then hit the hay."

***

Jack stripped to his underwear and crawled into a bed that was only marginally warmer in August than in January. But it was a bed. He was a little chilled, but he was a damn sight more comfortable than Vivian must be.

He tossed and turned, unable to settle. If he didn't drift off soon, it would be that much harder once Bowie's snoring kicked in. Bowie had kept his space in their original barracks rather than bunking with his new crew.

Bowie's words from earlier pinged around in his head. *You being at the controls wouldn't have made any difference. Result would have been the same.*

Based on what Bowie said about mechanical problems, Jack conceded the point. Different decisions might have changed the outcome. Sometimes the smallest decision, especially by the pilot, had spiraling repercussions. Still, the same result was more likely than not. Jack might not have done anything more than Tucker, especially in his mental state.

The news that Vivian had deployed to France, without leaving so much as a note, threw him offbalance. Marilyn's assurances about the army's inability to forward mail to the flak houses had only built up false hope. Returning to find no waiting letter sent his emotions skidding first to shock, then anger, followed shortly by forced indifference. But dammit, he cared, and he was tired of pretending otherwise. He would shelve his pride and reach out to her.

Jack rummaged in his trunk for paper and a pen. He climbed back in bed and began to write.

> *Vivi —*
>
> *I hope you've been blaming the army's slow mail delivery for lack of word from me. By now, even that excuse is probably wearing thin. I wouldn't blame you if you'd given up on me. I hope you'll hear me out and be able to forgive me.*
>
> *You were right. I was in worse shape than I realized. Those weeks at the flak house were what I needed.*
>
> *I'm proud of you for taking your work over there to the fellas who are slogging it out in the field. Keep yourself safe, honey. There are buzz bombs going off all the time here, especially in London, but it's gotta be far more dangerous where you are. Watch out for yourself.*

Viv, I'm so sorry. I can't take back everything I said, but I wish I could.

Just like that song says, sweetheart, "When the lights go on again all over the world," I'll find you. If you'll still have me, if you can forgive me, and love me again, I'll never let you go. I'll never let you down again.

All my love,
Jack

She might refuse to accept his apology. Worse, she might have already written him off and found someone else. He wouldn't blame her, but he would search for her after the war all the same.

Jack knew her APO number by heart and addressed the envelope in short order. He had folded the letter and stuffed it in the envelope when Gib bellowed, "Turn the fucking flashlight out! For fuck's sake, trying to sleep."

"Some of us were asleep until you yelled, asshole," said Chaz.

Jack smiled, clicked off the flashlight, and sealed the envelope. He placed it on the small table between his and Bowie's beds. He would post it first thing tomorrow. He might have a reply by week's end. If she forgave him, that is. He wouldn't blame her if she made him wait. He hoped it wouldn't be as long as he had made her wait.

***

"Up and at 'em boys! Time to rise and shine. Nielsen and Coates, report to ops right after chow."

Jack sat and stared around the room. The CQ slammed the door closed behind him, and the faint light of dawn disappeared.

Bowie pulled the cord to switch on one of the overhead light bulbs.

Jack rubbed a hand across his face. No mission today, so he had expected to spend the day lounging in a flight suit, not pulling on his full dress regalia. "Why do they want us in ops, do you reckon?"

Bowie stepped into his pinks. "No idea but get a move on."

Jack crouched in front of the small mirror mounted near Chaz's cot to knot his tie. Hank called his name. Davenport had taken one of the bunks vacated by another crew that shared these barracks.

Jack turned. Hank pointed to the letter to Vivian he had left on his bedside table the night before. "That need to get posted?"

No telling how long he might be at ops or wherever they might send him.

"Yeah, do you mind? Seems I'm going to ops this morning." Jack frowned at his tie, ripped the knot loose, and started over.

"Headed there anyway." Hank held up a small stack of letters.

CHAPTER TWENTY-SIX

August 28, 1944
Sceaux, near Paris, France

"Viva les femmes Américaines!"

Vivian waved at the throngs of cheering French citizens that lined the roads, holding American flags and pressing flowers, fruit, wine, and other treats on them. The Clubmobile convoy followed the army vehicles wending their way east toward Paris.

"This is better than when the men cheered for our arrival last month." Vivian leaned out the window to take a bouquet of sunflowers from a French woman. She passed the bouquet to Ruby.

Janie smiled and waved at a woman who passed her a small basket of apples. "Nah, nothing's better than our American GIs whooping and whistling because the Doughnut Girls were coming through."

"Yes, but were they more excited to see us or the doughnuts?" Vivian blew a kiss to a crowd of cheering French children.

It took the whole day to reach their destination outside Paris, owing more to the crowds than to road conditions or weather. The Germans had surrendered Paris three days earlier, and the French jubilantly celebrated the return of their capital.

Their new billet in Sceaux was a big improvement over the primitive field conditions they had endured since they landed in Normandy. The château had running water, electricity, and wood floors. Best of all, their new base was only six miles south of Paris.

The next morning, all the women of Clubmobile Group F woke at first light and donned their dress uniforms. The army provided a group of cars and drivers to take them into Paris for the day.

The Clubmobilers joined thousands of people lining the sidewalks of the Champs-Élysée to watch the victory parade. Their soldiers held aloft enormous American flags and marched in rows behind the British troops.

Vivian and the other women stood on tiptoe and craned to see over the heads of the excited crowd. Someone tapped Vivian on the shoulder.

She turned and looked up. Archie MacLeod's boyish face grinned at her. Vivian's lips turned up into her first genuine smile since the day before she left Leicester. His uniform shoulder loop now sported the golden oak leaf cluster that signified his rank of major. "Archie!" She gave him a quick hug.

"Thought that was you, Vivian. How long have you been here?"

"I came with the first Clubmobiles to cross over in July. What on earth are you doing here?" Last she knew, MacLeod had been stationed with division headquarters near Cambridge. Bomber crews would remain based in England.

"Narrowly avoided orders to accompany Iron-Ass LeMay to India. Reckon the tigers and cobras are any match for him?"

Vivian laughed. A cobra might indeed have a warmer personality than LeMay. "How did you manage a transfer to Paris rather than Bombay?"

MacLeod leaned closer and cupped his hands around his mouth to make himself heard better over the boisterous crowds. "Air brass are establishing new headquarters for the ETO, and I'm scouting facilities. Hope I can stay on once that's done. What about you?"

"Here for the duration. We've been following GIs across France for weeks, and I imagine we'll find ourselves in Berlin before it's over." Vivian waved her hand expansively at her friends. "We may look spiffy for the parade today, but it's the first time we've been out of battle fatigues since we crossed over." She didn't mention that their arrival at Sceaux yesterday had been their first opportunity to take a proper bath since they left England.

"For the duration, eh? I expect that isn't making your boy—"

She cut him off. "Let me introduce you to my friends, Archie. Gals, this is Major Archie MacLeod. He was with the 305th in Chelveston."

Vivian had avoided any mention of Jack to her new friends. Her guilt about his crewmates, which consumed her each night, was bad enough. Thinking about Jack was unbearable.

MacLeod waved his hand at the horde of people packed solid in every direction and raised his voice again. "You ladies need a better vantage point to see the parade. Follow me. I know just the spot."

He led them north for about two blocks, then threaded them through and around the crowd to several parked army jeeps. "Hop up on these. You'll be able to see so much more."

Their straight uniform skirts made it an awkward climb, but once Vivian, Ruby, Janie, and the others were seated on the hood of one of the jeeps, they could appreciate the expanse of the historic scene playing out.

Vivian's heart swelled with emotion at the sounds of the military band. She and the others applauded, waved, and whooped with appreciation at the impressive formations of marching soldiers. Vivian scanned the marching soldiers for her brother Bob. He was in France, though she had no way of knowing whether his division was part of today's parade.

When the last soldiers turned the corner, Gretchen said, "We should head to the Arc de Triomphe now that the parade's over."

"We want our doughnuts to be the first served in Paris," Vivian told MacLeod. They had brought doughnuts wrapped in waxed paper in a small box to serve to the anti-aircraft crews at the Arc de Triomphe. They gave MacLeod a few doughnuts as thanks for his help, and he bid them good-bye.

As they squeezed through the dispersing crowds, a Frenchman pressed a single-stem rose into Vivian's hand and kissed her on each cheek.

"*Merci*," she called.

She glanced at the distinctive pale pink rose, and her smile faltered.

The small package had caught up to her not long after she and Mabs had arrived at Chelveston. She turned it over in her hands, smiling and blinking back tears. He gave her the locket in New York. Was this another Christmas gift?

Nestled inside the small box were their ticket stubs from the showing of *Mrs. Miniver* they saw in Georgia. The stubs were pressed between pale pink rose petals. The pale pink Miniver rose was a motif in *Mrs. Miniver*. The principal character who died was youthful and idealistic Carol Miniver, not her husband of two weeks who had enlisted in the RAF at the height of the Blitz, not her father who had bravely taken his boat to join the rescue of Dunkirk the previous month. The altruistic young woman had been the one to lose her life.

The stubs and the delicate petals had been Jack's subtle reminder to keep herself safe.

Now she was in the thick of the action, in more danger than ever. Officially, the Clubmobiles followed at a safe distance, only moving into areas the military deemed secure. Yet their inadvertent slip beyond the front lines and the strafing near Saint-Lô was not an isolated incident. They had sheltered in ditches and under the *Yellowstone* several more times. Germans lobbed shells into their serving lines with some regularity, and the GIs praised them for their quick mastery of the technique of diving into foxholes. Once the shelling ceased, they clambered out of the foxholes and resumed serving.

Perhaps this rose was another reminder to take care of herself, even if not for Jack's sake.

Vivian hurried to catch up to the others.

The ack-ack crews were grateful for the doughnuts and tickled to have the company of American girls, so the women stuck around to chat with them.

"They beat us to the punch, can you believe it?"

Vivian and the others turned. Another large group of Red Cross Girls piled out of army jeeps, their arms laden with boxes of doughnuts.

"More doughnuts? Bring 'em here, dolls," called one of the ack-ack boys.

The women approached, laughing and waving.

"We wanted Group K to be the first to serve doughnuts in Paris," said a tall brunette woman striding ahead of the others.

Gretchen called, "Group F had the same idea, but these gentlemen seem happy to take seconds."

"Vivian!"

She searched the faces of the women heading their way, finally spotting Mabs's familiar bushy auburn curls.

Vivian dashed forward and pulled her friend in a tight hug. "What are you doing here? I didn't know you'd applied to come over."

"I didn't want to jinx my chances by saying anything to anyone, so I kept it quiet," Mabs said.

"What about …" Vivian trailed off. She had almost asked about the wedding Mel told her was planned for October. But she wasn't supposed to know about it.

"Mel? I couldn't tell him until I was already here, and that was so hard. I managed to see him one last time before I left, and I had to pretend nothing was about to change. We've talked it all through in letters these last few weeks, and he understands why I wanted to come here to help."

A sting of disappointment surged through Vivian's heart. Mail from England to the continent was getting through. She had half convinced herself Jack's silence wasn't intentional, that he had mailed letters that hadn't caught up to her fast-moving Clubmobile.

"Oh, that's swell." Vivian hoped her smile was a facsimile of convincing.

Gretchen and the tall brunette waved for everyone to follow them. They had directions to a hotel restaurant that might serve their large group.

"Viv, did you hear who played at Burtonwood after you left Leicester?"

Vivian groaned. "Don't tell me. Did Glenn Miller make it somewhere I might have seen him?"

"Not only Glenn Miller. Vera Lynn performed with his orchestra. Mel and some of the 305th fellas made it."

Walking through the streets of Paris, captivated by the exuberance of the celebrations and the excited talk of the other Red Cross Girls, Vivian kept her conversation with Mabs steered away from romance … and Jack.

She had called the Chelveston base three times to try and connect with Jack before she shipped out. She hadn't known any of the men who picked up her calls, though they each informed her that Lieutenant Nielsen was away from base. She gleaned "away from base" meant he was at a flak house. That was what she wanted. He would get the rest he needed. How peaceful could his stay be, with what had happened to his crew?

Vivian tried to write him a letter instead. She had crumpled up dozens of failed attempts. Smothering guilt about the fate of Jack's crewmates brought her up short every time.

She told no one about their breakup. In her letters to her parents, her brothers, and to Zanna, she managed to keep up a convincing pretense that everything was normal. She had avoided writing a letter to Mabs. Repeating the tangled web of half-truths she fed the folks back home was a bad idea, as Mabs might well have heard Jack's version from Mel. She also hadn't wanted to commit the truth to writing, for then she would have to grapple with her guilt and grief.

Pouring every ounce of energy she had into her draining work had kept Vivian from dwelling on her loss of Jack and his love and her complicity in the tragedy that befell his crewmates. Long days of hard physical labor, overlaid with ever-present danger, suited her. When she climbed into her bedroll each night, she was too exhausted to pine for Jack. She couldn't avoid her grief for his men, the men she had known and loved so well, but fatigue overwhelmed her most nights.

Seeing Mabs brought her intense grief perilously close to the surface.

If Mabs knew anything was amiss, she gave no indication. A group of army officers they met on the street joined them for lunch, and several liberated bottles of champagne flowed freely. After her second glass, Mabs whispered, "I've got news I wanted to share with you in person."

Vivian played it up, nudging Mabs, and widening her smile. "Ooh, do tell. Wouldn't involve a certain handsome navigator, would it?"

"Why yes, it would," Mabs said. "We're getting married." A sheen of color rose on her cheekbones, and her brown eyes sparkled.

Vivian hugged her. "Oh, Mabs, how wonderful."

"We'd planned to do it in October, but that was before I got the orders to come here. I hated it that I couldn't tell him we'd have to change our plans. But he understands why I wanted to help the ground troops slogging it out over here. Mel and I decided we'll marry whenever I get leave back to England. God knows when that might be."

Vivian took her friend's left hand to look at the ring.

"It was Mel's grandmother's ring. He wrote his parents and had them send it. He looked in London, but he didn't find anything he thought I'd like better." Mabs gazed fondly at the ring. Its center ruby was surrounded by smaller rubies set in a floral shape.

"It's beautiful." Vivian resisted the temptation to touch the locket she still wore.

Vivian raised her glass, clinked it against Mabs's champagne flute, and took a large gulp of champagne. She had a sinking feeling where the conversation would turn next.

Mabs whispered, "We could have a double wedding. You and Jack have probably been talking about it, right?"

Mabs didn't know a thing from Mel. Vivian should tell her now. If she found out later, she would wonder why Vivian hadn't confided in her. And yet … she couldn't do it. She couldn't say it out loud, couldn't bear Mabs's sympathy or the platitudes about giving him time and space she would offer.

"Gals, a perfume shop's open across the street. Who's interested in having a look?" Charlotte leaned over to their end of the table.

Vivian was grateful for the complete change of subject and that they would all be leaving. Terrible to think, but Vivian was relieved Mabs would move on with her group tonight. If they remained in each other's company for long, Vivian would have to tell her the truth.

CHAPTER TWENTY-SEVEN

December 15, 1944
Bastogne, Belgium

"Ready?" Vivian poked her head inside *Yellowstone's* back door.

"Just securing these last trays," Ruby said.

Vivian hopped in to give her a hand. Thousands of doughnuts cooled in wire racks for today's service to two different outfits in Luxembourg.

Today's route would take them within a few miles of the German border. Vivian omitted details when describing her work in letters back home. Mama was beside herself that Vivian was on the continent at all. She would have a conniption if she thought Vivian was anywhere near the actual fighting. Especially considering Bob and Danny were still in the thick of it. Bob's letters suggested he had seen some very rough duty in the last months. Vivian had the impression he was somewhere in this vicinity, and she eagerly searched the men crowded outside her Clubmobile each day, hoping for even a brief reunion.

Zanna's most recent letter contained interesting news about the raw deal dealt the women ferry pilots. The more useful the women aviators had become, the more likely male ferry pilots would be shipped off to combat, and they were having none of that. Zanna said the WASPs would disband this month, and the women would be sent home. She had made inquiries with the Red Cross and asked if Vivian could put in a good word for her. Almost as an afterthought, she mentioned Hank was now on active duty overseas. She didn't say where he was stationed.

Still no letters from the person she most wanted to hear from. She should accept it was over. Jack hadn't written. If only she could quell the tremor that ran through her gut at each mail delivery. Her disappointment affected her ability to appreciate the letters she did receive.

Vivian had tried several more times to write to him. It was no good. What could she say? His crew had perished in the frigid water of the Channel. Waves of guilt over her role in their deaths choked her every time she thought of them succumbing to a cold, watery grave. She had let smothering instincts inherited from her mother take over, with tragic and unalterable results.

She only wanted assurance that Jack was alive. He would be better off with someone else. If he had married her, he might have ended up like Daddy, constantly scrambling to meet unreasonable standards. Jack would be happier with a woman who could follow him to wherever his piloting jobs took him and keep a happy home for him and his children.

Perhaps she could write to someone at Chelveston who might report Jack's well-being. Vivian hefted the remaining sack of doughnut mix into one of the lower cabinets and latched it. Letter writing would have to wait.

Janie opened the back door of the *Yellowstone*. Her pale face peeked from under a head-wrap that shielded her from sleet and snow. "Do we have aspirin in here?"

Vivian pulled open a drawer and handed a bottle to Janie. "Too many rounds of something last night with the fellas of the 28th?"

"Champagne at first. They shifted to brandy when that ran out. I guess the brandy on top of champagne wasn't such a good idea." Janie opened her canteen and chugged water to wash down aspirin tablets.

"Should I drive today?" Vivian asked. Janie's headache wouldn't be helped by trying to drive the *Yellowstone* in these foul conditions.

"Oh, would you? Thanks." Janie sipped more water from her canteen.

"Glad we were on cooking detail last night," Ruby said to Vivian.

Vivian wasn't sure she agreed. Spending the evening making dozens of batches of doughnuts in the close quarters of Clubmobiles wasn't her idea of a good time. Besides, she enjoyed the camaraderie of dinner, drinking, and card games with the fellas.

French villages didn't have pubs, and the army and Clubmobiles moved too frequently to hold formal dances. Evening entertainment was more ad-hoc and casual, and it always involved large amounts of alcohol. In addition to the official army liquor ration, which the Clubmobilers also received, the men shared out from their supply of "liberated" bottles. Everyone carried a pocket corkscrew.

"Oh, before I forget, here you go." Janie pulled an envelope from her coat pocket. "Mail delivery came in."

Vivian's heart jumped. She hated herself for daring to hope, as she had for months, that Jack would write.

Janie passed the envelope to her.

Vivian's heart deflated. She averted her eyes from Janie and tucked the letter from Mabs in her pocket to read later.

"All right, we're set." Ruby placed their small decorated Christmas tree into a cabinet, shut the door, and hooked the latch.

Vivian buttoned her coat and stepped into the bitter cold. She climbed in the driver's seat, taking care with the holly garland affixed above the window.

Ruby spread a map on her lap and traced her finger over the route. "We'll serve Company A at Heinerscheid"—she jabbed her finger at a spot roughly twenty miles from where they sat—"and then we'll stop outside Marnach for Company B and the 630th TD. Oh, and if we have time and doughnuts left, there's a few machine gun crews at Reuler."

Icy patches cropped up on the narrow, winding road across the Belgian border and into Luxembourg. The *Yellowstone's* wipers had difficulty keeping pace with the sleet smattering the windshield in a pelting barrage. Under better conditions, even accounting for the *Yellowstone's* persnickety ways, they could have made this journey in half the time it took today. They regularly drove out fifty or sixty miles from their billet in a day's run.

Vivian was relieved when they reached the assembly area for Company A of the 110th Regiment. Serving the men with the cold blasting through the *Yellowstone's* open windows was preferable to continuing to creep along in these precarious road conditions.

Despite the frigid, foul weather, men surged from every direction at the sight of the approaching Clubmobile.

The women climbed out of the cab, waved at the men, and headed to the back door. In nicer weather, they would have opened the windows to the counter space and chatted with the men while they unloaded the doughnut trays and set up the coffee urns. Too cold today. Men stomped their feet to keep warm, chattered amongst themselves, and called out that they needed a hot beverage.

Vivian opened the serving counter, and Janie set their small Christmas tree in view. The fellas jostled good naturedly and called out questions a mile a minute, like usual.

"Coffee and a sinker served by a pretty gal. Say, that's all right, then," said a tall redhead near the front of the line.

"Worth the wait out here in the snow," called another man.

The mix of blowing sleet and snow stung Vivian's damp face. Ripples of burning pain shot up her calves, and she stamped her numb feet. Her discomfort was nothing to what these men faced. Many of them might be going out on guard duty for the night with no shelter from the biting wind. She was uncomfortable now, but at the end of the day, she would move back to their billet in Bastogne, where their Belgian hosts would serve them a warm meal topped off with hot coffee or tea.

***

"Is the weather getting worse?" Ruby asked. The *Yellowstone* chugged around a tight bend. They had made slow progress toward their second stop at Marnach.

"Yes." Vivian maneuvered carefully down the crest of a hill. She gripped the steering wheel in a tight hold, trying to prevent the *Yellowstone* from skidding on the slick road. It was the longest four miles she had ever driven.

Once they had served the men and closed up the Clubmobile, Ruby asked their commander Colonel Ackerman for directions to the latrines. Vivian and Janie nodded agreement. They hadn't asked at the first stop but now it was imperative. Bouncing on these rough roads with full bladders wouldn't be anyone's idea of fun.

As usual, he tried to put them off.

"We know it's not intended for women," Vivian interjected. "We know it's primitive, outdoors, muddy, smelly, and open on one side. Apparently no one in the army understands women also have to pee. Clear it out and post a guard."

Colonel Ackerman had waited for them near the Clubmobile after their visit to the latrine. "Roads are icy and getting worse. Think you ladies ought to shelter in Clervaux for the night. It's a resort town with plenty of hotels and inns. Shouldn't be any trouble to find you gals a room. Which one of you is driving?"

Vivian raised her hand, and he nodded at her. "Listen, follow my jeep, but take it slow. Clervaux's in a valley, and there are several sharp, and I mean *sharp*, hairpin turns as you wend your way for about a mile straight down into the town. Once you're there, the roads are very narrow. We could park your vehicle before all those curves, but I want to lead you all the way through town to a bivouac on the northern end. That's the road you'll need to take tomorrow to head back to Bastogne."

"Viv, I'm feeling okay if you want me to drive," Janie said.

"That'd be swell, Janie. Thanks." Janie was from Minnesota and familiar with driving in these conditions.

Ackerman hadn't exaggerated. Vivian was unnerved enough as a passenger as Janie cautiously descended around the series of S-bend curves into the picturesque town of Clervaux. If they hadn't been rattled by the precarious descent, they might have enjoyed the vista of the town, with its fairy-tale buildings and cottages nestled in a valley amidst a forest of snow-covered evergreen trees. They'd seen enough of Europe now to no longer be surprised to find medieval castles and enormous churches and cathedrals in tiny villages. A castle perched on a ridge overlooked the town center.

They made slow progress through the narrow town streets,

clogged with soldiers despite the weather. Men waved as the Clubmobile lurched past.

Janie parked the *Yellowstone* in a bivouac near the edge of town with assorted army vehicles.

They got out, and Ackerman trudged toward them. He pointed to the adjacent road. "That's the road you'll take to Bastogne."

Soldiers on leave had filled all the larger hotels, but Ackerman found them a room in a small inn. The proprietress welcomed them effusively in a smattering of French, German, and English.

"*Comment vous appellez-vous? Wie heißen Sie? Ich heißen Vivian.*" Vivian tried out both French and German.

"*Je m'appelle Ange Kayser et ce sont mes filles, Juliette et Caterina.*"

Good. French must be her stronger language.

The daughters, Juliette and Caterina, served them bowls of onion soup, bread, and hot tea. Service was as warm as the food.

"*Merci.*" Vivian smiled at Caterina, who cleared their dishes from the table.

Ange patted Vivian's shoulder and reached around her to retrieve the soup tureen.

"Friendlier here than in Bastogne," Vivian said to one of the GIs who had stayed for dinner.

He shrugged. "Hard to say. Sometimes these folks are more sympathetic to the Germans. These seem all right."

The GIs had a bottle of brandy. One of them poured drinks, while another shuffled a deck of cards. After the group finished off the brandy, the women bade good night to the men and went upstairs to their room.

Janie took their pitcher downstairs to fill it with water, and Ruby went to the bathroom. Vivian opened her musette bag to find her toiletry case. Her hands closed on the cool spine of a book buried at the bottom. She didn't remember packing a book this morning. Her eyebrows crinkled in curiosity as she drew it out. Her heart contracted. The Eleanor Roosevelt book Jack had bought her last Christmas.

Jack had shooed her to the front of the shop near the entrance. Said he would only be a moment. She saw him tuck whatever he had bought inside his coat while facing away from her.

He grinned and shook his head. "It's a surprise. For later."

"I thought you already had my gift," Vivian said.

"Who says this is for you?" he teased, evading her playful swipes at his coat.

But it had been for her.

Christmas in London was magical, even with the dreary weather and scarcity of wartime conditions. Vivian and Jack had attended Christmas Eve services, then secured a spot at a table by the fireplace in a small restaurant near their hotel. It had taken numerous letters—Mama claimed she kept forgetting—but Vivian had persuaded her mother to ship her men's wool socks, a soft cashmere scarf, and a pocketknife as gifts for Jack.

Vivian opened the smaller of her two gifts first: a filigree bracelet with enamel panels, hand-painted with delicate flowers.

"Saw a real pretty one with hearts all around. Um, a charm bracelet, that's what you call it. But I figured that might get in the way of your work."

"It's beautiful, Jack. You're spoiling me with all this jewelry." Vivian held her wrist out so he could latch the clasp.

"Started with the locket, and now I've got you something for your wrist. You know what's next, right?"

Vivian smiled and pointed at the last package. "Have you hidden a ring in that one?"

"That's something I spotted today and couldn't pass up." Jack passed it to her.

He snipped the twining open with his new pocketknife, and Vivian carefully loosened the paper.

It's Up to the Women read the Deco lettering emblazoned across the dove gray cover. By Mrs. Franklin D. Roosevelt.

"You've probably already read it. I know she wrote this one a long time ago," Jack said.

"I don't remember ever seeing this one." Vivian opened the book and ran her fingertips over the title page.

She leaned across to kiss Jack. "Thank you," she whispered against his mouth. "You know me so well."

Jack's eyes had been soft and tender. "I don't know why it would have been in a London shop but seemed you were meant to have it."

Vivian rocked back on her heels. She hugged the book against her chest and closed her eyes. Her aching heart swelled like an inflating balloon.

Just over a year ago. Only twelve short months ago, they had been so happy, so in love.

Janie set the pitcher of water on the bedside table, breaking Vivian's reverie.

"You all right?"

Vivian nodded and turned away. "Just tired."

She slid the book back into her bag and squeezed past Ruby, who had returned from the bathroom.

By the time she returned, Ruby and Janie had both climbed into bed.

Their room was barely warmer than outside. Vivian pushed her hands in her coat pocket to locate her mittens. Her hand closed on an envelope. Oh, the letter from Mabs.

She settled herself under the covers and propped herself against the wall. A small bedside lamp cast enough light for her to read. Vivian slit the envelope open with her fingernail and unfolded the letter, written on creamy hotel stationary from the Chateau des Thermes.

> *Liège, Belgium*
> *December 15, 1944*
>
> *Hiya Viv—*
> *What a life over here in the ETO, eh? Guess your group's been through the same experiences we have with the winter weather. At least I'm used to all this snow and ice. It's a lot like home in Kenosha. My crewmates are like you, from the South, and they aren't loving it.*
>
> *I haven't got much time, but I wanted to send this off to you in case you can get leave to join me. I got approval for leave in London for Christmas! I got a call through to Mel, and he's getting us a marriage license. Wedding will be Saturday morning—December 23 that*

is—at St. Martin's in the Fields. Do you know where it is? Near Trafalgar Square. We wanted to be married at Yelden. I can't get to London any earlier than Friday so we think we ought not to risk there being a problem with the trains and whatnot. If you can, I so want you to join and stand up for me.

The plan is I'll get a ride from Liège to Paris on Thursday and codge a seat on a flight from Paris to London the next day. Apparently, it's de rigeur to get on one of the transport flights or the C-47 medical flights, because if nothing else, you can take the jump seat in the cockpit.

Had you realized we're eligible to go home? We got here exactly two years ago this month, and Red Cross will send us back. Mel and I are going to talk it over, but I'm inclined to go on home, even if he has to stay through the end. I feel I've done my bit and then some. I know there's loads of girls who'd love to take my place over here. I feel a little guilty not seeing it through, but I'm so damn tired, Viv. I know you must be too.

I sure hope you can be there for our special day. I know it's a long shot, but let me know if you can swing it. Mel says he can bring Jack, if that sweetens the pot.

Love,
Mabs

Jack. He was alive. Warm tingles radiated out from Vivian's thrumming heart.

Was this their chance? A chance to see whether their relationship could be mended? She would ask Gretchen about a short leave when she got back to Bastogne tomorrow. A surge of expectation sent flutters billowing through her stomach. Two days, that's all she needed. Long enough to be there for the wedding. If she went, and Jack agreed to come, it was a start.

CHAPTER TWENTY-EIGHT

December 16, 1944, 5:30 a.m.
Clervaux, Luxembourg

"Do you hear that?" Janie's voice held a panicked edge.

Vivian rolled over. She was closest to the window, so she parted the curtains and peeked out. "It's too dark to tell what it might be."

In shadow, Janie's seated figure seemed poised for flight. "Not the usual sound, is it? Of shelling in the distance, I mean."

Janie was right. It was distinguishable from the familiar rumble and booms of artillery shells and anti-aircraft gunfire from a front line several miles distant.

This menacing, whirring whistle followed by a series of concussive blasts had a different rhythm.

Sssssszzzzzz ... Boom. Crackle, crackle, crackle.

Another loud crescendoing whistle passed close overhead. Vivian's stomach did several successive flips, not unlike the revolutions of a flour sifter.

Janie gave a small shriek. "It's a buzz bomb! Did it keep going?"

"No." Ruby sat, covers pulled over her head like a hood. "No, it's not a buzz bomb. We heard those in London, remember? A buzz bomb sounds more like a low-flying plane, only loads faster, and it's got kind of a propeller type sound in it."

Vivian rocked back off her knees. "It's not outgoing. That's the difference. What we're hearing now is incoming."

No one spoke as they listened to the next whirring shell. Wherever it exploded must have been close. Windows rattled, and the building shook.

"Shouldn't we hear outgoing? Response from our guys?" Ruby said.

Good question. If the Germans were attacking the American lines, why didn't they hear any defensive fire in response?

A *rap-rap* sounded at their door. One of the GIs from last night, his deep voice infused with a trace of agitation, spoke. "Ladies, you need to move to the cellar for safety. Bring your helmets and anything else you might need with you."

Vivian opened the door. A GI, wearing his helmet, stood in the narrow hallway. "What's going on?" she asked.

His eyes swept from Vivian to Ruby and Janie, who had scrambled out of bed and crowded behind Vivian. "Germans are attacking our line near here. Shouldn't last too long. Until it's all wrapped up, you gals should be below."

Everyone had slept in warm clothing. They scrambled to grab a few other essentials. Vivian stepped into her boots and patted her chest through her field jacket to confirm her locket was where it ought to be. She grabbed her journal, a pen, and a flashlight.

Ruby and Janie moved into the hallway, and Vivian was close behind.

Wait, her bracelet. She hurried to the window, parted the curtains, and retrieved the enameled bracelet from the windowsill. She tucked it in her pocket. Scattered bursts of fire illuminating the sky drew her eye, and she brought her face to the window pane.

Booming, exploding shells pounded closer.

She scurried to the door and stepped into the hallway. A sharp boom and thud sounded, followed closely by a waterfall of glass cascading over the plank floor. The same glass she had just pressed her face against. Vivian's heart flutter-kicked against her ribs.

The GI cursed. "Hurry." He motioned them down the stairs.

Ange and her daughters, bearing a teapot and cups, a loaf of bread, and a crock of jam, joined them in the cellar.

Vivian reached for the knife and cut a slice of bread while Janie dealt cards. Spreading jam on her bread, she explained the rules of gin rummy to their hosts.

Ange's hand shook as she picked up her stack of cards.

Vivian peered closely at her troubled expression in the flickering candlelight. "Don't worry. Our fellas will have the Germans dashing back in no time."

"*Les soldats Américains sont très courageux.*" Ange paused, her eyes cutting briefly to Juliette. "If only her birthday were not next month."

Juliette pressed her lips together and lifted her chin. "Letter or no, I won't go. I'll join *la résistance* if it comes to that."

"Letter?" Vivian passed a cup of hot tea to Ange.

"Conscription. Once eighteen, unless she is married or has children, a young woman must go work in Germany in their factories or on their farms. *Reichsarbeitsdienst,*" Caterina explained.

Juliette would be eighteen next month, and Caterina not far behind. Brutal work conditions would await both girls in Germany. Vivian translated Caterina's explanation for Ruby and Janie.

"They should come with us, at least until it's secure here again," Ruby said.

Vivian nodded. "Hopefully our fellas will have everything squared away before lunch, and it won't come to that."

Vivian guessed at least two hours had elapsed before two GIs clumped downstairs. The one who had rousted them from their room said, "I'm Jim, by the way, and this is Mark. Just us two here now. We were gonna try to get you gals on your way back to Bastogne, but now roads that direction aren't open."

"Do you know what's happening?"

If the roads weren't open, especially to the west, that sounded ominous. All territory to the west ought to be secure and in Allied hands.

"Phone lines are out, and our radios are jammed. From what we can tell, the Germans are on the move for miles up and down the front lines," Mark said.

"They've broken through our lines?" Ruby laid her cards down.

Vivian frowned. "If the roads aren't secure, does that mean German troops are west of us?" Had the German troops encircled Clervaux? Vivian's pulse skittered.

Jim held up his hands in an okay-calm-down gesture. "We're not getting full communication. Probably confined to a small sector near here, but hard to say. Reports suggest the roads out of here are under fire. Until that's contained, you'll shelter here."

Vivian's gut spasmed. Their ID cards reflected the substantive rank of captains. None of them had expected to ever have need of this honorific.

Jim didn't return with more news until midday. "Looking better. Krauts have stopped lobbing shells into the town anyways. Still don't know about the roads. Soon as we get word it's safe, we want you gals to be on your way outta here. For now, you can come upstairs. Maybe we can find something to eat?"

Typical man. He was hungry and hopeful Ange Kayser and her daughters could rustle something up.

Jim had good instincts. Vivian was astounded by the speed with which Ange and her girls served a scrumptious midday meal of cheese toast, potato pancakes, fried onions, and spicy sausage.

A messenger checked in with Jim and Mark early in the afternoon. He reported road traffic was confined to moving in additional troops, tanks, and supplies from the west. He advised the women should remain in place.

Another runner poked his head in before dusk to take stock of who was in the Hotel Bertemes. He was surprised to find three Red Cross women and their civilian hostesses.

They overheard him asking Jim in a heated whisper in the hallway why the women hadn't been moved out earlier.

"I informed headquarters they're here," Jim hissed. "I was told the roads needed to be clear for reinforcements. Can you run down the street and ask if we can put them on the road toward Bastogne yet?"

"Word is the brass have been told to hold our position here at all costs. There will be no retreat."

No retreat? Sleeting ice cascaded in waves in Vivian's stomach.

She approached Jim after the soldier left. "Since it's quiet, can I step outside for a few minutes? I could use fresh air after being cooped up all day."

He rubbed the back of his neck. "Uh … Yeah, but look, don't go far. Stay close, all right?"

The bite of crisp winter air on her face was a welcome change from the dank closeness of the old hotel.

Evidence of the earlier bombardment was all around: broken windows covered with canvases and tarps, holes blasted through walls, fire debris stacked about.

A vibrating, droning rumble from above attracted her notice. Clervaux was in a valley, surrounded by high ridges like the one they had traversed so slowly last night. That mechanized, growling sound thrummed louder. Vivian shaded her eyes and turned in a semicircle, settling her gaze at a point near the feudal castle.

Her heart skipped a beat. Tanks. Two tanks rumbled on the mist-shrouded ridge above the castle. Were they Shermans here to defend? Or German Panzers moving in?

Vivian pushed the door back open and beckoned to Jim. His eyes widened at the sight of the tanks. Before he could speculate, the question of their allegiance became clear. Shells landed at several points in the street. Her heart careened toward her dry throat.

Jim yanked Vivian by the hand inside and slammed the door.

***

Exploding shells, pulsating blasts from machine gun fire, and thundering booms filled the air throughout the evening. Vivian and the other women heard it from the basement where Jim had ordered them to retreat once the battle started again.

Jim and Mark appeared downstairs after midnight. "We want to get you gals to the abbey. Not sure if you saw it last night, but it sits high on a hill. Buys us time to figure out how we can get you farther away."

"How do we get to the abbey?" Vivian recalled seeing its spires in the distance as they crested the hill descending into Clervaux.

Juliette spoke in rapid French, addressing her mother and sister.

"Juliette says the path to the abbey begins a short distance behind this hotel. Wait, didn't we come here from that direction after we left our Clubmobile?" Vivian turned to Juliette and described the bivouac area where they had parked the *Yellowstone*.

Juliette reached for Vivian's journal. Vivian tore off a sheet and handed her a pen. Juliette drew a map and passed it to Vivian. The back end of the bivouac intersected with one edge of the road leading to the abbey.

Janie looked up. "Are you saying we could drive the Clubmobile to the abbey?"

"Drive?" Jim raised his eyebrows. "I dunno about driving. It's about a mile walk. Granted, it's uphill, but driving sounds like trouble."

"How so? The Germans are less apt to pick us off when we're on foot?" Vivian pointed at the map Juliette had drawn. "She says once we round the first curve here, the road cuts through a thick forest to the abbey."

Mark peered over her shoulder at the map. "Would give them a way to get themselves out."

Ruby picked up her musette bag. "If we have the means to go, we should try. Is the main road to Bastogne out of the question?"

Jim nodded grimly. "The road itself is fine, but Germans are swarming from that direction. They've crossed the railroad bridge on the other end of town, right where the road runs out. Too dangerous for you to drive that way."

"Juliette says we can take roads west of the abbey and head north until we intersect with the road to Bastogne. Well away from here." Vivian passed Juliette's latest map to Jim.

Jim looked from the map to Vivian and the others. "Makes me nervous. But it seems a worse idea for you gals to stay here, with the Krauts pouring in from all directions. They going too?" He gestured to Ange and her daughters.

"Yes," Ruby said. "They're in at least as much danger as we are from the Germans. And we'll need them to help us find our way through the forest roads."

Ange and her girls hurried up the stairs.

"They're going to gather canteens and food that we can stash in our coat pockets." Vivian slid her hands inside her pockets to retrieve her gloves.

"Earlier today, you had on a jacket with a bunch of unit insignia on it," Jim said. "You still got those on under your coats?"

Ruby nodded. "Field jackets. We've all got them."

Jim shook his head. "You want to be strictly Red Cross. You gotta ditch those. Leave 'em here. They don't add much warmth anyway. Come to the front hall when you're ready."

Once the men were out of earshot, Janie looked at the others. "I'm not losing that jacket."

Vivian agreed. Damned if she would give up her *Can Do* insignia badge from the 305th Bomb Group. Field jackets were the pride and joy of every Red Cross Girl. They had collected an insignia patch from every group and squadron they served. Vivian's jacket was adorned with at least two dozen patches.

Vivian pointed to their musette bags. "Let's stash them in there." They could toss those bags if they were in danger.

Rebundled, they met Ange and the girls, who passed them small parcels of food and canteens.

Jim's hand rested on the doorknob. "All right, listen, we're going to the left out of here. We'll edge along the street to the bivouac. Crouch and stay close against the buildings. Do exactly what I do. Mark will bring up the rear. If it's too hot, we're gonna divert to the road behind this one, the one that goes straight to the abbey. In that case, this plan to drive your vehicle out of here is nixed, and we'll take you there on foot."

Mark held up his hand before Jim opened the door. "The German tanks have got searchlights mounted on them, and they're shining those suckers everywhere, looking for movement. We're gonna stop short of any beam of light best we can. If you're caught in one, skedaddle out of it fast as you can."

Vivian exchanged a glance with Ruby and Janie. She inhaled and clenched her fists at her sides, determined to quell her tremors.

"Should go without saying, but we need to move fast. Do they understand all of this?"

Vivian had been translating in a low voice. She looked at Jim. "Ange says clusters of trees in between buildings could be good cover if we need to evade."

Jim pointed at Vivian. "You go behind me, with Ange or one of the girls behind you. That way you can translate for us."

He pulled open the door, stepped out, and looked both directions. After a slim pause, he motioned the others to follow. He moved swiftly to the left, his firearm trained on the street and his body hugged tight against the hotel front. One by one, they all followed suit.

The rumbling drone of German Panzers on the move filled the air. Blasts of machine gun fire sounded. Bullets ricocheted off the cobblestone streets and buildings. Greenish-white tracers arced overhead.

Vivian's heart hurtled into her throat. American tracers were red.

Tanks with mounted lights were positioned high on the ridges, and their trawling beams roved ominously from a point far above the ground. Anticipating the pattern of the shifting lights proved tricky. The pattern changed abruptly and nearly caught them. Jim slammed to a stop, and the others followed his lead. Ange pulled hard on Vivian's coat sleeve and pointed to a thick copse of trees to their left. They dove into it, huddling tight, the men ranged in front. The searchlight passed on, and they hurried back on their path.

At the next corner, Jim stopped short. None of them needed Vivian's translation to know a German patrol lurked in between the buildings. Vivian's heart arced toward her throat like the German tracers in the sky. Were they moving toward this road, this building? The German soldiers issued sharp, guttural commands with increased volume. One of them jiggled a doorknob and kicked open a door. Their voices died away, but jackboots thumped across wooden floors inside the hotel. Jim peered around the corner and circled with his arm to urge them forward.

Their feet crunched on hard-packed patches of snow, the sound amplifying. Vivian sucked lungfuls of frozen air. Her chest constricted and rebelled against her every breath. Gunfire, droning tanks, and explosions all around might mask the noise of their progress, but German soldiers would be on the alert, watching and listening for any sound of movement.

They found the bivouac despite the foggy mist clouding the air. They debated in whispers which of the hulky dark shapes of parked vehicles was the *Yellowstone*. Mark moved stealthily forward to check that no unwelcome visitors lurked within or around it. He would also start the engine. Would the persnickety *Yellowstone* cooperate and start after sitting idle all day in the bitter cold? Vivian's legs tingled and pricked. She resisted the urge to stamp her feet to shake feeling into her tense muscles. Too much time had elapsed. Had he been ambushed?

The rattling and whirring of the engine kicking to life blasted through the crisp air. Noises of the mounting battle surely overrode the gasps and coughs of the *Yellowstone* trying to wake up. Unless they were as near to this bivouac as Vivian's group, the Germans shouldn't hear it. They could be, and that made speed all the more vital.

Only as they half ran in a crouch, zigging and zagging behind and between other parked vehicles, did Vivian realize they hadn't discussed who would drive and who would ride in the front cab. Ruby and Janie didn't speak French. Juliette professed to know how to navigate them through narrow, country roads slicing through the dense terrain of the Ardennes. "Ruby, go in the back with Ange and Caterina. I need to translate Juliette's directions for Janie."

Jim held the back door open. "We'll ride back here. Stop at the abbey."

The *Yellowstone* chugged out of the bivouac, belching, sputtering, and struggling to rouse as usual.

"Hurry, hurry, hurry." Vivian's pulse danced a jitterbug. They needed to clear out of this bivouac without being spotted. Or intercepted. Or shot.

"Trying! I'm trying. You know what she's like when she first wakes up." Janie shifted gears. "The ground here is more mud than ice thanks to all these damn jeeps."

The dark, forbidding stand of forest to the left seemed less threatening than the backs of hotels and shops on their immediate right. At least one German patrol prowled those buildings.

They had gone a few hundred feet at most when Juliette signaled they must make a sharp right turn. Turning in the pitch-black without even cat-eye headlights would be a challenge.

Dishes and supplies clattered in the back when Janie swung the

Yellowstone into a tight turn. Vivian slammed hard against Juliette.

Janie took an immediate S-curve around the other direction, before straightening out for another few hundred feet. Juliette directed her with motions into another sharp right turn. Five hundred feet and another perilous S-curve.

"Juliette says that was the last sharp turn. We'll keep climbing with a few curves. You're doing great." Vivian reached around Juliette to pat Janie's shoulder. A sheen of perspiration covered Janie's pale face.

Vivian kneaded her shaking hands in her lap. "Look on the bright side. I don't suppose tanks can maneuver on this road." Tall, snow-covered firs and poplars crowded close against the *Yellowstone* on both sides.

"I wouldn't have thought they could manage that road we drove into Clervaux last night, but they did it." Janie shifted gears again.

"They may have come in a different way," Vivian said.

"Not comforting," Janie muttered.

They rumbled on. Janie tried to strike a balance between moving them fast out of harm's way and cautiously driving the awkward Clubmobile up an icy, dark road winding a hill in perilous curves.

"Juliette says this is the last turn."

The imposing facade of the abbey loomed ahead.

Janie stopped next to the low brick wall of the abbey. Tracers and flares periodically arced, flashed, and hung in the sky, illuminating the building's tall spire.

"Well, we made it this far. There it—argh!" Vivian clapped a hand on her mouth to stifle her shriek. Jim had rapped on the driver's side door to signal Janie to roll down the window. How did he get out of the rear of the Clubmobile so fast?

"Seen anything?" From behind Jim, Mark turned in circles, his weapon at the ready.

"Nothing but trees, and two American soldiers who scared us half to death." Janie held her hand over her heart.

"Mark will go poke around inside the abbey. I'll wait here with you," Jim said.

Jim moved in a circle around the *Yellowstone*. He exchanged terse passwords with Mark when he returned.

Jim leaned into the cab of the Clubmobile on Vivian's side. "All right, look, no one's in the abbey. You didn't see anything on the road. I reckon you should go on, if this girl thinks she can navigate you to the road that leads into Bastogne. If you wanna stay here, one of us can stay with you. If you're gonna go on, you're on your own. We've gotta report back."

Vivian asked Juliette again if she was sure she could lead them to the road.

"*Oui. Je sais que la route très bien.*"

Vivian exchanged a glance with Janie, who bobbed her chin once. "We'll drive on. Thank you for everything and … good luck."

Luck. They would need far more than luck. These men stood a good chance of being dead or captured by morning from the look of things in Clervaux. They were outnumbered, outmaneuvered, outmanned.

Was Bob caught up in this battle? His last letter had said he was in Luxembourg. It was a small country, and from the sound of it, entirely engulfed in this latest battle. Vivian's gut clenched.

"You have weapons?" Jim asked, cutting into her worries for her brother.

All Red Cross Girls were issued a sidearm. But they hadn't been given ammunition or instruction in how to use it. The Red Cross likely assumed they had met their duty toward giving the women self-protection by providing weapons.

Vivian didn't need a tutorial. She had grown up in rural Georgia with brothers who were avid sportsmen. She kept her weapon in the Clubmobile, but the others had probably left theirs in Bastogne. Vivian pulled her pistol from under the seat. "I don't have any ammunition."

Jim pulled a carton of rounds from his pocket and passed it to her. "You know how to load it and use it?"

She nodded.

He grinned. "Prove it, doll."

She closed the chamber, and Jim pursed his lips appreciatively. "Nice. I'll take your word you know how to use it." He pressed a second carton of rounds into her hand, ignoring her protests that he might need it more.

Jim saluted, patted the door of the Clubmobile, and waved. This was their signal to head out. They called out last words of thanks before rolling up their windows. Vivian turned and watched the dark silhouettes of their GI friends retreat toward the doomed village of Clervaux. She swallowed past a lump in her throat.

Tracers and sounds of battle fire faded soon after they forged on from the abbey. Juliette warned of an upcoming fork in the road. She told Vivian they should stay to the left to skirt around the village of Eselborn.

"How much farther to that road we're trying to hit, does she know?" Janie maneuvered through another sharp left curve, following Juliette's frantic hand signals.

"I'm not too good at metric conversions. Four or five miles?"

They moved away from the undisturbed peace of Eselborn, and the forest closed in on both sides again. Juliette said the route would stay straight for a time. Vivian puffed out a breath of air and watched it hover in the cab.

Was it her imagination or was the loud whirring of the *Yellowstone's* engine growing fainter and slower?

She opened her mouth to ask if Janie could see the fuel gauge when Janie cursed and guided the sputtering Clubmobile to a stop.

"I'm sure Jim could have topped off our fuel if we'd thought to ask. Dammit." Janie pressed her forehead against the steering wheel.

"Our focus was escaping a raging battle, Janie. Vehicle maintenance wasn't at the top of our list," Vivian said.

"Okay, now what?"

Now what, indeed. They were in the middle of a dense, dark forest, with the potential for enemy troops to come at them from any direction. Vivian rubbed her throbbing head.

"I'll hop out and tell the others what's going on." Vivian swung out and ducked to avoid the fir branches scraping against the cab window. She clicked the door closed behind her.

"It's me," she called and opened the rear door. "We're out of gas."

"We thought so. Any idea where we are?" Ruby asked.

"A forest somewhere in the Ardennes."

Ruby rolled her eyes. "Are we close enough to the main road to walk out and flag down a military vehicle?"

Vivian held up a finger and walked back to the cab to gesture for Janie and Juliette to come join their discussion.

Vivian exchanged remarks with Ange, Juliette, and Caterina and turned to her friends. "Juliette thinks we are halfway between the last village and the main road, so that would be about two miles. There's another small village between us and the road."

"Would one of the farmers have fuel for a tractor or car?" Janie said.

Juliette explained the small farms in this region wouldn't have a tractor or equipment requiring fuel.

Ruby stomped her feet on the hard-packed snow. "We're sitting ducks if we stay here and wait for the first army truck. This isn't a main route, so we might wait a long time."

"Right, but we have shelter here and could hide." Janie waved her hand at the impenetrable darkness of the surrounding forest.

Vivian inhaled a deep breath and let it out. It hung in the air before her, swirling. "We might not have enough warning to hide." Based on what they experienced in Clervaux, the Germans were pushing aggressively. "Ruby's right about the isolation too. Do either of you have your gun? Jim left me with another carton of rounds."

They shook their heads.

The risk of being apprehended with little warning proved persuasive. They closed the *Yellowstone*, taking only Vivian's gun, the extra rounds, and their musette bags. The terrain was hilly, which slowed their progress. Eerie fog and seeping mist heightened the sinister feel of the pressing forest, spooking their nerves.

After a half-hour's walk, they glimpsed dark silhouetted cottage roofs and barns in a clearing. "Lentzweiler," whispered Caterina.

"We could sneak into one of those barns to warm up. It may be hours before the army uses that road," Janie said.

Ruby circled her shoulders. "See what they think of that idea, Viv. Janie's right. It's the middle of the night. There won't be traffic until daylight. Besides, if we tried to stop a truck, they might mistake us for Germans and shoot us."

Ange directed them to a small barn on the outskirts of the village. She nodded fervently when Vivian asked if she was certain the family would be friendly if they were discovered. Not much point in escaping from the clutches of the Germans in Clervaux only to be turned over to them by a pro-Nazi farmer.

Snow-crusted evergreen trees towered over the barn, which nestled against the surrounding forest. Ruby lifted the simple wooden latch and pushed the door open. The creaking door magnified tenfold in the still winter night.

Vivian crept in first, with her pistol in hand. Faint light from the open door did little to relieve the darkness. Dark shapes with soft, huffing breath shifted on her left. Her nose confirmed what her other senses couldn't. This farmer owned at least a couple of cows.

As her eyes adjusted to the low light, Vivian turned slowly to each side. Three cows in stalls on the left. A few sacks of feed, pails, and tools to her right. A ladder leading to a hay loft straight ahead.

The others crowded in behind her. Ruby shut the door, and the barn was once again in complete blackness.

Janie clicked on their flashlight.

"Cows on the left, tools over here," Vivian whispered, watching the progress of Janie's sweep of the low light.

Janie flashed the light and illuminated piles of straw in the loft. It would be warmer up there. They had slept on straw in barns in France, albeit with their bedrolls.

Ruby had climbed two steps of the ladder, with Janie shining light on the rungs, when movement flashed above. Vivian grabbed Ruby's arm to stop her.

Vivian signaled with a quick bob of her head for Janie to train the light on the loft again. She moved her finger to the pistol's safety lever, ready to slide it in place.

Caterina handed a hoe and rake to her mother and sister, while she picked up an axe.

A soft, faint click sounded. A rifle moving from safe to fire mode. Vivian's stomach seized and tightened in a hard knot.

Should she say something? In what language? Her heart thudded in her chest like booming artillery, but Vivian's fingers held steady on the safety. "Who's there?"

A slight pause. "Aren't you supposed to say 'Knock, Knock' first? 'Who's there?' is our line, isn't it?"

Vivian lowered her pistol. Her quivering muscles slackened.

Knawk? Theah? No matter how proficient his English, no German could replicate a Boston accent like that.

"Let's start over. Knock, knock," Vivian said.

"Who's there?"

"American Red Cross Girls." Janie flashed the light across the loft.

Two GIs peered over the edge of the loft. "Red Cross? You got doughnuts and coffee?"

CHAPTER TWENTY-NINE

December 21, 1944
Herve, Belgium

"Approved leave or not, I doubt Mabs can leave Liège either. I'm sorry, Vivian, but it's a waste of time and fuel for you to go there, when I doubt you can get yourselves to Paris. She'll have to postpone her wedding until this is all over, and you can go then." Archie MacLeod took a clipboard from a clerk, scanned the document, and signed his name.

"What if I have a seat on a courier flight heading to Paris later today?"

Vivian and her friends had joined a card game with a group of airmen the previous evening. Assuming that excess consumption of brandy last night hadn't changed his plans, one of the pilots promised her a seat on a Sentinel carrying mail to Paris today. Once in Paris, it shouldn't be difficult for them to find a flight to London. Another practice against Red Cross regulations, yet often flouted by overseas personnel.

"I'm going to pretend I didn't hear that, Captain Lambert. And lest you've forgotten, you would need permission from both the Red

Cross and the army to take a seat on a military flight." MacLeod's eyes locked steadily with hers over the rim of his coffee mug.

"You could sign an authorization form," Vivian said.

MacLeod frowned. "I could, but as I'm sure you've guessed, I won't." He held up a hand to forestall her reply. "Those small planes and the pilots who fly them don't have the best safety record. If it were an emergency, that would be one thing. Seeing Jack Nielsen again is not an emergency, Vivian."

She bit back a petulant response. MacLeod had an unfortunate point. *The Sinker*, the newsletter for overseas Red Cross personnel, had reported the deaths of several women in plane crashes.

Vivian nodded and turned to leave.

"Vivian? When the war winds down, get in touch with me. We'll need people with leadership qualities and firsthand experience to work with the occupation forces." Major MacLeod passed her his business card, and Vivian slipped it in her coat pocket.

"Thanks, Archie." Vivian waved and showed herself out.

Vivian was exhausted from the rigors of their demanding work. But, unlike Mabs, Vivian couldn't see the appeal of returning to the States. Her options, once back home, would narrow. Remaining here afforded her the space and time to consider her path forward, with or without Jack. MacLeod's suggestion was worth keeping in mind.

She waited to cross a busy road. If only one of the army trucks roaring past could take her to Liège. Vivian was now less than a dozen miles from Mabs, but MacLeod was right. The army was far too busy fighting back the Germans to worry about transporting her anywhere for a pleasure jaunt. Gretchen had waved off her request yesterday, and there was little point asking her again.

Vivian had sent a telegram to Mabs yesterday:

> WAIT FOR ME IN LIEGE STOP
> TRYING TO ARRANGE TRANSPORT STOP
> BE WITH YOU SOON.

She shouldn't have sent it. Gretchen hadn't given her the slightest bit of hope. Vivian had pointlessly delayed Mabs, who might have enjoyed a night in Paris before catching a plane to London.

She could send another telegram and urge Mabs to go on without her.

No, Mabs would have left already. She might have waited for a while, but she wouldn't risk missing her own wedding.

***

Ruby poked her head in the bedroom door. "Janie and I are going out to the shops. See if we can find some things to spruce up the Christmas party for the fellas. Want to come?"

"Sure," said Vivian. Moping wasn't accomplishing anything positive.

They found a variety of festive holiday decorations for the Christmas party they had planned for the soldiers.

Vivian also bought boxes of Belgian chocolate, one for Daddy and each of her brothers. She hoped the one going to Danny in the Pacific wouldn't melt in the mail. And Bob. Her heart constricted. She hadn't heard from him since the Germans launched their attack last week. It was agony knowing he was undoubtedly caught up in this fierce fighting. For once, she watched the mail with more anxiety for a letter with her brother's signature cartoon illustrations adorning the envelope than for Jack's spiky scrawl.

Ruby and Janie went to a grocer, and Vivian wandered into a small shop with a display of lace goods in the front window. Mama would love the doilies or a tablecloth. Gosh, these were gorgeous. Vivian traced the delicate designs with a fingertip. She ought to buy one for herself too. No, a wedding gift. This was the perfect wedding gift for Mabs and Mel.

The veils draped over stands were exquisite. Vivian lifted the hem of one that caught her eye and admired the intricate handiwork.

"*Il serait beau regard sur vous. Voulez-vous essayer ceci sur?*"

Vivian flushed, shook her head, and let the veil fall from her hand. "*Non. Merci, mais non.*"

The seamstress smiled and pulled a few hairpins from her apron pocket. Her cool fingers gently pushed stray hair away from Vivian's face. She pulled the veil from the stand, attached it to a simple coronet hair comb, and pinned it in place. She stepped back, smiling, and waved Vivian toward a mirror. "*C'est absolument parfait pour vous.*"

She was right. Even paired with the Red Cross wool overcoat, everything about this veil was perfect for Vivian. Its fingertip length didn't overwhelm. Intricate flowers worked into the edges and hem were not the usual roses, but daisies, her favorite.

But Vivian wasn't getting married. Far from it.

"Ooh, la, la." Ruby stole behind her at the mirror and ran a finger down the length of the veil. "No wonder you've been all mopey. Did you and Jack have a secret plan to tie the knot this weekend?" Vivian had told Ruby and Janie about Jack, but she hadn't divulged many details.

"Golly, it's gorgeous, and it suits you to a T." Janie moved closer to the mirror.

"Wait until your fella sees you in that. His eyes will pop out of his head," Ruby said.

Vivian swallowed hard against a lump in her throat, and her chin quivered.

"Oh, honey, the war'll be over before much longer. You're worried about him, aren't you?" Ruby led Vivian to a nearby chair, knelt in front of her, and took her hand.

"His tour should be up by now. He's probably working in ops or something safe and easy. When did you last hear from him?" Janie pushed the veil behind Vivian's shoulders and fished around in her purse for a handkerchief.

Long pent-up tears streamed down her face. Vivian choked out the story bit by bit, relieved to finally share her misery with sympathetic ears.

Ruby squeezed her hand. "You'll see him at your friend's wedding. Or you'll see him in England when this is all done. I think deep down, you must think there's hope, or you wouldn't have let yourself think about this wedding as a chance to make up."

"I think you should write to him. Tell him what's in your heart." Janie unwrapped a chocolate truffle and handed it to her. "Here, chocolate makes everything better."

Vivian nibbled the chocolate and smiled gratefully at her friends. Neither of them had tried to absolve her when she told them about Jack's crewmates. They had simply listened. Maybe Janie was right.

She ought to write to Jack. If Mel had told him she would be there and she didn't turn up or offer an explanation, that wouldn't help. Her inability to leave Belgium provided her with an excuse to write to him after months of silence.

Vivian stood and beckoned the shop owner. "I'll let you help me remove this. I might have chocolate residue on my fingers."

The woman pushed the hairpins back into her pocket, and Vivian pointed to the two tablecloths she had selected earlier. "I would like to buy both of those. *Merci.*"

"And the veil?"

Vivian shook her head. "Not today."

They stopped in a coffee shop around the corner from their hotel. They had scarcely stepped inside when Ruby remembered a vase she wanted to buy for her mother. She asked them to order her usual café au lait and promised she would be right back.

When Ruby returned, she slipped her parcel into a bag with some of their other purchases. "I ran into one of those pilots we played cards with last night. The one with the Clark Gable mustache."

Janie raised an eyebrow. "Yes?"

Ruby lifted her coffee cup with a shaking hand. After taking a sip, she set it in the saucer and met Vivian's eyes. "Your pilot crashed. The one who offered you a ride in the jump seat. A takeoff crash."

Vivian's stomach twisted, and the blood drained from her face. If MacLeod hadn't chastised her and reminded her of the Red Cross women who had perished in plane crashes, Vivian might have been on that plane.

"Thank God you didn't go, but what changed your mind about that flight?" Ruby pushed another chocolate toward Vivian.

"MacLeod."

Her friends exchanged puzzled looks, and Vivian clarified. "Lieutenant Colonel Archie MacLeod. I knew him back in Chelveston, and I've run into him some over here. He's the one who found us a good viewing point for the parade in Paris, remember? I thought he might be able to help me get to Liège to travel with Mabs. I mentioned I could take a seat on a courier flight, and he reminded me those small planes and inexperienced courier pilots can be dangerous. Obviously, he had a good point." Her eyes sparkled with tears, and she bit her lip.

Janie stood, gave Vivian a tight squeeze around the shoulders, and gathered their purchases. "We ought to get back."

They had all become numb to death. If Vivian hadn't considered going on that flight, Ruby might not have mentioned her conversation at all. That pilot, a nice enough fellow, would have been just another casualty, another number to the ever-growing tally of senseless losses.

They entered the front door of their hotel, laden with packages, and found their entire group assembled in the lobby. Were they moving out again already?

Gretchen stepped forward, her face pale and somber. "I'm afraid we've had bad news while you ladies were out. A buzz bomb hit the hotel where some of our personnel lodged in Liège. The hotel collapsed. One of our girls was killed. Two others sustained severe injuries and are being treated now."

"Oh my God," Janie whispered.

"Liège?" Vivian's heart bounced and constricted in her chest.

Ruby hooked her arm in Vivian's. "Do you know the name of our girl who was killed?" she asked Gretchen.

Vivian knew before Gretchen took a step toward her. Where had all the air gone? Was everyone else having trouble taking in air?

"Mabel Kirk. From Kenosha, Wisconsin."

Vivian's knees buckled. Gretchen wobbled and faded in and out before her. Someone pulled Vivian to a divan in the hotel lobby. Janie sat next to her and pulled her into a tight embrace. Vivian's teeth chattered, and someone fetched a blanket. Ruby settled it around her shoulders.

Mabs. It couldn't be.

None of them were supposed to die. They operated in a combat war zone, and no matter what precautions they took, dangers were unavoidable. The Red Cross had recruited women with indomitable spirit. They were here to do a job, safety be damned. She, Ruby, and Janie had been lucky to escape capture or death days ago. Yet none of the folks back home likely imagined women serving with the American Red Cross might be war casualties.

A heavy weight compressed around Vivian's chest, and she fought to gulp in air.

"Are you sure?" Her throat was so dry. She swallowed and tried again. "Mabs might have already been on her way to Paris. Or maybe she's in London. That's where she's supposed to be now." That must be it. Mabs had already left, and when they couldn't find her, they presumed she was dead.

Gretchen knelt in front of her, took Vivian's trembling hands in hers, and shook her head. "It happened much earlier this morning."

Earlier this morning. She had waited. Mabs had waited on Vivian, and now she was dead. If Vivian hadn't sent that pointless telegram, Mabs would be in Paris or London, getting married as planned this weekend.

"I'm sorry, Vivian. They notified all of the group captains via telegram about an hour ago. Her funeral will be at the American cemetery on Saturday."

Saturday. Her wedding day. Had anyone called Mel yet?

"Do you know if anyone has notified her fiancé?" Vivian's voice sounded thin and raspy. "That's why she was going to London. They're to be … were to be … married on Saturday morning in London."

"I believe the Red Cross will notify her parents first. As she wasn't married, they are her next of kin," Gretchen said.

Mel needed to know. He needed to stay in Chelveston, surrounded by his friends. "Can I call him? I can't let him stand there in London waiting." She choked on the last words. Hot tears fell fast and furious.

Gretchen stood. "Yes, when you feel up to it, I'll take you to command headquarters. We can place a call to England from there."

Vivian made to stand, but Ruby gently pushed her back. "Rest here for a bit. Be sure you're ready. There's no rush."

"There is." Vivian shrugged out from under Janie's arm and stood. "I need to catch him while he's on base in Chelveston. He shouldn't have to hear this news on his own in London."

Ruby and Janie walked with Vivian, their arms linked with hers.

Gretchen gave the details to the secretary at the front desk. Ruby found someone to bring Vivian a glass of water while they waited. Her hands shook. Janie steadied the glass for her.

Once she established a connection, the woman motioned for

Vivian to take the phone. She took the receiver with a shaking hand. No one ever tells you how hard it is to break someone's heart, to deliver news this devastating. "Hello, I need to speak to Lieutenant Melvin Simmons. He's in ops. Yes, I'll hold the line."

A few minutes passed. Vivian crossed her fingers they wouldn't lose the crackling connection. The man came back to the line and reported Lieutenant Simmons had left for the train station.

Who did she still know on base? Jack. If he wasn't flying a mission or out at a pub, he wouldn't be anywhere near the phone at headquarters. The call was expensive, and the connection might be lost. Not to mention she couldn't, just couldn't, speak to Jack. Not right now. She would lose her tenuous hold on control for sure. "Is Vicar Chapman or Doc Burke near to hand?"

"Oh, yes, m'am. I saw Chappie a moment ago. Hang on."

A minute or so passed, and Vivian swiped at tears. The receiver clattered as Joe picked it up. "Vicar Joe Chapman here."

Vivian took a deep, gulping breath. "Chappie, this is Vivian Lambert. I … yes good to hear your voice too. I have some very …" Her voice broke, she squeezed Janie's hand, and took a deep, steadying breath. "I have very bad news, and I need your help." Hearing Chappie's kind voice twisted her insides in despair. But crying her heart out wouldn't do any good, not when time was crucial. Someone had to catch Mel in Wellingborough and keep him from boarding that train.

She pinched her forehead to stave off more tears. "I hoped I would reach Mel before he left for London. Mabs was killed in a buzz bomb attack in Liège earlier today. Please, Joe." A strangled suffocating sob burst from her, and she looked at the ceiling, fighting to regain control. "Joe, can you go and try to catch him before he boards?"

There was a pause, and an audible catch in Joe's voice when he answered. "I'm so frightfully sorry to hear that. I'll go straight away. Is there somewhere Mel can reach you?"

"I'm in Herve." She spelled it for him. "It's in Belgium."

Their hotel was a short distance from headquarters, and Gretchen persuaded Vivian to return there to rest. "They'll send someone to get you if a call comes through today."

Someone knocked on her door a couple of hours later.

"We're coming with you." Ruby pulled her coat off an armchair.

They hurried inside headquarters a few minutes later, and Vivian took the outstretched receiver with a shaking hand. "Hello?"

They both cried. She told Mel everything Gretchen had passed on. Vivian couldn't admit she had sent a telegram that might well have kept Mabs in Liège longer. She would talk to him about it. Not now. She couldn't bear to think about it.

"Her funeral will be here, at the American Cemetery at Henri-Chapelle," Vivian said.

"When?"

It seemed akin to stabbing a knife straight into his heart when she whispered, "Saturday. Our group captain says I'll be permitted to go. I'll do whatever I can, anything you'd like or think she would have wanted."

He promised to let her know if he thought of anything in particular, all the while insisting he would be at the funeral. Vivian didn't argue. Mel wouldn't be allowed to travel to Belgium, not with the Germans assaulting the Allied lines across the entire front. The world was in disarray. And so much worse off without Mabs and her kind-hearted spirit.

CHAPTER THIRTY

April 15, 1945
Mission to bomb munitions depot at Oranienburg, northwest of Berlin

Jack stared at the dark blue water of the Channel. Could he have set his ship down in those churning, white capped waves with a steady hand?

He wouldn't be doing it this direction, not on this mission. The French coastline was in sight, but no longer swarming with enemy fighters or flak batteries now that France was under Allied control. The Luftwaffe hadn't given up the fight, but the American bomber formation would fly much farther without interference.

"Co-pilot to waist: Oxygen check."

No response.

Hank nudged Jack's knee and motioned to the radio dial. Jack grinned, turned the radio frequency to music, and cranked the volume for a few seconds.

Curses emanated from every crew station at the loud blast of music in their headsets. Jack switched it off.

"Let's try again. Copilot to waist: Oxygen check."

"Waist to Copilot: Check, goddammit."

"Look lively and quit dozing back there then." Hank made tick marks in the log-book.

Hank did his job, but he hadn't assimilated into the tight circle of Jack's crew. Vivian was the elephant in the room. Jack hadn't removed her photos from the wall over his bunk or the framed photo on the bedside table.

Vivian hadn't written back. She must have moved on. Jack had a small spark of hope at Christmas. Simmons hinted Jack ought to come with him to London for his wedding. Jack secured a pass, daring to hope Vivian might have asked that he be invited.

She had called Simmons with the devastating news about Mabs. Jack watched the mail after that, but if Vivian needed comfort and solace, she must have found it with someone else. She might be engaged or married to another man by now. Someone like Hank Davenport. Someone with real prospects.

Jack couldn't bear to think about a future that didn't include Vivian. Emptiness loomed whenever he thought about what came next, despite the good news he received last week. A letter stashed in his trunk back at base fulfilled the dream he had chased since childhood.

> ...pleased to offer you a position as first officer pilot. Please provide details relating to your return to the States and expected date of discharge from the US Army Air Forces.
>
> Yours truly,
> E.V. Rickenbacker,
> President,
> Eastern Airlines

His bet had paid off. Eastern knew Jack had never finished his degree and still offered him a chance to keep flying. He could live in Charlotte or Miami. What would Vivian have thought? They had danced around discussions about what their life might hold after the war, both uncertain how her desire to run for office might mesh with his plans to be a commercial pilot. Maybe it took winning his dream for him to recognize the truth. Spending the rest of his life with Vivian meant more to him than anything else. That employment offer letter in his trunk wasn't his ticket to a happy future.

Hank's routine oxygen check shook Jack out of his reverie. The task at hand was to bomb Oranienberg and get his crew safely back to base.

"Navigator to crew: Estimate arrival at IP in thirty minutes."

Jack flew today as deputy lead on the right wing of *Texas Two-Step*, Bowie's ship. Bowie, Major Coates as of last week, was Squadron Commander for today's mission. Jack didn't begrudge Bowie his well-deserved and overdue promotion. Jack had worn the golden oak cluster insignia of a major for three months. But Bowie hadn't flown lead before, and today they were flying in a new formation. Bowie was a strong pilot, but he hadn't had much opportunity to be the leader. Jack and his men all knew Bowie's jokester manner belied his skill and knowledge, but would the other pilots in the squadron—especially the new ones—follow his lead?

The fighters—like a swarm of wasps—careened into the bomber stream.

They were in the thick of it, with the familiar call out of positions, evasive maneuvers, blasts from his gunners, and a ping-ping of shells around and against the ship.

"Navigator to crew: IP ahead."

Fighters peeled off, with the predictably intense flak taking over the defense function. Their ship rocked in the constant buffeting from the jarring blasts of exploding shells, rolling through the turbulent air like a dog sled gliding up and down hills.

Bowie must be over the target by now. Why weren't the bombs dropping?

"Pilot to bombardier: What's the holdup?"

"Bombardier to pilot: No visibility. Can't see a damn thing."

Texas Two-Step made a 360 degree turn to the right. They would go over again.

Jack held tight to his position, repeating the mantra "straight and level" in his head. No jinking, no matter how great the temptation.

His men expressed no enthusiasm about going around for another shot.

"Pilot to crew: Cut the damn chatter."

The intercom went silent.

Chaos was the only word to describe the scene playing out the cockpit window. The 384th had gone through earlier and released their bombs. Smoke streams from their drops mixed with the flak bursting all around. Squadrons and entire groups turned in all directions, some attempting to rejoin the bomber stream for another run, others headed for the rally point.

Flak assaulted them from all sides. With each successive attempt to run over the target, flak grew more intense, more accurate, more deadly. They were positioned near the end of the bomber stream. German gunners below had perfected their aim. Sweat dripped down Jack's neck. Overpowering gunpowder fumes permeated through his oxygen mask.

"Bombardier to cockpit: Looks like Bowie's bombardier can't get a fix on the aiming point again."

Dammit. They would have to pin the bombs and take them back. Or find another target of opportunity on the way home. They had risked their lives for no good reason.

Texas Two-Step did another turn as though to go again. Bowie broke radio silence: "Clouds are thinning. We'll make another run."

A third run? Fliers were superstitious by nature. They all had their talismans and their rituals. One of the biggest taboos was three on a match, but a third anything was considered straight-up bad luck. Superstition aside, a third run to the target objectively put men and machines in grave peril.

A loud and profane uproar broke out over the radio. Some pilots declared they were headed to the rally point.

Bowie was in command, and Jack's duty was to follow his orders. But wasn't his higher duty to protect his crew and his ship, even if he had to question his friend's call?

Jack toggled his switch to transmit to the squadron pilots. "Grubby Y here. A third run will run us low on fuel and subject us all to flak that's getting more accurate with every pass."

"Grubby M here. My bombardier is confident he can get a fix this time. We came to bomb this munitions depot today, and that's what we'll do." Bowie's voice held a harsh note. He had registered the babble of objections as a slur on his judgment, rather than an appeal to reconsider, and was overcompensating.

Jack's finger paused over the call button. Bowie needed an out, a way to save face. He pressed the button. "Grubby Y here. No one in ops would question a decision to turn back with cloud cover this heavy."

The war was all but won. It wasn't worth the risk to crews and planes to complete this particular mission at this stage in the war.

Bowie didn't respond but lined up his ship to go over the target again.

Jack's ship rattled harder than ever amidst the swirling, wispy black puffs of flak. Deadly shards of metal pinged against the thin skin of their ship like hail pellets pelting a tin roof.

Jack's hand hovered over the yoke. He would be disobeying a direct order if he turned for the rally point, and it was small comfort he would be far from alone in facing questions in debriefing.

Go by the plan, do our job, and stick together. Those were the words Jack had drilled into his crew from day one. It's what had gotten them through fifty-eight missions. Doing the job meant dropping the bombs on the target.

They would go. Bowie had made a call, and Jack trusted his judgment. His fellas trusted Bowie too. Would they trust him enough to take what they all knew was a perilous run? Jack had tuned his radio into the command frequency to communicate with Bowie and the other pilots, so he hadn't heard the intercom chatter of his men for several minutes. He flipped his radio back to intercom and gritted his teeth, bracing for a storm of criticism.

"No, his bombardier is right. Clouds are thinning. We can do it," Gib was saying.

That's all Jack needed to hear. He lined up behind Bowie for the bomb run. Ford and Stan reported three of their ships had taken off for the rally point, but the others were behind Jack, ready to make another go.

It happened so fast. If he had blinked, he might have missed it.

A burst of flak exploded directly in Bowie's path, a dead-to-right hit to the inboard engines. Smoking, *Texas Two-Step* fell through the clouds.

Jack's heart banged in his chest like the shrapnel shards exploding around their ship.

God, no.

He blinked, leaned forward in his seat, and stared intently through the swirling clouds. Too dense. He couldn't see what had become of *Texas Two-Step* and more importantly, whether any chutes blossomed out of her.

Their intercom was as silent as it had ever been.

Jack swallowed, only aware of the tears on his cheeks when he tasted salt. "Anyone see any chutes?" His voice cracked.

No one spoke for a beat or two. Finally Chaz's voice crackled through. "Fell too fast out of sight, Chief. Just … disappeared."

After another pause, Ira spoke. "What now, Chief? Are we going on?"

Jack's hand tightened around the yoke. The intercom went quiet again. His fellas were in shock. Or waiting for his decision.

Indecision increased the odds of buying the farm. Shell-shocked by Bowie's fall or not, his primary objective had to be the safety of his men and those crews now under his leadership. They were in the thick of the flak field, effectively committed to another bomb run. He could execute a sharp right turn and head to the rally point, but they would fly through heavy flak regardless.

"Matchsticks in a box, Chief," Lou said.

Jack's lungs sat heavy in his chest. He pressed his fingers to his chest and sucked in shallow breaths.

He pulled back on the yoke and pushed up on the throttles to accelerate.

He was the one tasked with making the decision, but Lou's repetition of Jack's signature takeoff reminder to his crew drove home the point. Jack had used the phrase to signify they were each equally important inside the ship, that each man had a job to do, that there should be no weight given to rank in the fury of aerial combat. What he hadn't fully appreciated until now was that he too was a mere matchstick in the box. They would pull together as a team and do their job.

"We'll continue with our mission objective. Gib, you're lead bombardier so get your sight lined up. I'll turn AFCE on when you're ready."

"Bombardier to pilot: Roger."

Jack navigated the flak field, while Hank monitored instruments and called out for a quick routine oxygen check.

Bowie and his men might have gotten out before centrifugal force trapped them inside a dying bomber. But if they had, they floated down in the heart of Berlin. A quicker and more merciful death if they perished with their ship.

Jack clenched his jaw and tried to banish images of Bowie and his crew, set upon by an angry mob of pitchfork-yielding German civilians. Hacked to pieces. Hung. Beheaded. Shot. They had seen it all in the German press clippings. German civilians were in no mood to take *terror fliegers* prisoner these days. Jack's heart juddered, and he tightened his grip on the yoke.

He blinked, and something red flashed out the cockpit windshield. A split second later, a sharp blast shook the ship.

Torque fell fast. The instrument panel confirmed the right inboard engine was out, but no evidence of an engine fire. Hank feathered the prop.

Vivian's Victory continued to nose down, dragged by the weight of her bomb load.

They needed to level off. Jack pulled with all his might on the yoke, which yielded an anemic response. He pulled harder, and she leveled off reluctantly.

"Pilot to engineer: Investigate elevator control cables and report back."

Hank took over the exertion of keeping the ship level and straight.

"Bombardier to cockpit: We're close to the AP. Can you turn on AFCE?"

"Pilot to bombardier: No good until elevators can hold up."

"Pilot to tail: Report on elevators?"

"Waist to pilot: Walt here, Chief. Stan and Lou are helping Ira try to wire the elevator cables back together. About half of them were knocked out."

Wire them together? Would that work?

Jack took the yoke back from Hank. Moments later, his rigid grip released perceptibly in response to whatever the men had done with those cables.

"Bombardier to pilot: AP looms ahead. I need the AFCE, dammit."

"Pilot to crew: How are we doing with those cables?"

"Radio to pilot: Walt's helping now too."

Another perceptible release in tension.

"Pilot to crew: I'm seeing some control return. Keep it up."

"Hurry, AP is coming up fast," Gib called.

"Pilot to crew: You heard Gib. Can you speed it up?"

"Engineer to pilot: Any difference?"

His tense hold on the yoke slackened another notch. Then another level. Not perfect, but the elevators were much more responsive. Good enough for this bomb run.

Jack turned on the AFCE at once and instructed Gib to take control for the bomb run.

"Pilot to bombardier: Got visibility?"

He stopped short of ordering Gib to release the bombs, even if he couldn't get an accurate fix on the target. Jack wouldn't want to risk bombing innocent civilians.

"Navigator to pilot: Clouds thinned. We've got it."

They swooped over three waves of flak turbulence in quick succession.

Gib didn't take evasive action. *Good. Hold steady. Hold steady. Hold steady.*

"Bombardier to pilot: Locked in. Twenty seconds."

Sweat dripped from under Jack's flack helmet.

Gib's voice sounded over the intercom with a terse: "Bombs away!" The bombs release light flashed red on the instrument panel, and the ship lifted at the nose as the bombs rained down. Gib closed the bomb bay doors.

Jack took over from the AFCE and turned them toward the rally point, exhaling. They had done what they came to do.

Whatever wiring and splicing his men had done helped, but *Vivian's Victory* couldn't lead the squadron formation home. She could make it home, Jack was confident about that. He had enough control from the elevators now, but with one engine out, they would be slower and lower than the others.

They would escape the flak soon. They would face a short engagement with Luftwaffe fighters before flying home over Allied-controlled territory.

The 305th's ships circled at the rally point, waiting for them. Jack squinted at tail numbers and nose art, and his heart sank. No *Texas Two-Step*. Jack's gut clenched. He said a silent prayer for Bowie and his crew mates.

The planes moved into formation and tightened up.

Mustang fighter escorts moved in protectively around the bomber formation, which proceeded on a southwesterly course from the rally point. Jack hoped at least one of them would hang back to help him and any others who couldn't keep pace with the formation.

"Engineer to crew: Bandits coming in. Twelve o'clock low and three o'clock high."

"Hey! What was that?" Lou shouted.

"Shot right through our little friends! Was that one of those blow jobs?" Ford called.

Blindingly fast, the Me-262 jets, nicknamed "blow job" by Allied airmen, were a relative newcomer in the skies over Europe. Scuttlebutt suggested the Germans didn't have too many of them, but they were out today. Jack's men spotted several more in a short space of time.

"There's more of 'em whizzing around. Wait, where the fuck did they go?"

"Waist to crew: Anyone got those blow jobs in sight? I don't see them anymore."

Unnerving to know they lurked, biding their time before exploding out of nowhere, cannons firing in close.

"Hey! Oh fuck no!" shouted Stan from the tail.

The smell hit him first. A sharp tang of smoldering metal filled his nostrils. The screams of his crew, fighting a raging fire somewhere in the belly, sounded tinny in his ears.

He and Hank fought a battle at the controls. *Vivian's Victory* had rolled right to left right after the impact tore into them, peeled over on her back, curled tight, and performed at least four complete revolutions like a diver doing a series of flips off a high board. Jack's focus narrowed to correcting her out of the spin. She continued to descend sharply even after his spin recovery pulled her out of the somersaulting action.

Jack fought hard to level the ship. She wanted to keep diving. He trimmed up and pulled back on the throttle.

She was now level, more or less. Flying precariously, but flying.

Control panel indicated they had two functioning engines. Jack swiped at sweat dripping into his goggles. How much time did they have?

Did the intercom work? He tried. "Pilot to navigator: Can you respond?"

"Here, Chief. Gib and I slammed around in here, but we're all right."

"Good. Where are we? We need headings east and west to Allied territory."

"Aye-aye, Chief."

"Bombardier to pilot: Not east. Let's not take a chance with the Reds."

Everything being equal, Jack would rather turn east and land behind Soviet lines. They would be taking a chance by continuing on the current course. If they undershot and bailed out over German-held territory, God help them all.

While Chaz calculated and Jack adjusted to get maximum power without overtaxing the remaining engines, Hank took status reports from the rest of the crew. They had put out the fire on the left side of the fuselage. Her tail was almost sheared off. Stan was gravely injured, and Tink was doing what he could for him. No medics at thirty thousand feet. Jack took successive shallow breaths, trying to force air into his taut chest.

Ford climbed out of the ball right after they came out of the spin. Hard to believe the ball turret hadn't been blasted away or jammed from the fire or the spin. Walt and Lou sustained burn injuries, and Ira and Ford were assisting them.

Jack heard all of this in a light buzz as he and Hank worked to trim and tease out whatever power she had left. Noisy blasts of frigid air tore through the cockpit from a hole in the left window. The blindfold cockpit checks from training now proved useful; the control panel had shattered in places.

"Navigator to pilot: That spin took us off-course: 205 miles east to Debno over the Oder River. 141 miles to reach Bielefeld: that's in American hands."

Turning east presented the most challenges. They would have to fly through the same flak batteries they had escaped and couldn't afford to take any chances with further damage. One more shot would finish her off instantaneously with no time for bailout.

"Chaz, I want the heading to Bielefeld. Engineer, do you copy?"

"Engineer to pilot: Copy."

"We gotta chuck out everything again, like we did after Schweinfurt. Leave the radio set for now. Everything else goes!"

"Will do, Chief. Engineer to crew: You heard Chief, toss everything out. I'm coming through."

Chaz relayed the heading for a course to Bielefeld.

"Pilot to navigator: Copy. Monitor course. May not make it that far."

They might not. *Vivian's Victory* was fighting valiantly, but this was her last battle. He needed a bailout plan for his crew. Jack's heart galloped, pounding hard through his constricted chest.

"Pilot to crew: I'll give the bail-out order when it's clear she won't go any farther. Inspect your chutes now. Tink and Ira will help Stan. You'll both bail out right after he does. Is Stan conscious? Can he pull the ripcord?"

"Radio to pilot: Yes, we think Stan can pull it."

Jack, Hank, and Chaz visually sighted landmarks on their maps while *Vivian's Victory* struggled onward. Staying aloft was a challenge, but Jack was hell-bent on getting as much distance as he could. His guys were not going down into a mob of angry civilians. Gib assisted Ira and the others in unbolting and tossing out all guns and equipment.

"Is that Brunswick?" Hank pointed straight out the windshield. A good-size town was visible through the cracks and mucky residue smattered all over the glass.

"Navigator to cockpit: Correct. Between us and the RAF, it's been bombed to rubble, and it's not in Allied hands yet. We would be most unwelcome."

The ship lost altitude more sharply than before. They would not make Bielefeld. His stomach swooped in sync with his ship. This was it.

"Cockpit to navigator: Do your maps or notes show the current front lines?"

"Navigator to cockpit: Negative. I have a general idea. What did you have in mind?"

"We've got less than twenty miles."

"Navigator to cockpit: Hildesheim might be all right."

Hank pointed to west of Hildesheim on his map. Cleared land where a crashing bomber would do little damage. Forests nearby to hide them until they connected with Allied troops.

Just north of Hildesheim, Jack could no longer ignore what his instruments said or the feel of his ship. They were losing altitude much faster now. Time for them to go.

Heart hammering, Jack pulled three sharp rings on the warning alarm bell to signal for bailout. "Bail out! Stan goes first, Tink and Ira follow."

Jack poured his racing energy into the exertion needed to keep the ship level. His men needed a stable platform to make their jumps safely.

His hand shook uncontrollably as he pulled one long ring on the alarm bell to signal for his crew to start their jumps. A searing shudder ran down his spine. *God help them. Please let this be far enough over the front lines.*

"Go see everyone's getting out, and call it out to me as they leave," Jack told Hank.

Hank stood, grabbed his chute from under his seat, and left the cockpit.

In that slight pause, with most of his crew preparing to leave, the guns all chucked out, and the landing gear down as a signal the aircraft was being abandoned, a lone German fighter whizzed by and fired off several rounds straight into the cockpit. A blistering flash of hot air crackled behind Jack's neck. The copilot's windshield and right window shattered and shards of glass sprayed in every direction.

Blinding pain shot up Jack's right arm. He couldn't feel the yoke and instinctively grabbed it with his left hand. The ship dipped. Jack gritted his teeth against the burning pain in his upper arm and awkwardly tugged hard on the yoke with his left hand. He should call Hank back.

His headset sputtered with Hank's voice. "Stan's out, and his chute popped. Tink hit the silk."

Jack swallowed against bile filling his mouth. He hoped the fighter who had tossed a few rounds at him wouldn't shoot his men as they floated toward earth.

He looked down twice to reassure himself his hand was still there. Jack had no sensation in his fingers, hand, or wrist, and sharp burning pain reverberated through his upper arm. He was useless now. He would never become a commercial pilot, not with this level of injury to his hand. Sweat leaked down his face, seeping in under his goggles and blurring his vision.

Seconds later, Hank reported both Ira and Lou had jumped, chutes open. Another few seconds. Walt and Ford were out, chutes functioning. Jack's heart thrust somewhere near his throat. Chaz and Gib had jumped. He didn't know which shook more, his good hand or the vibrating yoke.

The instruments faded on and off, some of them frozen in odd positions from the explosive impact of the bullets that cracked so much of the glass. The door between the cockpit and the bomb bay banged open and closed repeatedly, an eerie echo clanging through the empty shell of their beloved ship.

Almost empty. Hank reappeared in the cockpit. "What the holy hell happened in here?"

"Damn Fucke-Wolfe threw a few rounds at us. Good thing you got up when you did."

"You've been hit. Why the fuck didn't you call me back?" Hank squeezed in and grabbed his yoke. "My control. Can you get your chute and shoes with your other hand?"

Jack shook his head. "I'm gonna stick with the ship. Should be able to do a controlled crash landing in one of those fields ahead."

"The hell you are. Get your chute."

"Bail out, Davenport, and that's an order." Blood thundered in his ears. Jack used his left hand to rip off his green rubber oxygen mask. No idea why he still wore it; they had been under ten thousand feet for some time. He gulped lungfuls of air into his tight chest.

No, even if he was desperate to live, he couldn't jump. Not even at the current low altitude.

"We all know you're terrified of heights, but you gotta jump, Nielsen. That engine fails, you'll go down in a fiery ball."

They knew? He had taken pains to hide it.

"Swore I wouldn't leave until you jumped. You're surprised? You haven't fooled any of us. Especially those guys. Hell, they've been flying with you for over two years. 'Course they realized."

"I gave you an order, Davenport. Get the hell out." They lost more altitude in a lunging dip. "Look, you've gotta go. We can't keep her high enough for bailing much longer. Go!"

Hank grabbed Jack's shoulder roughly.

Jack yelped in pain.

Hank released him. "Shit, sorry. Hey, it's not just for the guys. Vivian would rip me limb from limb if I didn't make sure you got out of this plane. Get up, get your damn chute, and let's go!"

"Vivian won't care what happens to me." Jack let go of the yoke and reached across to the trim wheel by the throttle quadrant. He moved the wheel down, trying to correct the gradual descent until he convinced Davenport to bail out.

"She still cares, trust me."

"According to your sister?"

"Yes, from her." He paused. "Then, there's the letter Vivian wrote you at Christmas."

Jack cut his eyes away from the instruments to look at Hank. He frowned. "I haven't gotten any letters from Vivian. Not one."

"I swiped it, all right? I wrote to her right after that. Hoped if she didn't hear back from you, she'd give me a chance."

"She wrote once and gave up? Doesn't mean anything." Jack ignored the voice in his head reminding him he had been too proud to write a second time to her. "And her not wanting you doesn't mean it's got anything to do with me."

"Nice theory, but she flat out said she was still in love with you. Said you broke off with her, that she'd deserved it, but she still planned to find you after the war and see if you could work it out."

Jack's grip on the yoke slackened. His heart quivered with a spark of hope and thudded against his Adam's apple.

"Long as I'm doing a deathbed confession here, gotta tell you I never mailed that letter you wrote to her last fall. Remember? I picked it up off your table, told you I was going to the post. I was so fucking resentful I had been assigned to your crew. You. Of all the pilots and all the bomb groups? To be assigned to *your* crew? So I chucked it."

Hank pointed at the altimeter, which seemed to be functioning. Three thousand feet and descending. "Time's running out. Point is, she loves you, and you need to get yourself out of this ship for her sake. I've seen you mooning over her pictures. You still love her too."

Jack patted his jacket where her picture was buried deep in the inner lining. No sensation when he tried to put his right glove near Ace's tag in his pocket. He gulped. He wouldn't fly again.

Hank stood. "Get up, buddy. Time to go."

Jack was too dazed by these revelations to argue. He allowed Hank to maneuver him to his feet in the tight space, his right arm useless and pulsing with pain.

Hank reached around Jack's waist to set the autopilot. Jack stepped behind his seat to the narrow walkway leading to the front escape hatch. Hank retrieved Jack's chute from under the left seat, tossed aside the flak vest Jack had wrapped around it, and clipped it to Jack's harness. He put his chute on and prodded Jack toward the hatch.

Oh, God, Ace's dog tag. It would fall out of his pocket on the jump. He stretched his left hand awkwardly toward his pocket, but it was no use. He couldn't remove his left glove without his right hand, and he couldn't retrieve it from his pocket with the heavy glove on.

"We gotta go!" Hank yelled.

Jack dug in his heels, gulping for air. "His dog tag." He gestured to his pocket, realized his right hand might not be moving to signal anything to Hank, and jabbed toward his right pocket with his left hand. "Get it out. Please, help me get it out of my pocket."

"Your dog tag's around your neck. We've got to go!"

Jack shook his head side to side, tears slipping down his cheeks. He fought for the air to force out the words. "Not mine. Ace. Best friend. Right pocket."

Hank dug into Jack's pocket and pulled out the tag. "This?"

Jack nodded vigorously. He looked down so Hank could loop it around his neck.

The ship vibrated and took a swooping dip in altitude.

Hank lurched and skidded backwards against the jump seat. The dog tag clattered to the floor and rolled out of sight as the ship swerved yet again.

"I'll find it, I promise! You go!" Hank yelled above the yowl of wind coming in through the open escape hatch.

"No! No, no, no." Ace's dog tag wasn't worth Hank's life.

"No more time! Out!" Hank pushed him closer to the hatch.

Jack froze. His stomach lurched and dropped to his ankles, and his heart thrumped in his throat like a staccato fusillade of artillery. He swayed and gripped a handle on the hatch door with his good hand. "Go ahead," he yelled.

Hank shook his head violently. "You gotta jump!" he screamed in Jack's ear.

Waves of dizziness roiled him. Jack's legs were as numb as his injured hand. No. No way. There was absolutely no way he could jump out into the clouds.

Hank pried at Jack's fingers, locked around the hatch handle in a death grip. "Damn it, let go!" He pulled hard on Jack's waist, and they stumbled back to the narrow catwalk of the bomb bay.

Before Jack could clamp his hand around the handle again, Hank put the chute rip cord into Jack's uninjured hand and closed his fingers around it. Then he shoved hard with both hands in the middle of Jack's back.

Jack was out, free-falling in the icy slipstream, tumbling end over end. Out of control, exactly as he had always dreaded in his imagination.

The ground rushed toward him. *Slow down, slow down, slow down!*

The ring. The ripcord D-ring. Hank had put it in his hand. Jack jerked his hand downward.

The parachute burst out of the chest pack and opened above him with a resounding crack. His body jerked upward.

A loud, sustained bang sounded behind him. Jack turned his head, horrified to see his trusty, much-loved ship exploding in midair, engulfed in fiery flames. The engine had kicked off after all, like Hank warned.

Hank.

Had he gotten out? Had he cleared? Had he understood that Jack wouldn't want him to risk his life for that dog tag?

CHAPTER THIRTY-ONE

April 15, 1945
Hildesheim, Germany

Vivian set the tongs down. They needed to mix more doughnut batter, but for now, she was due a break from cooking duty. She would hand out ciggies, matches, and gum.

The last thing any of these men needed was doughnuts, cigarettes, or gum. But the Clubmobile crews had nothing else to offer. Janie had left to scour nearby facilities for ingredients to make a large vat of soup. Their Clubmobile group had arrived two days before, prepared to serve less than a hundred liberated POWs. Crowds swelled with each passing hour, and several thousand men were now crowded into this former Luftwaffe airfield north of Hildesheim.

Ruby waved Vivian over. "Most of them are British, and they prefer tea if we have it. I've heated water, but I need more tea bags. Can you see if you can find any? I know, I know. I don't know where."

Vivian put the tray of gum and cigarettes back in the Clubmobile and set out in search of the field director, who might be able to help locate more tea bags.

She pulled her poncho hood over her head and picked her way through the muddy field to the largest hangar, which served as the principal staging area for their supplies. Transport planes would fly these men out soon, but in the meantime, they needed water, food, medical care, and basic needs such as toothbrushes and razors.

"Hey, Red Cross, what are you off in search of?" A group of enlisted guys with the Medical Corps sat on wooden crates piled near the hangar, enjoying a smoke break.

Vivian strode to them and leaned against a wall to escape the rain. "Tea bags for our British friends. Any idea if I'd find them in there?" She pointed toward the supply hangar.

"That's where I'd look. But tea?" The man shook his head. "Give me a good strong cup of joe any day. Tea. Warm beer. No Cokes. We've got one up on those Brits."

"Well, I expect they might say the same about us," Vivian said.

"At least the Krauts have decent beer."

Vivian waved and moved toward the entrance to the supply hangar.

One of them called, "Say, did you see that B-17 blow up earlier?"

She turned. "Is that what it was? I heard a big explosion and saw something on fire in the sky."

"Yep. Poor guys. Hope some of them made it out. War's ending, and our guys are still dying. Why don't the damn Krauts give up?"

Vivian stared off in the direction where she had seen the doomed plane cascading down in burning fragments. Was Jack still flying? No. His second tour would be finished by now. Surely someone would have written to her if anything had happened to him. He might be back in the States, might have a new girl or even a wife. It had been nearly a year since he broke off with her. A year was a long time in the ETO.

Field Director Matisse located several cartons of tea, each containing hundreds of tea bags. He also gave her a large box full of razors, soap bars, toothbrushes, and toothpaste. She could restock each of the Clubmobiles after she delivered the tea bags to Ruby.

Emaciated, haggard British soldiers queued patiently while Vivian and Ruby set out cups and saucers, filling each one with steaming water and a tea bag. Vivian helped until the lines diminished enough for Ruby to handle it. After restocking each of the six Clubmobiles with the hygiene products Matisse sent over, Vivian sat on a bench sheltered with a canvas canopy. She unscrewed her canteen top and gulped water.

She was bone tired. They served last night until after ten o'clock and had woken before dawn to start the doughnut machines. She couldn't remember not being exhausted. They had all worked hard in England, but there had been regular leaves. Over here, leave time was harder to come by and complicated by the logistics of finding a secure location not too far afield from their base. Taking leave would also have rekindled memories of happier times with Jack. And after December, after her plans to go to London with Mabs and see Jack had ended in tragedy, Vivian hadn't bothered to take time off.

Ruby plopped down beside her. "We need more milk. Janie said you got tea bags from the supply hangar. Did you see milk?"

Vivian shook her head. "No refrigeration, but I can go check in the kitchen."

"Could you? That'd be swell."

Vivian pulled the raincoat hood tighter around her face. Rain came down in sheets now. Miserable weather to be working out in the field.

She stepped inside the building that housed the kitchen facilities and stamped her wet, muddy boots by the door.

"Hey, doll, whereabouts in Georgia did you say you're from?"

Vivian turned. One of the young doctors in the Medical Corps of the Twelfth Field Hospital shrugged into a rain poncho.

"Albany. Down in the southern part. Why?"

"One of the nurses said she thought that's what you had told her. We have an injured airman at the hospital. Says he's from Albany. About your age too. You might know him."

"What's his name?" Most of the hometown boys had signed up, but air crews tended to be mostly younger men, men closer in age to her brothers.

The lieutenant frowned. "Damn. Forgot his name. He's stable enough if you want to look in on him. A friendly Georgia face might be a welcome sight for this guy. Barely made it out of that B-17 that exploded near here earlier."

She was wet and supposed to be locating more milk. Her stomach churned at the idea of entering a field hospital. No way to avoid the smell and sight of blood. If she pinched her nose, perhaps she could stand it long enough to offer the man a little conversation.

Vivian hurried to keep up with the young doctor. The hospital consisted of a series of tents, and the last thing she needed was to find herself in one of the surgical tents.

"He's in that one over there. One of the nurses can show you. Suffered burns from the explosion, a broken arm from the landing."

Vivian stood outside the indicated tent and inhaled deep breaths of damp air. She could do this. She didn't need to stay long. She would say hello, establish who they might both know, wish him well, and be back to the kitchen in no time.

She flipped open the canvas flap and stepped inside. Vivian pressed her lips together, determined to keep herself from getting too strong a whiff of blood and wounds.

A nurse bent over a cot near the entrance looked up. "You're the one from Georgia?"

Vivian nodded, grateful she didn't have to explain why she was here.

"Follow me. Glad Doctor Nix found you already. We know you gals are busy too."

Vivian trailed behind the nurse. She averted her eyes and breathed in as little as possible. The nurse stopped at a cot several rows from the rear. Vivian stood back, the nurse blocking her view of the cot.

"Are you comfortable, sir? Warm enough?" He murmured something Vivian didn't catch. "One of the Red Cross Girls working nearby is here to see you. She's also from Albany. We thought it'd be nice for you to see a familiar face from back home." She turned to Vivian. "What was your name?"

"Vivian. Vivian Lambert." Oh, dear Lord, the smell was so overpowering.

"Viv?"

Vivian's eyes widened, and she peered around the nurse. Parts of him were heavily bandaged for burn wounds and his face was scraped up, but it was Hank. Tears sprang to her eyes.

"You two know each other? How lovely." She smiled at Vivian, moved a stool, and set it by Hank's cot. "Have a seat. You look a little pale."

"Vivian doesn't do well with blood." Hank's voice was hoarse and raspy, but his mouth turned up in a smile.

"I'm all right," Vivian whispered.

The nurse raised her eyebrows and fished a packet of saltine crackers out of her pocket. "These should help if you're feeling nauseous."

Vivian tore open the packet and pulled out a cracker. She nibbled on a corner. "Zanna said you transferred to active duty, but she didn't say you were in England. You didn't say anything either when you wrote me."

"I was a little vague on the details on purpose."

"Oh?" She took another nibble of cracker, savoring the salty taste in her mouth.

"I've been based at Chelveston, Vivian."

Something fluttered in her stomach. "Chelveston?"

"That's not all. I ... I've been copiloting for Nielsen's crew since I got there. And—"

"Jack's crew?" Vivian's heart tripped over her stomach. "The B-17 that exploded, the one you escaped from—are you saying that was Jack's ship?" The pilot was always the last one to leave. If Hank was burned from the explosion ...

Hank grabbed her hand. Vivian's eyes blurred, and her breath came in searing gasps. No. No, no, no. Not at the end of a second tour.

"He got out, Vivian! I pushed him myself. Saw his chute pop open. He should have been well clear of it before it blew to pieces." Hank's fingers laced tightly with hers. "He should be somewhere near here. Can't have landed too far off from where I did, and they found me right after I came down."

"You pushed him?"

Hank nodded, his lips crinkling up. "He would have never jumped otherwise. Chaz, Gib, all of them made me swear I'd push him if I had to. Jack's scared of heights. You didn't know?"

"I knew that. I never thought about what that would mean for him if his plane was in distress." It made sense. He had said it himself. As long as he felt in control in the cockpit, the height didn't trouble him.

But, in the case of bailing out or … or ditching. His crew ditching in the Channel—that's why he'd been so angry, so uncharacteristically furious. He had been terrified by the prospect of ditching or bailing out, and learning his men experienced his worst nightmare sent him over the edge. Wait. Did Hank say Chaz? And Gib?

"Chaz and Gib? Jack said his crew ditched last summer. Said if I hadn't interfered, he would have been flying that day. I think he thought if he'd been flying, they wouldn't have had to ditch, that they would've made it."

Hank's eyebrows knitted together. "Well, yeah, they did ditch last summer. Got their Goldfish Club membership and all. That was before I got to England. They got picked up by the LST guys pretty fast from what I heard. You thought they died?"

Had Jack ever said they died? Or had she jumped to that conclusion? A wave of dizziness left her lightheaded. Her muscles turned to jelly. "I've been blaming myself all this time. I should … I should go and try to find Jack." Vivian stood, but Hank didn't release her hand.

"There's more," he said.

She reluctantly eased back to the stool and tried to quell her rising impatience to look for Jack.

"You need to hear it from me."

Vivian waited for him to go on. Jack had gotten married. Or had a baby on the way. Or both.

"I told Jack, while I tried to talk him into jumping." Hank took a deep breath, wincing with the inhale, and closed his eyes.

Vivian released his hand and stood. "I'll go find a nurse for you."

His eyes popped open. "No," he whispered. "No, Vivian, I need to tell you." His voice was raspier than ever.

She nodded and sat.

"Jack wrote you a letter last fall, after he got back from the flak house. I told him I'd put it in the post with my mail. But I chucked it in the trash." He gulped and plunged on. "That letter you wrote him after Christmas, after your friend died? I swiped it. Figured if you didn't hear back from him, you might reconsider me. I should have told him months ago. When you wrote back to me, I could tell. You still loved him, you said so. But even if he wasn't an option, you weren't going to be looking at me. I knew the truth then, but I couldn't tell him. Or you. I'm so sorry, Viv."

Her heart pulsed with a crescendo of escalating flutters. Flutters and flips. Jack was alive. He was here, and he loved her. Hank didn't have to say it.

She should be furious with Hank. All these months where she and Jack might have been happy, though separated. She wouldn't have had to carry all this guilt about his crewmates. Yet, instead of anger, all she felt was surging optimism.

"I'm gonna go find Jack. I need to find him. I need to find him now." A sense of desperate urgency flooded through her. "I'll look in on you later, I promise." Vivian bent forward, kissed his cheek, and released his hand.

"Wait, one last thing." He reached his hand to his neck and tugged on his dog tag chain. "Pull it off for me, will you?"

Vivian frowned. Why would he want to give her his dog tag?

He raised his head off the pillow, wincing.

There were two chains looped together. She circled them both over his head and held them out to him.

Hank poked a finger at one with blackened edges. "Give that to Nielsen, all right?"

Vivian peered at it. Franklin Ralph Patterson. Ace's dog tag. A tingling zip of adrenaline surged in her chest. "I will."

She laid the other dog tag on his chest and kissed the top of his head.

Clutching Ace's dog tag, Vivian searched the cots, still not breathing deeply, and made her way to the tent's entrance. Where would he be? How would she find him? She stopped the nurse who had connected her with Hank earlier. "One of my friend's crewmates parachuted down before he did. Is there a roster of patients brought to this hospital?"

"The clearing station will have records of any soldier they've treated."

"Can you tell me how to get there?"

"I'm headed there now." Doctor Nix opened the tent flap and signaled for Vivian to proceed ahead of him. "You're looking for a crewmate of your friend, you say?"

"Yes. Hank said he left the ship first, so he should have landed near here. You don't think he could have ended up in German hands, do you?" What if he'd landed in a field, unnoticed by the Allies?

"If he didn't have severe injuries, he might have been treated at the clearing station. Since he's Air Corps, he would be waiting for transport back to England if he's mobile. Your first stop ought to be the clearing station."

Vivian's eyes roved over men clustered near the clearing station tent. Doctor Nix raised his eyebrows, and Vivian shook her head. He held the tent flap open for her, and she was poised to step inside when a man called, "Hiya, Red Cross."

Vivian was inured to the usual greeting, but a familiar drawling note in the man's voice prompted her to turn her head.

"Bowie?" Vivian's heart jumped.

He looked up, grinned, and pushed awkwardly to his feet. "Well, if this don't beat all. Didn't figure I knew a single soul in Germany."

Bowie hugged her and motioned for the men seated around him to stand. "Let me introduce you to my crew. Fellas, this lovely lady is Vivian Lambert. She was a Red Cross Girl at base long before y'all got there."

Maybe Bowie had seen Jack. She cut in over his introductions. "Bowie, I'm sorry, but have you seen Jack? You must have bailed out near where he did, right?"

"Jack? His ship went down?" Bowie's eyes clouded and his smile faded.

Vivian bobbed her head. "I saw Hank in the field hospital. He pushed Jack out himself, so he made it out. I was going in here to check—"

"I'll come with you." Bowie gestured for her to go ahead.

While they waited for the intake sergeant to be free, Bowie filled her in on what happened up to the point when *Texas Two-Step* took a hit. "Got her corrected out of that dive before it was too late. Flew west as fast as she could go, trying to make it to Allied territory. We landed here with no brakes, skidded off the runway into the grass, ground-looped, and nearly ran into some damn trees. It was quite a ride. And boy, we were sure relieved to see the US Army jeep headed our way after we came out. Wasn't too sure we landed over the front lines."

Vivian twisted her hands, only half listening to Bowie's story. Her stomach knotted, and she was of half a mind to barrel past the intake sergeant and resume her search.

The sergeant waved them forward. "Serial number and name," he intoned, his pen poised over a roster.

"Oh, I don't need admittance," Bowie said. "We're looking for a buddy who parachuted out near here. Hoping you could tell us if he's been checked through here."

Vivian had finished spelling—"N-i-e-l-s-e-n"—when she heard someone call her name.

He called again before she saw him. Seated on a gurney off to the side.

"Gib!" She hurried toward him. "Are you all right? Do you know about the others?"

"A few bruises, nothing too serious," he said.

Vivian hugged him. She still clutched his arms and had opened her mouth to ask about the others when a cultured Boston accent sounded behind her.

"Fancy meeting you here."

Vivian turned and threw her arms around Chaz, probably upsetting his New England reserve. "Oh, Chaz!"

Gib cast an appraising eye over Bowie. "Jesus, Bowie, last time we saw you, you were doing a funeral glide."

Chaz pulled Bowie into a loose hug and clapped him on the back. "We were all sure you had gone west." Airman slang for an aviator killed in combat.

Bowie stepped out of Chaz's hug. He couldn't resist the quip. "Well, I *had* gone west. Literally."

Chaz rolled his eyes. "Always with the jokes."

Vivian could stand it no longer. Her insides were hollowed out. She shook from head to toe. "Where are the others?"

"Lou and Walt got burns earlier, so they're about to move them to the field hospital. That's where Hank is, we're told," Chaz said.

"Tink and Ira were with Stan, but we're not sure where they've gone," Gib said.

"Only one more of us to account for. And speak of the devil."

Chaz put his hands on Vivian's shoulders and rotated her to face the other direction.

He wore no cap, and his fair hair glinted in the light filtering through the canvas tent. His blue eyes locked on her face and widened. He stopped midstep, frozen in place.

"Jack." It came out as a half whisper, half strangled cry. Her heart vaulted into her throat, and a sizzle of energy zipped through her.

Jack must have lost his shoes in the jump. He was wearing only his heated socks on his feet. The right sleeve of his bomber jacket was ripped, and his right arm hung limp at his side. What had happened to it, to him?

"Go on," Chaz whispered.

Jack's lips tugged up, hesitancy giving way to his trademark full-on grin.

Vivian ran to meet him, her arms outstretched, the cry of his name ripping from her throat. She stood on tiptoe and wrapped her arms around his neck. Her senses jolted fully to life.

"I'm not hurting you, am I?" she murmured into his ear. Only his left arm circled around her waist.

Jack shook his head and buried his face in her hair. Warmth spread rapidly, a tingle in her scalp goosing straight down her spine to her toes.

She tightened her hold around his neck and brought her mouth to his. His lips, familiar and soft, moved against hers, and Vivian's pounding heart leapt and soared.

Vivian pulled back and moved her hands to cup his face. Her right hand was still closed fast around Ace's dog tag.

"I have something for you," she whispered.

Holding her palm up and out toward him, Vivian unfurled her fingers to reveal the dog tag.

His fingers trembled as he lifted it from her hand and rubbed his thumb over the well-worn engraved name. He swallowed, and his Adam's apple bobbed in his throat.

Vivian ran her fingertips, light and feathery, along his jawline.

She expected him to ask how she had come by the dog tag. But when he spoke, in a voice thick and strangled with emotion, he asked, "Is he all right? Is Hank okay?"

"He will be."

Jack heaved a deep breath and exhaled.

Vivian lifted the chain from his hand. "Can I put it around your neck for safekeeping?"

He closed his eyes, nodded, and lowered his head.

She looped it around his neck and adjusted the chain, smiling at him.

A beam of sunlight splashed across their faces, filtering in through a gap in the overhead canvas. "I love you. I never stopped loving you," she whispered.

"I know. And I love you too."

"What do you mean you know? A little cocky, aren't you?" Vivian pushed playfully against his chest.

"How do I know?" He planted several small quick kisses on her lips. "Because, sweetheart, you've now got some of my blood on you, and you haven't noticed."

He might have been right, but Vivian was too busy kissing him to worry about it. Jack only stopped kissing her long enough to call out to Bowie.

Bowie waved him off. "I'll give you the story over a pint when we're back."

Jack and Vivian laughed and clung to each other as his gathering crewmates clapped and wolf-whistled, with medics, nurses, and other patients joining in.

CHAPTER THIRTY-TWO

May 15, 1945
Wiesbaden, Germany

Vivian hurried across Wilhelmstrasse, empty of all but milling groups of American military personnel. Only civilians staffing hotels and restaurants could avoid the strict six o'clock curfew, so she was spared the plaintive faces of hungry children lining the city streets. Vivian pulled open the heavy front door and stepped inside the ornate Art Nouveau lobby of the Hotel Rose.

She bypassed several groups of USAAF officers, though she waved and called out greetings to some of the men. Clusters of men congregated near the hotel elevators, so Vivian veered off to take the central staircase to the third floor.

Sheer luck that Jack had snagged a room here. Wiesbaden would be the European headquarters for the USAAF during the occupation, and all undamaged hotels were bursting at the seams with Americans. Much of Wiesbaden's central spa district had suffered bombing damage. Vivian had squelched her curiosity about whether it had been one of Jack's mission targets. He had done his job and didn't need an extra helping of guilt now that they could see the tangible effects. Last night at dinner, an officer at an adjacent table cleared up the question with an offhand reference to the RAF bombing raid in February.

They were here to visit some of Jack's friends from the 305th who were setting up base for post-war photo-mapping missions. Jack and Vivian would fly from here to England for their wedding.

If they weren't marrying and returning home, Vivian might have been tempted to stay. The Red Cross had a base of operations in Wiesbaden to provide recreation for the large number of expected occupation troops. Workers had hurried to convert the Kurhaus, a former opulent spa, into a club. The Red Cross's Eagle Club, opening in days, would include two ballrooms, several lounges, a concert hall, a restaurant and separate snack bar, conservatory and gardens, and various recreational venues.

She would find something worthwhile to do once they were home. Jack needed to go home and nab one of the commercial jobs. Surgery and extensive therapy in the weeks after his final mission repaired the nerve damage in his arm. He continued with strengthening and flexibility exercises several times a day, but a USAAF flight surgeon in Hildesheim declared him fit for flying duty. Fortunately, that pronouncement came after the German surrender. No more combat missions.

Vivian pushed the door open, stepped inside, and clicked it closed behind her.

Jack turned from the window and smiled. "Was wondering if I ought to get dressed to walk over to the Kurhaus and check on you." He wore a white undershirt and field pants.

She glanced past him out the window. Orange-red and surrounded by pink hues, the sun hung right at the horizon. It was later than she realized.

"I'm sorry, honey. I meant to only spend a few hours helping them set up the snack bar. But the gals talked me into taking kayaks out on the lake behind the new club. It's lovely back there, and we lost track of time." Vivian removed her jacket and hung it in the armoire.

Set in an expansive green space, the serene lake behind the Kurhaus provided a peaceful respite from the blight of widespread property destruction and hungry civilians in the war-torn city. Weeping willow trees overhung the banks. Vivian wouldn't have guessed so many of her favorite spring flowers from home would bloom in this climate, but flowering magnolias interspersed with a profusion of pink-hued rhododendrons and azaleas.

Jack tossed a letter on the writing desk.

She crossed the room and stood on tiptoe to kiss him. "Who was that from?"

He shrugged. "No one important."

She traced her fingertip around his lips. "What did you do this afternoon?"

"Mmmm." He locked his hands around her waist and tugged her against him. "Caught up with some of my buddies over at the new base. Had a few beers. Good air strips and nice setup for them. They're building new barracks and even some apartment housing. Sounds like the army will start letting fellas bring their wives and kids over by early next year."

Vivian nodded. "I heard that too. Our troops will be here for years."

"The troops *and* the Red Cross." Jack cocked his head, raised his eyebrows, and widened his eyes. "Archie MacLeod tracked me down at the base."

Vivian swallowed. "Oh?"

"Were you going to tell me?"

Vivian lifted her shoulders. "I already told him I can't accept it."

MacLeod's fianceé Sara Mercer was Director of Services for the American Red Cross in Europe. Archie and Sara had waited for Vivian when she arrived at the Kurhaus after lunch. Sara offered Vivian a promotion, a chance to oversee Red Cross service clubs for the entire western portion of the American sector of occupied Germany. A position with that much prestige would be hard to come by back home.

"Why not?" Jack's eyes locked in on hers.

"We're getting married, remember?" Vivian looked away. "Did I tell you I had a note from Chappie? He read the banns for us for the first time this past Sunday."

Jack's tightened his grip around her waist and brought his face closer to hers. "Marrying me shouldn't be the end of everything you want for yourself."

"Of course not, but I can find another job back home. Especially now that we know you'll be able to fly again, there's no reason to prolong our time here. You should be talking to the—" Vivian eyes, averted from looking directly at Jack, caught sight of the letterhead on the letter he had tossed to the side earlier. "Is that from Eastern Airlines?"

She pulled free of his embrace, picked up the letter, and read it. "Jack, this is such good news! Why hadn't you told me? And we wouldn't have to live in New York."

"I hadn't told you because I wasn't sure I'd be fit to fly again. I'm still not taking it." Jack pulled it from her hand and set it back on the desk.

"Of course you're going to take it. That's what you've been dreaming about since you were a boy. Are you holding out for another airline?"

He grasped both her hands and leaned in close. "Viv, let's stay here. Take this job with the Red Cross, and I can keep flying for the 305th. That photo-mapping work they'll do is important and will keep me busy."

Vivian opened her mouth to protest.

Jack laid a gentle finger over her lips. "No, listen, the letter says for me to let them know when I'm discharged from the service. I'll do that. That job will still be there for me, but this work you're gonna do won't wait."

She shook her head and looked down.

Jack released one of her hands so he could tip her chin up. His eyes blazed with a fierce love and determination. "Vivian, let's do this for you now, and I'll chase my dreams when we're ready to go home."

Vivian's vision blurred, and her heart jounced and swelled in her chest. *When we're ready to go home*. His words signaled they would make the decision together. His ambitions and plans wouldn't take precedence by default. Warmth rushed through her.

She choked out a half laugh. "Keeping me overseas for more time isn't gonna earn you any points with my mama. She's really gonna resent you now, Jack Nielsen."

He pulled her toward him. "We'll see about a stateside leave after the wedding. Can't have my mother-in-law on the warpath so early in our marriage."

Marriage. A thrill of excitement prickled at the back of her neck and swooshed in her stomach. After years of fending off boyfriends who wanted more than she did and her mother's escalating pressure, Vivian was shocked to find herself the quintessential giddy bride.

She wrapped her arms around his neck. The scent of his Burma-Shave soap lingered at his neck. Vivian leaned in and trailed featherlight kisses across his throat, up the side of his neck, and around his earlobe.

"Mmmm," he murmured, his breath warm against the side of her face. He pressed his soft lips to her cheek and tugged her closer. "You didn't answer. Will we stay here?"

Vivian's throat was so dry she wasn't sure she could speak. "But Jack ... Eastern—"

"Will still be waiting." Jack tightened his hold on her, and she fixed her eyes on the light almost-invisible dusting of freckles flecked across his nose. "You do want the job, don't you? Gives you a chance to hobnob with the kind of folks who could help you get into office."

"What if Eastern doesn't wait?" Would he resent her? Regret he hadn't asserted a male prerogative and put his own interests first?

Jack brushed a strand of her hair from her forehead with a gentle stroke of his fingertips. "There are other airlines."

Her lips parted, and he put a finger over the round oh of her mouth. "Shhh. If nothing else, honey, I stay in the military to keep flying."

The military. The military that stood at the ready to defend American interests at home and abroad. The military that would inevitably be drawn into another dangerous conflict. "Jack, I can't face another war. I can't risk losing you again."

He licked and rolled his lips, leaving an alluring sheen of moisture. "I know." Jack kissed her. "No more wars, I promise. I'd get out before it came to that."

She shifted her stance from one foot to the other and bit her lip. "You would? Even if you couldn't fly with one of the airlines?"

"I promise." Jack's lips quirked up on one side. "Was too hard on you. On us. I won't put you through that again." He leaned nearer, his breath so close to her mouth that Vivian could almost taste spicy, grassy hops. "All I want you worrying about is rubbing elbows with the kind of bigwigs who can help you get where you want down the road. So someday people will refer to me as Senator Nielsen's husband." His words as much as his low, throaty laugh sent shivers goosing across her shoulders and down her spine.

Senator Nielsen's husband. Vivian's breath quickened, and her pulse throbbed, fevered and frantic and frenzied. Her nerve endings tingled and pricked.

She sealed her mouth over his, consuming, moist, and greedy. An escalating surge of raw, hungry lust coursed through her chest, her loins. She threaded her fingers into his thick hair and pressed her body against his.

Jack stumbled back against the wall and tightened his arms around her. "Yowzah, Viv."

His eyes were wide and bright, his pupils dilated. Sweat beaded on his upper lip and at his temples. He panted from the primal fervor of her devouring kisses.

"What, you didn't think women have urges too?" She lifted on her toes and tilted her pelvis to crush against his groin. Vivian moaned, exhilarated to feel evidence of his desire, stiff and hard against her.

He tugged her shirt from her skirt and rucked the skirt and slip up to her waist. "Kablooey, that's all. Went from talking about jobs to this in no time flat."

"You want me to slow down?" Vivian unfastened her garters.

His voice, pitched low and husky and infused with a tinge of amusement, growled in her ear. "Oh, hell no, I don't want you to slow down." Jack cupped her bum in his hands.

Her fingers moved to the front of his fly and fumbled with the buttons. "Five damn buttons? Forget sex, isn't this a hassle when you need to pee?"

His chest vibrated with laughter, and his fingers closed over hers, deftly undoing them one by one.

She roughly pushed his pants and undershorts off his slender waist and down. He twisted and lifted his legs one by one to step out of them.

Jack groaned when she pulled his undershirt up his chest and urged his arms up so she could pull it over his head.

"Oh, God, I didn't hurt your arm, did I?"

He flung the shirt to the floor and pulled her tight against him once again. "Glad I can fly again, but I'm happier that I've got feeling back in my hand for this." He slid both hands under her blouse and cupped her breasts, swirling his thumbs over her bra cups.

Vivian groaned. "Hurry, Jack." She breathed, hot and fast and urgent, against his neck.

He pulled free of her embrace. "Got to get a rubber out of my bag. Hold there."

Jack returned seconds later and set a tin on the desk beside them. He unhooked her bra, then moved his fingers to the front of her blouse, unbuttoning from the bottom up. He made a low noise of frustration when he reached the collar. "You gotta start removing this damn pin when you walk in." He struggled with the fastening swivel.

Laughing, Vivian pushed his fingers away, released the bar, yanked the pin out, and tossed it to the desk. It clattered and slid to rest in front of his crush cap.

Jack pushed her blouse over each shoulder and arm in turn. Her shirt and bra pooled on the floor with his clothing. She pushed her skirt, slip, and panties to the floor.

He embraced her tight against his body once more. "Want you inside me," she murmured against his mouth. "Want you inside me and how."

Jack's hand pressed against her wet cleft. "You want to try this standing up?"

Vivian backed them toward the desk. She raised up on her toes, sat on the edge of the desk, and scooted back. "We Red Cross Girls are resourceful."

He hooked his fingers under her buttocks and pulled her closer to the edge.

Vivian planted her palms facedown on the desk and spread her thighs open. "Assertive. Not afraid to ask for what we want."

Jack exhaled and licked his lips, his eyes blazing with heat. He opened the tin, pulled out a condom, and rolled it on his penis. He then gripped the sides of her thighs and pushed inside her. "Demanding."

She moved to take him deeper inside her. "Confident."

Jack moaned and began to move. She hooked her feet over his shoulders.

Vivian wiggled forward, scooched her hands farther back, and tilted her chest, taking his shaft deeper. "And adventurous."

"Unpredictable." He shifted his angle.

Laughter bubbled up. "Innovative."

His eyes held fast with hers, and his lips twitched. "Unconventional."

"Deeper, Jack." She tilted her hips, aching for him to fill her.

He grasped her arms and pushed her into a supine position. She hooked her knees around either side of his waist and rubbed her stocking-clad feet down the backs of his thighs. "God, Vivian." He began to move faster, penetrating deeper.

He had her arms pinioned to the desk, but she brushed her fingers restlessly against the sides of his hips. Vivian pressed her feet flat against the backs of his thighs for leverage and arched her pelvis to meet his thrusts.

Jack panted, and his hip and thigh muscles tautened and shook and strained. Moments later, he choked out a cry, and Vivian felt his release inside her.

Her inner thighs quivered, and the muscles in her fingers clenched convulsively. Vivian rocked her pelvis and dug her heels against the back of his legs. "Don't stop, don't stop, don't stop."

Waves of mounting intensity built one upon the other. They rolled and gathered more speed, more depth, more power, before at last cresting.

Her muscles continued to convulse in concentric circles, widening and calming as the thunderous roar of blood pounding in her ears slackened and subsided. Her breathing regularized, and she opened her eyes.

Jack's face bent closer, his eyes alight. "I like these Red Cross Girl attributes. Innovative, assertive … what were the others?"

She compressed her lips to hide her smile. "Resilient," she whispered in her ear.

"Mmm. A useful quality."

Vivian kissed him. "And flexible."

"Can't disagree there." His raspy stubble scraped against her cheek as he trailed butterfly kisses down her neck.

She tightened her arms around him, looked into his eyes, and smirked. "And inexhaustible."

CHAPTER THIRTY-THREE

June 2, 1945
St. Mary's Church, Yelden, England

"Where on earth did your friend find this in Germany?" Janie picked up the pink Permalift bra Zanna had sent to Vivian as a wedding gift.

Zanna's antics that fall day years ago sprang to life in her mind's eye. Zanna must have remembered it too. The day Vivian met Jack.

"She owns one that's similar, but I know her size is far different than mine, so it can't be hers." Vivian took the pink bra from Janie, turned away from the others, and swapped it out for the one she wore.

"She must have had someone back home buy it. Or perhaps she bought it off some soldier who had it for his girl," Ruby suggested.

Knowing Zanna, the latter was more likely. She had trained with the Red Cross in January and arrived in Germany in February. By that point, Allied forces had extinguished the German counteroffensive and were on the march to Berlin. They hadn't seen one another. Zanna was attached to a Clubmobile group following Patton's Third Army much farther south from where Vivian had worked.

"I expect you'll be able to ask her yourself next month, right?" Dottie rummaged through Vivian's toiletry bag and pulled out three tubes of lipstick and a powder compact. Dottie, now working club service in London, got leave to come be part of the wedding. Their old crewmate Jean was still on the continent.

Vivian nodded. "We plan to stop off in Stuttgart to see her if we can."

"Where is that in relation to Wiesbaden?" Ruby handed Vivian the garter edged with blue ribbon. "Here's your something blue."

Vivian slid the garter over her ankle and up her thigh. She clipped her usual garters to the tops of her stockings and straightened. "Stuttgart's about two hundred kilometers south of Wiesbaden. They're both in the American zone, so we should be able to see her."

"If your new job, not to mention your new husband, don't keep you too busy," Janie teased.

Vivian opened the three tubes of lipstick and held them up one by one for opinions. "You're one to talk about being very important and busy."

Janie would be overseeing the gradual closure of the Red Cross clubs in Ireland. Ruby had accepted a position with Rainbow Corner in London, which was expected to remain open for several more years.

"And now the dress." Ruby held the dress for Vivian to step in. Dottie did up the buttons in the back.

Ruby tilted the standing mirror so Vivian could see the full effect.

Vivian took a deep breath. She moved toward the mirror, smiling at her reflection. The pink bra didn't show.

Vivian had assumed she would have to marry in her uniform. After she wrote her parents to tell them she and Jack would be married here, Mama sent a green-and-white striped peplum suit. Her years in the ETO had left her thinner than Mama realized. A village seamstress had made the necessary tucks and adjustments. The striped suit would be her going-away dress when they left for their honeymoon this afternoon.

She had an actual wedding dress, despite the ration and material shortages. Jack had given her the silk parachute he had used to escape his ship as material for her dress. The seamstress had created a gorgeous mix of the designer dresses from magazine clippings Vivian had saved in her trunk. A sweetheart neckline and ruched bodice fell to a point at the tucked waistline, and the skirt fell to the floor in a straight, smooth line. Long, fitted sleeves ended at a point at her wrist. The dress qualified as old since the parachute itself was made years ago.

She had planned to borrow a simple veil that had been worn by both Mrs. Tillman's daughters. Then Ruby turned up two days ago, bearing the very veil Vivian had tried on in Herve. "I went back that same day while you and Janie had coffee, remember? I knew you'd need it eventually."

The veil was every bit as beautiful as it had been in the shop in Belgium—more so when paired with her stunning, simple dress. She ran her finger over the delicate embroidered edge, Schiffli lace, according to the seamstress.

Vivian swallowed past a lump in her throat. She had learned about Mabs after her shopping trip.

"The veil is gorgeous and adds the right elegant touch with your dress. It's perfect. Mabs would approve." Janie lifted the veil off Vivian's shoulders and turned her pearl necklace so the clasp was once again hidden at the nape of her neck.

"I think of her when I see it." Vivian's chin trembled.

"Of course you do. She's here with you in spirit, and she'd be excited and happy for you and Jack," Dottie said.

Ruby dabbed a handkerchief at the corners of Vivian's eyes. She gripped her by the shoulders and smiled. "Mabs wouldn't want you to cry, especially not today."

Vivian bobbed her head and fought for composure.

"Your dress is old, veil is new, and the garter is blue. What did you borrow?" Dottie asked.

"Chappie lent her this comb for her veil. His wife wore it on their wedding day." Janie adjusted the pearl and crystals comb securing Vivian's veil. "Said he'd give it to Vivian, only he's saving it to give to his niece one day."

"It's beautiful. As are you. That's a lucky chap you've got." Mrs. Tillman stepped inside the room and handed her a bouquet. A simple nosegay with roses and peonies from local gardens, shades ranging from the palest translucent pink to a vibrant fuchsia. Some local women had made several similar arrangements of flowers for the tables at the reception, which would be held in the Chequers pub.

"Don't want to keep him waiting any longer. I expect we ought to walk to the church if you're ready," Mrs. Sanders said.

Vivian nodded at them in the mirror. Ruby and Janie each took one end of Vivian's dress to keep it from dragging in the dirt. They wore their best civilian suits, Ruby's soft dove-gray complementing Janie's periwinkle-blue and Dottie's pale-pink dresses. No actual bridesmaid dresses to buy or borrow, but the women conceded it was better than Vivian having her wedding attendants in Red Cross uniforms. The men would all be in uniform, but the women were overjoyed to have an occasion to wear pretty dresses. They carried smaller bouquets of pink roses.

They stepped through the cottage door, and Vivian glimpsed a familiar figure waiting by the gate.

Mel turned and smiled. "Nielsen is sure a lucky fella."

"I thought you had already left," Vivian said.

When she reached him, he took her hand. "I was finishing an assignment in London when I got word there was a wedding in the works, so I delayed a bit. Mabs would have wanted me to be here."

Tears pooled in her eyes, and Mel shook his head. "No, don't cry, Vivian. She would be over the moon for you and Jack, after all you've been through."

He pulled a handkerchief out of his coat pocket and passed it to her. She swiped at the moisture under her eyes. "I know she'd be happy. It's … Oh, Mel, I hadn't had the courage to tell you, and I should have."

Mel took her elbow and steered her a short distance away from the others. "What's all this about?" His eyes were soft and concerned.

"I sent a telegram to her in Liège, on the afternoon before she might have left. I told her to wait for me, that I was trying to find a way to get there. It's all my fault. She would have been in Paris, maybe London—"

"No. Vivian, no, listen to me." Mel put a finger under her chin, forcing her to meet his eyes. "I sent her a telegram earlier that same day. I thought travel was too dangerous. I knew she'd try to take a flight, and Glenn Miller had disappeared. All I could imagine was her going down over the Channel like he must have done. So I told her to stay put where she was, that we'd reschedule everything."

"But …"

"I know it was my telegram, not yours, that kept her there. Yours was still sealed in the envelope. She never opened it, Vivian. She stayed because I asked her to. I thought I was keeping her safe, and instead I lost her."

"I miss her so much," Vivian whispered. Her heart ached for Mel.

Mel's jaw tightened, and he hitched a deep breath. "She'd want you to be happy. You know she would."

He kissed her cheek. "I'm gonna go on ahead of you so I can get a seat before the bride appears."

Vivian expelled a deep breath. She hadn't realized until the press of guilt eased how much it had burdened her for months.

It was a short walk to the church from the Tillman cottage. Vivian was grateful the weather had been dry the past few days. There would be no need to traverse through the mud, that slimy gunk so ubiquitous to her service experience. They had been favored with a picture-perfect, sunny morning.

They passed under the gate's wrought-iron arch into the churchyard, and Vivian's heart jumped in her chest. Jack waited for her inside.

"Let's take a picture of you in your wedding dress by the church door, for your parents." Ruby arranged her dress and posed her for the best lighting and stepped off to the side so Janie could take a few pictures.

Mama had sent a letter full of love and good wishes with the peplum suit. If she was miserable her only daughter was being married overseas without her, she didn't let on. There would be a reception in Albany when Vivian and Jack came home for a brief stateside leave before taking their posts in Wiesbaden.

They would have a second reception in Jackson for Jack's family and friends. Phoebe had married last summer and given birth to a baby boy named Russell last month. Rose had gone to work in a town called Oak Ridge not long after she graduated from high school. Her letters didn't reveal much of what she was doing, but Jack had gleaned it was some sort of largescale government project.

Mrs. Sanders stepped ahead to hold open the heavy wooden door into the church. Ruby, Janie, and Dottie lifted Vivian's skirt away from the ground again. She passed through the door into the old Norman church, no longer marred with blackout curtains draped over its beautiful stained glass windows.

Commander Mustoe would be waiting to escort her down the aisle.

Bowie, Chaz, and Gib would stand with Jack, while the rest of his crew took seats in the front row. A compromise. Jack hadn't offered any opinions on much of the wedding plans. About a week ago, he made an offhand remark that suggested he expected his entire original crew would stand up with him. He was dead set on it. They argued for two days. She smiled, shaking her head at the mental image of what Chappie would have said to the sight of ten men arrayed together to the right of the altar. Three attendants each already pressed English norms.

The man waiting near the door turned expectantly. He wasn't Commander Mustoe.

"Bob!" Vivian stepped toward her brother, her arms outstretched.

He grinned but held up his hand. "No, no, no. I can't mess you all up by grabbing hold and hugging you. Not when you're looking so stunning." He leaned in and kissed her check.

Vivian handed her bouquet to Dottie and hugged him tight despite his protests. "Oh, Bob, I can't believe you made it. Why didn't you tell me?"

He never had shown up in front of her Clubmobile on the continent. Bob's unit suffered heavy losses during the Battle of the Bulge, and he had earned a long stay and lighter duty near Paris. She wrote to him right after VE Day to tell him they had set the wedding for the first Saturday in June, never dreaming he could find a way to England.

"Your fella got me a seat on a B-17 coming back over here yesterday. Wanted to surprise you. And, hey, don't cry." He pulled out a handkerchief and dabbed at her face.

Vivian looked down the aisle and blew Jack a kiss.

She took her bouquet from Dottie and linked her arm in Bob's.

The organist played the opening notes of Purcell's "Trumpet Voluntary." Dottie began her walk, followed by Janie, and then Ruby.

Ruby took her place facing the congregation.

A trumpet sounded the opening bars of the fanfare. Vivian took a deep breath and pressed her arm tightly against her brother's. Her heart swelled in her chest, exhilarating, expanding, exploding. Time to process.

Apart from the British women and children from surrounding villages, the assembled guests were mostly in uniform. A number of Red Cross Girls came from London and the bomber bases out this way, and what must be the whole of the remaining base of the 305th was here.

Vivian was only vaguely aware of the sea of uniformed guests as she walked down the aisle, her eyes fixed on Jack. He stood tall and straight, his shoulders pulled back, and his body angled toward her approach. Jack had combed his blond hair off his forehead. His lips curved up with the barest hint of what she now considered his bedroom smile, the smile he wore only for her. Her bouquet shook in her trembling hands. He was so handsome, and he was all hers.

He exhaled when she reached the altar.

"Who gives this woman to be married?" Joe asked Bob.

"I do." Bob took her hand, clearly intending to place it in Jack's, but Joe extended his own hand. Bob looked at Joe and then Vivian in obvious confusion. Was she marrying Jack or the minister, his expression seemed to ask.

Joe took Vivian's hand from Bob, winked, gave her hand an extra-strong squeeze, and placed it into Jack's. This must be a peculiarity of an English wedding ceremony.

Jack grinned at her. She clasped his hand tightly. However it got there, her hand was now in Jack's, and they would be married. She looked over her shoulder to smile at Bob, who had taken a seat in the front row of the left side where her parents would normally be seated.

The rest of the ceremony passed in a blur up to the point of their exchange of vows. Chappie had agreed to Vivian's request that their vows mirror one another, so she too promised to honor and cherish Jack rather than obey him.

Stan stood with help from Tink and walked on his crutches to give Jack her ring.

A beautiful emerald, surrounded by small diamonds and set in a platinum band with etched engraving. He had purchased the vintage Art Deco ring from a shop in London.

Jack slid it on her finger. A perfect fit.

"I now pronounce you husband and wife. You may kiss the bride." Chappie smiled at them both, his eyes sparkling with delight at their happiness.

Jack released her hand to cup her face, his fingers gently pushing the edge of the veil out of the way. He lowered his mouth to hers. She should have expected it, that neither would be content with a chaste, church-appropriate kiss. It had taken too much to get them here. The gentle press of his lips shifted as a surge of passion flared between them. She pulled him closer, her mouth opening under his. Her pulse fluttered.

"Honeymoon's in Cornwall, not here, right?" Bowie's voice held more than a hint of suppressed laughter.

They pulled apart slightly, laughing. Jack gave her several more small butterfly kisses.

Chappie had already told them that they would go with him into the vestry to sign the register while the guests waited. Jack and Vivian followed him in. Bowie and Ruby would sign it as the official witnesses, but no one had thought to tell the other attendants to wait. They followed Ruby and Bowie, crowding into the small space. Vivian laughed as the rest of his crew members peeked around the edge of the door.

Joe looked a bit taken aback at the assemblage. He laughed. "It's normally only five of us in here for this part, but no reason you can't all sign if you like."

When everyone had added their signature, Chappie told them to go back out, with Jack and Vivian last.

Once they reassembled, Jack and Vivian faced the congregation. Chappie spread his arms behind them. "I take great pleasure in presenting to you, Mr. and Mrs. Jack Nielsen."

The recessional music began, and Gib moved forward to take Dottie's arm. As they waited their turn for the recessional, Vivian focused on the sea of assembled faces. Hank was seated behind Bob.

She didn't know if it was customary in English weddings, but Vivian pulled Jack to a stop at the front pew so she could kiss her brother's cheek. Her eyes met Hank's. She took another two steps, clasped his hand, and gave him a swift kiss on the cheek. Hank smiled and nodded at Jack.

Vivian stepped out the church door into the bright, late morning sunshine on Jack's arm. All the horror and misery of the last few years was behind them. They would embark on a united future, a future brimming over with hard-won choices, potential, hope, and love.

THANK YOU!

Thank you so very much for reading Courage to be Counted. If you enjoyed Vivian and Jack's story, consider leaving a review on your retailer of choice or just talking about it in real life to your friends who enjoy historical romance. As this is my debut novel, every bit of publicity will help build my author platform!

STAY IN TOUCH!

Follow the link below to sign up for my newsletter. Through my newsletter, you'll receive deleted scenes and sneak-peak previews of upcoming novels. My newsletter will arrive in your inbox no more than once per month (or probably bi-monthly).

Sign up at:
www.elerigrace.com/contact.html

KEEP READING ON!

You can read the first chapter of the next Clubmobile Girls novel after the Author's Historical Note on the following pages.

AUTHOR'S HISTORICAL NOTE

Contemplating writing romances set in the WWII era and looking for a unique angle that might allow my heroines to be overseas close to the action (and the heroes!), I read Emily Yellin's *Our Mothers' War*, an excellent compilation of the range of roles women played stateside and abroad, and was instantly intrigued by the Red Cross Girls. They served all over the world (opening up the possibility of a series), and their work often took them close to the front lines.

History has largely forgotten the immense contributions of the Red Cross Girls. Margaret (Henry) Fleming, who served in Europe, wrote to Tom Brokaw after the publication of *The Greatest Generation*, upset that he hadn't included the memories of her wartime service she had sent him or those of any of the other intrepid young women who courageously served their country through the American Red Cross ("ARC"). Most of the women later pegged their overseas wartime service as the most profoundly meaningful experience of their entire life. They were marked and shaped by those years as much as the male veterans.

Not long after Pearl Harbor, the ARC mobilized to deploy thousands of women to overseas assignments. Though many Americans, then and now, associate the Red Cross with nursing, combat nurses were attached to either the army or the navy during WWII. ARC service fell into the categories of camp, club, and hospital (providing recreation to convalescing soldiers). Most of the women hired ultimately accepted assignments to staff on-post recreation clubs on bomber and fighter bases throughout Britain, Australia/New Zealand (and later New Guinea and countless Pacific islands), North Africa, India, and China, hostel-style clubs in cities serving as leave destinations, rest homes for combat-weary and convalescent soldiers, and canteens meeting and serving troop ships and trains. At its height, the ARC ran 2,000 clubs around the world, staffed with as many as 5,000 paid employees and countless local volunteers. Doughnuts and coffee were a staple of ARC club service; the ARC served as many as 1.6 billion doughnuts during WWII.

By late 1942, the ARC in Great Britain recognized a need for a mobile canteen that could serve units too small to warrant an on-post club or situated in far-flung locations. Greenliner buses, which could transport gallons of coffee and thousands of doughnuts, were modified to act as Clubmobiles. The army worked with the ARC to adapt the bus Clubmobile model for use in different terrain, leading to a jeep-mobile (used in remote areas in northeast Australia, on many of the Pacific islands, across the plains of India and in the deserts of North Africa), a truck-mobile modified for continental Europe after D-Day, an amphibious landing craft "duckmobile" in harbors around the world, and a train-mobile service in Iran. In addition to doughnuts and coffee, many Clubmobiles were outfitted with a Victrola and mounted speakers and carried items such as gum, candy, cigarettes, matchbooks, comic books, razors, and other items distributed to the soldiers. The ARC could distribute these items without charge because other Allied forces had no counterpart to the ARC Clubmobile service. By contrast, the military stipulated that the ARC must charge at least nominal fees for food service and other items distributed through on-post clubs, because British and Australian troops were charged for similar items in their clubs. Many soldiers didn't understand that distinction, and the ARC unfortunately must still contend with the resulting unfair stigma.

The baseline qualifications for the ARC's overseas positions were extraordinary for the time period, especially considering the need for rapid and expanding deployment all around the world. A woman could seek an interview if she was twenty-five to thirty-five years old, had a college degree, and had some career experience. Married women could apply, though most applicants were single. They were single when they *left* America, that is. Many women returned with an engagement ring or a husband after spending years working in such a male-dominated environment. Indeed, ARC interviewers closely assessed an applicant's ability to hold her own with men, not only whether she could tell a good joke or tall tale to boost morale, but also whether she could *take* an off-color or suggestive joke, play a hand of poker or shoot the dice in a craps game, and had at least passing knowledge of sports and cars. Charm, stamina, ingenuity, self-confidence, and creativity were among the valued intangible attributes of successful applicants. Even in 1942, the ARC realized these women would need to be assertive self-starters who could call on a range of varied life experience.

Many Red Cross Girls, particularly those who served in Europe, left memoirs or gave oral history interviews that were invaluable to me in relating Vivian's story. Vivian's experiences in setting up an Aero Club from the ground up, working dawn to dusk on Clubmobile runs, then dancing all evening at the officers' dances, taking leave trips to London and Scotland, and following close behind the fast-moving US Army forces through France and into Germany are grounded in historical fact.

Curtis LeMay was the commander of the 305th Bomb Group at its base in Chelveston from December 1942 to May 1943. I kept him at Chelveston a bit longer for simplicity. During his time with the 305th, LeMay pioneered the staggered combat box formation and other defensive tactical strategies eventually adopted by the Eighth Air Force in England. He was transferred to commands in India and Guam later in the war (readers can expect to see him again in my series). Bruce Bairnsfather, famous for his WWI "Old Bill" cartoon characters, was hired by the USAAF during WWII. He traveled around East Anglia, painting USAAF base common areas and portraits and bomber nose art, but lived with the 305th Bomb Group at their base in Chelveston. While they were both living on the Chelveston base, Bairnsfather and LeMay became close friends. Their friendship, striking because they each had so few close friends, was a lifelong bond.

By 1942, the RAF had undisputed air superiority over Britain; thus, Luftwaffe raids against American and British air bases in East Anglia were rare. However, on August 3, 1942, a German Dornier, beset by RAF Spitfires, dropped its bomb load in the center of the town of Wellingborough, and the men of the USAAF's 60th Troop Carrier Group, then based at Station 105 in Chelveston ten miles from Wellingborough, took refuge in the base air-raid shelters. Vivian shepherds the local boys into the base shelter in January 1943, not much more than a month after she, Mabs, and the men of the 305th Bomb Group move into Station 105.

Vivian's experience during the Battle of the Bulge is a dramatized composite of the harrowing ordeal of several Clubmobile crews who were caught behind enemy lines during the breakout of December

16–18, 1944. President Harry Truman later awarded the Bronze Star medal to Margaret (Henry) Fleming, who had been operating an ARC recreation club in the resort town of Clervaux, Luxembourg, and escaped raging tank battles under machine gun fire. Central Illinois WWII Stories, a video project of Illinois Public Media, created an emotional short documentary film that highlights the perilous danger faced by Jill Pitts and her Clubmobile crew in the early days of the Battle of the Bulge. It was not unusual for the Clubmobiles to traverse more than 50–75 miles from their bases in Belgium. As a result, several were caught off guard by the German counteroffensive.

Many Red Cross Girls married overseas or returned home with a fiancé. Their memoirs and interviews paint a vivid picture of an active social life (which was true also of combat nurses and WACs). They might easily arrange dates with two or more men on any given day, depending on their work shift. It is not a stretch to infer the women's embrace of a "seize the day" mentality, combined with the exhilaration of being overseas in a war zone, led many to greater sexual freedom and experimentation than might have been the case if they had remained stateside. Certainly some women related intense love affairs that fizzled once that layer of danger and intrigue was removed or broke off because the man confessed he was already married or engaged. But others met the love of their life and had a happily-ever-after ending similar to Vivian and Jack.

A nitpicky detail I feel compelled to share: Chaff was not actually used by the RAF until June 1943 and by the USAAF until December 1943, hence Vivian and Mabs wouldn't have decorated their 1942 Christmas tree with those aluminum strips.

Jack's service as a B-17 bomber pilot also adheres, as closely as possible, to historical facts. The dates and objectives of his missions as part of the 305th Bomb Group are correct, and his group did lose a significant number of their bombers on that ill-fated mission to Schweinfurt on October 14, 1943. Sadly, a third bomber from the 305th did not make an emergency landing on the coast or elsewhere.

Walhampton House, located near Lymington, Hampshire, served as a flak house for USAAF enlisted men, rather than officers; however, when I found a collection of photographs from 1944 online, it seemed worthwhile to tweak its historical use for my purposes.

Dog tag lettering was debossed rather than embossed, but I was concerned the word debossed would be an unfamiliar speed bump for readers. Debossed letters are recessed into the surface of the metal. Jack would have traced the lettering of Ace's dog tag on the reverse side, where the letters might be slightly protruded or raised.

Jack should have left all personal effects, including Ace's dog tag and Vivian's picture, at his base when he flew missions. Many men ignored regulations on this point and flew with mementos or photographs secreted into their pockets. Some of you may have wondered how Jack had his letter from Eastern Airlines in Wiesbaden, since he had left it behind in his trunk in Chelveston. Jack asked Bowie to retrieve it from his trunk and forward it to him while he recuperated from his injuries in Germany.

I did take some license with Jack's timeline in several respects. Jack and his crew spent more time in combat crew operations training than would have been normal, but I didn't want him to arrive in Europe until summer 1943. A typical combat tour could theoretically have been completed in nine months or perhaps a year. The first USAAF crew to complete a twenty-five mission tour of duty was the famous *Memphis Belle* in May 1943. Tactical changes, together with the arrival in force of P-51 Mustang fighters who had the range to accompany the bombers all the way to targets deep inside Germany and back by late 1943, improved the odds of survival. If Jack had arrived in March 1943, he almost certainly wouldn't have survived his tour. As foolhardy as it sounds, it wasn't unheard of for men to sign up for another tour, though it wouldn't have been usual for an entire crew to agree to another tour.

Courage to be Counted reflects my profound admiration and gratitude to those who have served or are currently serving our country through the military and related services. I hope readers will enjoy my depiction of Vivian and Jack's story in tribute to the courage, resilience, and spirit of the Red Cross Girls, and the forces of the USAAF, particularly the valiant crews of the Eighth Air Force.

Enjoyed the story?

Turn the page for Chapter One of
Eleri Grace's next Clubmobile Girls Novel

Copyright © Eleri Grace
All rights reserved.

CHAPTER ONE

January, 1943
U.S.S. West Point
South Pacific Ocean

"Aft starboard. Aft starboard. Aft starboard," Hadley chanted. She descended another flight of narrow, steep steps to the next deck.

First deck. The chaplain's office was on the first deck. Aft starboard on the first deck. That's what that crewman had said. From which deck had she started? Hadley gripped the cold steel railing of the stairs. No, ladder. A staircase was called a ladder on a ship.

Male voices sounded through the open doorway. Hardly surprising with nearly eight thousand troops on board.

If this wasn't the right deck, she would backtrack. Hadley stepped over the coaming and through the door.

Starboard was the right side, but only if she was facing the front of the ship. Which way was forward?

Silence to her right. Probably store rooms. Hadley turned left.

Swashhhh, plink, plink, plink. Hissssss. Swashhh, plink, plink, plink. Probably sailors hosing the deck.

Crewmen seemed to be cleaning something constantly. Perhaps the officers believed it was a good means of keeping sailors out of trouble. Hadley had discovered first-hand that the crew also amused themselves by directing their water hoses on unsuspecting passengers. Two nights after setting sail from San Francisco, Hadley and her Red Cross Girl cabin-mates had abandoned the stuffy confines of their cabin for the top deck. Hours later, the drenched women, wringing out sodden bedrolls, conceded open-air sleeping came with its own drawbacks.

Hadley continued through the passageway. She caught a whiff of Ivory soap a split-second before she slammed into him.

Him being a very tall, very wet, and very naked man.

"Woy!" Hadley clapped a hand over her eyes. The showers. She had blundered into the showers. Flush heated her neck and face.

"Looking for somethin' doll?"

"Wanna come join us?"

"I'll share my water point with you, honey."

A tingle of dizziness shot across her forehead. *Move. Get out of here.* Their catcalls would only become bawdier the longer she stood frozen with shock.

Hand still shielding her eyes, Hadley spun on her heel to retrace her route back to the ladder.

"Aw, don't leave yet, baby." Laughter rang through the steamy compartment.

She hurried forward blindly and skidded on the slick deck. Her feet whooshed out from under her, and she landed with a thud on the hard deck.

Red-hot pain pulsed through her hipbone. Hadley gritted her teeth. Water seeped through her skirt to her underwear. Why were her legs straight up in the air? Another stab of pain jolted through her hip. Owww.

Her skirt had rucked up to mid-thigh. Hadley pried her palm from the wet deck and tugged her skirt down.

Strong hands settled around her waist, lifted her to standing, and set her on her feet. There was the Ivory soap smell again, mixed with the distinctive mossy cedar of Aqua Velva aftershave.

"Can you walk?" His resonant voice put her in mind of a creamy café au lait.

Hadley took a tentative step, leery of slipping again. His firm, warm hand gripped hers and towed her forward.

Lordy, was he still naked? She chanced a sideways glance. He had wrapped a towel around his waist. Water droplets clung to his tanned, muscular chest and lean torso. Hadley swallowed and averted her eyes.

They reached the door leading back to the ladder she had descended. Hadley dropped his hand and stepped over the coaming.

"Thanks for helping me up," she muttered. She stepped on the lowest rung of the ladder.

"Hang on. Where were you headed? I'm guessing you weren't looking for the officer showers." Laugh lines on either side of his mouth creased with his grin.

Her cheeks heated again. Nautical terminology might as well be Greek. Hadley might not be seasick, but obviously she was a landlubber. She remained as lost on board this troop ship as when they embarked three days ago. As it was, most of the ship was off-limits for her and the other Red Cross Girls. They could roam relatively freely in "officer country," but couldn't venture to the lower decks where thousands of enlisted men slept and ate in shifts.

Glistening water droplets clung to the hair dusted across his well-defined chest. Hadley licked her lips and looked up into his hazel eyes. *What?* "Oh, er, the chaplain. I was told I could find him on the first deck . . . Starboard aft."

"You're in need of the chaplain already?" His grin deepened.

She stepped off the ladder and pulled a small notepad and pen from her jacket pocket. "I thought he could provide a verse of Scripture for the ship's newsletter. I'm the new editor."

He raised an eyebrow. "Editor?"

"Contributing editor," she corrected. The Navy officer who wrote and edited the weekly shipboard newsletter had declined her offer to take over the job. Hadley then showed him a scrapbook of clippings from high school and college newspapers and the *Times-Picayune*. Though worried she might be crossing that fine line between persistence and pestering, Hadley returned again, this time with her Underwood typewriter. Today was her first day on the job.

He pointed up. "One deck up. Bulls-eye 1-75-7-Q."

"Ok." She scribbled 1757Q on her pad and capped the pen.

The man jabbed a finger at the number and shook his head. "Not run together like that. One stands for first deck. Seventy-five is the frame number. Seven is the compartment number. Between starboard beam and starboard quarter."

Hadley stared at him.

He ran a hand through his damp hair. "Hold tight right here. I'll take you."

Before she could object that she only needed more conventional left-right directions, the man strode back toward the showers. He rolled his shoulders as though to release tension. Muscles rippled across his upper back.

He disappeared from view, and Hadley inhaled and blew out a breath.

He must be a naval officer to know the ship so well. Which meant he wouldn't be disembarking at Australia, New Zealand, India or wherever they were headed. Their ultimate destination remained a mystery.

The Pacific theater. Hadley rubbed the back of her neck and sighed. Of all the luck, she was bound for the Pacific. The Pacific rather than England. England, where communication lines were plentiful and easy to access. England, where women journalists were making a name for themselves. England, where credentialed war correspondents might be persuaded to help her obtain credentials or file stories on her behalf.

Hadley suspected her sense of being disconnected from civilization wouldn't improve after they docked, whether in Sydney or Bombay. She hadn't seen any bylines from female war correspondents reporting from anywhere in the Far East.

The man stepped into view again. His hair was considerably fairer now that it was dry. He wore the simple khaki uniform most officers donned on board the ship. No service cap, as was required at sea.

"Lieutenant Masterson at your service, Miss . . .?"

"Claverie. Hadley Claverie."

"Clea-Verhee." He drawled the syllables. "French?"

Hadley lifted her chin and smiled. "New Orleans." Steamy and sophisticated, stimulating and somnolent, free-wheeling and fettered,

New Orleans was home.

Masterson tilted his head to one side. "Never been. Jazz music. Parades. Big on parades there, right?"

A pang of nostalgia zipped through her heart. "Today's Twelfth Night. The start of Carnival."

"That's parade time?"

Hadley worried the beads on her bracelet. "Yes, but the parades and balls will all be cancelled, like last year." She might as well be in the middle of the Pacific Ocean for all it mattered. No floats and marching bands and riotously festive street celebrations this year.

"Maybe next year."

She widened her eyes. "You don't really believe the war will end this year, do you?"

"Nope. But you might be back within a year."

"My overseas assignment is at least two years." Hadley ran her finger over the Red Cross pin fastened on her jacket lapel. Unable to secure credentials with the *Times-Picayune* or another Louisiana newspaper, Hadley jumped at the chance to get overseas and near the action with the Red Cross. She would figure out how to file stories from her post.

He made an indistinct noise in his throat. Did he think she couldn't hack it? That women had no business near the combat zones?

"We signed on for the duration, same as men. Even if I serve overseas for two years, the Red Cross won't necessarily post me back to New Orleans. That's the way it works for you fellows too, doesn't it? You get enough points to rotate back stateside, but the military might station you anywhere."

"Gotta get the points." Masterson shot her a tight smile. "Without dying first."

Hadley's stomach twisted into a tight ball. Her best friend Camille's brother Philip had died in August on Guadalcanal. So many senseless losses already. She swallowed. "I —"

He shook his head. "Nah, I know what you meant. Didn't need to remind you that none of us are on a pleasure cruise."

"We all want to do our part." Hadley met his eyes. Maybe they weren't really hazel after all. The outer edges were a dark blue, with pale green yielding to amber closest to the iris.

"Do your part for duty, honor, country," he quoted a popular patriotic poster, mimicking the dramatic delivery of a newsreel announcer.

Hadley smiled.

Masterson gestured to the ladder. "Let's go find the chaplain."

She climbed the steep ladder-case, stepped off the top step, and looked over her shoulder. Well, well, well. Hadley had seen that look before. She tucked a strand of hair behind her ear and waited.

He paused on the top step and moistened his lips before swinging up to stand beside her. He pressed a gentle hand on the back of her arm and motioned to the left with his other hand. "This way."

Tingles radiated from where his hand rested on her arm. "How would I know which way to turn?"

"I'm gonna show you." He pointed to a yellow label plate affixed to the door on their right. The designation 1-12-3-C was stamped in black letters across the middle of the plate. "That's a bullseye. You'll see those on doors, hatches, and bulkheads throughout the ship. Now, see that first number is a one?"

She nodded.

"Number one means you're on the main deck. If it said zero two, you'd be two levels above the main deck. If it said three, you're two levels below the main deck. Now, the next number is twelve. That tells you the frame number. Frames are numbered from zero at the forward or bow of the ship and get higher as you move toward the aft or stern. Got it?"

"So is twelve closer to forward or aft?"

"You don't need to know that." Masterson guided her forward and pointed to the next bullseye. "See how the next bullseye is a higher number? That means you're moving aft."

Hadley paused to pull out her notebook and make a note. "Okay. What's the next number?"

He led them forward again. "Ah, that's the compartment number. That's where it gets more complicated. That number three means you're starboard from the centerline of the ship. The centerline is zero. Moving out from the center, you'll have even number compartments to the port side, and odd numbers to the starboard side. The numbers grow larger as you move out from the centerline."

"Even is port, odd is starboard. Numbers get bigger moving from center," Hadley scribbled.

"Yes, that's it. Now that last letter will tell you what the purpose of the compartment is. F stands for fuel. C, as we have here, is ship control."

Hadley stopped, tapped her pen against her notepad, and winked at him. "What's the code for showers?"

He laughed. "L stands for living space. That includes showers as well as heads, washrooms, berths and mess."

"Avoid L compartments." Hadley underlined it several times and capped her pen.

"Might not want to completely avoid L spaces, or you'll be plenty hungry before we reach port." His eyes crinkled at the corners.

"Oh, I know how to get to chow. It's not gumbo from back home, but better than what they fed us when we trained with the Red Cross in Washington." Hadley wrinkled her nose at the memory.

"Hmph. Navy's got the best chow in the US military, so you better enjoy it. Wherever you land up, it won't be this good," Masterson said.

Masterson clearly knew his way around a ship, yet her initial impression had been that he wasn't wearing a Navy officer's uniform. Hadley cut her eyes to look at his uniform insignia. No. Definitely no dark blue shoulder boards with gold stripes for the Navy. Perhaps she still didn't have a good handle on the various insignia. She pointed to the wings pinned above his right shirt pocket. "You're a naval aviator?"

"No." His mouth flattened to a thin line. He strode forward, walking faster now.

Hadley hurried to match his pace. "The wings indicate you're a flying officer, right?"

"USAAF pilot." He offered no further details.

"Oh, a fighter pilot?" Someone had told her that the fighter planes were transported to the combat theaters via ship. Bomber crews flew the planes to their assigned base of operations, making fuel stops as necessary.

"No." Jaw tight, he lengthened his stride yet again.

Why the sudden change in attitude? Hadley half-jogged a few

steps so she was once again alongside him. "I thought bomber crews flew their planes."

"They do. Gunners and ground crew go by ship."

Now she was really confused. He had wings and officer insignia on his shoulder. He clearly knew his way around a ship on a deeper level than might be expected of an Army Air Forces man. None of it made any sense. "But —"

"Here we are." Masterson pointed to the bulls-eye, stamped 1-75-7-Q. He pushed the door open and gestured for her to proceed inside.

The chaplain looked up. "Good morning. How can I help?"

Masterson cleared his throat. "Ms. Claverie needs some assistance for the ship newsletter."

"Ah, you must be in search of the daily scripture verse." The chaplain thumbed through sheets of paper stacked on his small desk.

"I leave you in good hands, then."

Hadley turned. An imprecation for him to wait and guide her back to her next destination died on her lips.

Masterson was gone.

***

Skip swiped at sweat beading at his temple. His heart thumped in his chest. He hurtled up the ladder, taking the steps two at a time. The weather deck would clear his head.

He stepped briskly toward the nearest side and tightened his hands around the cold taffrail. Skip had drawn no more than two deep lungfuls of cool morning air into his tight chest when he heard his name. Fuck. Though thirteen months had passed since Skip last saw him, he recognized the snarly voice, knew before he turned who he would find standing behind him.

"Just the man I needed." Commander John Buckley's cool gray eyes flicked over the wings pinned above Skip's right breast pocket.

"Sir?" Hyper aware that the sweat beads popping once again at his hairline were at odds with the brisk breeze ruffling his hair, Skip swallowed and clenched his fists at his side.

Commander Buckley's lips curved into a tight smile. "I hear one of the lovely Red Cross Girls aboard ship stumbled into the officer shower block earlier. Seems you took an interest in serving as her guide."

Skip pulled his shoulders back. "She was looking for the chaplain. Wrong deck. Got her squared away."

"Captain Donelson says she fancies herself a reporter and sweet-talked him into letting her help him with the newsletter."

"Hmm." Skip injected a note of casual nonchalance into his tone, tried to ignore the flutters of foreboding stirring in his gut. Buckley was not one to shoot the breeze.

"She will need an assistant. Someone who can act as guide around the ship, someone who can obtain information for her from areas of the ship where she has no access."

Skip made no reply. His clenched fingers were numb.

Commander Buckley's eyes sparked with self-satisfaction. "You, Lieutenant Masterson, are just the man for the job. Familiar as you are with ships, with the Navy, with the Navy's *customs and regulations*." He chopped his emphasis on the last phrases.

Flush crept up the back of Skip's neck. "Sir, I have responsibility to keep tabs on my group's enlisted men and ground crews and periodically check our cargo."

"So I heard. Normally, Lieutenant Masterson, flying officers *fly* rather than travel by troop transport. Normally, even the USAAF doesn't designate an officer to act as shipboard babysitter for men and cargo. I wonder how you managed to be tasked with a heretofore unnecessary job."

His jaw tightened. Skip had no intention of giving Buckley any details.

Buckley cocked a brow. "You won't say? Based on your history, Masterson, I can make a good guess. Some things never change."

Skip pressed his lips together, resisted the urge to take the bait. Buckley would make good use of any details Skip divulged in an angry outburst. Being shipboard again was torture enough.

He took a deep breath. "As I said, sir, I already have an assignment —"

"An assignment that appears to take little of your time, Lieutenant. I've noted you spend most of your day on this weather deck."

Yes, he did. He slept here too. Skip went to great lengths to avoid the choking confines of the vast ship interior. He had drawn one of the top bunks in his crowded berth. First night at sea, with his face inches from the overhead, panic, descending and enveloping like a thick fog, drove him to the weather deck. Shaking and gulping lungfuls of cool night air, Skip vowed to only go belowdecks for chow and a shower.

Buckley's lips curved up. "I will inform her that she can expect your assistance, effective immediately, and that she can meet you in the mess in an hour."

Dammit. She was attractive, with her inky black hair and dark eyes and trim figure. But she asked too many damn questions. Only ten minutes in her company, and she had managed to drill him with an uncomfortable line of questioning. No, he needed to evade this errand boy job.

Skip cleared his throat. "Sir, I'll be happy to find one of my top fellows to —"

Buckley shook his head. "No. You. None of your men are officers. They aren't allowed access to much of the ship beyond the lowest decks."

"I'm not Navy," Skip shot back. "Men with the most leeway and knowledge of this ship are its own crewmen."

"As you well know, our crewmen are busy, Lieutenant Masterson. They aren't sunbathing on the weather deck for hours every day."

Skip clenched his fists tighter. Sunbathing his ass. Surviving more like. "And if I have to neglect my shipboard orders to play Man Friday for this woman?"

"You have time for both jobs if I say you do, Lieutenant Masterson."

He took one more shot. "Sir, as you noticed, I've not spent much time belowdeck. I don't know the ship well enough myself to navigate it for Ms. Claverie."

"You'll find this ship not too different than others in your experience, Lieutenant. Like riding a bicycle." Buckley smirked. "Oh, and *Captain* Claverie will expect you in the officer's mess at ten hundred."

Captain? The woman outranked him? Swell. Just swell. He bobbed a tight nod at Buckley. "Yes, sir."

Buckley strode past him and disappeared from view.

Skip unclenched his fists. He glanced, from habit, at his watch, frozen at 08:06. His chest tightened as though secured in a bowline knot.

For Skip, the journey to Brisbane now held hazards and stresses far beyond any dangers from Japanese subs.

ACKNOWLEDGMENTS

I am grateful to so many individuals who helped make my dream of publication a reality.

Laura Mitchell, editor extraordinaire and inspiring writing coach, helped me transform my earliest manuscript into a much stronger story. I will always be grateful for her coaxing and prodding me to set fire to my characters and their emotional journey. Thank you for believing in me and my writing!

My childhood friend, Lonna Lambert McKinley, Museum Manuscripts Curator with the National Museum of the United States Air Force, ran down answers to countless questions relating to pilot training and certification and historical USAAF matters. Vivian's surname was chosen to honor her.

Ian D. White, Group Historian of the 305th Bomber Group Memorial Association UK, provided prompt and extensive answers to my questions about Station 105, the 305th Bomb Group, and local environs. He sent numerous historical photographs (some of which I use with permission on my website), allowing me to paint a more vivid picture of life on the Chelveston base to which both Vivian and Jack were attached at various points.

Donald L. Miller, noted historian and author of my favorite source on the Eighth Air Force operations in WWII, *Masters of the Air*, led a National World War II Museum tour to the bomber bases in East Anglia in May 2016 and was happy to respond to many follow-up questions, often within minutes. On this same tour, I had the great fortune to meet, among others, Paul Clifford, Jerry McLaughlin, and George Liao, each of whom lent support and advice from time to time. Local British people near the bomber bases we visited shared stories from their childhood. I am particularly grateful to the man who described how the American airmen would load canisters of ice cream ingredients into the bomb bay of a plane going up to altitude for a check-ride and send a gallon of ice cream home with the local children.

Jackie Walters, formerly a Historical Programs and Collections volunteer with the American Red Cross National Headquarters, generously answered questions, pointed me to additional sources, and digitized sources held only at the DC headquarters for the ARC.

Tab Lewis, an archivist with the National Archives in College Park, Maryland, helped me "hit the ground running" with a targeted pull list for the voluminous ARC records housed in College Park during a research trip in summer 2017 and quickly accommodated my requests once I was on-site.

Taylor Benson and Kimberly Guise, archivists with the the National World War II Museum in New Orleans, provided me access to the private papers for a Red Cross Girl in their collection.

Jackie Schriver and Terri Mote of the Bellaire City Library processed innumerable inter-library loan requests. Thank you to all the librarians, archivists, and curators who provided research assistance. On my website, I list many of the Red Cross Girl memoirs, Eighth Air Force combat memoirs, and other nonfiction sources I consulted in writing this novel. Julia Ramsey's master's thesis, "'Girls' in Name Only," provided a strong base for my research.

Holly Ingraham provided second-look editorial assistance, and Christa Desir did my copy-editing. I am so very grateful to them both for making the manuscript so much stronger and tighter.

Rafael Andres of CoverKitchen Book Cover Designers did an amazing job of creating custom-illustrated cover art that evokes the feel of WWII poster art and will be so easy to adapt to each new book in the series.

Many thanks for the tireless efforts of my formatter, Suz Whited. She went above and beyond the call of duty to provide wonderful interior design and formatting for both the print and ebook versions, and I'm so grateful for her help.

Many friends beta-read the manuscript for me in earlier stages, and I thank each of you for your feedback, including Marielle Kaifer, Mona Enderli, Carmen Pratt, Melinda Feeney, and Michelle Helm. My sister, Tracy Knight, spurred me to expand some of the emotional elements in Jack's story, and I hope she'll agree that her thoughts translated well to the page. My critique partner, author Caroline Leech, is always a sounding board for plotting, character development, historical details from the WWII era, and a plethora of nonwriting topics which we are often all too happy to discuss in lieu of getting on with actual writing goals. I treasure the camaraderie of our coffee-shop writing dates so very much! Her mother, Shirley Sibbald, also deserves special thanks for her quick answers to so many questions relating to life in Britain during the war years.

I must single out my friend Dulcie Wink for particular thanks. Dulcie showed early signs that she had the makings of a super-fan, particularly with her all-caps emails proclaiming, "I can't stop reading," interspersed with various OMGs and emoji. You boosted my confidence immeasurably, Dulcie, and I hope you enjoy this version of Vivian and Jack's story all the more. I'm also grateful that she introduced me to her Uncle Joe, a navigator with the 305th bomb group, before his death. What a small world.

Despite the input of all these talented individuals and more, there could well be historical errors that don't fall into intentional artistic license; and for those mistakes, I apologize in advance.

I am grateful to my parents, Hulon and Cheryl Turner, and my sister, Tracy Knight, for their unwavering belief in me and in my dream of pursing a writing career. My ex-husband Bryce also remains a steadfast supporter of me and my writing dreams.

To the courageous, spirited, and adventuresome women who served with the ARC during WWII, I hope I have done justice to your inspiring service and your stories.

Finally, to the most important people in my life (and those most affected by Mom's propensity to disappear for hours in front of the computer screen), I am so very grateful for the love and support of my children, Elizabeth and Harry. Had she been a young woman in 1942, there is no doubt Elizabeth, with her charm, compassion, and convictions, would have sought out a position as a Red Cross Girl. And though Harry has no particular love for vintage aircraft, his flight-simulating expertise and aviation interest proved indispensable. I will forever remember with amusement his handwritten comment in the margin of one of the combat chapters I asked him to read: "Your B-17 just exploded in midair at that speed." I no longer pull air speed and altitude references out of a hat.

Elizabeth and Harry, I love you both more than I can say.

ELERI GRACE writes historical romance novels featuring trailblazing Red Cross Girl heroines and flyboy heroes. Before penning her first novel, Eleri honed her writing skills as a corporate lawyer, a historical researcher, and an avid writer and reader of fan fiction.

Eleri lives in Houston, Texas with her two teenage children and two feuding cats. Courage to Be Counted is her first novel.

Contact Eleri Grace at:
www.elerigrace.com

Made in the USA
Monee, IL
20 August 2021

76184120R00225